HOLIDAY WITH THE MYSTERY ITALIAN

BY
ELLIE DARKINS

MILLS & BOON

First Published in Great Britain 2016
By Mills & Boon, an imprint of HarperCollins*Publishers*
1 London Bridge Street, London, SE1 9GF

© 2016 Ellie Darkins

ISBN: 978-0-263-92042-0

23-1216

Ellie Darkins spent her formative years devouring romance novels, and after completing her English degree, she decided to make a living from her love of books. As a writer and editor, her work now entails dreaming up romantic proposals, hot dates with alpha males and trips to the past with dashing heroes. When she's not working, she can usually be found running around after her toddler, volunteering at her local library or escaping all the above with a good book and a vanilla latte.

For Matilda

CHAPTER ONE

'LAST BUT NOT least, contestant number three, here's your question: As a gold-medal-winning ParaGames swimmer...' he paused for whoops from the enthusiastic audience '...I obviously spend a lot of time in the water. If you were a sea creature, what would you be and why?'

Amber suppressed an eye-roll. Seriously, this show couldn't be any cheesier if it tried. She had thought when she'd arrived that the flashing lights and tinsel-bedecked set were tacky enough, but this guy's titillating questions were taking the cringe factor to a new level. She just had to play along, she reminded herself, and get this over with. A charity gig was a charity gig, and when you worked in the media, even as a lowly newspaper columnist, you sometimes found yourself doing something completely embarrassing in aid of a kids' charity. Like appearing on a celebrity version of the country's best-loved dating show.

Luckily, with the answers she'd prepared, there was no way that this 'eligible bachelor' was going to pick her, even if the whole thing hadn't been scripted by the producers, so it was just a case of answering this last question, posing for a quick photo, and getting back to her laptop and her deadline. She still hadn't finished her latest column. Well, she hadn't actually started it yet—she had a mailbox full of 'Dear Amber' letters, and still had to choose the most interesting to feature on the magazine's website.

She took a deep breath and tried to remember the answer to the bachelor's final question that she'd written and memorised when she'd been emailed in advance.

'A killer whale,' she said, *sotto voce*. No doubt the man on the other side of the screen, not to mention the producers, had been hoping for something a little sexier. Something about mermaids and their shells and their penchant for handsome princes, or firefly jellyfishes lighting up the ocean. She'd considered several contenders for her answer, each designed to ensure that she would be the last contestant that this eligible bachelor would be interested in. ParaGames swimmer. That definitely rang a bell—Mauro someone. Welsh surname. She spent an hour every morning in her local pool, and had watched hours of footage of the international sports and para championships held in London a few summers ago. He'd won a clutch of medals, featured in a fly-on-the-wall documentary about his training regime and then been the face of various food and sportswear brands in the years since.

The voice too—she definitely remembered that: an unusual combination of Welsh and Italian accents that was unmistakable. Her brain flashed a pair of built arms, wide shoulders with droplets of water catching the light from a hundred flashbulbs.

She realised that the studio had fallen into silence around them, waiting for her explanation for her decidedly unromantic response. 'A killer whale,' she repeated, 'because they're intelligent, the women stick together and they can be ruthless predators when it's called for.'

For half a moment the silence in the studio stuck, but readers of her column knew what to expect from her. She called the shots as she saw them, and more often than not she saw the whole 'romance' scene as one big game that was rigged against fifty per cent of the players.

A deep, rich laugh from the other side of the screen stopped her train of thought, and she practically felt the noise flow through her, smooth and dark as the chocolate she kept permanently stocked in her kitchen. And in her desk. And in her bedside drawer just in case. Another flash of something from her memory. Hair slicked back and wet, a charming smile turned on a flustered television presenter. A shiver ran through her spine as she remembered the charm and the charisma that had exuded from this man, even down the camera from an echoing swimming venue. Good job she had sabotaged herself in this game. She had more than a sneaking suspicion that this man was going to be trouble for whichever unfortunate contestant got picked. She was best off out of it.

She sat cooking under the heat of the studio lights and looked longingly at the heaps of snow dotted around the studio. Sweat threatened to prickle at her brow and break through the industrial strength anti-shine powder she'd been caked with. Not that the poly-styrene decorations would have helped much—but then there wasn't a lot of genuine snow around in Septem-ber.

Due to 'scheduling reasons', they were filming this Christmas special in the autumn, and she had to admit that the fake festivities were messing with her mind. Christmas carol fatigue was an annual complaint, but she'd never suffered from it this early before.

Whichever contestant was 'picked' to go on this date would be summoned back in December for the live programme, when the footage they were shooting now, and the highlights of the date, would be shown.

As she waited for Julia to announce which 'lucky lady' had been chosen, she tried to think of the advice she'd given the woman in her last *Dear Amber* article, but the crash of the audience breaking into applause intruded into her thoughts.

The presenter announced, with a shake to her voice, 'And so it seems that our lucky contestant is Amber, a journalist from London!'

Amber wobbled on her stool as her jaw fell open. *Oh, please, no.* How could he have picked her? She'd said 'ruthless predator'! She'd not made a single sex-ual innuendo, no matter how leading his questions, not even the one about which swimming stroke was her fa-vourite—it had taken her an age to think of a response that didn't conjure images of breasts, butterfly kisses or caresses of a strong, muscled back. She knew for a fact that the producers had told him to choose one of the other women. Had he never seen this show before? He should be picking the person with the biggest hair— the one that the producers had pushed towards the most suggestive answers. She'd batted away their attempts to give her a makeover. She knew what she was working with, and a fake tan and big hair weren't going to change it. She glanced towards Ayisha, the show's producer, and from the look on her face it seemed that she was as shocked as Amber. It seemed that Mauro had just gone off-script.

She watched the two other women walk past the screen, and the groans of regret as Mauro met the women that he could be taking with him for their week in Sicily. Oh, God, a whole week with him. It had never even crossed her mind that he could pick her, and now she was signed up for a week-long holiday with a man that her brain had—goodness knew why—been stashing mental images of in a state of undress.

And then the music was rising to a crescendo and Ayisha was energetically motioning for her to get up. She took to her feet and straightened her spine, desperately trying to remember what they'd been told to do if they were picked. It had hardly seemed worth listening when she'd known that her prickly answers would keep Mauro well away. Keeping men at arm's distance was more than a habit these days: it was a reflex, as easy to her as breathing. Normally one flash of her 'don't even think about it' look was enough to have them backing away and leaving her alone, just as she liked it.

Perhaps that was the problem, she thought. He couldn't see her face, couldn't see just how desperate she was *not* to meet any sort of bachelor, eligible or otherwise. She stood on the spot where Ayisha had been gesturing and waited for the big reveal, her inner monologue not giving her a minute's rest in its utter contempt for putting herself in this situation.

The screen rolled back, with a wobble and a creak, and then she saw him, and realised she had been right. It was him, the athlete her brain had clocked and ogled, and then apparently saved half-naked images of in some deviant part of her mind, just in case it came in useful one day. His dark hair, not slicked back this time, but rebelling from a side parting, showed a hint of red—a dash of chilli hidden in the chocolate—and the shoulders dominated the rest of his body, making his waist look narrow, although she remembered abs that would make a lesser woman dribble. His wheelchair was small and space-age-looking, and the least interesting thing about this mountain of a man. An open shirt collar showed a triangle of tanned skin below his neck—and for just a moment Amber remembered that bronzed torso, thrust out of the pool by powerful forearms.

She shook her head. This should not be happening. He should not have picked the woman who had chosen her brain, when asked what her favourite part of her own body was. But the presenter of the show had grabbed her hand and was dragging her across to meet Mauro.

'Mauro, meet your date—Amber Harris. Amber, how do you feel to have been chosen?'

As if this was all a big joke, and she was the punchline. If he'd been able to see all three women she knew for a fact that he would have chosen one of the others.

'Erm…surprised,' she choked out, and didn't know whether to be pleased or not at the look on Mauro's face, the one that suggested that he liked catching her off guard, that maybe he'd done it on purpose.

'Well, Amber, just you wait until you see what we've got in store for you. You'll be jetting off on a romantic week-long break to sunny Sicily. Mauro has generously allowed us to use his luxury villa, complete with swimming pool, private beach and no fewer than seven beautiful bedrooms to choose from. Over the course of your week you'll be wined and dined by the owners of the Castello Vigneto, and tour the grounds of their beautiful vineyard before feasting on local foods and wines. You'll take jet-skiing lessons from Mauro himself, and can choose from any of the other water sports equipment available at his private pontoon. There will be a hike up the Mongibello, otherwise known as the live volcano Mount Etna, and to top it off we'll be flying you, by helicopter, to view the volcanic eruptions of the island of Stromboli! Amber, what do you say?'

Mauro watched Amber's shell-shocked expression as the presenter outlined the romantic week in Sicily that had been planned for his date. Well, he'd planned a large part of it himself, actually. When the charity had approached him about appearing on the show, he'd gone one better and offered the use of his home—it seemed to defeat the object of money-raising if they were to shell out on accommodation. And it was entirely unnecessary when he had his very own villa sitting empty most of the time. Anyway, as the patron of a charity that helped disadvantaged children through sport, he wanted to do more than just sign big cheques.

His villa in Sicily, the country of his mother's birth, was one of his favourite places on earth, so it was hardly a chore to spend a week there, especially a week in the company of a beautiful woman. Her blonde hair fell just to her collarbones in waves that seemed deliberately messy, and her eyes had grabbed his attention as he tried to work out whether they were more green or brown. But none of that was the reason that he'd decided to ignore the script the presenters had briefed him on, of course. Celebrity edition or not, he hadn't known who she was. The reason he'd picked her was simple: he'd been intrigued by her and wanted to know more. She was funny, for a start: he'd smiled at her answer to his first question, chuckled at her second and full-out belly laughed at her third.

And then there had been that attitude. The one that had said that she didn't for a second buy into the show's attempt at stirring up romance. The producers had told him that everyone involved knew that they were all just doing this as a money-raiser, that none of the women were actually interested in starting a relationship. But there had been one way to be sure that he wasn't getting involved with someone who had different expectations of this show from him—pick the woman that had Keep Out prickling her voice and written in neon letters so big he could see them above the screen that was keeping them apart.

She'd seen straight through his questions, straight through every pep talk and manipulation of the producers and refused to deliver the smut that *Holi-Date* had been leading her towards. She would have been a killer whale—who wouldn't have picked her after that?

She leaned in to kiss him on the cheek. Not exactly by choice—he was sure that he wasn't the only one who had instructions from the production team on what they were to do after the big reveal. What surprised him was that she was going along with it. The peck on the cheek was brief, gone almost before it started, but the scent of her shampoo, something earthy and familiar—rosemary, perhaps—lingered a second longer, teasing his senses. Two beautiful women had just sashayed past him—a singer from a girl band and a regular from one of the soap operas, apparently. But Amber...she marched. And though her expression wasn't quite a scowl, it wasn't the TV smile that everyone else in the studio was wearing either. No, she was definitely different. Good. Different was what he had wanted. Dating show or not, he wasn't in the market for a girlfriend, and no one had shown that they weren't interested in a relationship as eloquently as Amber had.

'And, Mauro, what do you think about your gorgeous date?' Julia, the presenter, asked him.

He took a moment to think about it. She was hot—there was no doubt about that. Slim legs were encased in dark jeans, and a hint of silk was revealed beneath her black blazer. The look was almost academic, it was so serious. And yet…something about it drew him in. Perhaps it was the thought of that silk, imagining the smooth warmth of it beneath his fingers if he managed to peel off that blazer, peel back the layers of protection that she had so clearly shown already that evening.

She hadn't given his chair more than a cursory glance—always a good start. Now she took a couple of steps back, guided by the presenter's hand on her waist, but her eyes hadn't left him yet. They'd dropped to his chest, he noticed, but they were making their way back up now, and…there. He had her again, her gaze locked into his. He wasn't going to let her go easily. He wanted to play with this—it wasn't as if he had to worry that she might want him to get involved.

'Oh, Julia, I'm very much looking forward to getting to know her better.'

Julia turned to the autocue and began to wrap up the show, but already he'd lost interest, could see only Amber as the audience were directed to clap and cheer. Then he realised he'd missed his cue. The two women were turning towards him and he realised they were meant to be making their way backstage. At this rate it'd look as if he was chasing Amber out of the studio—not the best of starts. He spun on the spot and caught up with her quickly then stopped at the mark they'd been given to turn and wave at the audience. He let out a breath of relief, and surprise. It took a lot to surprise him these days. He liked to think he'd seen it all—he'd spent the last ten years of his life *trying* to see it all in the wake of his accident. But somehow, after just half an hour in her company—and a large part of that without even being able to see each other—Amber had him chasing after her without his even realising how she'd done it.

He rarely had to chase. Normally, with women, he put in a little groundwork, a little charm; laid the bait and then waited for a bite. It never took long. Whether he was throwing a party, hanging out in a nightclub— hell, he'd picked women up in the supermarket—he always had this under control. He took advantage of every opportunity to experience something new, but always on the strict understanding that there was nothing more than a casual fling on offer. He didn't do commitment. Well, not to romance, at least. He was committed to his sport, his business, his charity work, and for ten years it had been clear to everyone involved that that didn't leave room for commitment to anything else.

As they headed back to the green room Amber kept her eyes dead ahead, and her shoulders seemed to stiffen and rise with every step that she took. Mauro hung back, nothing at all to do with wanting to keep an eye on that peachy *culo*, revealed with every swing of her jacket. But something about being close to Amber had made him concerned for her. That neon sign that had shown over the wobbly dividing screen looked different up close. There was hurt behind it, and a vulnerability that was making him wonder whether he had made a mistake in picking her. He had thought that it had been the straightforward, risk-free option, but now he wasn't so sure. He would give her space, he told himself. Space that she so desperately seemed to want.

She dropped onto the sofa in the green room and rested her head in her hands. Mauro moved in front of her and couldn't help but reach for one of her hands and brush it with his fingertips, before he remembered what he had told himself about giving her space. 'Hey, it's not that bad, is it?' he asked with a forced smile. It wasn't exactly flattering, that she seemed so traumatised at the thought of a date with him, but he knew from her answers on the show that this wasn't personal. She had had no intention of being the one to go on this date. He had thwarted whatever plan it was she had going on, and she was annoyed about it.

'I've made you angry?'

She looked him right in the eye.

'Maybe. Or maybe I'm angry at myself. I... It doesn't matter, anyway. Look—' she started gathering up her things, throwing her phone and bits of make-up into her handbag '—this has been...fun, and really nice to meet you and everything. But I've got to get back.'

'You're not staying for the party?' There were drinks planned—everyone on the show at a hotel in the city, where those from out of town were being put up. He wasn't staying at the hotel—he kept a penthouse suite in Mayfair for when he was in London—but it should be a fun couple of hours. From the looks he was getting from contestants numbers one and two he guessed that they would be at the party when he showed up. But for once the promise of a pretty face waiting for him in a bar didn't have its usual effect.

There was something about Amber that intrigued him. Some of the things he'd worked hardest for in life had been the sweetest: his first gold medal the sweetest of them all. But with women…what could he say? He'd never had to work that hard. Women fell for him easily, and before things got too complicated, he got out. His life was too full, too packed with ambition and drive to fit in a relationship as well, but the board of the sports charity had assured him that just turning up for this date, making nice for a week for the show, would help their fundraising efforts no end. It didn't mean that he was here looking for a relationship.

He was so distracted by trying to work out what was really going on with Amber that he missed her moving towards him, until she was so close that he could smell that shampoo again. Her lips brushed against his cheek, soft and plump, and he wondered what she would have done if he'd turned his head slightly, so that they touched against his own. So that he would have the taste of her on his mouth.

'I have to go. It was nice to meet you, Mauro.'

Something about the way she said it raised his hackles. Nice to meet him, but she wasn't planning on seeing him again, he thought. She was going to try and back out of their date. Well, he'd see about that.

CHAPTER TWO

AMBER TURNED UP to the airport with a fake smile plastered onto her face, her ears ringing with the warning her boss had just given her: go on this date or lose your job. OK, so it had been more nuanced than that, but that was what it came down to.

Recently, the feedback on her articles had been taking something of a dive. The comments on her online column had started off unpleasant and steadily descended into venomous. She'd stopped reading them, chalking them up to bullies with nothing better to do. But her boss had told her in no uncertain terms that the powers that be at the paper were paying attention.

And maybe they were right; Ever since her heart had been broken, she'd lost her home, and realised that the best advice she could dish out to anyone looking for romance tips was to get out, get your life together on your own, and make yourself happy. The words that had been bandied around in that meeting—cynical, bitter—when had she become that?

But how was she meant to undo the hurt and the anger that had been simmering under her skin? The pain that had become such a part of her that she wasn't sure if, never mind how, she was meant to shake it off.

This wasn't just about her feelings. If Maddie was right and her job was at stake…well, there was nothing that she wouldn't do to save her job. It was all she had. She'd literally lost the roof over her head when her relationship had broken down. Now her rent ate up most of her salary, and her travel card to get in from Zone Three took the rest. Even a month without work would be a disaster. She could *not* lose this job.

She'd thought she'd be able to beat the check-in queues by doing it online last night, only to be told at bag-drop that she had to go to the desk after all. It was taking an age—an immaculately manicured woman in an airline colours scarf was tapping at a computer and frowning at her passport.

'I'm sorry for the delay, madam.' She looked up and Amber forced her mouth back into a smile. There was nowhere she could escape the judgemental gaze of her readers. 'Some of the information from your passport was missing from the upgrade request, but it's all sorted now. Here's your boarding pass, and the executive lounge is just over there. Mr Evans asked me to let you know that he has already checked in.'

Executive lounge? With budget cuts at work, and the unmitigated disaster that was her personal finances, she'd got so used to travelling economy that she'd forgotten that there was any other way.

She determinedly ignored the flutter in the base of her stomach as she walked towards the lounge. There was no way she was going to allow Mauro Evans to have that effect on her. No way she'd be pulled into those sparkling green eyes and be tempted to flirt. The man was incorrigible—a playboy who was with a different woman on the front page of each week's trashy magazines, and remembering that was her best defence. She was sure that she was going to need one. She'd felt a pull of attraction from the second that she had realised who she was speaking to. A relationship, a fling, a flirtation was the last thing that she wanted, or needed. Especially with someone that the sidebars of shame told her regularly saw, conquered and came all in the space of a weekend. Every weekend.

Ugh, she didn't even know why she was worrying about this. It wasn't as if he was going to be interested in her. He had picked her for some perverse reason of his own. He must have wanted to annoy the producers of the show for some reason. Anyway, she had more important things to concentrate on.

She needed an image update. She needed her readers to see something different in her. Something that they could identify with. So far she'd been honest in her columns, brutally honest. But that wasn't what the readers wanted. *She* wasn't what the readers wanted. So while the cameras were rolling, she was going to have to be someone else.

Perhaps Mauro could help her out. No doubt he'd just gone into this whole thing looking for the image boost that came with charity work. She needed to show a softer side. Maybe there was a way they could both get what they wanted.

She didn't have to *do* anything. She didn't even have

to promise anything. All she had to do was let the light of Mauro's brightly shining libido reflect on her for a while. All she had to do was be friendly.

When had that started to be something she needed to work at? Since when had friendly seemed like such an effort?

Her boss was right. Something had to change, and a luxury holiday to a sunny destination—all on someone else's budget—seemed like as good a place as any to start a little soul-searching.

'Amber, you found us!'

Mauro greeted her as she stepped through the door to the lounge. He was already sipping from a glass of champagne, with the camera and a microphone pointed at him. The two members of the TV crew swung round at his words, and a camera was thrust in her face. She moulded her features once again into the smile that she'd practised in the mirror, and hoped that it looked more convincing that it felt.

'Mauro! This was a surprise. An upgrade?'

'The best way to travel,' he said with a smile, and the smallest salute from his champagne flute. 'Don't worry,' he added, and Amber guessed that some uncertainty had shown on her face. She'd thought that she'd kept her smile pinned in place, but he had seen through it. 'I matched the cost of the upgrade with a donation to the charity, if that's what you're worried about.'

Maybe she *should* have been worried about it. This was a PR exercise after all. But that hadn't been what she was thinking. What she'd been thinking was that his white shirt highlighted the hint of red in his hair and the golden warmth of his skin. That his hair looked as if it had been carefully undone, perhaps by some other woman's hands as he left her bed that morning. That the smile on his face was warm and open, as genuine as hers was strained.

'A great surprise, I should have said.' She forced the words out. 'Here's to the start of a great week.' Ayisha, the TV producer, had passed her a glass and she matched Mauro's toast with one of her own.

'To us,' Mauro said, with a searching look.

'To us,' Amber agreed, fixing her smile in place again, trying to hide the effect that Mauro was having on her.

God, he was attractive. Far too attractive for his own good, or for hers. He had been sent to test her. That was the only way she could think of it. One week, trying to show a softer side. Showing that she wasn't the bitter old hack that the Internet had labelled her. But did the dating gods really have to send this guy to help? Someone who it seemed she was physically programmed to react to. Someone whose eyes seemed to twinkle into the depths of her own, who seemed to sense her discomfort, however hard she tried to hide it.

She sat beside him, and he reached for her hand, pulling her towards him for a friendly kiss on the cheek. A day's worth of stubble scratched her cheek— he'd lain in bed too long that morning perhaps. Had something more tempting than a close shave kept him there?

Good for him if it had.

Just because she was sworn off romance and men,

and sex by default, that didn't mean everyone had to live her celibate life. If he was getting some, she was pleased for him, really. And not in any way the teeniest, tiniest bit jealous. She settled into her seat and glanced at the screen showing flight details. Another hour until they had to be at the gate. Were they meant to make small talk until then? With the camera rolling?

'I think I might just have a look round the shops until they call our flight.'

She needed something to read, something to bury her nose in during the flight, to keep her eyes from wandering over to Mauro.

'Great idea,' Mauro said, draining his glass. 'Lead the way.'

'I meant—'

'You were trying to get away from me?'

He said it with a laugh, but the question in his eyes was serious enough.

'Of course not. I'm just surprised that you're so keen on shopping.'

'Casual sexism? I'm shocked at you, Miss Harris.'

She smiled, not quite sure whether he'd shamed her or charmed her into it. 'Well, shopping it is, then. We'll meet you back here before we go to the gate,' she told Ayisha, pre-empting any thoughts of them following. She was going to have to get used to a camera watching her every move, of making sure that every word and action was projecting the image that she needed it to, but she couldn't just turn it on from nowhere. She needed to practise without the cameras on her. One misstep and she was sure that they would be all over her.

'So, then, what's it going to be?' Mauro asked. 'Handbags? Clothes? Are you going to disappear into the make-up for an hour?'

'Who's sexist now?' she asked. 'None of the above.' Her interest in make-up hadn't survived her relationship with Ian. She'd never seemed to get it right, however hard she'd tried—too slutty, too shabby, too colourful, too drab. In the end, she'd stopped trying.

She strode purposefully across the concourse towards the bookshop, dodging tourists dragging cases behind them with no sense of spacial awareness.

'What? My witty repartee isn't going to be entertaining enough for you?' Mauro asked as he zipped into a space in front of her, using his chair to clear a path through the throngs of holidaymakers. 'I'm clearly not making a great impression.'

'What can I say?' Amber replied with a shrug of her shoulders. 'I'm a writer. Which by default makes me a reader. We get a free pass to have our nose in a book whenever we want.'

'Even when there's something better to do.'

She laughed.

'Wow. I'm surprised you got that ego of yours in the terminal. And, for the record, I have absolutely no intention of *doing* you.' There, if she was going to try and flirt for the cameras then that needed to be said. She could pretend to be attracted to him now with a clear conscience. There was no leading him on if she'd already told him it wasn't happening. He'd understand friendly banter. No doubt flirting came to him as easily as breathing.

He raised an eyebrow. 'We'll see about that.'

'I want to be honest with you, Mauro. I'm here for the charity, because my work insisted on it, and for a week in the sun. I'll smile for the cameras and if you want to get to know each other while they're rolling then fine. But that's all. No funny business.'

He held her gaze for a second longer than was comfortable. What was he seeing? What was making him search her features like that, as if he was trying to get inside her head?

Managgia, she was driving him crazy already. He'd fixed her with his most challenging look. The one that had got impossible contracts signed, and unattainable goals achieved. And she still hadn't shown him who she was. She was carrying this front of hers like some sort of armour, and all he wanted was a glimpse at what was behind.

He'd heard the real her on the show, he was sure. The take-no-prisoners, 'I'd be a killer whale' Amber. The one whose caustic humour had hit him so hard he'd had to go off script, just to see what happened if he called her bluff.

So where was she now? Because she damn sure wasn't in this airport with him. Instead, in her place, was a woman trying to appear...*ordinary*.

Was she soft underneath? he found himself wondering. Like the silk shirt she'd worn beneath that blazer the first time he'd met her. The one that had gaped slightly between the buttons, that had skimmed gently over her generous breasts, hinting at the shape below just enough to keep him awake last night, concealing him enough to drive him crazy.

What had happened to make her so…closed? So controlled? Where had these defensive walls around her appeared from?

At least she had made it clear that she hadn't expected anything from him this week. It was why he had gone off-script and chosen her, of course. When he had been swimming competitively it had been his time in the pool that had controlled his schedule, his time, his life. Now it was time in the boardroom, trying to steer his sports marketing company from one market-leading success to another. There was no room in that life for a relationship. It simply didn't fit. If he was going to achieve everything that he wanted in this life—everything that he needed to—then he had to be focussed.

Since his university friend had driven the car they were travelling in into a tree, leaving him with a spinal injury and a brush with death that had been closer than was comfortable, he'd been determined to do more. To see more. To *be* more.

Before the accident, he'd been a naturally talented but under-committed athlete. The thought of leaving this world with just a mediocre list of achievements to his name: a bronze medal in the university swimming championship. Scraping a two-two in his Sports Marketing degree. A girlfriend he had liked a lot, but not loved. Not enough, anyway.

After the accident? It had all changed. It had to. He wanted to leave a mark on the world. So he'd watched the ParaGames from his hospital bed with an interest that had bordered on obsession. Four years to get himself fit, to be the best in the world. And he'd done it. Six gold medals over two games. And then after a day in the pool or the gym it was packing as many more achievements and successes as was humanly possible: flying lessons, professional development courses, a one-night stand with a beautiful woman. Anything new, anything remarkable, anything to make his life meaningful. To drive him further and further from the mediocrity that had almost been his epitaph.

And after he retired from swimming, he'd attacked the business world with zeal. The seeds he'd planted when he was competing started to grow, and somehow, ten years later, he had money rolling in from sponsorship deals, which he'd used to set up his own sports marketing business, his half-dozen medals hanging in his Sicilian home, and a passport that had seen almost as much action as his super-king-sized bed.

This front of Amber's was meant to keep people at a distance, he guessed. To keep herself apart, private. She must not realise how much he could see. How her hurt radiated from her like an inflamed wound; how her strength and her vulnerabilities were so tangled together he couldn't seem to see one without seeing the other.

He had thought that he was picking the least complicated option, when he had chosen Amber. That she was someone who couldn't be less interested in a relationship with him. And yet now, with this strangely fragile front she was presenting to the world, she suddenly seemed more complicated. More dangerous.

And now she was off again, without a backward glance at him, elbowing her way through the crowded shop to the till. He followed in her wake, through the path that her elbows had created between the tourists, and caught up with her.

He gripped his wheels tightly with his fingers. Because despite every well-reasoned argument he made about why he absolutely, definitely could not get involved with her, it was taking all the self-control he possessed to stop himself reaching out and brushing his fingertips over her skin. Pulling her down to sit on his lap so that he could explore today's silk blouse, tug at the ends of that prissy pussycat bow and satisfy his need to know what it hid beneath. Whether she was peaches and cream or strawberries; firm and toned or soft and yielding.

Because it didn't matter how much he wanted to know, the fact remained that trying to find out would be a very bad idea indeed. She was the walking embodiment of complicated, and he didn't need that in his life.

He pushed through the crowds after her, wondering how he had found himself chasing again. It wasn't a situation he found himself in often. He'd got used to a slightly embarrassed deference when he was with other people—he'd heard, 'Oh, no, after *you*…' so many times that it made him wince. He was so different from the youth he had once been in so many ways— the money, the medals, the chair—that he wasn't sure which of the three it was that had that effect on people. All he knew was that whichever it was it didn't have an effect on Amber. It seemed there was actually a chance that he might have a normal conversation this week. One with someone who wasn't an employee, or a fan, or trying to get into his bed or his bank account. How refreshing. How utterly tempting.

He forced the thought away as they left the shop and the crowds thinned.

'Now we have something to keep us entertained on the flight, what next?' he asked. 'More shopping? More champagne?' Keeping themselves busy seemed like the best defence against his thoughts wandering in inappropriate directions, like sliding down the neckline of her silky blouse.

She glanced at the screen in the centre of the terminal. 'They've announced the gate number. We get priority boarding, right? Might as well head straight over.'

'Sure, if you want.' What he wanted was to take her shopping for one of the teeny tiny bikinis he could see in the window of the shop opposite. What, so that he could torture himself by looking at something that he couldn't have? He'd need his self-restraint locked down before they reached his pool later, with sunshine and Prosecco in abundance.

He just hoped that she was going to be taking care of her own sunscreen. The thought of smoothing his hands over her shoulder blades, lifting her blonde hair to one side and tracing the nape of her neck with his fingers, rubbing cold lotion into hot skin… He imagined her, muscles relaxing under his touch, leaning her weight back against him as his hands skirted her sides, dipped into the hollows of her waist, found twin indentations at the base of her back. Would she object if his hands drifted lower still, if they dipped into the waistband of that tiny bikini?

'Mother—' Amber stopped and grabbed her foot, pulling it up to nearly waist level and inspecting the grubby mark across her shoe, which looked suspiciously like a tyre mark. 'Watch your wheels, Mauro!'

Damn. He'd caught her toes like a complete novice and all because he'd let his thoughts get carried away, imagining something that he could never allow to happen. She was still standing on one leg, grimacing, and gripping her toes as if she were worried they might fall off.

'I'm sorry, Amber. Here, let me see.' Before she could protest he'd wrapped an arm around her waist and pulled her down onto his lap. Caught off guard and off balance, she fell into him without protest, her bum landing on one thigh, her injured foot propped on the other.

'Mauro! What the hell; let me up.'

His arm was still wrapped tight around her waist— even as he was doing it he knew what a bad idea it was, but he'd just run her down, and it wasn't as if he were a waif. Between him and the chair they were well capable of doing some serious damage to a little toe.

'How about we wait until the smart wears off, *cara*? Don't tell me it doesn't hurt—I can see that it does.'

'It doesn't hurt so bad that I need to be in your lap.'

'It's nothing,' he said, wishing that he could believe what he was saying. 'It doesn't mean anything. Just think of me as a convenient seat. One of the underrated benefits of using a wheelchair, in my opinion. I'm very useful to have around when there's swooning going on.'

'Swooning? I didn't swoon, you tried to cripp—'

He saw the blood drain from her face as she realised what she had been about to say and stuttered to a halt.

'I mean—I meant—I didn't—'

Oh, he would enjoy this. Finally, a crack in this Ice Queen's façade. This was the most out of her comfort zone he'd seen her since that screen had pulled back and she'd realised he hadn't taken her 'back off' bait.

He raised an eyebrow, waiting for her to speak.

'I wasn't thinking.' The words rushed out of her as she desperately tried to backtrack and swerve around the very politically incorrect word that had nearly escaped her mouth. 'I would never use that word if I was talking about...'

Flames were devouring her face and there was an earnest, beseeching look in her eyes. OK, that was probably enough.

'Relax—' he nudged her shoulder with his own '—I know that you didn't mean anything by it. It'll take a lot more than accidentally dropping the C-word into conversation to offend me.' He'd learnt pretty quickly after his accident that it was the intention behind a particular word that would offend him, rather than the word itself. In his opinion, *that* word used among friends was far less offensive than being labelled 'brave' by someone who knew nothing at all about him.

In her horror at what she had been about to say, the fight had left her body, and she now sat comfortably in his lap, leaning just ever so slightly into the arm around her waist. Maybe sitting a little too comfortably. He might have lost a lot of the sensation from his legs, but his spinal injury was incomplete—doctor-speak for the fact that his spinal cord hadn't been completely severed—and those nerves that were still attached? Boy, were they doing an awesome job right now. And his eyes? There was nothing wrong with those. Nothing wrong with his nose, either, which was drinking in the rich scent of her hair by the lungful; or his hands, which were begging for permission to take hold of that stubborn chin, angle her luscious mouth down towards his own, and take the kiss that he'd been completely unable to stop imagining from the moment that he had first seen her, however much he had tried.

Or maybe he didn't need to use his hands at all, because she was turning towards him all of her own accord. Those big hazel eyes were locked on his, until they dropped and he just knew that she was looking at his lips. He flicked a tongue out to moisten them, to tempt her into reacting to him. Her skin flushed again as she watched him, her eyes not leaving his mouth. He moved closer, a centimetre, and then another, waiting for the moment when she blinked, when she realised he was getting too close, and froze up on him. When there was nothing but a couple of millimetres between them he breathed in another lungful of that intoxicating scent and closed his eyes, desperate for the moist warmth of her lips on his.

And then the wind was knocked from his chest and they were wheeling across the floor. Someone must have barged his chair out of the way. His hands went to his wheels as her arms tightened around him.

Brakes, Mauro. He'd never been so relieved to have made such a schoolboy error. If he'd put on the brakes he wouldn't have just been barged across the terminal building. She'd still be sitting in his lap, her lips on his, rather than scrambling herself upright. He was going to have to be more careful if he wanted to keep his life exactly as he liked it, with nothing getting in the way of his ambition and his achievements. The only relationships he had space for were simple, honest flings where both parties knew what they were getting and were happy with the bargain.

A relationship with Amber would be anything but simple. Something about the brittleness of the front she showed the world told him that she had been broken. It was as if the pieces of her didn't fit together quite right, leaving chinks to the hurt and vulnerable woman underneath. 'What the hell? Did someone just *push* you?' She spun around, looking for a fight. Nice deflection, he thought, wondering why she was so angry at herself.

'Leave it, Amber.'

There had been a time when he'd have chased anyone trying to push him around—literally or metaphorically—and shown him just how much damage a bloke with a spinal-cord injury was capable of inflicting with his fists. It just so happened that when you used a wheelchair you were at the perfect height for one or two particularly vulnerable targets. But he'd long accepted that some people would act like idiots around him. He could either let the anger consume him, as it had sometimes threatened, or he could learn to rise above it. To be the bigger man and show the world what he was capable of with his medals rather than with his fists and fury.

He glanced up at the flight information screen and realised that they had no time to pick a fight anyway. There wasn't even time to head back to the lounge and meet Ayisha and the cameraman—they'd have to hope that they would make their own way there without them.

'Come on,' he said to Amber, his resolve cracking for a second and brushing his hand against her hip. 'They're calling our flight.'

As the car swung into the driveway of the villa Amber caught her breath. The low-slung walls of the building were rendered in white, which in the late afternoon sun seemed to glow a warm orange. Three sides of the building wrapped around a central swimming pool, with expansive glazing, so every part of the house had a view of the water. Through the floor-to-ceiling windows, Amber could see straight through the building, through more windows, to the clear blue-green of the Mediterranean. She stopped as she was climbing out of the car for a moment, stalled by the beauty of Mauro's home.

Somehow, even though Ayisha had told her to expect luxury, she'd been expecting the sort of villa she and her ex, Ian, had stayed in during happier times; the sort with slightly noisy plumbing and grass growing between uneven paving stones in the garden. This—this was something else.

Imagine being able to call this your own, she thought, her mind wandering back to her bedsit in a grimy part of London. She was grateful to have a roof over her head at all, but to think that this was real life for Mauro, not a week of playing house... Their lives couldn't be more materially different. It was bad enough that he was a millionaire, successful in every aspect of his life, whereas she was just holding onto her job by a thread. They had to rub it in her face with this beautiful house as well. Not that he was going to be interested in her, with her bargain basement clothes and her grubby flat. Not that she wanted him to be.

She turned to look at Mauro.

'This is beautiful.'

'Thanks,' he said with a nonchalant shrug. 'Come on, I'll show you around.'

She wasn't sure why, but somehow she found the idea that they were staying in his house more unsettling than if the production company had hired somewhere neutral. As if it handed him a massive advantage over her. And that wasn't the only thing unsettling her. There was the memory, too, of what had happened in the airport. The way that she had sat in his lap, hypnotised by his mouth. The slight smile tugging at the corner of his lips, the way his tongue had moistened them, readying them to meet her own.

If they'd not been interrupted...

But thank God they had, and she didn't have to think about how that sentence could end.

As Mauro gave her a guided tour of the property, she was blown away by the sheer luxury of the place. The gleaming chrome of the coffee machine, the soft, supple leather of the sofas, the expansive cotton and silks on the beds. Every now and then a detail caught her eye—a handrail, a switch to lower a kitchen counter, a tile underfoot that felt particularly grippy—that made her realise all the subtle adaptations that had been made to the villa in order for it to function perfectly as Mauro's home. A million miles away from the clunky white bars and red strings she'd seen in the disabled loos at work.

'And I thought you might like this room.'

He opened the door into one of the guest suites and Amber caught her breath at the view of the ocean from the wall of windows. The water stretched green-blue as far as she could see. The view drew her in, closer to the windows until her fingertips were resting lightly on the glass. There was nothing between her and the horizon. No one but a handful of fishermen in their brightly coloured boats between her and the edge of the world. Mauro crossed the room and pressed a button on the side wall, upon which the glass doors concertinaed until the whole wall was gone and there was just a few hundred feet of terrace and sand between the bed and the ocean.

'Mauro, it's incredible.' Amber's voice caught in her throat, and she cursed herself. She didn't even understand why she was feeling so emotional. Perhaps it was the fact that she'd lost her home, that she didn't even have that West London shoebox to her name any more. Perhaps it was the knowledge that all of this had come from Mauro's many successes, when she was barely keeping a job using the one talent that she had. Maybe it was the fact that she'd spent the last eight hours on edge, desperately trying to keep her hands to herself, her libido in check, and her thoughts from wandering to Mauro.

At least he seemed to be shying away from the issue as well. Since that moment in the airport they'd both been studiously well-behaved. It all added up to exhaustion, physical and emotional.

'I was going to offer you dinner. My housekeeper will have left something in the fridge, or I can arrange something to be brought in.' He took another look at her. 'Or I can let you crash and see you at breakfast?'

She knew the relief on her face had shown when he gave her a concerned smile.

'I'll leave you to it.' He showed her how the controls for the window wall worked and let her know that he'd be in the pool if she needed anything.

Once he was gone she sat heavily on the bed, still in awe of the understated splendour of Mauro's home. If she had been unsure before about whether she wanted to succumb to Mauro's advances, this had been the wake-up call she had needed. Their homes couldn't be more different, their *lives* couldn't be more different. She absolutely would not get involved with him.

CHAPTER THREE

MAURO WOKE TO the smell of rich Italian coffee percolating through the house—Amber was up already, then. He gave a half-smile. He hadn't expected her to be awake first—had thought that she would be making the most of the holiday with a long, lazy lie-in. He had planned to be in the pool, fifty laps in, before she emerged and wanted to float on a lilo with a cocktail in hand. So she'd caught him out already. He didn't like it, the way that she kept him guessing, kept proving his assumptions wrong.

It had made him wonder what else he'd been getting wrong lately.

His bedpost certainly wasn't lacking in quantity of notches, but, now that he thought about it, there hadn't been much variety, much challenge. He'd left hospital after his accident with the single goal of achieving and seeing as much as any person could in a lifetime, and now a whole aspect of it seemed…samey. Dull.

But those meaningless flings had been exactly what he had wanted. His ex-girlfriend had made it perfectly clear that his ambitions and commitment to his sport didn't leave room for a partner or romance. He had failed at it once, and he had no interest in revisiting that disaster.

He pulled himself up in bed and transferred to his chair with a quick push of his arms. They still had a little time together before everyone else arrived. Once they'd had a quick breakfast and he'd done his laps for the day they were to meet Julia, Ayisha and the cameraman for that day's filming. The usual stuff, he supposed—by the pool, on the beach, and a 'romantic' dinner for two. And in the meantime? He still couldn't satisfy his curiosity, his need to understand more about her.

He wheeled through to the kitchen and found Amber sitting at the table, espresso cup in hand.

'Morning,' he called out to her as he came into the kitchen and headed for the coffee pot, still hot on the stove. There was something about being home in Sicily that brought his Italian blood out; if he were in England, he might start the day with a cup of tea and toast, but as soon as his feet were on Sicilian soil it was espresso or nothing.

He pulled up to the table with his coffee and reached for one of the pastries she'd piled onto a plate in the middle of the table. He expected his fingertips to meet flaky, buttery pastry, but instead they landed on impossibly soft, slender fingers as Amber reached for the *cornetto* at the same moment. He pulled away at the same instant that he registered her flinch. He couldn't help the sting of rejection at that tiny movement; whether he wanted her to be interested in him or not, that small pull away from him hurt. It was just his pride, he thought as he met her eyes, daring her to acknowledge the contact, the electric flicker that he had felt when their skin had touched.

But she backed away from the challenge, lowering her eyes and snatching her hand back.

So she really wasn't out here to play that game. Good. He decided to get them back on more neutral ground. 'All ready for your day as a reality TV star?'

She groaned, and he laughed at the look of horror on her face.

'I'm not sure I'm ever going to be ready,' she admitted. Her face had relaxed, and he could tell that she was relieved he hadn't called her out on what had just happened between them. Well, she didn't have to worry on that front. Ego had made him hold her eye just then, but that didn't mean that he had any intention of actually exploring that spark further.

'So why sign up in the first place?' he asked. She looked as if she had been regretting her decision ever since, after all.

'Sign up? I'm not sure that's how I'd describe it. It was more like…railroaded, or threatened. Definitely something that doesn't count as volunteering. And it's for charity. How could I say no? It's not like I ever thought…never mind.'

Oh, he knew exactly what she'd never thought, whether she was going to finish that sentence or not. She'd never thought she'd be here, never thought that she would be the one chosen. Well, in fairness she hadn't been. The TV company had had it all worked out—of course he'd been meant to pick contestant number two—but then with the cameras rolling and a live audience—what could they do when he picked the wrong woman? His agent had given him an earful, of course, but it had been worth it.

And what were a few booked flights and cancelled reservations when you had earned a fortune and were willing to use it to get what you wanted?

'Sorry I spoilt your masterplan. What can I say? I like a challenge.'

He instantly regretted his words, because he absolutely didn't want her getting the wrong idea. It wasn't that he wouldn't seduce her in a heartbeat if he had thought that she might be up for a fling. But it couldn't be more clear that a simple dalliance wasn't on the cards with her. There was too much hurt behind those eyes, too many defences built around her. The ghost of romance past haunting her expression.

And as much as he wanted to back away slowly, keep his distance from the big scary emotions that were clearly behind that controlled front, there was something in there calling out to him. Some vulnerability that made him want to protect her. To find out if there was anything that he could do to help.

He didn't want to think too much about why.

Perhaps, if nothing else, he could give her an ego boost. She clearly needed one. He could see it in her dropped eyes, the way she pulled her shoulders in to protect herself. Someone had given this beautiful woman cause to doubt that she looked like an absolute goddess. And as he couldn't give the person who had done that to her the hiding he no doubt deserved, then maybe he could at least get her to see what he saw, without any danger of either of them wanting to be any more involved.

'So you're not dating anyone? There's not some boyfriend hiding away somewhere while you raise money for the kiddies?'

'No.'

That wasn't a 'not right now', or a 'nobody special'. That was 'never', 'definitely not' and 'not ever' all rolled into one. He had been right: there was a world of back story behind that one word.

His voice dropped to a gentle murmur. 'Do you want to talk about it?'

What was he doing? Talking about a bad breakup ranked right up there with sticking needles in his eyes on his list of enjoyable activities. But there was something about this woman that he couldn't ignore. He couldn't brush her pain away and pretend that he hadn't seen it. If spilling her heart over her breakfast was what she needed he had a horrible feeling that he was signing up for the whole messy performance.

She took a long gulp of her coffee, and painted on something approximating a smile. 'There's nothing to tell, really. I broke up with someone a year and a half ago and have no intention of repeating my mistakes. I think maybe I'm just one of those people who are happier alone. Independent.'

Perhaps. Or perhaps not. Because as she spoke he could see the lurking shadows of grief and disappointment in her expression. The memory of someone who had let her down. Had left her feeling…less than she was.

'Or maybe you just need to—'

'Get back on the horse? Because there are plenty more fish in the sea? And someone better is just around the corner? Sorry but I've heard the clichés all before. Perhaps some people are just better suited to not…riding. Sorry, I'm better at the metaphors when I've had more coffee.'

She laughed, but it sounded hollow, thin. He had been right when he'd assumed that a quick fling would never be on the cards.

'I'm going to head out to the pool for a few laps before the cavalry turns up,' he said, trying to get them onto safer ground. 'Can I tempt you with a dip?'

For a second he thought she was going to say no, but then a smile appeared on her lips, a real one this time. 'Actually, that sounds good. I'll go get changed and meet you out there.'

The day was already warming up as he made his way out to the pool, unseasonably balmy for this time of year. He was going over his conversation with Amber again. He wanted to make her see how beautiful she was. After a decade of mutually satisfying but emotionless seductions and flings, this was new ground. He might have had a sensitive side once. It'd just been so long since he'd had any call to get in touch with it he wasn't sure that it was even still there.

He lowered himself into the pool and lay back in the water, letting it take his weight as he soaked up the warmth of the early autumn sun. His eyes drifted closed as he enjoyed the freedom to power himself around the pool, moving effortlessly in the water in a way his body didn't allow him on land. He heard her before he saw her, the flip-flop, flip-flop of her sandals on the tiles at the water's edge, the soft rustle of cotton as her towel hit the sunbed. Looking up, he saw the fluffy dressing gown she was wearing, and realised that he had been hoping for something else, something revealing, maybe. A better look at that body that she normally kept so well hidden beneath skimming silk.

She dropped the robe only at the last minute, as she slipped into the water. He had the briefest glimpse of a utilitarian one-piece in black and white, with thick straps and a racer back. Most definitely built for speed rather than decoration. Disappointed as he was, he had to admit to feeling a little pleased at finding that they had something in common.

'You're a swimmer?' he asked. Maybe he should have guessed from her strong shoulders and her toned limbs, but it seemed that his mind had been elsewhere since they met.

She shrugged, crossing her arms in front of her. 'Maybe when you're not in the pool to show me up. Given present company, let's just say I like to swim.'

'So if I were to challenge you to a race?'

'Then I would politely decline the chance to further inflate your ego by letting you whip me.'

He laughed out loud as he crossed to the side of the pool. Now there was an image he would normally enjoy.

'How about a few friendly lengths, then?'

She pulled her goggles down over her eyes. 'Fine, but no splashing.' For a moment, she paused and sniffed the air above the water. 'No chlorine?'

'It's salt water,' he told her. She *was* a swimmer, then. Any fantasies that a rebellious part of his mind might have had about a little heavy petting in the deep end were being firmly quashed.

She pushed off from the side of the pool and sliced through the water with a stroke that was perfectly decent if a little loose in places. He saw the hesitation at the end of the length and knew with an athlete's instinct that her tumble turns were not going to be the smartest part of her repertoire. He watched her for a couple more lengths, tracking the movement of her limbs as she executed each turn, looking for places to pick up a little speed, lose a little resistance. It was what had made him a champion—that ability to deconstruct every move in the pool, looking for tiny improvements, all of which added together made for six gold medals and a whole ream of world championship titles.

At the end of her fifth length she paused with her hand on the wall, and threw him a look over her shoulder, as if she had only just remembered that he was there, still watching.

She gave him a long look, and then her eyes narrowed. 'Come on, then, out with it.'

'Out with what?'

'Either you've seen something wrong with my performance here, or you're blatantly ogling me. And I've already told you that I'm not interested.'

How dared she? It was taking all his self-control *not*

to watch her in anything but a professional manner, and he was pretty damn impressed with himself for managing it. He wished he *had* been ogling her if that was all the thanks that he got. The only way to prove it was to tell her exactly what she had been thinking.

'You really want my advice?'

He saw the hesitation in her eyes, and the way that her shoulders dropped forward defensively, automatically. She'd taken criticism before, and often. It was clear in the way that she smoothed her features so that her expression was carefully blank before she looked up and met his eye.

She needed him to be kind.

The knowledge struck him in his gut, and he knew without having to be told that someone, somewhere, had been beating on this woman's self-confidence until all that was left was the presence of mind to pretend that she didn't care.

'Well,' he said, choosing his words carefully as he crossed the pool to her side. 'Your basic stroke is great: you really power through the water. But if you want me to help you with your tumble turns, we can save you some time there.'

Her shoulders dropped, just a fraction, and he let out the breath he had been holding. A smile crossed her face, slowly, chased by a look of fierce determination.

'Let's do it.'

'That's it. Perfect. Amazing!'

Amber let her body go loose as she rested her head on her arms at the side of the pool, a small smile turning up the corners of her lips. Her lungs were burning and limbs aching. She'd performed turn after turn after turn, tucking tight and exploding out until she knew— even before Mauro said a word—that she had nailed it.

She didn't care about the exhaustion. It was totally worth it. She'd struggled with those turns since she'd first taken up swimming, and if this was what it took to get them right, she'd be out here in the pool with Mauro every morning.

She'd wanted to die, at first, at the thought of stripping off in front of a world-class athlete, conscious of the wobble of her thighs. Conscious, too, that her swimming had always been the one part of her life that Ian's criticism had never been able to touch. For half an hour, every morning, she had been able to put one arm in front of the other, kick as hard as she could, shake off the tension and anxiety of living in fear of his next piece of 'advice'.

'You really got it that last time. You want to try one more?'

She shook her head, knowing that she had given the pool everything that she had. 'I'm spent for the day. Anyway Ayisha and the others are going to be here soon, aren't they? I think she said something about lunch nearby. Are they going to interview us both? Try and make us say something embarrassing about each other?'

'What could we possibly have to say? We've both been on our very best behaviour.'

Well, she wasn't sure if that was exactly true—that time when she'd sat on his lap in a public place, that didn't feel exactly like something a good girl would do. And the way that his eyes had followed her in the pool… She could tell the difference between public and personal interest, and his professionalism had slipped more than once. The heat in his expression had warmed her cheeks. When she looked up now and met his eye, what she saw there could have set the whole pool simmering.

'Well, this is cosy!'

Amber spun in the pool at the sound of Ayisha's voice, to find herself looking straight down the lens of a TV camera. She forced her smile into place and held it there until it felt as if her cheeks were cracking.

'We were just—'

Amber forced herself to keep her features neutral as Mauro draped a casual arm around her shoulders. 'Ayisha, hi,' he said. 'We were just finishing up here.'

She shrugged the arm off, as casually as she could. She knew that she needed to show a softer side on camera, but that didn't mean she had to get all up close and personal. Not yet, and definitely not when she was undressed and exposed.

'I'll see you inside.' The words came out almost as a squeak, but Amber remembered to keep her smile in place as she boosted up out of the pool, grabbing for her robe before she was fully out of the water. She couldn't help but be aware that the camera was rolling, that she had to be on her guard, protecting herself and her reputation whenever that red light was on show. 'I just want to shower the salt off and then I'll be out.'

She pulled the towelling tight around her as she

walked from the pool, wondering how much the camera had caught between her leaving the meagre privacy of the water and the safety of her robe. Ian had told her often enough how out of shape she was, even with her exercising every morning, and the last thing that she wanted was her wobbly bits exposed on TV. She pulled her shoulders forward slightly, hiding the curve of her breasts from the camera, and headed as quickly as she could towards the open door of the villa.

CHAPTER FOUR

SHE WAS STILL rubbing at her hair with a towel when she came out of her bedroom. She could have lingered in there longer, but leaving Mauro with the TV crew didn't seem like the best of ideas. She knew from being in the studio with him that he was capable of being deliberately provocative, saying whatever he thought would get the biggest reaction. It was as if he was so used to his Casanova persona that he didn't think at all. Just flirted on reflex, made suggestive bedroom eyes at any woman in a fifty-metre radius. But he could be different in private, she had noticed. He was still polite, of course. There was still that heat between them when their eyes met, however much they were both trying to ignore it. But there was a distance between them as well, a barrier that he held strong when they were alone, but that seemed to disappear in public. As if he didn't mind *appearing* to be close to her, but making it very clear when they were alone that he was strictly off limits. Well, that was fine by her. It was exactly what she needed if she was going to use this show to save her career.

Mauro had pulled up to the kitchen table in his chair, and another steaming cup of coffee was sitting in front of him. Julia was sitting on the other side of the table, chin resting on her hand as they chatted.

Julia fancies him, Amber thought. Oh, she was hiding it well. The flirtatious persona Julia had oozed in the studio was nowhere to be seen now the camera was off—she was the very definition of professionalism. But the nervous touches of her hair and the frequent glances at Mauro's lips gave her away. A surge of red-hot emotion shot from Amber's belly to her jaw, and she took a deep breath, trying to identify it. Jealousy? How could she be jealous when she had no interest in Mauro? Well, as long as it didn't impact her image on the show, then Mauro and Julia could get up to whatever they wanted. Except that thought made her stomach turn; made her want to stake her claim so that the other woman would back off.

The intensity of the feeling took her breath away.

She couldn't allow this to happen. Couldn't allow that feeling, that urge, to hold any sway over how she behaved. She'd come to Sicily with only one goal—to save her career. She needed to show the British public a softer side to her character, and flirting with Mauro was the best way to do that. But the more time she spent with Mauro, the harder it got. Every time she saw his professional gaze slip and a flash of bedroom eyes instead, every time she felt the press of his skin as he straightened an ankle, turned a hand, in the pool, she was more and more sure that this wasn't just play-acting. Her body wanted him, and it didn't care that her head was screaming for her to stop. To hide and protect herself. Not to let her feelings anywhere near a man who had blown through woman after woman without looking back.

'Don't worry, no camera this time,' Julia said, breaking her dangerously racing thoughts and pushing a cup of coffee towards her.

'I was just filling Mauro in on the plans for the rest of the day,' Ayisha chimed in from behind her. 'We'll head out to a restaurant from here, film you guys over lunch. Then we'll pull you out individually for some interviews. This afternoon you two will hit the beach with us in tow. Some sunbathing, some water sports, then we'll wrap it all up and you'll be on your own this evening. Sound OK?'

But her brain had got stuck on water sports, a safe avenue of thought at last. 'How will we…?'

'What, you think using a wheelchair means you can't jet-ski?' Mauro raised an eyebrow in her direction and she suspected there was more to this question than met the eye. A test, maybe. Was she going to expect limitations from his chair? Or would she, rather as he did, she suspected, see his life in terms of what he *could* achieve, rather than what he couldn't.

'To be honest I've never really thought about it before.'

There was no point lying and saying that she'd spent long hours wondering about the ability of paraplegics to participate in adventure sports. But that didn't mean that she was going to underestimate him now. 'Somehow I suspect there isn't anything that you can't do if you set your mind to it.'

He held her eye and his mouth twitched up at the corner. If that was a test, she guessed that she'd just passed. As he refused to look away, she felt the start of that smile radiate from his face to hers, as her mouth seemed to mirror his without any input from her.

'Right, we're off,' Ayisha said reluctantly, looking from one of them to the other, and the moment was gone. 'If we're not going to be filming here then we need time to set up at the restaurant. Are you absolutely sure that we can't—?'

'Certain, I'm afraid. It's just not going to work, having cameras in the house,' Mauro said. 'We'll meet you there.'

Amber's hands fidgeted as she waited for Mauro to return. What had just happened? For a moment it was as if she and Mauro had been completely on the same wavelength. As if they had shared exactly the same thought, with no conflict or tension between them. It made her nervous. Because fancying the man and pretending to flirt with him, that was something that she could handle when she knew absolutely that there would never be any chance of anything emotional developing between them. But that look had suggested something different. It had hinted at common ground, and them being connected.

The slick sound of Mauro's wheels on the tiles warned her that he was back.

'I thought you might be happier if we kept the cameras out of the house as much as possible,' he said as he picked up his coffee cup and then drained the contents.

She was touched that he'd thought of it. Who was she kidding? She was more than touched. Ian had never considered her feelings like that. Looking back, she realised he'd actually tried to make her uncomfortable, if he'd had the opportunity. He'd liked her off balance. Because that was when he'd been there for her. He'd liked to create situations that were impossible for her to tolerate, just so that he could 'rescue' her.

Now Mauro was doing the opposite, trying to smooth the distress from her life, and she didn't know how to handle it. Why? Why was he being so kind?

Could it just be the playboy at work? Was this simply a seduction technique, a ticket to an easy, grateful prize?

'I'm not a complete idiot, you know.' He turned towards her and caught her hand. 'I saw how uncomfortable you were when they all turned up. It's not fair for you to have to deal with that at home. I want you to feel comfortable here.'

She took a step backwards, snatching back her hand. Comfortable? How was she meant to feel comfortable with all this tension between them, with the memory of being so close to him that she could feel his breath on her lips, waiting for her to lean in.

How could she feel comfortable when Mauro had just told her that he saw not only her face and her body, but that he saw something deeper too? He saw what she was thinking, what she was feeling. Most dangerously of all, he saw what she was trying to hide.

They needed safer ground, something less personal, less dangerous to discuss. 'I've never been on a jet ski,' she said, hoping that talking about him would lead them away from anything too personal.

'You'll be a natural, I'm sure. The hardest part's getting the wetsuit on.'

Oh, for God's sake… A wetsuit. What more humiliation were they planning on throwing at her this week? 'If you can do it, I'm sure I can…' She stopped speaking as she realised what she was saying. 'Mauro, I didn't mean that you wouldn't be able to because… Because…'

He held her gaze for a long moment. 'Are we going to talk about the elephant in the room, or are we going to keep tripping over it?' So maybe talking about him wasn't safer ground after all.

'Elephant?'

'Why don't we assume,' Mauro said, 'that I'll take it as given that you're not going to intentionally be insulting me because I have a disability? You don't have to tiptoe—see, you can mention toes and everything—around me.'

'I'm sorry.' She shook her head as she sat beside him and poured another cup of coffee from the pot. 'I don't know why I said that. It's not like I've not met someone with a disability before. Maybe it's the cameras. They make me nervous.'

'There are no cameras on us now.'

She froze with her hand outstretched, cup of coffee halfway towards him. He had caught her gaze as he had spoken, and now he refused to drop it. Blood rushed again to her cheeks and she knew that they must be blazing red. He hadn't even touched her, and already her skin was burning for him. She managed to tear her gaze away, and glanced for a split second at his hand, resting on the table. It was only a couple of inches away. It would be nothing to set the cup down, reach for his hand and let her fingertips brush gently against his skin. But he twitched away, even as the thought crossed her mind, and she breathed a sigh of relief. It was too much. Too risky. She placed the coffee in front of him and withdrew her hand to the safety of her lap. 'I'm sorry. No more tiptoeing, I promise.' She stood suddenly from the table, and headed to the door. 'I'd better go get ready if we're meeting them there.'

'So about this elephant,' Amber said later that day.

He concentrated on the electronic controls of his beach wheelchair, rolling steadily across the sandy planks of the boardwalk as they made their way across his private beach, heading towards the building that housed his water sports equipment. The heat of the sun was fading, and the afternoon was pleasantly warm in the sheltered cove.

He'd not had a chance to talk properly to Amber since she'd so abruptly fled the kitchen after breakfast. He'd thought maybe he'd have a chance over lunch to ask what had upset her, but they had been too busy fielding questions from Julia and Ayisha. Now they finally had the opportunity to finish the conversation they had started back at the villa, but she wanted to talk about him, instead of herself.

'That journalistic instinct finally winning out over social awkwardness?' he asked with a grin that he hoped told her he didn't mind answering her questions.

'Can I ask what happened?'

'Why not?' It was refreshing, after the way that she'd been watching her words around him. 'After all, this is a date, isn't it? We're meant to be getting to know each other.' Why had he said that? This wasn't really a date. It was closer to being a business arrangement. If he were to start thinking of it as a date… Well, he just couldn't; it was as simple as that. He had no interest in starting anything with Amber Harris. Every line of her muscles screamed of past hurt and vulnerability, and he was the last person that she needed in her life.

No, this definitely wasn't a date. If it had been a date, he'd be letting himself hang back in his chair, just a little, so that he could watch the swing of her hips as her feet sank in the golden sand with every step. He'd reach out and brush her hand with his free one, savouring each spark of energy, which he just *knew* would grow with every touch of her.

If this were a date, he wouldn't be fighting the mental images that were bombarding him in the aftermath of their little coaching session in the pool this morning.

But this wasn't a date. Because she was afraid, and sad, and, oh, *so* not ready for a fling. And he was ambitious, and driven and single-minded and selfish, and— according to his ex-girlfriend—the very last person that any sane woman wanted in her life.

His chair gave out a low electric growl as it fought over the sand, but he didn't hesitate, pushing the machine forward at full speed, 'There's not a lot to know,' he told Amber as they reached the edge of the water. Amber let the waves lap at her toes, and he tried not to think too much about the fact that he'd never paddle in the ocean again. There was no point dwelling—there were so many things that he could still do. So many things that he'd achieved that he'd never dreamed of doing before his accident.

He shrugged as he continued speaking. 'I was driving home from training with a teammate. The car came off the road and hit a tree; part of the car door got wedged in my spine.'

She drew in a short breath in shock. 'Well,' she choked, 'that's one way of putting it.'

'Honestly—' She was looking out at the water, her eyes on the horizon, but suddenly he wanted her attention. All of it. If he was going to talk about the most transformative time in his life, he needed…connection. He didn't want to just throw the words out into the air and hope that they reached her. He needed to see, to know, that she understood. He caught her hand, and, though she tensed, she didn't pull away. He held on tight, not because he wanted romance, but because he wanted—no, needed—her to get this. If she couldn't understand this, then she couldn't understand *him*, and suddenly nothing seemed more important.

'No one believes me when I say this, Amber, but I'm lucky. I'm alive; I have enough money that I can get pretty much anywhere I want. I have the equipment to keep in shape and I have the sort of perspective that only comes from a near-death experience. You're not going to be one of those terrible, terrible people who tell me you'd rather have died, are you? I'm not sure I could take that. Not coming from you.'

'Not from me? Why not? What's special about me?'

What was special about her? Well, actually he had a list of what was special about her. It started with the way her skin felt as it slipped, wet, under his fingers, and went from there. But why the hell had he said that when they'd been talking about his accident? Why should it bother him any more than normal if she was one of those people who just didn't understand him, who couldn't see how much life he had left in him? He shouldn't care. He'd promised himself ten years ago that he was going to do the things he needed to in life. Anyone who wasn't OK with that had been left behind and had no one but themselves to blame.

But he couldn't bear to hear her speaking as if there were nothing remarkable about her. It made his blood boil to think that someone had let her down so badly that she could have lost sight of the truth of herself so completely. And just then he couldn't bear for her to think of herself that way. He grabbed for her other hand and pulled her in, resting both her hands on his arm-rests so she would have no choice but to meet his eyes.

'What's special about you? Oh, *cara*, where do you want me to start?'

With her leaning in so close, it would be nothing to reach out and caress her jaw, just a whisper of a finger-tip from her chin up to behind her ear. But his hands re-membered the slide of her lithe calf, her delicate ankle beneath his hands that morning, and they yearned for more. He reached for her, and his fingertips hit the soft vulnerable skin behind her knee. He let his hand rest there just for a moment as he registered the shock in her eyes. Then he raised his hands and threaded his fingertips through the salt-textured waves of her hair, until her breath was warm on his lips; until her eyes were enormous green pools just inches from his.

Just as he was closing his eyes, could practically taste the sweetness of her lips, a flash of light caught his eye and snapped him from his Amber-induced trance.

'Ayisha.' With that one word, the sensual softness disappeared from Amber's lips as they formed a concerned expression. But by the time she lifted her head, they had stretched into a sham of a smile.

A frown furrowed his brow. Why had she done that? Why fake it? It wasn't as if she'd ever made a secret of the fact that she hadn't wanted to come on this date in the first place. Perhaps she was just being polite. But... no. It was more than that. You didn't become someone else just because you were being polite. And that was what had just happened. Amber had disappeared behind the mask of this grimacing stranger.

'Looks like we're interrupting again,' Julia said with a singsong intonation that made the red light on the front of the camera behind her redundant. Of course they were filming—and the timing couldn't be worse.

'What gave us away?' Ayisha asked. He could see from the expression on her face that she was just as annoyed as he was that they'd interrupted what had looked certain to be a *very* interesting progression.

'Sunlight reflecting off the lens,' he told her, trying to regroup his thoughts, and calm his body.

'Argh, gets us every time,' Ayisha complained. 'Well, don't let us stop...uh, whatever it was we interrupted. You two feel free to pick up right where you left off.'

Tempting as that was, he had a feeling that he and Amber needed to finish this conversation—and anything else that had been about to happen—without an audience. 'Oh, we were done here,' Amber said with a strained cheerful intonation to match her smile, and again Mauro felt a flicker of anger and hurt that she was faking it like this, faking it with him.

'OK, then, if you're sure, we could actually do with cracking on a bit. We need to do some long shots first, because the light's great with you two down by the water there. So if you want to continue your...conversation we'll be way back up the beach so just ignore us. We just need to have a little look round, set up a couple of things and then we'll shout you over after we've got those shots for some interviews. All sound OK?'

His eyes narrowed as his gaze followed Julia, Ayisha and Piotr as they retreated down the beach, all the while with that little red light letting them know that they were still being watched, however far they might go. When he looked up and met her eye, it was clear that Amber had retreated from him, and it wasn't just that her hands were no longer resting on his chair but loosely at her sides. He ached to grab them again, even while he knew that it would be a terrible idea. For a brief moment there had been an intimacy between them, but he knew from the strained look that had replaced her manic fake smile that this wasn't just complicated, it had layers of obstacles that he didn't understand. Maybe he should be mad at her for lying to him, for being fake with him, but mainly he just wanted to help her. Protect her.

'That woman has terrible timing,' he said jokingly, hoping to lighten the mood.

'Oh, really?' Amber replied.

That was how she was going to play this? As if that moment had never happened? Well, good. It had worked for them so far, he supposed. They'd both brushed off that kiss that never happened in the airport. He supposed it made sense that they'd try the same now. But they couldn't go on like that for ever; they couldn't ignore indefinitely whatever it was between them that was making him feel like this. As if he wanted to know her. To understand her. As if the more time he was spending with her, the more he wanted out of this week. More than he had ever been able to give before.

Perhaps they were going about this all wrong; if they confronted this head-on—acknowledged that there was an attraction—they'd be able to move past it.

'It's not going to work, Amber.'

She raised her eyebrows in an attempt at playing dumb.

'I know that you feel something between us.' Out of the corner of his eye, that red light still winked at him from down the beach. Damn it. She was standing away from him; in any other circumstances it would have been a comfortable distance. Close enough for conversation, not so close that he had to strain his neck looking up at her. But right this second there was nothing comfortable about it. He wanted her close if they were going to have this conversation. He wanted her hands back on his chair. Right up in his personal space with nowhere to hide. This could only work if they were both honest with one another. If there was anything left unsaid, he knew that it would just allow this atmosphere between them to fester. But he also knew that if he tried to touch her with the cameras on them, she would bolt.

So when she leaned in, her hand on his, and whispered into his ear, he could barely catch his breath with the shock of it. 'It's just attraction. Just physical, Mauro. It doesn't have to be a big deal.'

It's just—

What?

She was still uncomfortable. That much was clear in the tension showing in the muscles above her collarbones. The slightly fixed look at the corners of her mouth. She was faking this flirtation. Oh, the attraction was real enough. Her body wanted him and his was begging him to give himself to her. It seemed stupid even to try and deny that. But those casually thrown away words. They weren't her. Goddamn him, though, if he wasn't going to take advantage of this moment and try and crack through to whatever was going on underneath. Maybe he'd actually get at something close to the truth.

'Just attraction? Amber, this "just physical" thing

you're talking about is testing me to breaking point. So if it's no big deal, why haven't we both stopped all this dancing around and got it out of our systems? Because we both know that there's more to it than that.'

Just saying it out loud fired a charge of electricity into the air, and it crackled between them, looking for earth, any opportunity to shoot through them and tie them together. But it was easy to throw words like that out there when you knew there was no chance of them hitting the mark. Amber might be saying all the right things, pretending that she was going to give in to attraction, but he knew that she didn't mean it. Not yet, anyway.

The more he saw of her, the more he saw of how much she kept hidden from the world, the more intrigued he was. He still wanted her to open up to him, still wanted to try and get to the bottom of the pain in those eyes, to help ease the burdens of her past. He didn't want to think too much about why. About why he couldn't just cheer her up and show her a good time and move on. Something about her spoke to him. Called out to him, and he couldn't just ignore it.

Perhaps if he opened up, spoke more about himself, perhaps then she'd start to trust him. He'd lay himself out there, and could only hope that she'd accept the challenge and reciprocate.

With a wrench in his gut he turned his chair away from her and wheeled along the water's edge. Away from that prying red light. 'You wanted to know about the chair. After the accident, they couldn't tell me a lot about what was going to happen. With all the swelling and everything it takes a while before they can really see what the extent of the injury is.'

'Did you think that you might walk again?' He glanced up and her face looked a little more relaxed. She'd jumped on the change of topic, and he guessed she was pleased that he wasn't going to call her out directly on her attempt at flirtation.

He didn't mind answering her questions. From someone else, it might have felt intrusive, but from her it was matter-of-fact. She was simply trying to understand him better rather than looking at the freak show.

'God, I hoped so. I think I spent most of those first few weeks praying to anyone who would listen that I would be able to. But my spinal cord had taken too much of a beating. So I have a little sensation in places; I've worked on what movement and strength is left so that I can manage a few paces with crutches if I need to. But mostly I feel happiest in my chair. In the right building it can get me from A to B quicker than if I was walking. The beach is a challenge, but the right equipment makes it possible, and it's worth it to get into the water and on a jet ski.'

They continued for a few metres in silence, and he guessed that she was choosing her words with care, this time. 'I'm not sure what I can say that won't sound patronising. But I find it incredible that you can think of it that way. No wonder you charge a fortune for your motivational speaking.'

'Don't start thinking I'm some sort of poster boy. I just did what I had to and thought what I had to in order to survive. It's all any of us do.'

'Not everyone,' she argued. 'Not every person who uses a wheelchair is into extreme sports.'

'No, but they do what they have to—just like everyone who doesn't use a wheelchair.'

'And you need extreme sports to get by? Let me guess: classic case of needing to feel near death to feel alive?' Oh, she really thought she had him pinned down, didn't she?

'No, it's not that. Trust me, when you've felt as close to death as I have, you're happy keeping it at a respectful distance. Well, I am anyway. It's not the danger I love; it's the experience. It's pushing to find the limits of what my body can do, of what my mind can take in. It's finding something new in every day, to mark that day as special. To make it matter.'

They stopped again and looked out over the water. A light breeze was playing with her hair, making the sun catch all its shades of gold and silver.

'And you're telling me that has nothing to do with your accident,' she said.

'It has everything to do with the accident.' Of course it did: he wasn't a machine. It wasn't as if he could have carried on with his life without the accident having an enormous effect on him. His need to achieve, to *experience*, had infected every part of his life. His girlfriend hadn't been able to understand. She had seen the man that he had become after his accident and decided that she wasn't that interested after all.

'It changed me. What would you expect? Look: I nearly left this world as a mediocre twenty-something wasting his days on mediocre experiences. I've been pretty damn close to my highest achievement in life being winning the one hundred metres freestyle at school sports day. It's not the way I want to go. I don't need the money or the fame, though I'm not going to argue that they don't make my life a hell of a lot easier than it might be otherwise. But I need to know I'm doing something. I'm *being* someone.'

She fixed him with a shrewd look, and he felt a curl in the base of his stomach. If she was sussing him out, he had the feeling he wasn't making the good impression that he'd been aiming for.

'You like the thrill of the chase, then. The new and the unfamiliar.'

He was right, and she was getting close to the bone. Was she digging around this subject with intent? Did she want to know what he had to offer? Part of him wanted to keep his mouth shut, lie by omission, say whatever it took for her to trust him and take him to her bed. But he couldn't do that. If Amber decided that was what she wanted, then he wanted her to decide it while in possession of all of the facts.

'You think that's why I've never settled down? Well, maybe you're right. Maybe it is. But I didn't set out to be a playboy, Amber, if that's what you're getting at. I had a girlfriend. I think I loved her, actually. But that wasn't enough. It wasn't enough to compensate for the man that I became after the accident. There's not room in my life for both. I can't have this drive and ambition, and have enough time and energy left over for a relationship as well. She made that pretty clear when she packed her bags and left me. I've discovered since that when you've made it your life's mission to see everything you can, it doesn't leave a lot of time for seeing the same thing twice.'

'Or the same woman.'

He looked up at her, trying to gauge from her features whether she was judging him. 'I'm not looking for commitment, Amber. But you know that I want you.'

'I know.'

He held her gaze, challenging her with that intimacy, with the connection that he knew that they both felt.

'And if I thought for a second that a fling was on the cards then, trust me, I'd be pulling out my best moves right now. But I think we both know that that's not what you want. All I want to know is—what *do* you want? Why are you here? The truth.'

He wasn't sure why he thought that he deserved honesty from her. Really, if he thought about it, she was little more than a stranger to him. But he had shown her parts of himself that he didn't open up to just anybody. It wasn't too much, surely, to expect the same from her.

Then she broke their connection and her eyes flicked over his shoulder. He glanced behind him and saw Ayisha and Julia deep in conversation, and a winking red light on the camera that told him they were still being watched.

He could show her that she should trust him. That she wouldn't regret taking a chance and confiding in him, but he'd rather do it without an audience. Anyway, there were other ways to put a smile on a woman's face, to put some colour into her cheeks. He turned his chair and powered along the beach again, his free hand at the small of Amber's back. A couple of hundred yards later they reached the cabin where he kept his water sports equipment.

'Come on.' He tugged her hand as he drove up onto the boardwalk in front of the cabin. 'We can talk later. Now: I'm going to teach you to jet-ski.'

Amber pulled the elastic from her hair and collapsed on the sand. Adrenaline still coursed through her veins, making her heart race and every grain of sand feel like a pinprick on her skin.

'Mauro, that was… Immense. Incredible. Some other big word I can't think of right now. I don't know how to thank you.'

He had a grin plastered on his face, making his green eyes twinkle, and showing off the smile lines around his mouth.

'You don't need to thank me,' he said.

Which was a good thing, because her perverse imagination was having a few rather inspiring ideas about how she might show him her appreciation. Call her a cavewoman, but there was something about seeing him with that powerful machine between his legs, seeing him leap over waves and twist and turn in the water, that had her hotter than anyone who'd just spent an hour in the ocean had any right to feel.

Ayisha came up to meet them where they'd stopped on the sand. 'Amber, we're just going to do these interviews before we let you get changed, if that's OK with you?'

Spell broken again. Thank goodness. Because the

longer this day was going on, the harder she was finding it not to sink into those green eyes of Mauro's, to
remind herself of everything that she had lost the last
time she had let herself be so careless, the last time
that she had let her guard down. Getting involved with
Mauro would be like asking for her heart to be tram-
pled all over again. He was a playboy—he didn't even
bother to deny it. Acting on this attraction would lead
to nowhere but trouble. But she couldn't think about
that now. She was going to have to smile and flirt her
way through this interview.

She settled into the chair set up in the little gazebo
on the sand, and tried to pull herself together, to make
sure that she was showing exactly what she needed to
make the audience find her likeable. The viewers at
home—all the ones who bought her paper, read the
website and held her career in their hands—needed to
see that she was a warm-hearted person. Someone to
be trusted, to come to for advice. Someone with something interesting and witty to say. Without readers, she
had no job. And her boss had made pretty clear before
she'd left that she had precious few of those readers
left. She needed to make this work.

Not that it was going to be difficult to make anyone believe that she fancied Mauro. She was pretty
sure that it was obvious to anyone that she was having
X-rated thoughts about him. The problem was going
to be keeping it likeable, and that meant keeping her
memories at bay.

Broken and broke, she'd been left by the man she
had thought she was going to spend her life with. Noth-

ing could induce her to want to repeat that. No, a relationship was definitely out of the question. But it wasn't as if Mauro wanted that anyway. He'd told her he only ever had casual relationships. So even if she had wondered, in her weaker moments, whether there might be anything to chase between them, at least she could rationalise herself out of it.

'So, let's go back to that first time you met. What were your first impressions of Mauro?' Julia's question broke into her thoughts, and Amber rushed to smile, though she guessed it looked creaky. The TV presenter's excited tone told Amber—if she'd had any reason to doubt—exactly the answer she and the audience wanted to hear.

With her fake smile still fixed in place, Amber gave her what she wanted. 'Well, he's gorgeous, obviously.' She followed her words with a little laugh, which sounded tinny even to her. Relax, she ordered herself. Don't go too over the top. Julia was nodding encouragingly. 'And he knows just how gorgeous he is—never misses an opportunity to remind me of the fact.'

'Well, that sounds like Mauro, all right. So what did he do? Can you give us an example?'

'Well, this morning, for instance…' She improvised hastily, feeling the blood rushing to her cheeks. The blush would work in her favour, she thought—show that she really was human. 'He turned up to breakfast with no shirt on.'

Julia made a performance of fanning herself with

her script. '*Really*, that is interesting. Not the worst start to a day, I imagine.'

'It was quite a sight,' Amber agreed. The smile this time came naturally, and she took a deep breath, forcing it into her shoulders and spine, helping them to relax. 'Unfortunately, he was just on his way to the laundry room. You can imagine my disappointment.' She let the cushions of the chair take her weight and mould round her body, finally feeling able to speak without a shake in her voice. This is all there is to it, she told herself. Just talk about how you fancy Mauro, and don't overthink the rest of it.

God, she hoped it was working. If she could just convince Julia, and the viewers at home, that she could be warm-hearted, open to romance, perhaps they'd call off the Internet witch hunt and she could salvage her career.

'So other than the fact that he looks good without a shirt—which, let's face it, we all knew from his swimming career—how are things going? Any sparks?'

The memory of his hands on her body, his breath on her lips, of his arms around her when he pulled her onto his lap, was at the forefront of her mind. She forced herself to keep looking at Julia, when her instinct was to drop her eyes, to try and hide exactly what she was feeling. Where was the line? She needed to show a softer side of herself, but that didn't mean she had to reveal everything.

Thankfully it seemed Ayisha had seen that she had got the best out of her for now. 'I think that blush speaks for itself! That's great, thanks, Amber. That's all we need right now. I'm going to get Mauro in here and then you two are done for the day. Make sure you rest up tomorrow; you've got Mount Etna to conquer in a few days.'

CHAPTER FIVE

A WHOLE DAY passed in a blur of sun, swimming and sleep by the pool while Mauro caught up with some business on the island, and he still hadn't appeared by the time she decided to turn in for the night. But the next day she was aware of him before she was even out of bed: she awoke to the rhythmic swish-swish of a powerful swimmer in the pool. As the glass wall of her bedroom concertinaed open, the briefest hesitation in his stroke told her that he'd heard her, and he slowed to a halt at the end of the lap, before crossing to the side of the pool nearest her room with a lazy backstroke.

'Morning, sleepyhead.'

He was right—she could tell from the warmth of the tiles beneath her feet that she'd slept later than she'd planned. Must be all the sun, she reasoned. She rarely slept past six at home, was in the pool by seven and the office by eight. Judging from the hungry ache in her belly it must be nearly nine now. Long past her habitual breakfast of toast and black coffee.

'Sorry, I did wait for you, but I needed to make a start on my laps.'

'No, my fault.' She dropped to sit by the side of the pool, pulling her robe tight around her swimsuit while she let her feet play in the water. 'I can't believe I slept so late.'

Mauro placed an elbow either side of her knees. Her instinct was to pull away—but his hand brushed against her calf, and she found herself incapable of moving. Or perhaps…perhaps that was an excuse. Perhaps she wanted to stay right where she was, testing her limits, her resolve.

'I must have worn you out on the jet ski,' Mauro said with a roguish grin. 'Was one lazy day not enough? Should I have gone easy on you?'

'Never.' She smiled, but faltered when Mauro's hand dropped to her ankle, absent-mindedly caressing the delicate bones, and then found the sole of her foot with his thumb. Just…there. There was her limit. She pushed him away gently with her free foot.

'Right,' he said, raising an eyebrow. 'Where's the fun in holding back?'

She rolled her eyes at his obvious double meaning.

'So are you getting in the pool?' he asked. 'We can work on those turns some more.'

Did she want to be barely clothed, in close proximity, with him watching her every move… A dropping sensation in her tummy told her that that was a very bad idea. But he was a medal-winning athlete, offering to help her. It could be just professional interest. She looked down and met his eye, and knew instantly that there was nothing professional about what he was thinking. But she couldn't resist the lure of the cool water, the slight smell of salt in the air, the chance to stretch her limbs and loosen her joints.

She started to untie the belt of her robe but Mauro's eyes on her stopped her dead. It was bad enough that he was going to see her in her swimsuit *again*; she couldn't bear to have him watch her with that quiet intensity while she undressed.

'Erm…any chance of some privacy, Mauro?'

She tried to keep the words light, but suspected that the shake of her voice had given her away.

'Privacy? You have your suit on, don't you? There's not going to be anything I haven't seen before, you know.'

She'd expected flirtatious, playful Mauro, but instead his face was serious as he regarded her through narrow eyes. 'You didn't like that the camera caught you in your swimsuit the other day either.'

She laughed, but it sounded brittle.

'Who wants to be on telly in their underwear?'

'Well, plenty of people don't seem to mind too much, from what I've seen. But… I don't know. I just feel like there's something you're not telling me.'

'Mauro, there's a million things I haven't told you. You barely know me. Come on, I thought you were going to help me with these turns again.'

She shrugged off her robe and his questions and slipped into the water. She swam half a length under the surface, letting the water muffle the outside word. Only when her lungs were screaming for air did she finally surface, opening her eyes to see Mauro just a couple of metres ahead of her.

She took a deep breath before she turned, aware in every part of her body of Mauro waiting at the end of the lap, his eyes following the movement of every limb. She'd never felt more exposed, more vulnerable, in front of him.

Pushing away from the wall, her body was strong and straight, and she swam another couple of laps, letting the familiar rhythm of her front crawl wipe away her tension at Mauro's question. It wasn't what he'd asked—it was why he'd asked it. He must have seen something, worked out some of her past to make him wonder.

The next time she reached the end of the pool where Mauro was waiting, he reached out to her, his hand just brushing against her arm.

She pulled up, resting her arms on the side of the pool. She hadn't realised until she stopped and found herself out of breath that she'd been going at sprinting pace, swimming faster and faster to try and slow the racing of her mind.

'It's looking really good,' Mauro said, in response to her raised eyebrow. 'Even better than when we worked on it before.'

'You stopped me to tell me that?'

'Is that not OK?'

'I thought this was a training session.' That was how she'd talked herself into this, after all.

'OK…' He gave her a shrewd look. 'Let's get to work, then. This time, I want to see those arms dead straight before you push off.'

As she neared the wall again, she glanced ahead

to gauge her approach, trying to time it to the perfect arm's reach. She exhaled through her nose as she somersaulted, curling her knees into her chest. Just as she tensed her legs to power into the start of another lap, she felt a heavy pressure on her waist, immobilising her. Her eyes flew open in surprise, until her gaze rested on Mauro, holding onto the side of the pool with one arm, the other curled around her.

'It's OK—it's me,' he said, as if anyone else could have that effect on her body.

He'd misinterpreted her reaction: it wasn't panic making her suddenly breathless. It was the heat of his arm on her waist, burning into her skin where the suit was cut out at the back. It was the way he was supporting her whole body in the water, the way that her muscles had relaxed into his care, her body trusting him completely even if her mind wouldn't.

'I wanted to show you…' His voice trailed off, but she didn't move. Didn't uncoil her body, didn't seek the safety of the floor of the pool. 'You could tuck in a bit tighter, and straighten…'

His fingers brushed the inside of her arm, the oh-so-sensitive skin just above her elbow, barely a whisper of a touch. But it was enough to unravel her practised poise, until her toes were drifting down towards the glassy mosaic tiles at the bottom of the pool, her body was seeking the touch of his, and her arm—where the fine hairs were still erect from the touch of Mauro's hand—was draping itself loosely around his shoulders.

'Tighter,' Mauro said, and she wrapped both arms

around him, testing how it felt to follow his commands—and her desires—without trying to rationalise.

He spun suddenly in the water, trapping her against the rough wall of the pool, his forearms braced either side of her: holding her, protecting her. When she met his eyes, it was to find that she was already half drowning in him. But where she was water, he was fire; the heat in his eyes was unmistakable, and directed solely at her.

'Amber…' Mauro began, but his voice trailed off as he broke their gaze, and he moved closer, until she couldn't resist closing her eyes in anticipation. She waited for his lips to meet hers. Instead of soft pressure of skin on skin, warm breath tickled behind her ear, and his nose nudged her hair aside. In a voice barely more than a whisper, he spoke in her ear. 'Amber, you're so beautiful.'

Instantly she stiffened. 'Don't. Don't say things like that.' She ducked under his arm, away from the spell he had cast over her.

'Like what?' Mauro asked, his expression punch drunk as he twisted around to face her.

She turned and swam, pushing her anger through her muscles until she was powering through the water.

'What's wrong?' he asked when she stopped to catch her breath.

'Nothing.' Nothing that she wanted to discuss with him at any rate. It was safer if they just forgot about this. If they pretended that that hadn't just happened. Surely he could understand. She turned and started another lap, but he was ahead of her before they were halfway across the pool. She didn't want to know how much of a head start he'd given her.

'Why?' he asked as she caught up with him.

Instead of answering, she took a deep breath and performed a tumble turn. After Mauro's coaching, she barely made a splash. But a strong hand touched at her ankle. It was for only a second, but long enough to break her rhythm. She whirled around.

'For God's sake, Mauro. Just let me swim!'

'Why are you angry that I paid you a compliment?'

'I'm not angry.'

'Then what?' he asked, genuine bewilderment showing on his face. 'Can't you at least be honest with me? I don't know what happened back there. I don't even know what I wanted to happen. But I know that I hurt you, somehow, and I want to know what I did so that I don't do it again. I'm not looking to cause you pain, Amber.'

She sighed, shaking her head. 'I'm not angry that you complimented me, Mauro. I'm angry that you lied to me.'

'When? When did I lie?' he asked.

'You called me beautiful. And I know that that's not me. So don't do it. *Please.* Don't flirt just because you think that you should. Or because you can't help it. It makes me feel crappy, and it's not going to get you anywhere.'

'I'm sorry,' he said, with a shrug of his shoulders as he leaned back against the side of the pool, but the apology was just as much a reflex as the compliment had been. 'I didn't mean anything by it.'

'And that's the point, isn't it? It didn't matter who you were saying it to. It could have been anyone. I bet you've used that line a dozen times before, haven't you?'

'Amber, I think you're being—'

'I'm sorry, Mauro, I need to get showered.'

She boosted out of the pool and walked away, knowing that she was running because she was scared, because she was disappointed in him and in herself. And knowing that she was being unfair by walking out before they could finish their conversation.

By the time Mauro came into the house from the pool, she was showered, caffeinated, and had regained some of her composure.

'I'm sorry,' she said, as he wheeled into the living space where she was sitting with an espresso and the English newspapers.

He shrugged. 'No need to apologise. But, you know, I've given it some thought,' he said. 'And I honestly think you're a very beautiful woman.'

'Well, OK…' Amber said with a small smile. 'As long as you've thought about it.'

'Oh, my goodness. You look like a…like a goddess,' Mauro said, when she emerged from the bathroom later that afternoon. Had he learned nothing from their conversation? There *was* something Grecian about the dress that she'd chosen for their tour of the winery, and the formal dinner tonight. Pleated silk swept down from an empire line almost to the floor, and a cleverly cut neckline balanced out her swimmer's shoulders.

She'd assessed the result in the mirror before she had left the room. Acceptable, yes. Maybe even attractive, which—given the cost of the dress and the cosmetics, all courtesy of Ayisha—was the very least she could have hoped for.

But a *goddess*?

'Don't,' she warned.

They had walked on eggshells that morning after their argument in the pool, and she didn't want to spoil the entente that they were delicately balancing by re-hashing it.

'I thought about it before I said it, I swear.'

She shook her head as they walked out of the villa and towards the waiting car. 'Please—I don't want an argument. I just want you to cut the bull,' she said as she slid into the car beside him and pulled the door shut, lowering her voice, though she wasn't sure if the driver could understand English. 'I know that this whole week is a weird, fake scenario. We keep trying to pretend that nothing is happening, but I'm not sure how successful we're being. And just when I think that we're starting to understand each other you go and spoil it by spinning all this rubbish about how beautiful you think I am.'

'Why is it rubbish?' he asked. 'Why am I not allowed to think it's true? I'm not playing games, Amber. I'm not telling you you're beautiful because I want something, or because I think you want something. I'm just trying to be honest.'

She rubbed her forehead with the palm of her hand, squeezing her eyes tight. 'But I know I'm not beautiful, Mauro, so every time you say that to me, it's like a shot of iced water down my back.'

'Oh, you *know* you're not beautiful, therefore my opinion isn't valid.' His voice was irritatingly calm as the driver eased the car around a series of curves in the road. 'I'm sorry, Amber, but it doesn't work like that. I'm afraid I get to decide for myself whether I think you're beautiful, and I do.'

'But I'm *not*.' Her voice broke as the tears that had been threatening all day finally came through. 'If you think I am it's because I've just spent an hour applying every lotion and cosmetic that Ayisha could find in Palermo when she realised I didn't have any of my own. This isn't some sort of false modesty. I scrub up all right, that's what Ian used to say to me. I can look half-decent if I put enough time and effort in. But we both know I'm not beautiful, so just cut it out.'

'Ian.' He was quiet for a long, thoughtful minute. 'Your ex?'

Stupid—she hadn't even meant to mention him. The last thing she wanted was to dissect her disaster of a relationship with Mauro, but from the determined look on his face she guessed that he had other ideas.

'He never told you you're beautiful?'

She rested her elbow on the car door, and let her head rest against her hand, losing the energy to be angry. 'Please just leave it. I don't want to talk about him.'

'Fine, we won't talk about him. We'll talk about you, and how you've got to the ripe old age of whatever you are without being able to take a compliment. This Ian, what else did he say?'

She turned to look out of the window, at a sky that was just turning pink. 'I'm not going to talk about it, Mauro, so we can just drop this.'

'So it wasn't what he said, was it? It was what he did. What was it? Did he cheat?'

At that, another tear escaped the corner of her eye as she fought a losing battle with herself.

'Yes, he cheated.' She turned back to him and fixed him with a stare. He met her gaze, and she read pity there. She didn't want him to feel sorry for her, but if he insisted on the whole sordid story, then fine. He could have it. Maybe that would be enough to put an end to his flirtation. To the temptation she was finding harder and harder to resist. 'Is that what you want to hear? He cheated and he left me, and he cleared out our bank accounts and sold my house from under me before he went. It wasn't enough to break my heart. He had to take my home and practically everything that I owned as well. And that is why I'm not in the least interested in a relationship, Mauro. I've taken just about as much heartbreak as a person can, and I'm not stupid enough to get involved with someone else, especially someone who is as proud of you to love women and then leave them.'

'Whoa, a relationship? Involved? Who mentioned involved?'

'The flirting, Mauro. The compliments. The attention. I know you're just trying to get me into bed.'

He stayed silent as they pulled through a pair of

magnificent gates and wound up the road towards a castle of warm yellow stone. Silent while the car stopped in front of a magnificent wooden door. Silent until they spotted their hostess waiting for them in a stone archway.

Mauro looked across at her, his face hard and unreadable. 'She'll wait.' His tone said, *We will finish this conversation,* as clearly as if he'd spoken the words out loud. 'I have *not* been trying to get you into bed. That's the very last thing I want, actually.' His words felt like a slap to the face, and she knew that the hurt must have shown in her expression. 'No, not because… You're beautiful, Amber. And sexy, and yes, a goddess. I'm not going to take that back. I mean it. But that doesn't mean I think we should be *involved.* I don't have space in my life for a relationship; you don't want something casual. It would never work. But that doesn't mean you shouldn't believe me when I tell you how goddamn desirable you are.'

He said it with such sincerity and passion that she couldn't help one corner of her mouth turning up in a half-smile.

'That's better,' he said, swiping at her tear with his thumb and reaching for her hand. 'I'm sorry if my compliments upset you. I honestly didn't mean them to. I'll try harder to stop, if they make you uncomfortable. We can be friendly, can't we? We have our week-long first date, with a national audience along as chaperones; we smile pretty for the cameras come December, and then we get back to real life. Every now and then we'll think back to the completely strange week that we had here. You meet Mr Right, settle down and have a dozen beautiful children; I'll continue to have my fun and grow old disgracefully.'

'I'll think about it,' she said. And then, because she couldn't help herself, she leaned forward and brushed the gentlest, briefest of kisses on Mauro's cheek.

Late in the evening, after they'd feasted on the local foods and sampled plenty of Castello Vigneto's wines, Amber took another sip of the rich, deep *vino rosso* that she was sampling and let her eyes drift closed so that she could concentrate on the sheer joy of it. Dinner had been magnificent, the vineyard both beautiful and impressive, and the fruits of their host's labours was like nectar.

And the help of a little Dutch courage, or Sicilian courage she supposed, was very, very welcome. Because she strongly suspected that she still owed Mauro an apology.

She looked longingly at the wine left in the bottle, and, for just a minute, could imagine the delicious, empty oblivion it would bring if she downed the lot. But her problems would still be there when she sobered up. She was staying in his house, after all—and somehow she didn't think that a monster headache would help their situation. She rubbed at her temples, hoping for a quick fix for the tightness behind her eyes. Nope. Nothing but an apology was going to ease it.

Mauro had disappeared with Fabrizia, their hostess, ten minutes ago. Apparently she had a painting that she thought he might be interested in buying, and Amber had wandered away to sit with her thoughts and her wine as they'd negotiated in rapid-fire Italian that she had found impossible to follow.

She crossed the room to go in search of them, but she drew up short in the shadow of the doorway at the sound of Fabrizia's voice, no longer the rattle of a negotiator, but a seductive drawl that was recognisable in any language. Amber peered out of the doorway and saw Fabrizia leaning close to Mauro, one hand resting on the arm of his chair. A shiver passed through her at the sight of that hand, of her leaning forward into Mauro's personal space, making her intentions clear, however subtly.

She held her breath, a sharp pain in her chest preventing her from calling out. Memories crashed back: finding those photos on Ian's phone. The sultry tones on his voicemail. Promising things that made Amber sick to think about. The memory of that day battered through her with full force and she started shaking.

How could she get out of here? How would she get back to the villa without them realising that she had seen them? Perhaps he wouldn't even miss her—it looked as if his plans for the evening had just got a whole lot more interesting. She shrank back into the room, but couldn't drag her eyes from the scene in front of her. But as she watched, Mauro took Fabrizia's hand from his chair, and, with his other hand on her upper arm, gently pushed her away. Fabrizia smiled, a little chagrined.

'If you change your mind…' she added in English. For my benefit? Amber wondered. Does she know

I'm listening? Does Mauro? Was that why he turned down what must have been a very tempting offer?

Why? Why would he deny himself another notch on his bed post? He'd been honest enough with her about what he wanted in his romantic life.

She watched as he rubbed both hands over his face and looked up to the ceiling for a second. On her tip-toes, she retreated back into the drawing room, not wanting him to know just yet that she'd seen that little interlude. Not until she tried to work out what it meant. She poured herself another glass of wine and was taking a sip when she heard Mauro approaching behind her. 'Are we OK?' he asked, his features showing his trepidation. 'I know we've not had a chance to talk about earlier, in the car. I didn't mean to upset you.'

'And I didn't mean to fly off the handle. I am sorry.'

'You sure you don't want to talk about it?'

Her gut reaction was a screeching no. But she'd just seen him turn down easy, meaningless sex. And she wanted to know why. She didn't want to tell him that she'd seen. Didn't want to show her hand just yet.

'I'm sorry I overreacted. I suppose I'm not used to compliments. It made me suspicious.'

His brow furrowed as he frowned. 'You know, I'm starting to think I might like to meet this ex of yours. There's one or two things I'd like to say to him.'

No compliments for him, she assumed.

'I'd count myself lucky not to have met him. I wish I could turn back the clock.'

He reached for her hand. 'That bad, huh. No happy memories?'

'I used to have some,' she remembered, letting her hand rest in Mauro's, enjoying the slow-growing warmth of the touch of skin on skin. 'Some of the things we did were amazing. The places we visited… I wish I could still remember them fondly. But what came after—what he did. What he'd been doing all along, actually. It tainted them, made everything we'd ever done… It made me suspicious of how I remembered it. There had been another woman most of the time we'd been together. When I first found out about her I wondered why he'd stayed with me at all. If he wanted her then why not just be with her? When I found out that he cleared the bank accounts and forged my signature to transfer the house to his name, I had my reason. Why leave with nothing when you can play the long game and make some money out of it?'

'Surely the police—'

'Have done everything they can, given that I have no proof. And it isn't quite enough, apparently. My solicitor pushed things as much as he could, but he doesn't come free, there's no real evidence, and funds…'

'Ran out.'

She nodded then hung her head, trying to hide the tears threatening her eyes. Mauro reached for her hand and she let him take it in his own. Now the whole sorry story was out there, the fight had gone out of her.

'I saw you just now, with Fabrizia.'

He raised an eyebrow.

'Yes?'

'I would have understood, you know. If you wanted

to take her home. It looked like a difficult offer to refuse.'

He dropped her hand as if it were suddenly hot.

'Don't you dare, Amber.'

'What? I would have understood.'

Understood, yes. Been happy about it? No. In fact, she'd have been sick with jealousy.

His voice was hard and expression stern. 'You're trying to make me him, Amber, but I'm not. I might be many things, and lover of women is well up there. But I do not—ever—cheat. I never lie—I have always been completely honest with you. I am not your ex, and I would never, ever treat you that way. Let's get that straight right now.'

She lifted her hands in exasperation. He wasn't getting it. And it wasn't as if it would be cheating when they weren't even together. When they'd both already said that they didn't want to be together. 'I didn't mean that, Mauro. I wasn't comparing you to him. This is different. I mean, it's not like this is real—'

'Enough, Amber. I don't want to hear any more.' Mauro reversed away from the sofa, putting himself out of reach. She was about to speak again, but he held up his hand to stop her. 'This might not be a real date, but that doesn't mean that you're not here at all, that I'll treat you like you're nothing.'

CHAPTER SIX

'BUT YOU COULD HAVE…with Fabrizia…'

'Yes, I could have. But I didn't want to. I want to be here with you.'

He didn't want a relationship. For ten years now he had been certain that his lifestyle wasn't compatible with that sort of commitment. But after less than a week with Amber, he was questioning that decision. He had meant what he said—he didn't want to get involved. But he wasn't sure how he was meant to walk away from her either. He was fascinated by Amber in a way he hadn't experienced before.

He wheeled nearer to her again, leaned closer still until there was no escaping his scrutiny. He wasn't going to let her get away with hiding from him. 'The way that we got here, that might have been a set-up, but that doesn't change the fact that I'm enjoying getting to know you. Why do you find that so hard to believe?'

He could see the indecision in her face. See her trying to rationalise their way out of this in the way he was trying so hard to avoid. Enough. He had to make her understand.

He knew that she wanted him: it showed in the quickness of her breath, the flush of her cheeks and the flicker of her tongue to moisten her lips. What she wanted wasn't in doubt. Whether she could trust him, trust herself, to take it was another question.

He took her hands and pulled himself closer, until his chair was butting up against the overstuffed upholstery. She didn't believe him when he told her that she was beautiful—maybe she would believe him if he showed her instead. One kiss. He could give her one kiss without it leading to more.

He shifted from his chair onto the sofa, wanting—needing—to be closer to her. He would have to be, if this was going to work. He cupped one cheek with his hand, and bit back a groan as she turned into his palm, hiding her face from him. The light from the candles set around the room caught at her face, dancing golden warmth across the tops of her cheekbones, highlighting the delicate point of her chin, and—like a beacon—the plump dip above her top lip, the very top of her cupid's bow. He wished she'd look up at him, but her eyes were fixed on the patterned upholstery.

He touched her other cheek with his fingertips and gently tilted her face up. She finally flicked her gaze up to him, but darted it away just as quickly. He ached to kiss her, but didn't just want to do this; he wanted her to know why.

'Amber,' he started, but she placed a finger across his mouth, silencing him. He still held her face in his hands, and she leaned forwards, until her nose nudged at his, and he could rest his forehead against her brow.

For a moment, he couldn't breathe. Amber caught at her lip with her teeth before she let out a long sigh, closed her eyes and leaned in. She bumped her mouth against his, and for that fraction of a second it was as if every nerve in his body ended in his lips. Her mouth was soft and full, the lower lip just a little plumper than the top as it slipped too briefly against his. Electric shivers of desire burned through every place that their skin touched, and he yearned for her, for more. He knew that he had to be patient; he trusted that if he gave her space she would come to him.

Just as he was about to lose his mind with aching anticipation, she whispered his name. When he opened his eyes, all he could see was Amber. Her lashes, thick and long and a deep charcoal black, cast feathery shadows on her cheekbones, hiding her feelings from his view.

She still didn't know.

If she truly knew how beautiful she was, she wouldn't avert her gaze like this. She would be a beacon, bold and fearless, demanding everything that was her right.

He nudged at her chin, and smiled as she finally raised her eyes, defiance in her features. He couldn't tell her what he thought of her, so he would show her with the heat in his eyes as he looked at her; the way that he let his fingertips dance over the lines of her face, tracing where the candlelight caught at her features, light and shadow. He rubbed his thumb gently across her bottom lip, making sure that she knew that

that spot, just there, had been keeping him awake at night.

Just as he was about to lose reason and reach for her again, her hands threaded into his hair and she pulled his lips to hers.

Fire burned through him again, great walls of flame spreading through his veins as she opened her mouth to him, tasting and testing and demanding. With the taste of her, any pretence of self-control was lost. He pulled her closer and her legs across him, folds of bronze silk moving with her, sliding under his hands. With the curve of her bottom nestled in beside him, and the whole sweep of her thigh just waiting for his hands, he finally lost the power of thought. She tasted of espresso and vanilla, of rich red wine and Marsala, and as she shifted on his lap he turned her to press her tight against his chest. And then she was on top of him, a knee either side of his hips and her long, beautiful, perfect spine beneath his hands.

She murmured his name again as he broke their kiss, but it was lost in a sigh as he pressed his lips to her throat. He opened his eyes and lean shoulders filled his vision; he noticed for the first time the light spattering of freckles, coaxed out by the Sicilian sun. They were like stars dotted across the sky, he thought as he brushed his lips against one galaxy, and then another. He followed a constellation down to her collarbones, and breathed in the smell of her rosemary shampoo as his kisses found her neck.

He didn't care that this was a terrible idea, didn't care that it couldn't go anywhere. All he could care about was this, right now: the slide of silk beneath his palms as he ran his hands over calves, thighs, and cupped firm buttocks. The sound of her gasp as his palms explored higher: the smooth sweep of her waist and then back to the warm bare skin of her shoulder.

As he shifted round, tried to fall back against the arm of the couch and pull her with him, he remembered where they were, remembered that Fabrizia could walk in at any moment and find them. He closed his eyes again, but it didn't work. Real life had found them, and the *clip-clip-clip* of stiletto heels on a stone floor broke into his consciousness. Fabrizia, nearby.

Amber must have heard it at the same moment he did, because she sat up, breathing fast, and clutching at the neckline of her dress. They both looked across at the door in the same moment, and Amber jumped up.

When Fabrizia walked in, Amber still had her back to the doorway, and Mauro could see her rearranging her expression as she was brushing imaginary creases from her dress.

As she gathered her bag and wrap, and gave their thanks for a wonderful evening, Mauro realised that Amber couldn't hide the golden glow, like an aura around her that he had helped to light, and she was keeping burning.

They said goodnight to Fabrizia, and he wondered whether Amber would call out the woman who had tried to seduce her date. But in the end, she had settled on a classily subtle smile and a kiss on each cheek, as the memory of their kiss so clearly radiated from her expression.

* * *

Why had she done it?

She had known from the day that she had met Mauro that he would bring nothing but trouble, and now here was where she paid the price.

With the clarity of the morning after, she knew that a kiss like that *had* to come at a price. For those few minutes last night, she'd forgotten who she was. She had been the imperious goddess that Mauro told her he saw, oozing confidence and sex appeal. But it had been safer there, where they had known, deep down, that an interruption must come sooner or later. Alone in the villa, they had no such safety net.

'Mauro…' she had started to say when they'd returned.

'Do we need to talk about this?' he'd asked.

'I think we do. It's not that that wasn't…nice.'

'*Nice?*'

The expression on his face told her exactly what he thought of that descriptor and she grinned shyly.

'We both know what it was,' he said.

'OK…' she conceded. 'I know what it was, and nice doesn't even start to… But it was a one-off.' She nodded her head emphatically, but wasn't sure who she was trying to convince more. 'Considering that we have both said that getting involved isn't what we want, let's just say that it was a mistake. A very enjoyable one,' she added at the sight of his raised eyebrow, 'but we should forget that it happened. And keep it just between ourselves, of course. I don't want anyone to know, Mauro.'

Last night that had seemed like the only sensible thing to do. This morning, she had to ask herself, was that really what she wanted? She had come here with the intention of showing a softer side of herself on camera, maybe flirting a little to get the job done. But now that there was something real between her and Mauro, every instinct that she had was telling her to hide it. To bury it. To shove those feelings somewhere she didn't have to think about them. Somewhere they couldn't hurt her. She knew that it didn't make sense. But there was no room in what she had with Mauro for examination. For expectations. If anyone else were to find out what had happened, if they were to start asking questions, then she was going to have to think about them. She was going to have to think about how she *felt* about what had happened, and she just couldn't.

That kiss had been nothing more than enjoying Mauro's body—part of the weird fantasy life that the TV company had constructed for her this week. That, and their killer chemistry. He had told her that he thought she was beautiful, and just for a few minutes she'd chosen to believe him, to see how that might feel. Now those moments of madness were over, she just had to bury the memory somewhere deep, where it couldn't hurt her.

And she had to do it fast, because in less than an hour she was going to be on camera, talking about how their date was going. If she got it wrong, her job could be at stake. Ayisha kept telling her to be herself—but she was herself when she was writing, and look where that had got her. As good as unemployed, the last time that she looked. The whole point of her being here was to be someone else, someone that the public liked more than they liked her.

If she was herself on screen today, then what would the public see? What questions would she have to answer? What parts of herself would she have to expose?

In a steaming hot shower, she pushed her memories away, deep into a distant, hidden corner of her brain. Somewhere she hoped they could stay safely during their interview. Good practice, she told herself. For when they left this place and her time with Mauro was just a fond, distant memory. Not something that would affect her in real life.

She dressed in a light silky beach dress, burying the memory of Mauro's lips where her collarbones were exposed. Tying the shoulder ties a little tighter to cover the cleavage that Mauro had touched so reverently. The plan was for them to have a lazy day on the private beach and in the grounds of the villa. A luxurious picnic had been packed, along with several bottles of ice-cold Prosecco.

She had said little to Mauro since they'd discussed their kiss—it had hardly seemed necessary. They'd said everything they'd needed to already, after all. They both knew that they didn't want to be involved. They both knew that the kiss had been a mistake.

When she breezed out of the bathroom with her carefully practised air of nonchalance, it was to find Mauro wearing a killer smile and another crisp white shirt, waiting for her in the kitchen. He whistled through his teeth as she approached, and Amber fought hard to keep the reaction of her body down to a brief stutter of her breathing and the lifting of the hairs at the back of her neck. Not bad, she thought. She might carry this off yet.

'We're going to be late,' she said.

'Everything OK?' Mauro asked, and she could hear the concern in his voice. 'Is there something I've missed?'

'Nothing, nothing. I'm fine, Mauro. I just don't want to keep them all waiting. The sooner we start, the sooner it's over with.'

He followed her out of the door, but she could still feel his eyes on her. Not the sensual caress of his gaze from the night before, but a harder, more calculating stare. She shrugged off the feeling of unease. She was imagining things.

They walked down to the beach and found the crew waiting for them at a gazebo, where a loveseat with white linen covers was being set up for the interview. Gauzy white curtains fluttered on three sides of the structure, protecting the seat from the warmth of the afternoon sun.

'Mauro, Amber, great timing,' Ayisha greeted them. 'The light's perfect so we need to be shooting in about ten minutes. Get yourselves on the sofa, we'll throw some make-up on you both and then get started.'

'Both of us?' Amber asked, feeling the foundations of her protective walls take a little pressure. The last thing she wanted to do was share her true feelings about Mauro with the world. That would mean acknowledging her feelings, acknowledging that, much as she tried to avoid it, something stronger than simple physical attraction was developing, something that had the power to hurt her if she dared to acknowledge it.

She would only be able to keep herself safe from hurt if she could block last night from her mind, but how was she meant to do that if she had Mauro sitting next to her? Close enough to touch, to kiss, to smell. To remind her of everything that they'd shared while she pretended to all the world as if none of it had ever happened.

But she didn't see what choice she had. By the time that she had opened her mouth to protest, Ayisha was already deep in conversation with Piotr, and Mauro was moving over to the loveseat. Amber sat herself primly at the other end, shifting further and further away, until the rattan arm of the chair was biting into her waist.

'Relax, *cara*, I won't bite, you know,' he said in a low voice that reminded her of last night. Reminded her that she hadn't minded all that much when his teeth had trapped the flesh of her shoulder, just hard enough to make her gasp.

It took all her self-control to keep her face neutral as she looked over at the TV crew, praying that there were no microphones on them that she couldn't see.

'Don't, Mauro.'

'Don't what?'

Did he really not know what he was doing to her? Or was this an act—was he trying to lead the conversation back to that kiss?

'I just need to relax and get this over with, and I can't do that if I'm thinking about you biting, or thinking about yesterday, or about…you at all. So just don't, please.'

I can't do this if I'm thinking about you. Why had she said that? She wasn't thinking about him. She'd spent every minute today studiously *not* thinking about him. And now she'd gone and said that and he was going to think that it was this whole big thing, and then they'd have to have a conversation, *another* conversation, about how much neither of them wanted a relationship, and then she'd have to die of awkwardness about the whole thing as they went through the motions of the last few days of the holiday.

'I'm sorry,' Mauro said, and Amber gave a small smile at the sincerity in his voice. 'This interview's going to be fine. Just be yourself.' She rolled her eyes with a huff, and he frowned.

'What?' she asked.

'Don't do that. Don't put yourself down like that.'

'I didn't—'

'You did. You rolled your eyes when I told you to be yourself.'

'Well, yeah. It's not the greatest advice. Turns out, when I'm myself, pretty much everyone hates me. Or hates my work, at least. No, I need to try being someone else: I'm just not sure who yet.'

The line reappeared between his eyes, the one that told her that he wasn't happy, but before she had a chance to ask why, Ayisha had appeared in front of them with her tablet computer, demanding their attention.

She smiled, or tried to. The corners of her mouth

turned up, but she knew it hadn't come anywhere close to reaching her eyes.

'Come on,' Amber said. 'Game faces on—let's get this over with.'

She pulled her mouth into even more of a grimace, but he couldn't return her attempt at a smile. Game face? What game exactly was she playing? She'd told him already that she had been railroaded into this by her boss at work, but that didn't explain why she couldn't just be herself on camera. It didn't explain why he could see the protective defences being erected around her as clearly as if they had been barbed wire. She had been herself on the first show, he was sure of that. So what had changed? This forced smile, this fakery—it wasn't *her*.

But if a game face was what it took for her to relax, to take a deep breath and shuffle closer to him on the seat... He'd play along—for now.

Before he could say any more, the make-up artist was drenching them both in powder, complaining about the shine from the sun lotion that Amber had used to protect her skin. As soon as it had been banished, Julia was in front of them, they were miked up, and a steady red light was warning him that they were both being watched.

'So then, you two,' Julia began. 'Here we are more than halfway through your date. Can you tell us how it's going? Do we need to book a church for the wedding or separate flights home?'

Mauro forced himself to keep his eyes on Julia, and

not to share a conspiratorial look with Amber, however tempting it might be. He waited for Amber to speak, but no words came. He stepped in, trying to cover their awkwardness with breezy self-assurance.

'Ah, Julia. You can't expect us to tell you all our secrets, can you? A man's allowed a little honour, after all.'

'So coy, Mauro,' Julia said with her trademark tinkling laugh. 'That's not what we're used to from you. Surely you've got a little gossip for me.'

'Well, I think you can safely say we don't need the separate flights. Can't we, Amber?'

He glanced across at her and knew instantly it was a mistake. She looked up at him at the same time, and when their eyes met he knew that heat flashed between them. That they saw not each other, sitting formally awkward here, but memories of heat and passion, of eyes locked together in intense desire, fingertips and lips exploring and tasting. And then that, all that, was gone, and in its place Amber's eyes flashed horror and then fear.

'Of course there's nothing going on,' she said to Julia, her voice just a little too loud to be considered natural.

He knew that they needed to cover this. Whatever her motivation for this act she was putting on, he guessed that it must be important to her. Well, he'd always heard a believable lie was as close to the truth as possible. The best way to cover up what had happened between them was to act his usual, flirtatious self. As if this were nothing. 'Not for want of trying on my part,' Mauro said, stretching an arm around the back of the seat with a mock yawn. 'I've tried my hardest to seduce this beautiful woman, Julia, but so far she's resisting my charms.'

'Oh, really, I imagine that's taking quite some personal discipline. Are you finding it as difficult as Mauro seems to think you should, Amber?'

Come on, play along, Amber. He willed her to do it, to pick up his thread and weave the story that would keep their cover. They could still save this. He brushed her shoulder with his knuckles, knowing that the move was make or break. The physical contact could tip her over the edge; make her so mad that she spilled their secret. But, as he had hoped, instead she leaned back against his arm, and turned to give Julia a blazing smile.

'A man with his reputation? I don't think he deserves an easy time of it, do you? He should have to work for at least one of his conquests, I think.'

Julia laughed and leaned in close, resting her hand on Amber's in a show of intimacy. 'And are you planning—' she waggled her eyebrows like a pantomime dame '—on being conquered?'

'Oh, you can't expect a girl to answer that,' Amber answered in a sultry purr. 'You have to allow us some secrets, Julia.'

Mauro bit back his surprise. A few minutes ago he had been sure she was about to lose it at the thought of giving themselves away, and now here she was flirting like a pro. Why had she changed the rules? Where

was the sharp, witty, spiky woman that he was growing to—?

Growing to what? He stopped himself short with
that thought.

Not love. Never that.

Love was standing still. *Love* was saying goodbye
to ambition and achievement—not to mention saying
goodbye to every other woman he might ever meet.
Love was losing sight of all the pleasures and experiences that he might have if he kept looking for the next
woman, the next adventure. His lifestyle wasn't compatible with love, and he wasn't prepared to give it up.
He wasn't prepared to fail another relationship, another
woman. Letting Louise down had been bad enough.

He conducted the rest of the interview on autopilot.
Aware somewhere in the animal part of his brain that
Amber hadn't let go of his hand. She was gesticulating
with the other, telling some anecdote from their wine
tasting. If the story had really happened, he didn't remember it. She was playing a part, playing up to the
camera and to Julia. It hadn't bothered him the first
time that he had seen her do it. But he knew her better
now. Knew what she was hiding, knew that she was
being this other person because she didn't think that
the real her was good enough. And she was using him
to do it. Using him to pretend that Amber Harris wasn't
the goddess that he knew her to be.

He didn't like it.

Because it wasn't just her own life she was rewrit-
ing. His memories, his experiences were being white-
washed too. Last night, with its heated touches, and

soft silk and moist lips, if she was making out as if it never happened, then he was missing out too. She was leaving his life with a giant hole where once there had been sweet seduction.

And all because her confidence had been so battered that she couldn't face up to what they felt for each other.

He wanted the real Amber here with him. He wanted her *really* answering questions about what they were doing. About how she felt about him. About where this was going to go. He shouldn't have to ask her that. This thing was meant to go wherever he wanted it to—which was precisely nowhere. Since when did he need The Talk? He had to pull himself together.

They wrapped up the show, and he held his temper and his tongue until they were on the boardwalk up to the villa and safely out of view of the camera. 'What happened back there? Who was that on the seat with me? Because I didn't recognise her one bit.'

That was it. Deflect attention from his own feelings. Perhaps if he could make this all about her then maybe he wouldn't have to admit how conflicted the last hour had left him.

She sighed and shrugged her shoulders. 'The way you looked at me, Mauro. We might as well have just told everyone what happened last night.'

'I get why you want to keep it quiet,' he said, 'but it wasn't that bad.'

'It was worse.' She wrapped her arms around her waist as she walked beside him. 'I just hope that it doesn't make the final cut on the show.'

Some chance—the whole show only existed to capture moments like that, and he didn't think that this being a celeb version would get them an easy ride. 'You know if it was that obvious they'll definitely use it.'

'I can only hope that they don't.'

He let out a sigh of exasperation.

'Would it be so bad? It was just a kiss.'

For a moment her face fell, and he knew exactly why. If she had described what had happened between them last night as 'just a kiss', he would have been fuming. He knew, deep down, that it was so much more than just the meeting of two mouths. 'If everyone knew that something really had happened, rather than just a bit of flirting?' Her face showed him that for her, yes— it really would be so bad. 'To have everyone watching to see what happens to us. To have the story grow, be manipulated. To be asked what's happened between us when we've both decided to move on and leave it behind us? It'd be awful.'

'So why all the flirtation, Amber?' The words burst out of him in frustration. 'It doesn't make any sense. You don't want people to know that we've kissed, but you want everyone to know that we're thinking about it? What, are you worried people will think we've slept together?'

'It's nothing to do with sex.' Her voice was irritatingly calm, as if she could reason her way through every question about what was happening between them. Make sense of it all when he was struggling. 'Why do you have to bring everything down to that level?'

'Bring it down? Based on our kiss last night I think the sex would be pretty damn transcendent.'

Transcendent? *Managgia*, he was in real trouble. It was bad enough that he was thinking that way, never mind saying it out loud.

'*Transcendent?* Mauro, what's going on? Are you OK?'

He stopped in front of her, blocking the way so that she would have no choice but to look down at him. 'You know what? No. I thought we were being adults about this. I thought we were being honest. I told you what I want from you, from this. From us. But I don't think you were honest with me. And you certainly weren't honest in that interview. If you're going to use me like that then you could at least have the decency to tell me what's really going on.'

She dropped down to sit on a bench beside him.

'Who says there's anything going on?'

'I do. There's something you're not telling me and I want to know what it is. Why were you acting like that?' He pulled at her hand and lifted her chin with his thumb so that she couldn't escape his gaze. So that she couldn't hide what she was really thinking.

'It's what the show wants,' she said. 'I was just playing along.'

She was lying; it showed in her eyes.

'And since when have you cared about what the show wants? You didn't care when you were talking about killer whales, did you?'

'Yes, but that was before—'

She stopped herself with tightly pursed lips, stood

up, and made to walk away. He still had hold of her hand though, and he kept it tight in his.

'Before what? Finish your sentence. Please,' he added, when he saw the stubborn set of her chin.

'That's not what I was going to say.'

'Bull. This thing only works if we're honest with each other. I thought I'd been pretty clear that I don't mess women around, and I don't like to be messed around in return.' That was the reason for the ache in his chest and the churning of his stomach. He just didn't like to be made a fool of. He would feel like this with anyone who was being dishonest with him. It didn't mean that he…that he loved her. It couldn't. 'Either we're honest with each other, or we end this now.'

'Please, Mauro—' she reached for his hand '—it really doesn't have to be a big deal.' She threw her free hand up in a show of nonchalance. He didn't buy it for a second. Finally, they were getting to the bottom of what was going on. 'It's just…after we filmed the first show? My editor told me a few home truths. Apparently my work isn't going down well with the readership. I need to…lighten up. Show a softer side. If I don't? Well, the bosses are looking for places to trim headcount, and I'm going to be easy pickings.'

The churning in his stomach stopped, and for a moment it felt empty. Less than empty. As if a gaping hole had left him incomplete. 'And you're using me to do it. But it doesn't make sense. If you want everyone to know you have a softer side, then why all the secrecy? Just tell them we're having a torrid affair. The tabloids will love it.'

'Because if we tell people what's going on, then how are we meant to move on after that, Mauro? When we leave here I just need to be able to move on and forget it. And if the whole world sees what happened, I'm not sure how we do that. Just because I'm showing a softer side doesn't mean I have to share my whole life. I just need people to *think* that we could be…whatever. I don't want people to actually know. It's nothing to do with real life. It's just a show.'

'But don't I get a say? Don't I get a voice in this? You weren't alone last night, you know. They're not just your memories you're playing with. You told me that Ian tainted your memories, when you found out what he had been up to. Well, what do you think it does to mine when you deny it ever happened?'

She had dropped back onto the bench beside him and her elbows were resting on her knees. Worry lines marked her face, and suddenly he could see the pressure that she had been under, the genuine fear that she might lose her job.

'I'm sorry,' she said. 'I didn't think. I didn't realise that it would hurt you. All this, it all happened before that kiss, and we had both said that nothing was going to happen between us, and then last night *did* happen, and I didn't have time to come up with another plan. I didn't realise that it would hurt your feelings if I just went along with what I knew Ayisha wanted.'

He was hurt. Hurt that she had saved smiles and laughter for the cameras and not for him. That she felt closer when she was pretending to like him than when they were really alone together. He wanted to bring some light to her eyes, wanted to make her laugh, make her smile. But even after everything that they had shared last night, she still had to fake it.

'Let's just go,' he said. They needed to forget this, forget the kiss, change the subject. Because if they didn't it was going to gnaw away at him in a way that he didn't understand. 'Let's sit by the pool and drink Prosecco and watch the stars come out.'

'So do you have a thing about stargazing?' Amber asked as she sat back beside Mauro on the double sun lounger. 'Or is this just an excuse to get me on my back?'

He looked at her in surprise, but saw from the grin on her face that she was joking.

'I'll have you know,' he said, reaching for one of the glasses of Prosecco on the table beside him and passing it to her as she settled beside him, 'that I am quite the astronomer. See there—that one…that's the plough.'

'That's Orion,' Amber said with a laugh, lying back beside him. 'But nice try.'

'OK, you rumbled me. I like to just lie here and think. There's nothing like a clear sky to help you clear your mind.'

'I'll drink to that.' She took a sip of Prosecco and pulled a soft wool throw over them both. 'What are you thinking about?' she asked. 'Is it your ex?'

Where had she got that idea? He'd not thought about her for years, not properly, anyway. Well, not until this week. For some reason, memories of their relationship had been clearer in his mind than they had been for an age. Especially those last months when it had become clear to them both that what they had wasn't working, and wasn't going to last.

'Maybe it was.' It made as much sense that it was memories of him and Louise that were clouding his mind as anything else.

'How did it end between you two?'

Trust Amber not to ask if he wanted to talk about it, just dive in there with the hardest question. Well, he couldn't exactly expect an easy ride from a journalist. Amber wouldn't be Amber if she weren't constantly challenging him. He'd berated her earlier for not being honest with him, so he had no choice now but to tell her the truth—she deserved that. Maybe it would help them both, he thought. Show her why he was so sure that he wasn't meant to be in a long-term relationship, make her see that there was no point trying to think that anything might happen between them. She didn't have to worry about keeping her distance from him: his lifestyle would make it easy for them.

'Louise ended it. She said that there wasn't space in my new life for her, and that it was best we just went our separate ways.'

'Was she right?' Amber shifted onto her side, propping her head on her hand as she looked at him intensely.

'She was. By the time she called it a day, I had been away for five weeks, travelling and training. I hadn't had time to see her. It made sense to end it.'

'Five weeks without the chance to meet up? It is quite a long time.'

'Exactly. She was right.'

'But other couples go longer,' she added with a brief shrug of her shoulder.

He remained quiet.

'Or they find time to fit in an hour together. Or they talk over Skype, or they…' Her voice trailed off. 'I'm not… I'm not saying that you weren't right to end it. But—'

'But what?'

'Your colleagues, your other competitors. Do they manage to have relationships?'

'Some of them.'

'And don't you wonder how they make it work?'

Of course he had. But he had always just assumed that they were different. That they had something that he didn't. And he told Amber so.

'You think they're less committed? They don't train as hard? They don't take their work as seriously?'

'No, of course not.'

'Then what could be different?' she asked, and he had no reply. 'Perhaps…' She hesitated. 'Perhaps the relationship is different. Perhaps they make it work because they can't imagine life if they *didn't* make it work.'

He considered it. When Louise had broken it off with him, could he have fought harder? Could they have done something different?

'What is she up to now?' Amber asked. 'Let me guess, she's a stay-at-home mum. Husband works in finance. Holiday snaps from the Caribbean and skiing in the Alps shared on Facebook every year.'

He raised an eyebrow.

'If you hadn't had your accident, do you think you would have stayed together? Would it have been you in those photos?'

He tried to think back to what he and Louise had planned together before his accident; what they had said they wanted. Was that what she was aiming for all along? The cute kids and the holidays and the house in the suburbs? Because that was never going to be him. Whether he had been injured or not, he knew that he couldn't have been happy in that life. 'So…what? You're saying that me and Louise were doomed from the start?'

'Of course not. I'm saying that perhaps your relationship was perfect for that time in your life. But as you grew older, maybe you would have grown apart anyway. Perhaps your accident sped that up, but, even before then, could you see yourselves growing old together?'

He stayed silent for a few long moments. Was she right? Had he been wrong all this time, and it wasn't him that had sabotaged the relationship? Perhaps they just hadn't been meant to be. And where did that leave him with Amber? If his lifestyle wasn't stopping them, then what was?

CHAPTER SEVEN

By THE TIME she emerged from her bedroom the next morning, dressed in combat trousers and T-shirt, ready for their hike on Mount Etna, she'd made a decision. Last night, looking at the stars with Mauro, had been foolish.

She'd let her curiosity get the better of her, asking about Mauro's ex, and it had steered them into very dangerous waters. Today, she had to be sensible. She had to put that kiss behind them and forget any crazy ideas she had had about Mauro and her. So today was all about Operation Forget the Kiss. She hadn't meant to make Mauro change his mind about relationships, but show him that his assumptions about his last girl-friend might have been off the mark. Somehow, after Mauro's thoughtful silences, she suspected that she needed to be more careful than ever.

But she had her defences firmly in place, so she'd spend her last couple of days enjoying the island and not fantasising about her and Mauro.

'Morning,' she said, flicking him a wave on her

way to the coffee maker already steaming on the stove. 'Sleep well?'

'Like a baby,' Mauro answered. 'Were you up early? I thought I might see you in the pool.'

'I got in a quick session before you were awake. I didn't want to presume on any more free coaching.' And she hadn't trusted herself to be in the pool with him. That was a key part of the plan—be sensible. There was no reason why two adults couldn't get through two days together without locking lips. Even two adults who found each other attractive. And were living together. And had already kissed once anyway. They just had to make a resolve and stick to it.

He didn't comment further on the fact that she hadn't waited for him, and she took that to mean that he understood why she had done it.

'So I never asked,' Amber said. There she went again, being sensible. If they strayed into risky topics, like, say, whether they should be in the pool together, then she should change the subject as quickly as possible. 'This hike that we're heading out on. How's that going to work? Not in that chair, surely?'

'I've got a hand cycle,' Mauro replied, smiling and looking at her closely. 'It's been a while since I've taken it out so I'm looking forward to it.' His words sounded stilted, and she wondered if he was thrown off course by her attitude this morning. He shouldn't be. It was what they had talked about yesterday. But for some reason, it seemed Mauro still wasn't happy about it. Well, it was nothing. He'd get over it, she was sure. There'd be someone else along to entertain him and distract him soon enough. He wouldn't be lonely for long.

'Are you looking forward to the walk?' he asked. 'You've brought boots and stuff?'

She'd not worn her walking boots since a weekend to the Lake District that had involved a lot more wine than walking, but she hoped that the hours that she put in keeping fit in the pool would mean that she'd make it to the top of the mountain unscathed.

She nodded as she took a bite of her pastry—she really could get used to Italian breakfasts. 'Yep, Ayisha let me know that I'd need walking gear. It's been a while but I'll be fine. Have you been before? To Etna, I mean.'

He nodded. 'Yeah, I've been going ever since I was a kid. It's like nowhere else on the planet, Amber. It's so raw up there. Exposed. There's nowhere to hide.'

A shiver ran down her spine and she wondered whether that had been meant as a challenge.

She wasn't sure how to respond. So this was what it was like when you tried to pretend the most mind-blowing kiss of your life had never happened.

Etna loomed on the horizon as they drove through the heart of the island, the fields all around them scorched by a summer of fierce sunshine. Silence filled the car as they ate up the miles, the mountain growing ever larger before them. Amber kept her eyes on the landscape, too afraid of what it would lead to if she brought her attention closer to home. She had tried to strike up conversation, they both had, but with the black hole in the middle of their small talk all attempts had fizzled into nothing.

She jumped nearly out of her skin when Mauro's hand brushed against hers when they both reached for the bottle of water in the holder between them.

'Whoa. What's wrong?'

'Nothing,' Amber said quickly. 'You do remember, Mauro, that I still don't want Ayisha or the cameras to see what happened between us?'

How was this so hard? All they had to do was pretend that they had never kissed; pretend that she didn't know the scent of his skin and the taste of his lips. When they had talked about it before, it had seemed so simple. The kiss was meant to get their lust out of their system; once she had acknowledged the attraction, had answered the million questions that her brain had had about what it would be like to kiss Mauro, it should have been enough. She should have been able to laugh and joke with him, without their mutual attraction hanging over them.

But the memories of those few moments in the Castello Vigneto still wouldn't leave her be. It had seemed so simple to say that they were just going to pretend that it had never happened; two days later, she still couldn't do it. She stared out of the window again, making the most of this time they had alone. As soon as they reached the base camp, the TV crew would catch up with them and they'd have to get back to faking it.

She shook her head as she looked out of the window, contemplating the ruins her career—not to mention her heart—would be in if today didn't go well. She was worse off than when she had arrived. At least at the beginning she'd had nothing to hide from the cameras.

She glanced over at him as the car started to climb, and his jaw was set firm, his eyes fixed on the road ahead. The gleam of white on his knuckles gave away his tension and she felt a stab of unease at this hint that he was finding it as hard as she was to pretend that nothing had happened. They had to get through the next couple of days, and then they had to walk away from each other. Anything else would only lead to one or both of them getting hurt, and neither of them wanted that.

They were both going to have to get their game faces on if they were going to get through today. She needed it to go well, and for all that to happen she needed Mauro's co-operation.

'Is everything OK?' she asked.

'Of course,' he replied with a smile that didn't reach his eyes. 'Why wouldn't it be?'

Well, that was one way of assuring that she wouldn't say it out loud.

'No reason. You just seem a bit quiet, that's all. So it's not...' She didn't want to be the one to bring it up again, out into the open where they couldn't ignore it any longer. But she could feel the tension between them, could feel that their grand plan to pretend that it had never happened wasn't going to hold water. And she didn't want it there on the screen, where it might come back to bite her.

'It's nothing. Honestly.' He took his eyes off the road for a moment to turn and smile at her. 'Just concentrating on the road.' As his gaze returned to the windscreen she followed it with her own. Just as well he wasn't letting himself be distracted. The road was unlike any she'd travelled on before, with one hairpin bend after another as they climbed higher and higher up the mountain.

Mauro was driving them up to the Rifugio Sapienza, the start of the *funivia*—the cable car—where there was a collection of shops and restaurants, halfway up the south slope of Etna. It would be their base camp for the day. From there they would hike up to the next checkpoint, where the *funivia* finished, and then go on to the craters at the summit. From what she knew of Mauro, they wouldn't be taking any shortcuts.

As they climbed they passed villages that had been brushed at the edges by fingers of lava. The rivers of rock were black against the vegetation, a record of decades and centuries of rebellion by Mother Nature against the ingress of human habitation upon her territory.

Wide expanses of scrubland stopped dead as they reached the corpse of another river of fire. And then the balance shifted. No longer was the lava eating into the vegetation, but it had taken over completely, and there was nothing but rock to see on all sides.

'It's awesome,' Amber said, her gaze fixed on the changing landscape.

Mauro raised an eyebrow.

'No, seriously,' she went on. 'As in, I'm full of awe. The lava—it must have just destroyed everything in its path. Can you imagine sitting in your house in the village, and looking up and seeing that coming towards you?'

He nodded, but didn't speak. Yet more proof that, however they might try, there was no banishing the awkward. But if they could just keep it on hiatus until the cameras had finished shooting for the day that would be enough.

They continued up the side of the mountain, switchback after switchback, and by the time that Mauro's four-by-four pulled up at base camp, the landscape was positively lunar. Hillocks of coarse black rock were all around them, big enough to hide the summit of the mountain from view.

Rifugio Sapienza was more touristy than she had been expecting. Chalets housed gift shops, hiking equipment stores and restaurants, and tourists milled around, dressed in various states of propriety, from full climbing gear, with walking poles and backpacks as big as she was, to tourists who had come in coaches from the beach resorts, dressed in jeans and white plimsolls, and looking decidedly concerned about the potential of lava dust to cause serious harm to both.

Mauro stopped the car and looked over at her. 'You ready for this?' he asked.

'Which?' Amber laughed. 'The hike or the cameras.' He gave her an understanding smile, and as she looked over at him their eyes met and she felt that familiar spark, the familiar pull towards him. If she had thought that the not knowing, the wondering what that connection meant, was bad, having the answers was far worse. A couple of days ago she would have wondered what it would feel like if he pulled her across the centre console and into his lap. Today, knowing the answer to this question, it made the reach for the door handle almost impossible.

'So…' Mauro's gaze was locked on her eyes, refusing to let her go. 'It's still as we discussed yesterday? We pretend that—'

'Nothing happened,' Amber said, urgently. 'Exactly. Just like we said.'

Fumbling for the door handle while she still couldn't look away from Mauro, she all but fell out of the car. Well, it might not be the most dignified exit, but it got the job done. Got her out of danger, out of proximity with those soulful green eyes, with all the memories and promise that they held.

As she leaned back against the car she heard the click of the boot opening and the mechanical whirr of a motor. It was Mauro getting his bike out, she guessed. The one with the rugged tread on the tyre and the hand pedals. He'd trekked up Etna plenty of times, he'd told her, both before his accident and after, so he shouldn't have any problems dealing with the terrain here. Shame—a flat tyre calling the whole thing off could be just what today needed.

As Mauro rounded the corner of the car, Ayisha stepped out from the restaurant and started asking Mauro about his cycle.

'And you're sure that you don't need a guide?' she asked. 'Because we've got a guy on standby and it'll be no trouble at all to have him accompany you, just in case you run into any problems.' She shifted awkwardly for a moment. 'Uh, so to speak, you know.' Amber waited for the laugh from Mauro that usually smoothed over this type of awkwardness, but it didn't come. And when she looked at him, those lines across his forehead were deeper than ever.

'We'll be fine.' His tone clearly brooked no argument.

'OK, no guide, that's not a problem, Mauro. It'll be just you guys, and me and Piotr will follow behind with our guide. Julia will be waiting back here for us. We'll do a couple of really quick interviews before we send you off, and then we'll try and keep our distance as much as possible. You'll both have mikes and sports cameras on, so we can hang back a bit without missing anything.'

She looked from Mauro to Amber, and Amber knew that she had picked up on the tension between them. How was she going to play it in the interviews? Amber wondered. Would she try and help them paper over the cracks so that they could get a fairy-tale ending, or as near as possible, for their Christmas TV special—or would she go for the fireworks? Push them and play them off against each other to get the dynamite material that Amber knew they could deliver. God, she hoped it would be the first one, because she and Mauro had been managing—just about—to keep smiles on their faces and the elephant out of the room this morning, but she suspected that it wouldn't take much for their awkwardness to spill over into something more dramatic. She shut her eyes against the sun and leaned back against the car. God, she just wanted this to be over. She wanted to be home. To start forgetting.

CHAPTER EIGHT

'IF YOU TWO are ready, we'll wait for you in the restaurant—the camera's all set up in there. I'd say take your time, but our guide just let us know that they're expecting the visibility to be bad later. Something about the clouds coming down. Long and short of it is that we need to get cracking if you're going to make it up there safely.'

'No problem. We'll meet you there in a minute,' Mauro said. The car journey had been a special kind of torture: he had been in that enclosed space, filled with the scent of sea salt and rosemary from Amber's hair, but completely unable to reach out and touch her. Screw the mountain roads. He would have pulled over into any layby that they'd passed if he'd thought that he could wind his fingers through her blonde waves and drag her close. If he'd thought for a second that that would have been a good idea.

If only she hadn't made everything so much more complicated by asking about his relationship with Louise. If he'd been able to go on believing that another commitment just wasn't possible, then he wouldn't be second-guessing himself and his decisions. He'd just have to get through it. Stick with it for two more days and then she would be going back to London and he wouldn't have to spend all his energy resisting her any more.

'Mauro,' Amber said, walking towards him, 'why do I have the feeling this isn't going to go well?'

He turned his lips up in a smile that he hoped was reassuring. 'It's going to be fine. You've got nothing to worry about.' But his words did nothing to smooth the lines on her forehead.

When they sat down in the restaurant, Amber painted on a fake grin, and he knew that she was going to play nice for the cameras. As the interview went on she smiled and flirted, and hinted at some of the fun that they'd had together, all the while steering clear of anything that might be considered the truth. He could feel his muscles growing tighter and his pulse starting to pick up. With every lie, the truth felt further away. The magic of that night at the vineyard was diluted, until, one lie soon, it would be as if it never happened. It would be taken from him. And it was her fault that he was feeling like this—if she'd not asked about Louise, made him reconsider everything that he'd thought about the place for relationships in his life, he'd have been able to walk away from her the same way he had from every other woman for the past ten years. He was almost sure of it.

It felt like a betrayal.

He managed to hold his tongue the whole time the camera was rolling, smiling in the appropriate places, albeit with a fair amount of subtle prompting from Julia. But the whole while, he just wished that they could talk, properly. That she didn't have to worry about protecting herself, because he would never hurt her. That maybe, if they were both brave enough, they could stop denying what was going on between them and take a chance on making a relationship work.

As soon as he heard the words, 'That's a wrap, guys,'—or maybe he just imagined them—his hands were on his pedals, powering himself out of the restaurant and out onto the surface of the volcano, leaving the whole team following in his wake.

'Mauro!'

Amber called him from the door of the restaurant, but he was too riled. They were meant to be acting as if that that kiss had never happened, and if she made him speak to her now there was no way he could do that.

He could hear rapid footsteps behind him as she picked up her pace to catch him up, but he didn't break his rhythm on the pedals. Powering himself forward, grateful for every minute he'd spent in the pool and in the gym keeping his arms and his upper body in shape.

'Mauro, would you wait up?'

But there was no need, because she'd already caught him up. Goddamn this gravel and the slow going.

'What did I do?'

He glanced at her waist, where she still wore the battery pack for her microphone.

'Nothing,' he said as levelly as he could. 'You heard Ayisha. The visibility's going to be bad later. We need to get going, that's all.'

Amber glanced over her shoulder. He followed her gaze and saw that Piotr had caught them up. Hell. Were they going to have no privacy at all today? All this, the interviews, the camera trailing them, the microphone still clipped to Amber's shirt, it all served to show him what a farce all this was. How fake the whole week and everything in it.

How much of the kiss with Amber had been real? Perhaps she had been faking with him as well. Except he knew that couldn't be true. There had been a connection and a bond between them that was impossible for him to have imagined. And if that hadn't been real, then there would be no reason for things to be awkward—and they definitely were awkward.

But enough was enough now. He'd smiled through the interviews. He'd provided the villa and the resources and the activities. He'd even kissed her, for God's sake. What more did they all want from him? He just wanted to get on, get up this mountain, and then get on with forgetting that he'd ever met her.

Amber glanced again at the camera, and then studied his face for a few long moments. Her expression hardened, and something twisted in his guts as he realised that he had hurt her. And it didn't matter that she had hurt him first. He had promised her that he wouldn't and now he had broken that promise. He reached for her hand, and pulled her gently towards him. From the corner of his eye he could see that Piotr and Ayisha had suddenly pulled off their headphones and found some very interesting buttons to press on their equipment and were showily paying no attention at all to the two of them.

'I'm sorry,' he told her. 'Let's just forget it and go have fun. I've been waiting to show you this all week. Does that sound OK?'

She nodded, and he let go of the breath that he'd been holding.

'OK, then.' He indicated a path. 'We need to head that way. We'd better make it a fast walk if we're going to make it up there on schedule.'

He looked up at the sky, and let the sun warm his face. It was much cooler up here, at about eighteen hundred metres, and would only get colder the higher they climbed. It was a beautiful day, though. There were just a few clouds in the sky at the moment, a clear bright white against the rich blue of the sky. With the black of the lava all around, the contrast was striking. They headed away from the cable-car terminal and towards one of the paths up the mountain, along with the other rucksack-carrying, walking-shoe-wearing climbers.

His hand cycle drew a few curious glances, and they stopped a couple of times to chat to the other walkers. They trod on for an hour or so, until he realised that Amber was struggling. She'd said that she had done some walking before, but he knew that the altitude could make even an easy stroll difficult if you weren't used to it. Her face was flushed, but she didn't seem out of breath.

He tried to interpret the expression on her face. Her eyes were fixed forwards, deliberately not looking at him as they made their way higher and higher. When he glanced over his shoulder he couldn't see Ayisha—true to her word they must have been hanging back a way behind them. They were both still wearing microphones, though, so any feeling of privacy was just an illusion.

'So what do you think?' he asked eventually, not sure how long they could keep walking without making any conversation at all.

'About what?'

He laughed, despite himself. 'Uh, about the volcano?'

He could already feel the cool of the altitude biting into his fingers. Amber had pulled on another layer since they had left the cable-car station, and the clouds were thickening above them. The other hikers had gone on ahead, what with four working limbs, and without the encumbrance of an all-terrain cycle, they seemed to be making better time than him. He glanced at the compass app on his phone, just to make sure he was still on top of their navigation and was pleased to see they were dead on course.

'Are we on track?' Amber asked, and he nodded.

'Just keep heading uphill,' he said with a smile.

They walked on, but the clouds on the horizon were starting to concern him. And the day that had started in bright sunshine was rapidly turning darker. Another couple of hundred metres passed without either of them saying a word, and he could tell from the sound of Amber's rapid breaths that she was starting to find the terrain hard going.

'Do we need to stop?'

He hadn't meant for the words to sound interrogative, but they had, he realised too late.

'I'm fine,' she bit out.

'Really,' he softened his voice. 'It's no problem if you need to take a break. I could do with a breather too.'

She snorted and he shrugged his shoulders. OK, so he didn't need to stop, but that didn't mean that he minded if it was what she needed.

'OK, then, how about if I said I'd like to stop and admire the view?'

It wasn't a lie: the view really was worth stopping for. They'd long ago left behind any signs of life; the few straggling plants that had valiantly fought for survival further down the mountain were nowhere in evidence here. But the contrast between the barren rock, the bright blue sky on one side, and the wall of white cloud on the other was unlike anything he had ever seen anywhere else on the planet. He stopped when they reached the top of the hillock they were climbing, and looked around him to get his bearings. He knew from experience that mountains could be deceptive, with one false summit following another, and when he looked around him he realised that this hike might not be as simple as he'd planned. This wasn't the summit, but he couldn't see the higher peak either. The wall of white was in front of them now, as the clouds rolled down.

He turned and looked back, and could still see the path. They could turn around and head straight back. But it was a long way down, and there was no guaranteeing that the clouds wouldn't catch up and over-take them long before they reached Rifugio Sapienza. The *funivia* terminal wasn't far—the safest thing to do would be to just keep going. And yet when he looked for the path, he just couldn't see it. They'd have to rely on the compass, the map and his memory of this trail.

'Mauro…' Amber's voice was full of trepidation. 'Please tell me you know where we're going.'

He turned to look at her and saw genuine concern in her face. Cracking a smile for the first time since they'd escaped the cameras, he told her that every-thing was fine. 'It's no more than half an hour from here. We'll have to trust the compass and the map, but we'll be fine.'

The tension lifted from her face, but a crease ap-peared between her eyebrows as they both heard the shout from behind them.

'Aiuto! Sono caduto!'

They both whipped around at the sound of the shout, but could see nothing behind them except for a wall of white.

'Che succede?' Mauro called back. *'Serve aiuto?'*

All they heard in response was a groan of pain.

Amber looked down at Mauro. 'What did you say? What's happening?'

'I'm not sure. Someone shouted for help, it sounded like he said he'd fallen, but I don't know more than that.'

'We have to go back,' Amber said.

'It might not be safe.' But another loud groan from the injured man decided for them. 'He's probably on the trail,' Mauro said. 'And he can't be that far behind or we wouldn't hear him.'

'What about the crew? Won't they have caught up with him?'

'It depends whether they turned back. I couldn't see them behind us last time I looked, and I don't know how far behind they were. But I think we have to assume that if he's shouting there's no one else there to help him.'

Amber turned on the spot, taking in the blank whiteness on all sides, before setting her face in an expression of resolve. 'Well, then. Let's get going.'

'Still no signal,' Mauro said, checking his phone as they were making their way back down the path. 'Normally I'd say one of us should go on ahead to get help, but with the visibility like this we need to stick together. At least until we find him and know what we're dealing with.'

They retraced their steps along the trail, the shouts of the injured man getting louder and more desperate as they grew close, and as he came into view it was obvious why.

The man was sitting on the ground, cradling his arm, which was bent at an ugly angle. His face was a ghostly white, bordering on grey, and his forehead was clammy with sweat. Amber dropped to her knees beside him, and murmured soothing words as she pulled an emergency blanket out of her daypack.

'It's OK,' she told him. 'We're here, and we'll get you some help. You're going to be fine.' His expression didn't change from that of shocked terror. She brushed the hair from his forehead as she sat beside him, and he flinched away from her touch.

'Can you tell me your name?' she asked gently as she shook out the blanket. 'Do you understand English? Mauro, can you translate?'

'No…need,' the man replied, shivering. 'Enzo. My name is Enzo.'

'OK, Enzo,' she carried on, in the tones one would use with a spooked horse. 'You're looking a bit chilly, a bit cold. I'm just going to wrap this around you to keep you warm. Is that OK?'

'Amber,' Mauro whispered behind her. 'Did you see his arm? We need to support it in a sling if he'll let us.'

'Mm hmm,' she said, in the same soothing tone. She appreciated his help, but she didn't need it. She could see exactly what Enzo needed, and how to help him. 'Not just now, Mauro.'

'Here we go then, Enzo.' She wrapped the blanket around him as gently as she could, keeping her hands well away from the nasty-looking kink in the bones of his left arm. 'All done,' she said. 'You're doing really well. You've got nothing to worry about. Me and Mauro are going to take care of you until Mountain Rescue arrives, and everything's going to be fine, OK?' She laid a gentle hand on his shoulder. 'OK?'

Waiting until he met her gaze, she smiled, and then turned back to her bag. 'Now then, something to warm you up.' She pulled out the flask of coffee that they had packed back at base camp and poured a cup. Holding it up to Enzo's lips, she encouraged him to take a couple of sips. 'That's it,' she said with another smile. 'You're doing great.'

Finally, she turned to Mauro, who was still behind her.

'What?' she asked when she saw him smiling.

'Nothing,' he said. 'Just…that was pretty amazing. That's all.'

She went to dismiss him with a wave of her hand, but then stopped herself. 'Thanks. But that was the easy part. We need to decide what to do next. What do you think—do we sit and wait?'

'I'm not sure that we can,' Mauro said. 'Did you see the colour of his hand? It looked to me like his circulation was compromised. The forecast had this fog sticking around until nightfall. There's not a good time for someone to find us, so I think we're going to have to get ourselves found instead. Do you think he can move?'

'Not like this.' She turned her back to the injured man and dropped her voice to a whisper. 'You saw how much pain he was in when I was just wrapping that blanket around him. You're right about needing to get that arm in a sling, but he's not going to like it. Are you sure that there's no other way?'

'Our other option is to wait till morning. What do you think?'

'Too cold,' she said immediately. 'And he's in too much pain. We have to move.'

'Agreed.'

She turned to Enzo, wondering how much he had heard, but, from the glazed expression on his face, his distress and panic were going to be as much of a hindrance as his physical injuries.

'OK, Enzo. We have a plan to get us all to safety, but we're going to have to move. Do you understand?' She glanced up at Mauro to translate, but it wasn't necessary.

'No, not moving,' Enzo said with a shake of his head and a panicked expression. 'Hurts.'

'A sling,' Amber said. 'If we can strap his arm tight and immobilise it, it should keep the pain to a minimum. Is there one in the first-aid kit?'

'No, but we can make one from a spare shirt, if he'll let you.'

She nodded thoughtfully. 'He's going to have to trust me. OK, Enzo. I know you're scared, but we really need to get ourselves somewhere warm and safe. It's not far. Mauro knows exactly where we're going, but we need to go soon, before it starts to get dark.'

'My arm…'

'We're going to make you a sling, and make sure your arm won't hurt while we move. Can you do that for me?' she asked, brushing the hair off his forehead again and turning his face up to her. 'Can you trust me? We're going to do this together.'

She pulled a spare T-shirt out of her pack and showed it to Enzo. 'OK, here we go. Just a T-shirt. Nothing to be worried about.'

With Mauro murmuring instructions behind her, she eased the neck of the shirt over Enzo's head.

'There we go. Now we need to put your hand through here,' she said, indicating the armhole as Enzo shrank away from her. She sat back on her heels, giving him some space. 'I don't need to touch,' she said gently. 'The armhole is right there by your hand. Do you think, when you feel ready, you can get your fingers through it?'

Behind her, Mauro spoke a few words of quiet Italian, and she guessed that he had translated her words. Enzo looked up and met her gaze, but made no signs of moving.

'I can't,' he said.

'You can.' She laid a hand on his uninjured arm. 'I know you can do this.'

Slowly, carefully, he moved his hand into the armhole, and with frequent glances at his face, to make sure that he was OK, Amber eased the rest of the fabric around his elbow, taking some of the weight off the injured limb.

She grabbed a bandage from the first-aid pack and gently wrapped it around the sling, so that the broken arm was pinned to Enzo's chest. He finally let out a sigh of relief as she finished and Amber was relieved to see some colour returning to his face. She replaced the blanket around him, and turned to talk quick and low to Mauro.

'How far to the station?'

'The route we were going to take? Thirty minutes. There's another route that should only take ten, but…'

'But?'

'It's steep.'

'I can manage.'

'I don't doubt it.'

'Oh.' She looked at his cycle. It had never even occurred to her that he had planned their route to take
his disability into account. She had got so used to him
being able to do anything that she could that she had
almost forgotten that his way of seeing the world was
different from hers.

'There are a couple of steps. Nothing that you and
Enzo wouldn't be able to manage, but I can't get the
cycle up them.'

'I can send Mountain Rescue back for you,' she said,
and it wasn't until the words left her mouth that she
realised that she'd come to a decision.

'I'm not letting you go alone. It's dangerous, Amber.'

She glanced over at Enzo. 'Do you really think he
can walk for thirty minutes? Show me on the map. I've
a compass on my phone. I can do it.'

They both looked over at Enzo. Although some colour had returned to his face, it was still creased with
pain and he was cradling his injured arm like a baby
bird.

'He'll have to wait, I'm not letting you go,' Mauro
said.

She couldn't suppress a small smile at that. 'We'll
be fine. You know it's the right thing. I know that I can
do this, and I'll send a team back for you.'

'We...not get lost,' Enzo said from behind them. 'I
climb many times.'

'There you are,' she said, leaning in close so that
Enzo couldn't hear them. 'Please, I'm going to go
quickly. For his sake. I'll see you back at the *funivia*
in no time.'

Mauro nodded, knowing that she was right and—more importantly—that they didn't have a choice. He forced a smile, tugging on the front of her jacket. With one firm hand on the nape of her neck and the other on her back, he stole a quick, hard kiss on the lips.

CHAPTER NINE

AMBER PACED THE floor of the *funivia* station, looking again at her watch. Forty-eight minutes had passed since she had left Mauro, alone, on a volcano in zero visibility. She had told him that she was sending Mountain Rescue back for him, and two volunteers from CNSAS, the Sicilian rescue organisation, had headed out to find him. They'd only been half an hour away, he had said. Well, she was going to hold him to that. She was giving him ten more minutes, and then she was going back for him.

Ayisha and Piotr were down at Rifugio Sapienza already, having turned back when they found themselves in poor visibility. Enzo was being cared for by medics, and someone had pushed a cup of hot coffee into her hands but she had batted everyone away, her eyes fixed on the windows, as she waited for Mauro to appear. What would she do if he didn't? How would she feel if he had kissed her goodbye on the mountain, and then he'd had an accident himself? What if he was out there hurt?

He had kissed her.

Despite everything that they had said, despite the fact that their attempts to forget their last kiss had been laughable, he'd gone and done it again.

She looked out of the window once more, hoping for a glimpse of him. Still nothing. She glanced at her watch again. Forty-nine minutes.

Looking over at the mountain rescue team, Amber wondered what they would do if Mauro and the other members of their team didn't turn up. Would they really leave him out there until morning? Well, they might, but she planned on sticking to her word. He could have five more minutes' grace and then she'd be going out there after him.

She started sorting through her pack, working out what extra supplies she would need, when the door to the station flew open, and Mauro wheeled in, the two CNSAS volunteers behind him.

He was bent over the crank of his cycle, his chest heaving, and his face red and shiny from exertion. She dropped her pack and crossed the room, half running.

'Oh, my God, I was just about to come and find you.'

'I'm not—' he was panting, trying to catch his breath '—that late. Had to stop—and check the map.'

She dropped into his lap and framed his face with her hands. 'You had one more minute, I swear.' She leaned in and touched her forehead against his, hesitating for just a second before closing her eyes and brushing her lips against his. Tingles of pleasure shot from where their mouths met down to where his hands had found the small of her back and were holding on tight.

'I'm so glad you're safe,' she breathed, pulling away and then pressing her cheek against his. 'I was worried.'

'So I see.' His hands left her back to wrap tight around her waist. 'But there was no need. I told you.' She stayed still for a few moments, their breathing in sync, as she let her fear subside. But as the adrenaline leached from her system and her heart rate started to slow, she became suddenly self-conscious, nestled in his lap. Glancing over his shoulder, she saw two of the mountain rescue staff grinning at them. She started to slip away, but Mauro's arms pulled her back in tight.

'Don't,' he said, pressing a kiss on her jaw. 'Stay there.'

She looked past him again, and the others in the room were blatantly watching them still.

She smiled, and leaned in close so that they wouldn't be overheard. 'Maybe we should wait until we're alone?'

'And what if I can't?'

She bit her lip, playing with that thought for a moment. What if they couldn't wait? What if they didn't want to? What if she didn't care what anyone else thought?

What if she didn't care that she might get hurt?

'I think we have to try,' she said at last. 'We can talk later, back at the villa.'

He narrowed his eyes as she slipped off his lap. 'You're not interested in taking a risk, are you? Even after we kissed. Even after you started falling for me.'

'I'm n—'

'Don't deny it, Amber. I've seen the way you look at me.' He wheeled closer, back into her personal space, until he barely needed to speak above a whisper. 'I've seen how scared you are, as well. I know that you could only be that afraid because you know that I could hurt you.'

She took a deep breath before she spoke again. 'I've never said that I'm falling for you.' After all she'd decided that she absolutely, definitely wasn't. But the very fact that she'd had to put so much effort into forgetting that one kiss, surely that told her everything that she needed to know about how she felt about Mauro Evans.

So she was falling for him—so what? She wasn't some slave to her libido, or even to her heart. She had to be more careful than that, otherwise she was going to get hurt. It was what Mauro had agreed to—he'd said all along that he didn't want to get involved, so why was he angry about it now?

'But even if I was, what I feel doesn't have to have anything to do with this. Can't you see that? I went with my feelings before, and I got burnt. I don't want that to happen again.'

'And what about this?' he asked, gesturing at the two of them.

She sighed, shaking her head in confusion. 'I need to be sure, Mauro. I need to know that you're not going to hurt me, and I'm afraid your history doesn't exactly work in your favour. What's changed, Mauro? Why would I be any different from all the women you have discarded before me?'

'What's changed? You should know—meeting you,

that's what's changed. You're the one who started asking questions about me and Louise. Making me wonder whether I'd got this wrong from the start. And now you're the one who's backing out. Why is that? Is it really because of what Ian did to you? Do you really want to give him that level of control over your life? Let him ruin your future, as well as your past?'

'This has nothing to do with him.' She gritted her teeth, and fought down the anger that always reared its head when she thought of her ex. 'It's the opposite; it's about what I want.'

'And what is that, Amber?'

'I want to not get screwed over, Mauro. You know that I have feelings for you. You know that I can't pretend that that night at Castello Vigneto didn't mean anything. But you're the one who's just pulled a U-turn and I've not had time to catch up. I just need time to think—is that unreasonable? Please, Mauro, it's been a very long day and I don't want to fight. Can we just drop this?'

She watched Mauro take a deep breath, and the lines on his face deepen. He wasn't happy, but she could tell that he didn't want to fight either.

'I want to find out where this could go, Amber. Aren't you curious?'

'Oh, that's what it is, is it? That's what's killing you.' She gave a weary, hollow laugh. 'Here I was thinking it was me that you wanted, but I'm not sticking around because you've just realised that you need to conquer the world of committed relationships next. I'm not going to be your next gold medal, Mauro, because in a month or two, when the shine has worn off, you're going to revert to type and you'll be gone.'

Was she right? Was everything that he was feeling, the pull in his gut every time that he saw her, the need to have her skin against his, the way she filled all his thoughts when they were apart, the way that making her smile made him feel as if he'd just won another gold—was it just novelty?

He couldn't believe that in a week, a month, a year from now, he would feel any different. He didn't have the answers. He didn't know if they *could* make this work. But he knew—he felt—more than anything that walking away now would be something that he would regret for the rest of his life.

He couldn't let Amber just push any mention of what they had aside, as if they didn't matter. But it was clear that her past was holding her back, and if she couldn't come to terms with that, she was never going to give him, give *them* a chance.

One of the park staff called them both over, and explained that they would be able to descend in the cable car. Amber was silent as they were ushered into the *funivia*, and he sent up a silent prayer of thanks that they were alone at last. She had barely said a word since their argument. More than anything, he wanted to reach out and take her hand, to anchor himself to her, but he knew that wouldn't help matters.

'You were amazing out there,' he told her, nodding towards the expanse of thick white fog on the other side of the plastic windows.

A light lit behind her face, and she glowed with a self-confidence he had only seen glimpses of before. 'Thanks. It felt good to help. Maybe I should consider a career change if the show doesn't go well.'

She smiled, but he knew how much her job meant to her. Could she really be so blasé at the thought of losing it?

'There's something I don't understand. Surely your editor wouldn't have hired you if she hadn't thought you were talented. So what's changed?' He asked the question, but it didn't take a genius to guess the answer. Ian, her ex, had happened, and he'd sapped her of her confidence.

'I just couldn't write the way I used to. How could I give romance advice when every time I thought about what Ian had done I grew more convinced that a relationship doesn't bring anything but heartbreak?'

'So you were trying to protect your readers, by telling them not to get involved. The same way you tried to protect yourself. Maybe you're not doing them any favours. Maybe it's time to drop some of those walls, let someone in.'

She looked out of the pod again, out into the clouds, a small smile on her lips.

'Maybe you're right.'

Amber stared in the mirror in her bathroom, a lip crayon stalled halfway to her mouth. Ayisha and her team were waiting for her down on the beach for their last interview, and she knew this one had to be different. She had come out here to save her career, and she still wanted that. She needed her job. But she didn't want to pretend any more. She didn't want to be bitter and defensive, but she didn't want to go back to being the woman she had been before Ian had hurt her either.

Mauro had been right. Since Ian had left she'd given him too much control over her life. First had been the chippy, icy front, and the defensive barriers she'd constructed to stop herself getting hurt. That she'd projected into her work in an attempt to protect others. And then this week pretending it had never happened at all, trying to remember who she'd been before she'd met him, acting out an approximation of that stranger on screen.

She wanted to be the woman who had moved on from that heartache, and come out stronger the other side. She just wanted to be herself.

If she could do that, then she'd be home and free. Well, she'd be home, anyway, waiting to see how the show would be received, whether she would be keeping her job. She lifted her hand and painted some subtle colour onto her lips.

A soft knock on the bathroom door was followed by Mauro poking his head into the room. 'Everything OK?' he asked. 'I think they're ready for us.'

She turned to smile at him. 'Let's do this.'

Mauro came over and gave her a quizzical look. 'What did I miss?'

'What do you mean?'

'You look different.'

She shrugged—and held up the crayon. 'A different colour. I'm impressed. I didn't think you'd notice.'

'No, not that,' he said, reaching up and tilting her chin down. 'No, it's something else. something...*more*. Whatever it is, I like it.'

'Good,' Amber said, replacing the crayon in her make-up bag and zipping it shut. 'Are you ready? Or have you come to pinch my make-up?'

He laughed. 'You are in a good mood. Lead the way, and don't you dare try painting my face.'

'Well,' Julia said, once they were settled out on the loveseat and the camera was rolling. 'That was some dramatic stuff up on the mountain. Can you talk us through what happened?'

Mauro looked so relaxed, Amber thought. And so gorgeous with the sun catching the red in his hair and the gold in his skin.

'Dramatic? It was terrifying!' Amber said, collapsing back in the seat. 'Well, the short story is that we found an injured hiker while we were trekking, and we had to get him to safety.'

'Wow, it sounds like he was lucky you were there,' Julia said after Amber explained about Enzo's broken arm. The presenter leaned forward, eating it up. 'Your trekking experience came in useful, then, Mauro. It's lucky you were there.'

Mauro shrugged and held up his palms, his expression all modesty. 'It did, for the practical stuff, but it was Amber who was really amazing.'

'Oh?' Julia smiled in encouragement. 'Can you tell us more?'

'Well, when we found Enzo, he was understandably distressed—a bit panicked. To start with he didn't want either of us to touch him, but we had to immobilise his broken arm. It was Amber who managed to persuade him to let us help, and then she was so determined to get him quickly to safety that she trekked the last part on her own through dense fog.'

'Wow, pretty brave stuff, Amber.'

'Thanks,' Amber said. 'It didn't feel brave, though. It was just what needed doing. It felt pretty scary actually.'

'But she did it anyway,' Mauro interjected. 'Nothing was going to stop her once she realised what had to be done.'

'And what did you think, when you were watching Amber walk away with Enzo?' Julia had leaned in again, and Amber could see from her expression that she knew that she was on to something, that she'd touched on something potentially explosive.

'I thought she was incredible,' Mauro said simply, looking over and meeting her eye. She was rooted to the spot, blood rushing to her cheeks, making her glow with embarrassment and pride. 'She didn't doubt herself for a second. She just did it.'

He wouldn't let her gaze go, and in his expression she saw everything that they had both been too scared to say out loud. She saw the depth of his feelings for her. She saw herself through his eyes, and she found that she liked the filter—she was the woman who had come through the other side of adversity. She saw a survivor.

Despite Mauro's modesty, she knew that she would never have found safety without his guidance. And he wouldn't have got Enzo to safety without her. It had only worked out because they had worked together. They had both understood what they brought to the situation and had used their gifts accordingly.

As the interview wound down, she felt a frisson of excitement. She still couldn't see how it could work; couldn't see how they could fit a relationship into two lives with no space. But for the first time, she could really see the new her and Mauro clearly. She could see who he really was, past the playboy reputation. And she could see how he felt about her. She didn't know where things were going from here, but she felt for certain that this was the start of something, not the end.

CHAPTER TEN

AMBER SQUEEZED HER headphones a little tighter against her head, trying to block out the noise from the blades of the helicopter.

'It's so… *Loud* doesn't seem the right word. I can *feel* the noise,' she shouted.

'Amazing, isn't it?' Mauro replied over the headsets. 'I love that feeling.'

He had always got a hit of adrenaline from the way that it overwhelmed all his senses—what you could hear was the least of it. His belly vibrated with it. He could practically taste it. And tonight there seemed to be something extra, some new vibration in the air that he hadn't felt before. He glanced across at Amber, who had her hands pressed over her earphones as she looked out of the window.

Not that there was much to see at the moment. The sun had set an hour ago, and the airfield offered little more than runway lights and the windows of the control tower by way of visual interest. All of that would change when they were up in the air, he hoped. He'd been waiting to see Stromboli erupt for nearly a year—

during its last great show he'd been on the other side of the world and missed it.

There wasn't room in the cabin for a camera crew, so one of the sports cameras had been rigged up in one corner, so unobtrusive he kept forgetting it was even there. After that interview, he suspected there was a fair bit to say. And they were running out of time. Amber would be flying back to London first thing tomorrow. He felt a dip in his stomach as the helicopter lifted off the ground, and Amber reached for his hand in her excitement.

'Ugh, do you ever get used to that?'

'To what?'

'Hovering,' she shouted, 'just above the Earth like that. It feels weird.'

'Weirder than the enormous jet that we flew out here on?' He laughed at her excitement; her smile was infectious.

'Of course! On the plane you can barely see outside. It's basically a tube carriage with wings and—if you're lucky and fight for the window seat—a marginally better view. This is…this is really *flying*.'

'Maybe I have got a little too used to it.'

When had that happened? he wondered. The last time he'd flown, he was sure that he had had that same tremor of excitement that he'd always felt, but tonight, he'd been distracted. It was Amber. She was the reason, he realised. He'd been more interested in her than the sensations of flying. More interested in the light in her eyes when they'd taken off, the little gasp of breath that she'd given when the skids had left the ground and they'd held just above the Earth, weightless.

Normally he was so excited, waiting for that moment when the aircraft tilted slightly, and the world tipped on its axis, before they were away. For a man who had to exert an enormous amount of energy just getting himself from his bed to his chair in the morning, the freedom he felt in a helicopter was unrivalled. The only thing that came even close was being in the pool. He had already had some flying lessons, with a gadget that adapted the controls for him to operate with his hands. Next year would be the year that he got his licence, he decided. He'd base himself in London for a few months, where he'd taken his first lessons, and get the hours that he needed clocked up.

And maybe see Amber while he was there.

Where had that thought come from? When they were on Etna she'd been as insistent as ever that their kiss had been a mistake, an aberration, and mustn't be repeated. But there had been something in her expression when they had given that interview to Julia that made him think she was having second thoughts. It was what he had been hoping for: that she could see that she could trust him. That he was nothing like her ex. But now he had an inkling that it might have worked, that she might be considering this thing between them after all, his heart started to race.

The pilot's voice broke into the headset, and Mauro snapped back to the present.

'We're just approaching the south side of Stromboli

now,' he told them both. 'As you can see, she's pretty lively tonight.'

Rivers of lava were spitting out of the mountain and flowing down the side of the rock, tracks of light and colour in a black night. But they held Mauro's attention for only a few moments. Amber's gaze was fixed out of the helicopter's window, the light of the volcano reflected in her eyes and a look of wonder on her features.

'It's spectacular,' she whispered.

'Beautiful,' Mauro agreed. But he was far more interested in watching Amber, the way that she pressed her hand against the glass as if she wanted to get closer, to be part of the sky itself.

As the helicopter turned, Amber turned too, to look out of the other side, and her body pressed up against his arm in the close confines of the cabin. The heat from her skin nearly burned him, as if he had been plunged into one of those rivers of fire.

The experience was all her.

He had been anticipating this experience for months, since long before he had met Amber, but he knew with unbridled certainty now that it would not have been complete without her. Nothing could compare to the experience of seeing this vision with her by his side. An emptiness opened up in his chest, and he wondered how many other experiences had been lacking for want of her company. He thought that he had travelled the planet to see its most incredible sights. He had kept moving, constantly looking for the next big adventure, always wanting to better the last. Would they all have had this extra sparkle, the extra intensity? There was something about tonight that didn't feel real. It recalled those days after his accident, when the doctors had thrown every drug they could at him to help control the nerve pain.

He'd never dabbled with drugs recreationally, and now he knew why. Because once you had something that heightened every sensation, made every colour brighter, every emotion more intense, it was hard to know how you came back from that. How you could go back to the life you led before. Next time he saw a volcano erupt, or a glacier slide into arctic waters, or jumped an epic wave on his jet ski, would the experience be dulled by the lack of Amber to share it with?

Sweat broke out on his forehead as panic started to set in. He had tried having a relationship before, and he had failed. His life didn't work with anyone else in it.

A huge plume of fire shot from the island, and Amber grabbed for his hand, squeezing it tight. And just like that, the pounding of his heart stopped, his chest relaxed, and he let out the breath that he was holding. He didn't have all the answers, and it didn't matter. Because if she was willing to give this a go, they would work it out together.

He would make it work: for her. He would compromise: for her. He would find time and space in his life. For her. It was all for her. She was the woman who made his world bright, his heart beat stronger, his laugh come louder. He knew, deep in his gut, that he wouldn't have shared this experience with anyone else.

Amber looked him in the eye.

'Are you OK?' she asked.

He had to convince her to give him a shot. She was scared, and she had every right to be after what she had been through, but he couldn't give up on them yet. His eyes dropped to their clasped hands and he smiled. 'Better than OK,' he said. 'I'm great.'

She opened her mouth to speak, but then glanced over at their pilot.

'Giorgio, can you give us some privacy?' Mauro asked him. The man flicked a switch on his headset and gave them a thumbs up.

'I was just going to say—' she started to speak and he dropped his gaze to watch her slide her fingers sensuously between his '—that this is just about the most incredible thing I've ever seen.'

The husky tone of her voice and the sight of her hand in his hit him straight in the gut. If this woman was the one, life could definitely be a lot worse.

Shutting out his worries with the closing of his eyes, he leaned towards her. Their last kiss had been gentle, hesitant. This was one fired by the lava spewing beneath them. He grabbed a handful of her hair, pulling her closer as his lips moved towards hers, heat and passion flowing through his body.

She drew in a sharp breath, and for a second he froze, scared beyond measure that she was about to push him away, but then her body went supple and relaxed beside him as she pulled him across to her, and he heard a low moan of desire in his headset. Her lips parted, and her hand moved to slide sensuously up his thigh—he dropped his eyes to watch, and the sight of that seductive caress sent a shiver up his spine. But it wasn't enough. He moved her hand from the dead zone on his thigh to a spot where he could feel the warmth of her fingers, and then he closed the distance between them and took her lips in a searing kiss.

Her hands were in his hair, they were dancing across his shoulders, teasing at the hem of his shirt and pulling at the buttons. Her mouth was on his, demanding and passionate, testing the limits of his patience and his control. And her moans and breaths were in his ears, magnified by the headset so they could be heard even over the thrumming hum of the helicopter blades.

He cursed the safety harnesses that pinned them to their seats, wishing that he could snap her buckle open and drag her into his lap. With her straddling him, there was no telling what they could get up to. But as the helicopter swooped around reality hit him and he remembered where they were, and that they weren't alone. Thank God he'd thought to tell Giorgio to turn his headset off.

With a strength of mind he hadn't known he possessed, he pulled away from her. She wouldn't meet his eye as they both caught their breath, so he snuck a sweet kiss high on her cheekbone, bringing a smile to her lips.

'To be continued,' he said with a grin, before tapping their pilot on the shoulder. 'Ready to head back to base, *amico*.'

Once they were back on the ground, Giorgio gave him a hand getting back into his chair. 'Thanks for letting me borrow the heli,' Giorgio said in English as Mauro stretched his arm to shake hands.

'Any time. Thanks for the ride.'

'Wait,' Amber said as Mauro's driver took them down dark Sicilian lanes. 'You let him borrow it? The helicopter's yours? You know I forget sometimes that you're the guy who can casually go out and buy a helicopter. Can you fly it?'

'Yes and no,' he replied, though his fingers were caressing her knee, and every so often wandering further afield. But she couldn't let this rest. People she knew just didn't *have* helicopters. She couldn't even afford a car. 'I'm working towards my licence. I just need to log some more hours.'

She didn't ask *how* he flew, given that she'd already seen him driving a specially adapted Range Rover. You could adapt pretty much anything, she guessed, if you had enough money and motivation. She closed her eyes and leaned back against him, her whole body focussed now on those fingertips tracing circles on the sensitive skin at the backs of her knees, and the soft skin of her thighs. Something had happened while they were in the air. She couldn't put her finger on what, but the way Mauro had looked at her—equal parts passion and fear—made her nervous.

She opened a bottle of Prosecco when they got back to the villa and carried it outside with a couple of glasses. Mauro was waiting for her on a lounger by the pool. She sat beside him, her elbows propped on her knees and her arms tight in against her body. It was ridiculous, really, to feel shy after what they had just shared. He reached for her hand and threaded his fingers through hers. She wasn't sure what she had been expecting of him, but, after their passionate kiss in the helicopter, it hadn't been this quiet contemplation.

'That was pretty incredible,' he said simply.

Was he referring to the helicopter? The volcano? Or the kiss? It was the 'but' in his voice that gave it away. He was definitely talking about the kiss. Oh, God, were they going to be sensible and reason their way out of this—again? She had been so carried away by the fireworks and the helicopter and the kiss, all their concerns hadn't seemed to matter any more. And once they'd landed, she'd expected them to flood right back in, but it seemed they'd left them up there. All that had landed was her and Mauro, two people who liked each other, who both seemed pretty keen to see where that might go.

'Mauro, I don't—'

'But,' he went on, 'I think we should give ourselves some time to think about what we want.' He reached for her hands, and held them tight in his own.

'You know how I feel about you. I think you're incredible. You're talented and you're kind, and you're beautiful. And, God, this new confidence you've found from somewhere is so sexy it's nearly killing me. I want to find a way for us to make this work. But you've been telling me all week that you don't want to get hurt again, and I think it's the right thing to do to think about this properly.'

She wanted him—so much. She wanted to drag him

into the villa, into bed, and show him just how much. She reached for him again, but he wheeled back a fraction, just far enough that he could reach up and frame her face with his hands. 'You know, I'm really hoping that I'm not going to regret this. But I need you to think about this, to be sure. Because if you come to me, Amber, and tell me you want me, I'm not sure I'm ever going to let you go.'

'So what do we do now?' she asked, her body burning in frustration as it realised it wasn't going to get what she wanted tonight. But she could wait a few weeks, if that was what Mauro needed.

'Well, I don't know about you, but I'm going for the world's coldest shower.'

CHAPTER ELEVEN

It HAD BEEN six long weeks since she had seen Mauro, as he had kissed her goodbye on the terrace of his villa. He had had to fly straight to New York to take care of some business, he had said, and wouldn't be back in London for several weeks at least.

And then a month had passed, and more, with no word from him. And she'd braced herself for the fact that maybe she'd misunderstood what had happened that last night. Here she was in the make-up room of the TV studios, with less than an hour to go until she was on screen, and she hadn't heard a word from him since she had left his villa. A small, tinsel-bedecked TV in the corner of the room was showing what was happening out in the studio, and the knot of fear and nerves in her belly was growing larger and larger.

She'd thought at the time that their last kiss had been a promise, a commitment of more to come. But perhaps it had been goodbye. A curl of embarrassment started in her stomach and radiated out to her skin. What would the production team have done with the footage of those last days in Sicily? The heartfelt conversations they had had on Etna, and the awkward silences in the interviews that had followed, not to mention the kisses at the cable-car station and in the helicopter. It hadn't been until the next day that she'd remembered that there had been a camera in the corner of the cabin.

It would be fodder for an explosive reunion, she supposed.

She'd thought that she might have bumped into Mauro by now, or that at least they'd see each other in the green room before they went on air, but she'd just been told that that definitely wouldn't be happening. They wouldn't lay eyes on each other again until they were on screen. Maximum drama, Ayisha had said. Maximum humiliation was just as likely.

Amber sat in the green room and closed her eyes, trying to block out the streams of conversation flowing around her. She tried to take a deep breath, but the sparkling, sequinned dress that the wardrobe department had thought was suitably festive had other ideas.

Even if Mauro had decided that he didn't want to be with her, she couldn't be sorry that she'd gone on the date. Finding a man like Mauro had been incredible. But finding herself again—that was a miracle. Something she could only ever be grateful for, even if she never saw him again. She hadn't expected to lose her heart to him, but she'd done it all the same.

She'd known it on the plane, wishing he were beside her.

She'd known it when she'd lain alone in her bed that

night, thinking of Mauro's arms, how delicious they'd feel wrapped around her.

She'd known it when she'd arrived at the studios earlier that day, remembering the first time that she'd met him. The flip of her stomach at the sound of his voice as she'd remembered seeing him soaking wet by the side of a pool.

She'd fallen for him. And she wanted him—even though it frightened her.

He was worth the risk.

Like the London drizzle after the Sicilian sunshine, everything in her life had seemed grey and dull since she had returned from their date. She wanted the heat and the spark that only came from being with him. From sharing their experiences. From seeing things together.

And if she'd managed to convince him that she didn't want him, then she was going to have to undo the damage herself. If she wanted him, she was going to have to make it happen.

But what was she meant to say, how was she meant to act with the whole country watching? She was just going to have to tell him, she realised. Tell him that she still wanted him, that she loved him, and hope that he still felt the same. Be honest with herself, and with him. And if he rejected her? Then he rejected her. She couldn't control him, or his feelings. All she could do was share hers with him and hope that that was enough.

Ayisha appeared at the door of the green room with her tablet computer.

'All right, Amber, we'll be live in about fifteen minutes. Anything you need to ask before we get started?'

Amber shook her head. It was too late for second thoughts now.

The studio lights were dazzlingly bright, as she waited out of view of the cameras. The set had been dressed for Christmas, and fairy lights glinted and twinkled, reflected off the silver glitter of the decorations and icicles, and in the pillowy white of the fake snow.

The heat of the lights on her skin reminded her of watching Mount Stromboli erupt from the window of the helicopter. Just the memory of that night was enough to push her forward to centre stage when she heard her cue, when a very large part of her wanted to run and hide, away from the intrusive glare of the cameras and audience.

'Please welcome... Amber Harris...and Mauro Evans!'

She stumbled towards the couch in the middle of the stage with her eyes fixed on the enormous Christmas tree just behind Julia, too afraid to look at Mauro, who she knew would be coming in from the opposite side. She needed to keep herself together. If she looked at him, she knew that she'd lose her composure—she just had to hold her nerve a little longer.

Once she was centre stage, the long sequinned dress no longer felt out of place. The lights were winking and shining off her the same as they were from the decorations. The Christmas tree was at least twenty feet tall, with baubles as big as grapefruits of glass and silver and glitter; candles burned on every surface and Julia was waiting for her in an enormous wingback chair upholstered in white velvet, beside a matching couch, just big enough for two.

It was a fantasy Christmas wonderland, and at its centre she felt intoxicated by it.

And there, still with his ice-white shirt, was Mauro. The audience broke into enthusiastic applause, and at last Amber risked a glance at him from beneath her lashes. She couldn't risk looking at him full-on. Not yet. She closed her eyes completely as she leant in to kiss him on the cheek, just as she'd been briefed by Ayisha. Just like that first time, when she'd done the same thing, almost on this very spot.

The closed eyes didn't help. They did nothing to block out the feel of his rough cheek against her smooth skin. Or to block out his scent, so delicious, so familiar, with that hint of sea salt that was as much a part of him as his charm.

She'd not swum since she'd been back in London. She couldn't face the reminder of him. Of the electric crackle of chemistry between them, a spark that held so much promise. If they have the courage to pursue it. Eventually she couldn't put it off any longer and, just for a moment, she drank him in. That dark red hair, its wildness not quite subdued by whatever product had been dragged through it. The white shirt still effortlessly chic, and perfectly highlighting his golden skin. And his eyes. Green, and deep, and full of emotion.

Not the cheeky twinkle that had flirted with her that first night that they met, but wells of something deeper and more serious. Secrets hidden from their audience, and something hidden from her as well. The last time that she'd seen him, he had laid all his cards on the table. Had told her everything that he felt for her, and asked for honesty and truth in return. And now here he was, guarded. Hiding something.

'Look at these two, don't they make such a gorgeous couple?' Julia turned to the audience with a sparkling smile while a member of the production team encouraged the audience to clap and cheer. 'We're all so happy to have you both here with us. So, before the commercial break our audience saw that magic moment when you surprised us all, Mauro, and picked Amber to accompany you to your beautiful home in Sicily, but, just for you two, let's see again where all this started.'

While the VT of their first meeting showed, Mauro moved from his chair to the couch beside her, but he refused to meet her eye. She still had no idea what he was thinking.

She watched their first awkward meeting and felt a blush rise on her cheeks. She was so guarded. So prickly—she remembered, of course, but what she hadn't seen then was the look on Mauro's face with each of her answers, entertained and intrigued. Proof, right in front of her eyes, of how badly her plan to push him away had been doomed to failure from the beginning.

'And now, what we've all been dying to see. How did you two get on when we sent you away for a week of sun, sand and…ahem…?'

'Jet-skiing?' Mauro supplied.

She breathed a sigh of relief at the sound of familiar humour in his voice. Maybe this would be OK after all. But then her spine grew straighter and straighter as they watched their week together unfolding on screen. Some moments when she'd known the cameras were rolling—and then some she hadn't.

They'd been there, somewhere behind them, when Mauro had caught her toes with his wheelchair in the airport, and captured the moment when he'd pulled her into his lap. Her cheeks warmed and her breath caught when she remembered how close she'd come to kissing him. How she'd been overwhelmed by the heat of his body, the way that his chest and his arms had so totally engulfed her.

She risked a glance at Mauro, and their eyes met as he looked across at her for just a moment. A shared smile melted some of the frost between them.

And then she'd leapt off his lap like a scalded cat, and just like that the moment between them had been lost.

Those first couple of days in Sicily, they'd caught lingering glances and shared smiles. The end of that first swimming lesson, when she'd been so aware of Mauro's eyes on her body. She had felt more exposed that day, with one man watching, than she did now, with her swimsuit-clad body broadcast to the nation.

God knew, the footage made no secret of where the producers thought this story was heading. They didn't have the money shot, so to speak—no smoking gun, but there was plenty of circumstantial evidence.

And then the fog descended—literally and metaphorically—during their hike up Etna; and the fires raged on Stromboli, and a great big question mark hung over where they were going next. The producers had been kind—it could have been a lot worse—and not a shot of that kiss in the helicopter was broadcast. But it was clear what direction this interview was going to take—they were obviously hoping for Christmas fireworks.

'So then, you two. I think we saw some sparks flying there. What's been happening since that was shot?'

'Well, Julia, I'm sorry if this comes as a disappointment…' ah, that voice with its rich mixture of Welsh and Italian; a combination that shouldn't work but in reality was dangerously seductive '…but I've actually been in New York since that was filmed. So this is the first time we've seen each other since.'

'Oh, how exciting!' Julia declared with a clap of her hands—Amber admired her ability to sell a lie. If she'd had half her talent, this whole charade would have been a hell of a lot easier from start to finish. 'Reunited right here, with us. Tell me, then, Amber, what's it like seeing Mauro again?'

She opened her mouth to speak, but found that her tongue was dry and her lips paralysed. A prickle of sweat beaded in her palms and she shifted on the couch, willing herself to speak.

It had to be now. If she didn't tell him how she felt tonight, then this could all be over. If this show hadn't been booked, maybe she never would have seen him again. And if she couldn't even speak, she was going to lose him—and deserve it.

'Uh, well, it's…nice.' Nice? She wanted to scream at herself. After everything, that was all she could come up with—nice?

But what if she laid out her every emotion in heart-rending detail, and then he turned her down? If she could just have a clue as to what he was feeling she knew that she could do better. She opened her mouth to try again, but Julia was already jumping in with another question.

'OK… So, Amber thinks it's "nice" to see you, Mauro. How are *you* feeling seeing Amber again?'

He glanced across at Amber, and she could feel her cheeks warm. 'Well, it's not often that she's lost for words. I'm pretty surprised by that.'

Still he evaded her eye.

'Well, you two are playing your cards pretty close to your chests.' Julia raised her eyebrows theatrically towards the audience and got a ripple of laughter and applause in response. 'How about we look at this another way: have you got plans to see each other again?'

She could see that Mauro was about to speak, but there were things she needed to say before they could answer that question. She laid her hand on his, and felt a shot of heat and electricity straight to her heart. She drew in a steadying breath and spoke.

'Mauro, wait.'

Finally, *finally* he turned and properly held her gaze. As his green eyes bore into hers, she could see surprise. But that wasn't all. There was still a spark there, a look so familiar from their time together in Sicily that it gave her the courage to speak on. From the corner of her eye she saw genuine shock on Julia's face at the way that she had silenced Mauro, and rushed to fill the vacuum with the speech that she'd started rehearsing weeks ago. If she wanted Mauro to know how she felt then she had to tell him—and now. If she waited, she'd lose her nerve, and might never have the opportunity again.

'Look, Mauro. I know what I said before, when we were at Etna…' She glanced up at Julia, wondering if Mauro was going to make her spell it out, air all their dirty laundry. His face showed no emotion, and she knew that she had no choice but to lay it all on the line. 'I was scared. We both know it. I was terrified because of when I got hurt before, and I was worried that it was going to happen again with you, and I let that keep me away. Because you were right, Mauro. We both know that you were. I'm falling for you. Damn it, I've fallen. I've fallen headfirst, stupidly, recklessly in love with you.'

Her words were met with a shocked silence. In her peripheral vision she could see Julia staring at her in shock. But she was distracted by that for only a fraction of a second. She couldn't drag her eyes from Mauro, who was looking at her with careful regard. She wasn't sure what she had been expecting, but this sangfroid was her worst nightmare. If he'd been repulsed, told her to forget it—she would have been devastated. If he'd declared his own feelings she would have been elated. But this—this meant that she had to go on. She drew herself up a little taller, pushed her shoulders back, opening up her chest, and started speaking again.

'That week with you was the best week of my life. Even though I spent half the time pretty terrified, and a lot of it mad either with you or myself. And Etna was a bit of a disaster, and you kept asking me to be brave about my feelings for you and I couldn't do it. It's just so incredible to have found someone that makes me want to risk all that again—risk *feeling* again—that I don't want to give it up. I don't want to give *you* up, Mauro.'

She waited again. That was it. That was all that she had to say, and if it wasn't enough… Well, there would be nothing she could do other than accept it. Lick her wounds. Hibernate. Work out how she was going to rebuild her life again. Because even if Mauro didn't still want her, she wouldn't go back to where she was before she'd met him. It wasn't fair to him, wasn't fair to what she'd learnt in their week together to act as if it had never happened. Even if he wanted to forget the whole thing, she wouldn't. She'd never forget that week, and she'd never forget the man who made her realise that she could be whole again, even after her heart had been broken.

But now she had said everything. She couldn't force him to want her. All she could do now was wait and see.

She looked long and hard into his eyes.

'Of course I still want you.' The light and sparkle was back in his face, and she could feel the heat crackling between them in a way that made her realise how cold she had been ever since they'd got back. 'What kind of guy do you think I am?'

'Oh, my God!' She grabbed his face and kissed him hard on the lips. 'You are so infuriating! You've been avoiding me for weeks and you choose now—'

He smacked her a kiss back, and then dropped his voice until it was little more than a breath. 'You wouldn't want me all biddable, would you?' he murmured and a shot of heat went straight from her lips to between her legs.

He was right, of course. He wouldn't be the man that she loved if he had been anything other than absurdly confident that everything would go his way. She leaned in again for another kiss, when a melodramatic throat-clearing behind him reminded her that they were still on live TV. A rush of blood heated her cheeks, and she knew that they must be blazing red.

'So it seems like we've got some catching up to do here!' Julia declared. 'Are you going to fill us in on what's been going on?'

She looked across at Mauro. She didn't want to use him, to exploit their relationship, but they both knew that she had got into this because she needed to improve her image, and now they had the perfect opportunity to do that, just by sharing their happiness. But it wasn't just her decision to make.

'Well, I think we can just put it down to me being irresistible,' Mauro said with a smug look on his face. 'I've said all along that it was inevitable, you know. She couldn't help but fall in love with me.'

Amber laughed and leaned in close as his arm wrapped around her shoulders. At last. At last she had him exactly where she wanted him. At last, she was exactly where she wanted to be. 'Well, there's not a lot I can say to counter that, is there,' she said, 'given that I was absolutely hopeless at resisting?'

Julia looked on them indulgently for a second, before glancing across at Ayisha, who was mouthing something from behind the camera. 'But back to the interview... Amber seems to think that you've been avoiding her, Mauro? Surely that can't be true.'

'Yeah, I noticed that,' he said. 'I haven't—I swear. I had work in New York and then something came up that demanded my personal attention in Mexico. I only had time to fit in one last errand in London before I came to the studio, so I've genuinely not had a minute of free time since I last saw her. But seriously, Julia, I owe you, big time. If you hadn't invited me to come on here, I wouldn't have met the woman of my dreams, the woman I want to spend the rest of my life with, if she'll have me.'

Amber's jaw dropped open. The rest of his life? She'd been so elated that he'd not just rejected her on live TV she hadn't even thought about where this might be going past that first kiss.

'The rest of your life?' Her voice shook as she asked the question, but she had to do it. She had to know how he felt about commitment, whether they were just empty words or whether he actually meant them. About the fear that he might be missing out on something else. She'd seen genuine panic in his eyes when they had been growing closer on the island, and she couldn't quite believe that he could have such a complete turnaround.

Mauro reached into his jacket pocket, but Amber was distracted by a squeal from Julia—the woman looked as if she'd just been slapped. Or told she had a winning lottery ticket. She wasn't sure which.

'Julia, are you—?' Amber started. 'Oh, my God.' At the sight of the small velvet box in Mauro's hand, the words caught in her throat, and she found that she couldn't carry on.

'Mauro…'

'Amber,' he replied. His voice steadier than hers. 'Do you think you can see past the fact that you've told me more than once, in no uncertain terms, that you don't want to get involved with me, and the fact that I was such an idiot it took me nearly a whole week to realise that I can't live without you *and* the fact that I told you that I absolutely, definitely, wouldn't ask you to get involved with me…' As he took a breath a hush descended on the studio.

'Would you do me the very great honour of marrying me?'

The silence seemed to expand within her as the attention and expectation of every person in the room became fixed on her, and on her answer.

Can you trust him?

That little voice in her head was still there. Mauro or no Mauro, she hadn't managed to silence it completely. She hadn't meant to fall in love. Not with him, this playboy who had told her straight that he was never in it for the long haul.

All around her was snow and ice and light, all of it

beautiful, all of it fake. This set was a fantasy, an illusion. Only one thing in it was real.

As she looked up into his eyes she could feel the connection between them, feel that their souls had somehow, in the heat and steam and chaos of a volcano, melted and become one. That it was as impossible to separate them now as it would be to prise the lava from those hillsides.

Her gaze was locked onto Mauro, and just as she was about to speak she saw a tiny crease line his forehead, and that was what did for her. That tiny crack of self-doubt, the softness that she knew was inside him, hiding inside this crazy man who had no fear, even at the thought of proposing marriage live on air.

'I'd be crazy not to,' she said with a smile. 'Yes, Mauro, I'd very much like to marry you.'

Mauro let out a whoop as he wrapped his arms tight around her waist and dragged her unceremoniously onto his lap.

'I promise you I'm going to make you the happiest woman in the world for the rest of your life,' he said as he opened the ring box.

Amber gasped at the sight of the stone, blazing orange and pink in a band of icy platinum and diamonds.

'It's a Mexican fire opal,' Mauro said. 'It reminded me of—'

But she cut him off with a kiss before he could finish the sentence.

'It's beautiful,' she said, coming up for air. 'Absolutely beautiful.'

She leaned in to kiss him again, and for a few long

moments the rest of the world disappeared, forced out of her consciousness by the volume of her shock and delight. Gradually, though, the silence of their little bubble faded, and reality started to crash back into Amber's world.

'Congratulations, you beautiful pair,' Julia gushed. 'When's the wedding—and where? I'd better be on the guest list, because if I'm not then I'll be gatecrashing!'

Mauro and Amber both laughed.

'I think it's a little early to be announcing a venue, but I promise you we'll let you know.'

From the corner of her eye Amber spotted Ayisha still gesticulating wildly, and she guessed that Mauro's little stunt had taken the show careering off course. Well, if you couldn't bend your schedule for a little romance, then what were any of us doing here at all?

Julia was still gushing at them both, and Amber noticed a tear had escaped the corner of her eye as she pressed her hands into Mauro's with more congratulations. But Mauro was extracting his hands, gently, she noticed. And then one giant paw had enclosed her fingers.

'Now, if you don't mind, Julia, I think my fiancée and I need to be going.'

Without another word he had shoved her off his lap, moved to his chair, and grabbed her hand. He wheeled off the studio stage, only pausing at the last minute and giving the show's signature wave, and then they were behind the scenery, and away from the public glare.

From the corner of her eye, Amber noticed a runner approaching them, but when Mauro's fingers curled into her hair and pulled her down for a kiss, her eyes closed and the world melted away.

The kiss burned through her with the intensity of a wildfire. But a niggling thought dampened the flames.

'You're sure, though, Mauro. Because I know you, and I remember everything you said in Sicily. I can't go into this lightly. If I'm getting married, it's going to be for ever. I need to know that that's what you want too.'

Mauro loosened his arms from around her waist, and she stood, suddenly unsure. Wondering whether she wanted to hear what he had to say. Maybe she should have just gone along with it, regardless. Maybe she could learn to be happy in the moment, as Mauro was, rather than worrying about what their future might bring.

But no. She girded herself, and stuck to her principles. If she was going to make a commitment, she had to mean it, and she had to know that Mauro meant it too.

He reached for her hands, preventing her from withdrawing any more.

'Amber, *amore mio*, I've never been more sure about anything. I love you. These past few weeks have been hell without you, but I owed it to you to think it through. To give you time to think about things too. That day after the mountain everything was so... heated. It wasn't the time to make big decisions.'

'Whereas live TV...'

'That bit wasn't exactly planned. I was going to wait until later, but then you said what you did and I couldn't help it. I want you. I want us, and I want it to start right now.'

He meant it. There was no doubting the expression on his face when he looked at her, no mistaking the hope and fear and doubt in his eyes.

She leaned in for another kiss, soft and gentle this time, a promise of everything that was to come.

'Right now?'

He nodded.

'Then you'd better take me home.'

EPILOGUE

AMBER THREW ANOTHER log into the fire, and watched as the flames licked up the side, yellow, orange and red all dancing in the grate.

'Home,' she'd said to Mauro. 'Take me home.'

She'd not given any thought to the word as it passed her lips, and it was only when they had climbed into the waiting car that she'd even questioned where they were going.

'My place?' he'd asked.

She'd agreed without thinking about it. Of course his place. What were they going to do? Huddle round the solitary space heater in her flat? She'd spent that night at his penthouse suite in Mayfair, and then another. And another. In the weeks since the show aired she'd only gone back to her flat for clothes and basic supplies.

And then his friend had lent him this house for Christmas—it was only a few streets away from his hotel, but their first Christmas together warranted somewhere more festive, he'd said. And she couldn't fault the house on the festive front. The tree in the hallway, lit with flickering LED candles, looked as if it could have been in that exact spot for a hundred years. Garlands weaved between the spindles of the banisters, and a huge green wreath greeted guests at the front door opposite the gated park. Even the British weather had delivered, and she could see snow gathering on the windowpanes.

The floorboards were original, sanded and waxed to a perfect glow, and covered with luxurious rugs, plush underfoot. And under her back, she thought. And her elbow, as she lifted herself to look at Mauro, who was still snoozing beside her on the floor. She pulled the blanket up higher over them, and traced her fingers across Mauro's chest, outlining the pectoral muscle and drifting through the auburn-tinted hairs.

'Mmm...' he said, his voice still full of sleep. 'Are you trying to wake me up?'

'Maybe.' She smiled and glanced at the clock, just as the minute hand hit the twelve. 'Merry Christmas,' she said, dropping a kiss on his cheek.

His eyes flew open and he pushed himself up, toppling her off him in the process. 'It's midnight already?' he asked, looking flustered. 'How did that happen?'

She wrapped the throw around herself, taken aback by Mauro's change in mood.

'Uh, well, you suggested that we get a brandy and come and sit down here by the fire, see in Christmas morning, and then you said...'

His face softened, and then broke into a grin. 'I

know. I remember; I'm sorry.' He kissed her, a smile still on his lips. 'I'm just excited.'

'About Christmas Day?' She laughed and leaned in against his shoulder. 'You big kid.'

'Don't get too comfy.' He pulled the throw away from her, leaving her chilly, and he reached for his shirt, discarded beside them, and wrapped it around her shoulders. 'I need you to do me a favour.'

'Now?'

'Yes, now. It's Christmas, it has to be now.'

Amber pushed her arms into the sleeves, and stood with an air of resignation. She knew that once he'd got an idea in his head, it was impossible to change his mind.

'My jacket,' he said. 'Over the back of the chair in the hall. There's an envelope in the inside pocket. Can you grab it for me?'

She did as he asked, and when she got back to the rug, he was sitting up, his back against the couch, the throw blanket tucked over his lap. 'Come back in,' he said, holding up one corner, and she crawled in beside him, nestling into his heat again.

'Here.' She handed him the envelope, curiosity starting to niggle at her.

But he handed the envelope straight back to her.

'Merry Christmas,' he said.

She took the envelope from him and turned it over in her hands before she opened it slowly, carefully, with half an eye still on Mauro's face. He looked nervous, she thought. And excited. And all of a sudden she was nervous too, about what she was going to find in that envelope. Was she going to like it?

She pulled out the sheaf of papers and started reading. Then skipped to the next page. And the next. She didn't understand. How could he…? He couldn't have…

'A house, Mauro?'

'This house!' he declared, kissing her on the lips. 'Merry Christmas, Amber. I hope you like it.'

'Oh, my God.' She couldn't speak past the orange-sized lump in her throat. She forced it down, and tried to string a sentence together.

'Mauro, I can't accept this house. This is crazy. You've bought me a *house*. In *Mayfair*.'

He smiled, still apparently not seeing that there was anything weird about this situation.

'Look,' he said, tucking her hair behind her ear, 'I know what happened to you before. I know how much your independence means to you. But I want us to be together. I want us to live together.' He dropped another kiss on her lips. 'Most of all, I want you to feel safe, secure. That's why I bought you this house, but I hope you'll let me live with you.'

She couldn't take her eyes from the deeds. From the space where her name was in bold black ink. The owner of this house. Mauro was right. For nearly two years she'd been living in fear of ending up with nowhere to call home, and now he was telling her that she would never have to feel that again.

Except now…everything was different. She didn't just want a roof over her head. She wanted a home, and she knew that a house could never be that again without Mauro there too.

'Of course you'll live with me,' she said. 'But this… this is too much.' He opened his mouth to speak, but she had to have her say. 'I want us to live together, Mauro. With both our names on the deeds.'

'But I thought that you'd want—'

'And it was so thoughtful of you. But let's do this together. Take this leap together. I want to go into this marriage knowing we're equals. I trust you. I love you.'

He leaned down and kissed her hard, pulling her onto his lap and wrapping his arms around her. 'I love you so much,' he said. 'And we're going to make this such a happy home. Merry Christmas, Amber.'

'Merry Christmas, Mauro,' she whispered against his lips.

She relaxed into his body, the fire, the brandy and the heat of her fiancé warming her to her bones, and she knew without question that this was only the first of a lifetime of Christmases they'd welcome in this room.

* * * * *

"You have to get the groceries for me."

"Nope. It's May." He stuck his hat on, so his hands were free to pick up his second boot and shake the cell phone out of it.

"It's May? What kind of answer is that? Do you fast in May or do a colon cleanse or something?"

He looked up at her joke, but his grin died before it started. Judging by the look on her face, she wasn't joking. "The River Mack rounds up in May."

She looked at him, waiting. He realized a woman from Hollywood probably had no idea what that meant.

"We're busy. We're branding. We have to keep an eye on the late calving, the bulls—"

He stopped himself. He wasn't going to explain the rest. Managing a herd was a constant, complex operation.

Sophia flapped one hand toward the kitchen behind her. "I have nothing to eat. You have to help me."

He stomped into his second boot. "Not unless you're a pregnant or nursing cow."

At her gasp, he did laugh. "I keep every beast on this ranch fed, but you, ma'am, are not a beast. You're a movie star, a woman who can take care of herself, and you're not my problem."

She looked absolutely stricken. Had he been so harsh? "Listen, if I'm going toward town, I don't mind picking you up a gallon of milk. That's just common courtesy.

I expect you to do the same for me."

"I can't leave the ranch."

"Neither can I. Now if you'll excuse me, I've got a barn full of animals to feed before I can feed myself."

* * *

Texas Rescue:
Rescuing hearts… one Texan at a time!

A COWBOY'S WISH UPON A STAR

BY
CARO CARSON

First Published in Great Britain 2016
By Mills & Boon, an imprint of HarperCollins*Publishers*
1 London Bridge Street, London, SE1 9GF

© 2016 Caro Carson

ISBN: 978-0-263-92042-0

23-1216

Our policy is to use papers that are natural, renewable and recyclable products and made from wood grown in sustainable forests. The logging and manufacturing processes conform to the legal environmental regulations of the country of origin.

Printed and bound in Spain
by CPI, Barcelona

Despite a no-nonsense background as a West Point graduate and US Army officer, **Caro Carson** has always treasured the happily-ever-after of a good romance novel. Now Caro is delighted to be living her own happily-ever-after with her husband and two children in the great state of Florida, a location that has saved the coaster-loving theme-park fanatic a fortune on plane tickets.

This book is dedicated to You,
the reader who
spent time to meet me at the book signing,
or spent time to send me the note to say
you love the love stories that
I spent time to write.
Thank you.

Chapter One

It was the end of the world.

Sophia Jackson strained to see something, anything that looked like civilization, but the desolate landscape was no more than brown dirt and scrubby bits of green plants that stretched all the way to the horizon.

She might have been in one of her own movies.

The one that had garnered an Academy Award nomination for her role as a dying frontier woman had been filmed in Mexico, but this part of Texas looked close enough. The one that had made her an overnight success as a Golden Globe winner for her portrayal of a doomed woman in a faraway galaxy had been filmed in Italy, but again, this landscape was eerily similar.

Doomed. Dying. Isolated.

She'd channeled those emotions before. This time, however, no one was going to yell *cut*. No one was going to hand her a gold statue.

"Are we there yet?" She sounded demanding, just like the junior officer thrust into a leadership role on a space colony.

Well, not really. She had the ear of an actor; she could catch nuance in tone and delivery, even in—or especially in—her own voice. She didn't sound like a commander. She sounded like a diva.

I have the right to be a diva. I've got the gold statue to prove it.

She tossed her hair back with a jingle of her chandelier earrings, queen of the backseat of the car.

In the front bucket seats, her sister's fiancé continued to drive down the endless road in silence, but Sophia caught the quick glance he shared with her sister. The two of them didn't think she was a young military officer. They didn't even think of her as a diva.

She was an annoying, spoiled brat who was going to be dropped off in the middle of abso-freaking-lutely nowhere.

Her sister, Grace, reached back between the seats to pat her on the knee. "I haven't been here before, either, but it can't be too much farther. Isn't it perfect, though? The paparazzi will never find you out here. This is just what we were hoping for."

Sophia looked at Grace's hand as it patted the black leather which covered her knee. Grace's engagement ring was impossible to miss. Her sister had been her rock, her constant companion, until very recently. Now, wearing a different kind of rock on her left hand, Grace was giddy at the prospect of marrying the man who'd encouraged her to dump her own sister.

Sophia mentally stuck out her tongue at the back of the man's head. Her future brother-in-law was a stupid doctor named Alex, and he'd never once been impressed with Sophia Jackson, movie star. Since the day Sophia and Grace had arrived in Texas, he'd only paid attention to Grace.

Grace's hand moved from Sophia's knee to Alex's shoulder. Then to the back of his neck. The diamond played peek-a-boo as her sister slid her hand through her fiancé's dark hair.

Sophia looked away, out the side window to the desolate horizon. The nausea was rising, so she chomped on her chewing gum. Loudly. With no class. No elegance. None of the grace that the world had once expected of the talented Sophia Jackson.

Pun intended. I have no Grace, not anymore.

Grace didn't correct her gum-smacking. Grace no longer cared enough to correct her.

Sophia was on her own. She'd have to survive the rest of her nine-month sentence all by herself, hiding from the world. In the end, all she'd have to show for it would be a flabby stomach and stretch marks. Like a teenager in the last century, she was pregnant and ashamed, terrified of being exposed. She had to be sent to the country to hide until she could have the baby, give it up for adoption, and then return to the world and spend the rest of her life pretending nothing had ever happened.

If she had a world to return to. That was a very big *if*.

No one in Hollywood would work with her. It had nothing to do with the pregnancy. No one knew about that, and she wasn't far enough along to even begin to show. No, the world of movie stardom was boxing her out solely because of her reputation.

A box office giant, an actor whom Sophia had always dreamed of working with, had recently informed a major studio he would not do the picture if she were cast opposite him. Her reputation had sunk that low. They said there was no such thing as bad publicity, but the publicity she'd been generating had hurt her. Her publicist and her agent had each informed her that she was unmarketable as is.

Ex-publicist. Ex-agent. They both left me.

Panic crawled up the back of her throat. They were all leaving her. Publicist, agent, that louse of a slimy boyfriend she'd been stupid enough to run away with. And worst of all, within the next few minutes, her sister. She was losing the best personal assistant in the world, right when she needed a personal assistant the most.

There was no such thing as loyalty in Hollywood. Not even her closest blood relative was standing by her side. Nausea turned to knots.

"Oh, my goodness," her sister laughed. The tone was one of happy, happy surprise.

Alex's laugh was masculine, amused. "Just in case you needed a reminder that you're in the middle of a genuine Texas cattle ranch…"

He brought their car to a stop—as if he had a choice. The view through the windshield was now the bulky brown back of a giant steer. A thousand pounds of animal blocked their way, just standing there on the road they needed to use, the road that would lead them to an empty ranch house where Sophia would be abandoned, alone, left behind.

Knots turned to panic. She needed to get this over with. Her world was going to end, and she couldn't drag this out one second longer.

Let's rip this bandage off.

"Move, you stupid cow!" she hollered from the backseat.

"Sophia, that's not going to help."

But Sophia had already half vaulted over Alex's shoulder and slammed her palm on the car horn. "Get out of the road."

The cow stared at her through the glass, unmoving.

God above, she was tired of being stared at. Everyone was always waiting for her to do something, to be crazy or brilliant, to act out every emotion while they watched passively. Grace was staring at her now, shaking her head.

"Move!" Sophia laid on the horn again.

"Stop it." Alex firmly took her arm and pushed her toward the backseat. His stare was more of a glare.

He and Grace both turned back toward the front. Sophia had spoiled their little delight at a cow in the road, at this unexpected interlude in their sweet, shared day.

I can't stand it, I can't stand myself, I can't stand this one more minute.

She yanked on the door handle and shoved the door open.

"Sophia! Stay in the car." Grace sounded equal parts exasperated and fearful.

Sophia was beyond fear. Panic, nausea, knots—a terrible need to get this over with. Once the ax fell, once she was cut off from the last remnants of her life, she could fall apart. She wanted nothing more than to fall apart, and this stupid cow was preventing it.

She slammed the car door and waved her arms over her head, advancing on the cow. Or maybe it was a bull. It had short horns. Whatever it was, it flinched.

Emboldened—or just plain crazy, like they all said—Sophia waved her arms over her head some more and advanced toward the stupid, stationary cow. The May weather was warm on the bare skin of her midriff as her crop top rose higher with each wave of her arms. On her second step, she nearly went down as her ankle twisted, the spike heel of her over-the-knee boot threatening to sink into the brown Texas dirt.

"Move, do you hear me? Move." She gestured wide to

the vast land all around them. "Anywhere. Anywhere but right here."

The cow snorted at her. Chewed something. Didn't care about her, didn't care about her at all.

Tears were spilling over her cheeks, Sophia realized suddenly. Her ankle hurt, her heart hurt, her stomach hurt. The cow looked away, not interested in the least. Being ignored was worse than being stared at. The beast was massive, far stockier than the horses she'd worked with on the set as a dying frontier woman. She shoved at the beast's shoulder anyway.

"Just *move!*" Its hide was coarse and dusty. She shoved harder, accomplishing nothing, feeling her own insignificance. She might as well not exist. No career, no sister, no friends, no life.

She collapsed on the thick, warm neck of the uncaring cow, and let the tears flow.

Someone on the ranch was in trouble.

Travis Chalmers tossed his pliers into the leather saddlebag and gave the barb wire one last tug. Fixed.

He scooped up his horse's trailing reins in one hand, smashed his cowboy hat more firmly over his brow, and swung into the saddle. That car horn meant something else needed fixing, and now. He only hoped one of his men hadn't been injured.

The car horn sounded again. Travis kicked the horse into a gallop, heading in the direction of the sound. It didn't sound like one of the ranch trucks' horns. A visitor, then, who could be lost, out of gas, stranded by a flat tire—simple fixes.

He kept his seat easily and let the horse have her head. Whatever the situation was, he'd handle it. He was young for a foreman, just past thirty, but he'd been ranching since the day he was born, seemed like. Nothing that happened on a cattle operation came as a surprise to him.

He rode up the low rise toward the road, and the cause of the commotion came into view. A heifer was standing in the road, blocking the path of a sports car that clearly wouldn't be able to handle any off-road terrain, so it couldn't go around the animal. That the animal was on the road wasn't a surprise; Travis had just repaired a gap in the barb wire fence. But leaning on the heifer, her back to him, was a woman.

What a woman, with long hair flowing perfectly down her back, her body lean and toned, her backside curvy—all easy to see because any skin that wasn't bared to the sun and sky was encased in tight black clothing. But it was her long legs in thigh-high boots that made him slow his horse in a moment of stunned confusion.

She had to be a mirage. No woman actually wore thigh-high leather boots with heels that high. Those boots sent sexual signals that triggered every adolescent memory of a comic book heroine. Half-naked, high-heeled—a character drawn to appeal to the most primal part of a man's mind.

Not much on a cattle ranch could surprise him, except seeing *that* in the middle of the road.

The horse continued toward the heifer, its focus absolute. So was Travis's. He couldn't take his eyes off the woman as he rode toward her.

She lifted her head and turned his way. With a dash of her cheek against her black-clad shoulder, she turned all the way around and leaned against the animal, stretching her arms along its back like it was her sofa. As the wind blew her hair back from her face, silver and gold shining in the sun, she held her pose and watched him come for her.

Boots, bare skin, black leather—they messed with his brain, until the car door opened and the driver began to get out, a man. Then the passenger door opened, too, and the heifer swung her head, catching the smell of horse and humans on the wind. The rancher in him pushed aside the adolescent male, and he returned his horse to a quicker lope with a *tch* and a press of his thigh.

That heifer wasn't harmless. Let her get nervous, and a half ton of beef on the hoof could do real harm to the humans crowding her, including the sex goddess in boots.

"Afternoon, folks." Travis took in the other two at a glance. Worried woman, irritated man. He didn't look at the goddess as he stopped near the strange little grouping. His heart had kicked into a higher gear at the sight of her, something the sound of the horn and the short gallop had not done. It was damned disconcerting. Everything about her was disconcerting. "Stay behind those doors, if you don't mind."

"Sophia, it's time to get back in the car now," the man said, exaggeratedly patient and concerned, as if he were talking a jumper off a ledge.

"No."

"Oh, Sophie." The woman gave the smallest shake of her head, her eyes sad. Apparently, this Sophie had disappointed her before.

Sophie. Sophia. He looked at her again. Sophia Jackson, of course. Unmistakable. A movie star on his ranch, resting against his heifer, a scenario so bizarre his brain had to work to believe his eyes.

She hadn't taken her blue eyes off him, but she'd raised her chin in challenge. The *no* was meant for him, was it?

"Walk away," he said mildly, keeping his voice even for the heifer's benefit—and hers. "I'll get this heifer on her way so you can get on yours."

"No. She likes me." Sophia's long, elegant fingers stroked the roan hide of the cattle.

"Is that right?" He reached back to grab his lasso and held the loops in one hand.

"My cow doesn't want to leave me. She's loyal and true."

It was an absurd thing to say. Travis didn't have time for absurd.

"Watch your toes." He rode forward, crowding the heifer, crowding Sophia Jackson, and slapped the heifer on the hindquarters with the coiled rope. She briskly left the road.

Sophia Jackson looked a little smaller and a lot sillier, standing in the road by herself. He looked down at her famous face as she watched the heifer leave. She actually looked sad, like she didn't want the heifer to go, which was as absurd as everything else about the situation.

Travis wheeled his horse away from Sophia in order to talk to the driver.

"Where are you heading?"

"Thanks for moving that animal. I'm Alex Gregory. This is my fiancée, Grace."

Travis waited, but the man didn't introduce the woman in boots. He guessed he was supposed to recognize her. He did. Still, it seemed rude to leave her out.

"Travis Chalmers." He touched the brim of his hat and nodded at the worried woman, then twisted halfway around in his saddle to touch his hat and nod again at the movie star in their midst.

"Chalmers, the foreman?" asked the man, Alex. "Good to meet you. The MacDowells told me they'd explained the situation to you."

Not exactly.

Travis hooked his lasso onto the saddle horn. "You're the one who's gonna live in Marion MacDowell's house for a few months?"

"No, not us. Her. Sophia is my fiancée's sister. She needs a place to hide."

He raised a brow at the word. "Hide from what?"

"Paparazzi," Grace answered. "It's been a real issue after the whole debacle with the—well, it's always an issue. But Sophie needs some time to…to…" She smiled with kindness and pity at her sister. "She needs some time."

Sophie stalked around the car on spiked heels, looking like a warrior queen who could kick some serious butt, but instead she got in the backseat and slammed the door.

"Time and privacy," Alex added. "The MacDowells assured us your discretion wouldn't be an issue."

His mare shifted under him and blew an impatient breath through her nose.

"Should we go to the house and have this discussion there?" Grace asked.

Travis kept an eye on the heifer that was ambling away. "I'm gonna have to round up that heifer and put her back on the right side of the fence. Got to check on the branding after that, but I'll be back at sundown. I go past the main house on the way to my place. I'll stop in."

"We weren't planning to stay all day." The woman threw a look of dismay to her fiancé.

They couldn't expect him to quit working in the middle of the day and go sit in a house to chat. He ran the River Mack ranch, and that meant he worked even longer hours than he expected from his ranch hands.

Heifers that wandered through broken fences couldn't be put off until tomorrow. May was one of the busiest months of the year, between the last of the calving and the bulk of the branding. Travis hadn't planned on spending any time whatsoever talking to whomever the MacDowells were loaning their house, but obviously, there was more to the situation than the average houseguest.

"All right, then. Let's talk." He swung himself off the horse, a concession to let them know they had his time and attention. Besides, if he stayed on horseback, he couldn't see Sophia in the car. It felt like he needed to keep an eye on her, the same as he needed to do with the wandering heifer.

On the ground, he still couldn't see much through the windshield. He caught a glimpse of black leather, her hands resting on her knees. Her hands were clenched into fists.

Travis shook his head. She was a woman on edge.

"Sophia just needs to be left alone," her sister said.

"I can do that." He had no intention of staying in the vicinity of someone as disturbing to his peace of mind as that woman.

"If men with cameras start snooping around, please, tell them nothing. Don't even deny she's here."

"Ma'am, if men with cameras come snooping around this ranch, I will be escorting them off the property."

"Oh, really? You can do that?" She seemed relieved—amazed and relieved.

What did these people expect? He took his hat off and ran his hand through his hair before shoving the hat right back on again. His hair was getting too long, but no cowboy had time in May to go into town and see a barber.

"We don't tolerate trespassers," he explained to the people who clearly lived in town. "I'm not in the business of distinguishing between cameramen and cattle thieves. If you don't belong here, you will be escorted off the land."

"The paparazzi will offer you money, though. Thousands."

Before Travis could set her straight on this insinuation that he could be bribed to betray a guest of the MacDowells, Alex cut in. "That's only if they find her. We've gone to great lengths to arrange this location. We took away her cell phone so that she wouldn't accidentally store a photo in the cloud with a location stamp. Hackers get paid to look for things like that. That's how extreme the hunting for her can be."

"She's got a burner phone for emergencies," Grace said. "But if you could check on her...?"

Travis was aware that the front doors to the car were wide open, man and woman each standing beside one. Surely, the subject of this conversation could hear every word. It seemed rude to talk about her as if she weren't there.

"If she wants me to check on her, I will. If she wants me to leave her alone, I will."

He looked through the windshield again. The fists had disappeared. One leather-clad knee was being bounced, jittery, impatient.

"How many other people work on this ranch?" the man asked.

"Will they leave my sister alone?" the woman asked.

Travis was feeling impatient himself. This whole conversation was moving as far from his realm of normal as the woman hiding in the car was.

That was what she was doing in there. Rather than being part of a conversation about herself, she was hiding. This was all a lot of nonsense in the middle of branding season, but from long habit developed by working with animals, Travis forced himself to stand calmly, keep the reins loose in his hands, and not show his irritation. These people were strangers in the middle of the road, and Travis owed them nothing.

"I'm not in the habit of discussing the ranch's staffing requirements with strangers."

The man nodded once. He got it. The woman bit her

lip, and Travis understood she was worried about more than herself.

"But since this is your sister, I'll tell you the amount of ranch hands living in the bunkhouse varies depending on the season. None of us are in the habit of going to the main house to introduce ourselves to Mrs. MacDowell's houseguests." Travis spoke clearly, to be sure the woman in the car heard him. "If your sister doesn't want to be seen, then I suggest she stop standing in the middle of an open pasture and hugging my livestock."

The black boot stopped bouncing.

Grace dipped her chin to hide her smile, looking as pretty as her movie star sister—minus the blatant sexuality.

"Now if you folks would like to head on to the house, I've got to be going."

"Thank you," Grace said, but the worry returned to her expression. "If you could check on her, though, yourself? She's more fragile than she looks. She's got a lot of decisions weighing her down. This is a very delicate situa—"

The car horn ripped through the air. Travis nearly lost the reins as his mare instinctively made to bolt without him. *Goddammit.*

No sooner had he gotten his horse's head under control than the horn blasted again. He whipped his own head around toward the car, glaring at the two adults who were still standing there. For God's sake, did they have to be told to shut her up?

"Tell her to stop."

"Like that'll do any good." But the man bent to look into the car. "Enough, Sophie."

"Sophie, please…"

One more short honk. Thank God his horse trusted him, because the mare barely flinched this time, but it was the last straw for Travis. Reins in hand, he stalked past the man and yanked open the rear door.

Since she'd been leaning forward to reach the car horn, Sophia's black-clad backside was the first thing he saw, but she quickly turned toward him, keeping her arm stretched toward the steering wheel.

"Don't do that again."

"Quit standing around talking about me. This is a waste of time. I want to get to the house. Now." She honked the horn again, staring right at him as she did it.

"What the hell is wrong with you? I just said don't do that."

"Or else what?"

She glared at him like a warrior, but she had the attitude of a kindergartner.

"Every time you honk that horn, another cowboy on this ranch drops what he's doing to come and see if you need help. It's not a game. It's a call for help."

She blinked. Clearly, she hadn't thought of that, but then she narrowed her eyes and reached once more for the steering wheel.

"You honk that horn again, and you will very shortly find the road blocked by men on horses, and we will not move until you turn the car around and take yourself right back to wherever it is you came from."

Her hand hovered over the steering wheel.

"Do it," he said. "Frighten my horse one more time. You will never set foot on this ranch again."

Her hand hovered. He stared her down, waiting, almost willing her to test him. He would welcome a chance to remove her from the ranch, and he wasn't a man to make empty threats.

"I don't want to be here, anyway," she said.

He jerked his head toward the steering wheel. "You

know how to drive, don't you? Turn the car around then, instead of honking that damned horn."

The silence stretched between them.

Her sister had leaned into the car, so she spoke very softly. "Sophie, you've got nowhere else to go. You cannot live with me and Alex."

Travis saw it then. Saw the way the light in Sophia's eyes died a little, saw the way her breath left her lips. He saw her pain, and he was sorry for it.

She sagged back into her seat, burying her backside along with the rest of her body in the corner. She crossed her arms over her middle, not looking at her sister, not looking at him. "Well, God forbid I should piss off a horse."

Travis stood and shut the door. He scanned the pasture, spotted the heifer twice as far away as she'd been a minute ago. Those young ones had a sixth sense about getting rounded up, sometimes. If they didn't want to be penned in, they were twice as hard to catch.

Didn't matter. Travis hadn't met one yet that could outsmart or outrun him.

He had a heifer to catch, branding to oversee, a ranch to run. By the time the sun went down, he'd want nothing more than a hot shower and a flat surface to sleep on.

But tonight, he'd stop by the main house and check on a movie star—a sad, angry movie star who had nowhere else to go, no other family to take her in. Nowhere except his ranch.

With a nod at the sister and her fiancé, Travis swung himself back into the saddle. The heifer had given up all pretense at grazing and was determinedly trotting toward the horizon, putting distance between herself and the humans.

Travis would have sighed, if cowboys sighed. Instead,

he spoke to his horse under his breath. "You ready for this?"

He pointed the mare toward the heifer and sent her into motion with a squeeze of his thigh. They had a long, hard ride ahead.

Chapter Two

She was alone.

She was alone, and she was going to die, because Grace and Alex had left her, and even though Alex had flipped a bunch of fuses and turned on the electricity, and even though Grace had carried in two bags of groceries from the car and set them on the blue-tiled kitchen counter, Sophia's only family had abandoned her before anyone realized the refrigerator was broken, and now the food was going to spoil and they wouldn't be back to check on her for a week and by then she'd be dead from starvation, her body on the kitchen floor, her eyes staring sightlessly at the wallpaper border with its white geese repeated ad nauseam on a dull blue background.

Last year, she'd worn Givenchy as she made her acceptance speech.

I hate my life.

Sophia sat at the kitchen table in a hard chair and cried.

No one yelled *cut*, so she continued the scene, putting her elbows on the table and dropping her head in her hands.

I hate myself for letting this become my life.

Was that what Grace and Alex wanted her to come to grips with? That she'd messed up her own life?

Well, duh, I'm not a moron. I know exactly why my career is circling the drain in a slow death spiral.

Because no one wanted to work with her. And no one wanted to work with her because no one liked her ex, DJ Deezee Kalm.

Kalm was something of an ironic name for the jerk. Deezee had brought nothing but chaos into her life since she'd met him…wow, only five months ago?

Five months ago, Sophia Jackson had been the Next Big Thing. No longer had she needed to beg for a chance to audition for secondary characters. Scripts from the biggest and the best were being delivered to her door by courier, with affectionate little notes suggesting the main character would fit her perfectly.

Sophia and her sister—her loyal, faithful assistant—had deserved a chance to celebrate. After ten long years of hard work, Sophia's dreams were coming true, but if she was being honest with herself—*and isn't that what this time alone is supposed to be about? Being honest with myself?*—well, to be honest, she might have acted elated, but she'd been exhausted.

A week in Telluride, a tiny mining town that was now a millionaires' playground in the Rocky Mountains, had seemed like a great escape. For one little week, she wouldn't worry about the future impact of her every decision. Sophia would be seen, but maybe she wouldn't be stared at among the rich and famous.

But DJ Deezee Kalm had noticed her. Sophia had been a sucker for his lies, and now she couldn't be seen by anyone at all for the next nine months. Here she was, alone with her thoughts and some rapidly thawing organic frozen meals, the kind decorated with chia seeds and labeled with exotic names from India.

There you go. I fell for a jerk, and now I hate my life. Reflection complete.

She couldn't dwell on Deezee, not without wanting to throw something. If she chucked the goose-shaped salt shaker against the wall, she'd probably never be able to replace the 1980s ceramic. That was the last thing she needed: the guilt of destroying some widow's hideous salt shaker.

She stood with the vague idea that she ought to do something about the paper bags lined up on the counter, but her painful ankle made fresh tears sting her eyes. She'd twisted it pretty hard in the dirt road when she'd confronted that cow, although she'd told Alex the Stupid Doctor that she hadn't. She sat down again and began unzipping the boots to free her toes from their spike-heeled torture.

That cow in the road…she hoped it had given that cowboy a run for his money. She hoped it was still outrunning him right this second, Mr. Don't-Honk-That-Horn-or-Else. Now that she thought about it, he'd had perfect control of his horse as he'd galloped away from them like friggin' Indiana Jones in a Spielberg film, so he'd lied to her about the horn upsetting his horse. Liar, liar. Typical man.

Don't trust men. Lesson learned. Can I go back to LA now?

But no. She couldn't. She was stuck here in Texas, where Grace had dragged her to make an appearance on behalf of the Texas Rescue and Relief organization. Her sister had hoped charity work and good deeds could repair the damage Sophia had done to her reputation. Instead, in the middle of just such a big charity event, Deezee had shown up and publicly begged Sophia to take him back. Sophia had been a sucker again. With cameras dogging their every move, she'd run away to a Caribbean island with him, an elopement that had turned out to be a big joke.

Ha, ha, ha.

Here's something funny, Deezee. When I peed on a plastic stick, a little plus sign showed up.

Sophia had returned from St. Barth to find her sister engaged to a doctor with Texas Rescue, a man who, unlike Deezee, seemed to take that engagement seriously. Now her sister never wanted to go back to LA with her, because Alex had her totally believing in fairy tale love. Grace believed Texas would be good for Sophia, too. Living here would give her a chance to rest and *relax*.

Right. Because of that little plus sign, Grace thought Sophia needed some stress-free *alone time* to decide what she wanted to do with her future, as if Sophia had done anything except worry about both of their futures for the past ten years. Didn't Grace know Sophia was sick of worrying about the future?

Barefooted, Sophia went to the paper bags and pulled out all the cold and wet items and stuck them in the sink. They'd already started sweating on the tiled countertop. She dried her cheek on her shoulder and faced the fridge.

It had been deliberately turned off by the owner, a woman who didn't want to stay in Texas and *relax* in her own home now that her kids were grown and married. Before abandoning her house to spend a year volunteering for a medical mission in Africa, Mrs. MacDowell had inserted little plastic wedges to keep the doors open so the refrigerator wouldn't get moldy and funky while it was unused.

Sophia was going to be moldy and funky by the time they found her starved body next week. She had a phone for emergencies; she used it.

"Grace? It's me. Alex didn't turn the refrigerator on." Sophia felt betrayed. Her voice only sounded bitchy.

"Sophie, sweetie, that's not an emergency." Grace spoke gently, like someone chiding a child and trying to encourage her at the same time. "You can handle that. You know how to flip a switch in a fuse box."

"I don't even know where the fuse box is."

Grace sighed, and Sophia heard her exchange a few words with Alex. "It's in the hall closet. I've gotta run now. Bye."

"Wait! Just hang on the line with me while I find the fuse box. What if the fuse doesn't fix it?"

"I don't know. Then you'll have to call a repairman, I guess."

"Call a repairman?" Sophia was aghast. "Where would I even find a repairman?"

"There's a phone on the wall in the kitchen. Mrs. MacDowell has a phone book sitting on the little stand underneath it."

Sophia looked around the 1980s time capsule of a kitchen. Sure enough, mounted on the wall was a phone, one with a handset and a curly cord hanging down. It was not decorated with a goose, but it was white, to fit in the decor.

"Ohmigod, that's an antique."

"I made sure it works. It's a lot harder for paparazzi to tap an actual phone line than it would be for them to use a scanner to listen in to this phone call. You can call a repairman."

Sophia clenched her jaw against that lecturing tone. From the day her little sister had graduated from high school, Sophia had paid her to take care of details like this, treating her like a star's personal assistant long before Sophia had been a star. Now Grace had decided to dump her.

"And how am I supposed to pay for a repairman?"

"You have a credit card. We put it in my name, but it's yours." Grace sounded almost sad. Pitying her, actually, with just a touch of impatience in her tone.

Sophia felt her sister slipping away. "I can say my name is Grace, but I can't change my face. How am I supposed to stay anonymous if a repairman shows up at the door?"

"I don't know, Sophie. Throw a dish towel over your head or something."

"You don't care about me anymore." Her voice should have broken in the middle of that sentence, because her heart was breaking, but the actor inside knew the line had been delivered in a continuous whine.

"I love you, Sophie. You'll figure something out. You're super smart. You took care of me for years. This will be a piece of cake for you."

A piece of cake. That tone of voice…

Oh, God, her sister sounded just like their mother. Ten years ago, Mom and Dad had been yanked away from them forever, killed in a pointless car accident. At nineteen, Sophia had become the legal guardian of Grace, who'd still had two years of high school left to go.

Nothing had been a piece of cake. Sophia had quit college and moved back home so that Grace could finish high school in their hometown. Sophia had needed to make the life insurance last, paying the mortgage with it during Grace's junior and senior years. She'd tried to supplement it with modeling jobs, but anything local only paid a pittance. For fifty dollars, she'd spent six hours gesturing toward a mattress with a smile on her face.

It had really been her first acting job, because during the entire photo shoot, she'd had to act like she wasn't mourning the theater scholarship at UCLA that she'd sacrificed.

With a little sister to raise, making a mattress look desirable was as close as Sophia could come to show business.

That first modeling job had been a success, eventually used nationwide, but Sophia hadn't been paid one penny more. Her flat fifty-dollar fee had been spent on gas and groceries that same day. Grace had to be driven to school. Grace had to eat lunch in the cafeteria.

Now Grace was embarking on her own happy life and leaving Sophia behind. It just seemed extra cruel that Grace would sound like Mom at this point.

"I have to run," her mother's voice said. "I love you, Sophie. You can do this. Bye."

Don't leave me. Don't ever leave me. I miss you.

The phone was silent.

This afternoon, Sophia had only wanted to hide away and fall apart in private. Now, she was terrified to. If she started crying again, she would never, ever stop.

She nearly ran to the hall closet and pushed aside the old coats and jackets to find the fuse box. They were all on, a neat row of black switches all pointing to the left. She flicked a few to the right, then left again. Then a few more. If she reset every one, then she would have to hit the one that worked the refrigerator.

It made no difference. The refrigerator was still dead when she returned to the kitchen. The food was still thawing in the sink. Her life still sucked, only worse now, because now she missed her mother all over again. Grace sounded like Mom, and she'd left her like Mom. At least when Mom had died, she'd left the refrigerator running.

What a terrible thing to think. Dear God, she hated herself.

Then she laughed at the incredible low her self-pity could reach.

Then she cried.

Just as she'd known it would, once the crying started, it did not stop.

I'm pregnant and I'm scared and I want my mother.

Sophia sank to the kitchen floor, hugged her knees to her chest, and gave up.

Would he or wouldn't he?

Travis rode slowly, letting his mare cool down on her way to the barn while he debated with himself whether or not he'd told the sister he would check on the movie star tonight, specifically, or just check on her in general. He was bone-tired and hungry, but he had almost another mile to go before he could rest. Half a mile to the barn, quarter of a mile past that to his house. A movie star with an attitude was the last thing he wanted to deal with. Tomorrow would be soon enough to be neighborly and ask how she was settling in.

The MacDowell house, or just *the house*, as everyone on a ranch traditionally called the owner's residence, was closer to the barn than his own. As the mare walked on, the house's white porch pillars came into view, always a pretty sight. The sunset tinted the sky pink and orange behind it. Mesquite trees were spaced evenly around it. The lights were on; Sophia Jackson was home.

Then the lights went out.

On again.

What the hell?

Lights started turning off and on, in an orderly manner, left to right across the building. Travis had been in the house often enough that he knew which window was the living room. Off, on. The dining room. The foyer.

The mare chomped at her bit impatiently, picking up on his change in mood.

"Yeah, girl. Go on." He let the horse pick up her pace.

Normally, he'd never let a horse hurry back to the barn; that was just sure to start a bad habit. But everything on the River Mack was his responsibility, including the house with its blinking lights, and its new resident.

The lights came on and stayed on as he rode steadily toward the movie star that he was going to check on tonight, after all.

Chapter Three

Travis couldn't ride his horse up to the front door and leave her on the porch. There was a hitching post on the side that faced the barn, so he rode around the house toward the back. The kitchen door was the one everyone used, anyway.

The first year he'd landed a job here as a ranch hand, he'd learned real quick to leave the barn through the door that faced the house. Mrs. MacDowell was as likely as not to open her kitchen door and call over passing ranch hands to see if they'd help her finish off something she'd baked. She was forever baking Bundt cakes and what not, then insisting she couldn't eat them before they went stale. Since her sons had all gone off to medical school to become doctors, Travis suspected she just didn't know how to stop feeding young men. As a twenty-five-year-old living in the bunkhouse on canned pork-n-beans, he'd been happy to help her not let anything get stale.

Travis grinned at the memory. From the vantage point of his horse's back, he looked down into the kitchen as he passed its window and saw another woman there. Blond hair, black clothes…curled up on the floor. Weeping.

"Whoa," he said softly, and the mare stopped.

He could tell in a glance Sophia Jackson wasn't hurt, the same way he could tell in a glance if a cowboy who'd been thrown from a horse was hurt. She could obviously breathe if she could cry. She was hugging her knees to her chest in a way that proved she didn't have any broken bones. As he watched, she shook that silver and gold hair back and got to her feet, her back to him. She could move just fine. There was nothing he needed to fix.

She was emotional, but Travis couldn't fix that. There wasn't a lot of weeping on a cattle ranch. If a youngster got homesick out on a roundup or a heartbroken cowboy shed a tear over a Dear John letter after a mail call, Travis generally kept an eye on them from a distance. Once they'd regained their composure, he'd find some reason to check in with them, asking about their saddle or if they'd noticed the creek was low. If they cared to talk, they were welcome to bring it up. Some did. Most didn't.

He'd give Sophia Jackson her space, then. Whatever was making her sad, it was hers to cry over. Tomorrow night would be soon enough to check in with her.

Just as he nudged his horse back into a walk, he caught a movement out of the corner of his eye, Sophia dashing her cheek on her shoulder. He tried to put it out of his mind once he was in the barn, but it nagged at him as he haltered his mare and washed off her bit. Sophia had touched her cheek to her shoulder just like that when he'd first approached her on the road this afternoon. Had she been crying when she'd hung on to that heifer?

He rubbed his jaw. In the car, she'd been all clenched

fists and anxiously bouncing knee. A woman on the edge, that was what he'd thought. Looked like she'd gone over that edge this evening.

People did. Not his problem. There were limits to what a foreman was expected to handle, damn it.

But the way she'd been turning the lights off and on was odd. What did that have to do with being sad?

His mare nudged him in the shoulder, unhappy with the way he was standing still.

"I know, I know. I have to go check on her." He turned the mare into the paddock so she could enjoy the last of the twilight without a saddle on her back, then turned himself toward the house. It was only about a hundred yards from barn to kitchen door, an easy walk over hard-packed earth to a wide flagstone patio that held a couple of wooden picnic tables. The kitchen door was protected by its original small back porch and an awning.

A hundred yards was far enough to give Travis time to think about how long he'd been in the saddle today, how long he'd be in the saddle tomorrow, and how he was hungry enough to eat his hat.

He took his hat off and knocked at the back door.

No answer.

He knocked again. His stomach growled.

"Go away." The movie star didn't sound particularly sad.

He leaned his hand on the door jamb. "You got the lights fixed in there, ma'am?"

"Yes. Go away."

Fine by him. Just hearing her voice made his heart speed up a tick, and he didn't like it. He'd turned away and put his hat back on when he heard the door open.

"Wait. Do you know anything about refrigerators?"

He glanced back and did a double take. She was standing there with a dish towel on her head, its blue and white cotton covering her face. "What in the Sam Hill are you—"

"I don't want you to see me. Can you fix a refrigerator?"

"Probably." He took his hat off as he stepped back under the awning, but she didn't back up to let him in. "Can you see through that thing?"

She held up a hand to stop him, but her palm wasn't quite directed his way. "Wait. Do you have a camera?"

"No."

"How about a cell phone?"

"Of course."

"Set it on the ground, right here." She pointed at her feet. "No pictures."

He fought for patience. This woman was out of her mind with her dish towel and her demands. He had a horse to stable for the night and eight more to feed before he could go home and scarf down something himself. "Do you want me to look at your fridge or not?"

"No one sets foot in this house with a cell phone. No one gets photos of me for free. If you don't like it, too bad. You'll just have to leave."

Travis put his hat back on his head and left. He didn't take to being told what to do with his personal property. He'd crossed the flagstone and stepped onto the hard-packed dirt path to the barn when she called after him.

"That's it? You're really leaving?"

He took his time turning around. She'd come out to the edge of the porch, and was holding up the towel just far enough to peek out from under it. He clenched his jaw against the sight of her bare stomach framed by that tight black clothing. She hadn't gotten that outfit at any Western-wear-and-feed store. The thigh-high boots were gone. Instead, she was all legs. Long, bare legs.

Damn it. He was already hungry for food. He didn't need to be hungry for anything else.

"That's it," he said, and turned back to the barn.

"Wait. Okay, I'll make an exception, but just this one time. You have to keep your phone in your pocket when you're around me."

He kept walking.

"Don't leave me. Just…don't leave. Please."

He shouldn't have looked back, but he did. There was something a little bit lost about her stance, something just unsure enough in the way she lifted that towel off one eye that made him pause. The way she was tracking him reminded him of a fox that had gotten tangled in a fence and wasn't sure if she should bite him or let him free her.

Cursing himself every step of the way, he returned to the porch and slammed the heel of his boot in the cast iron boot jack that had a permanent place by the door.

"What are you doing?" Her head was bowed under the towel as she watched him step out of one boot, then the other.

"You're worried about the wrong thing. The cell phone isn't a problem. A man coming from a barn into your house with his boots on? That could be a problem. Mrs. Mac-Dowell wouldn't allow it." And then, because he remembered the sister's distress over the extremes to which the paparazzi had apparently gone in the past, he dropped his cell phone in one boot. "There. Now take that towel off your head."

He brushed past her and walked into the kitchen, hanging his hat on one of the hooks by the door. He opened the fridge, but the appliance clearly was dead. "You already checked the fuse, I take it."

"Yes."

Of course she had. That had been why the lights had gone on and off.

She walked up to him with her hands full of plastic triangles. "These wedges were in the doors. I took them out because I thought maybe you had to shut the door all the way to make it run. I don't see any kind of on-off switch."

The towel was gone. She was, quite simply, the most beautiful woman he'd ever seen. Her hair was messed up from the towel and her famously blue eyes were puffy from crying, but by God, she was absolutely beautiful. His heart must have stopped for a moment, because he felt the hard thud in his chest when it kick-started back to life.

She suddenly threw the plastic onto the tile floor, making a great clatter. "Don't stare at me. So, I've been crying. Big deal. Tell all your friends. 'Hey, you should see Sophia Jackson when she cries. She looks like hell.' Go get your phone and take a picture. I swear, I don't care. All I want is for that refrigerator to work. If you're just going to stand there and stare at me, then get the hell out of my house."

If Travis had learned anything from a lifetime around animals, it was that only one creature at a time had better be riled up. If his horse got spooked, he had to be calm. If a cow got protective of her calf, then it was up to him not to give her a reason to lower her head and charge. He figured if a movie star was freaked out about her appearance, then he had to not give a damn about it.

He didn't, not really. She looked like what she looked like, which was beautiful, red nose and tear stains and all. There were a lot of beautiful things in his world, like horses. Sunsets. He appreciated Sophia's beauty, but he hadn't intended to make a fuss over it. If he'd been staring at her, it had been no different than taking an extra moment to look at the sky on a particularly colorful evening.

He crossed his arms over his chest and leaned against the counter. "Is the fridge plugged into the wall?"

She'd clearly expected him to say something else. It took her a beat to snap her mouth shut. "I thought of that, but I can't see behind it, and the stupid thing is too big for me to move. I'm stuck. I've just been stuck here all day, watching all my food melt." Her upper lip quivered a little, vulnerable.

He thought about kissing just her upper lip, one precise placement of his lips on hers, to steady her. He pushed the thought away. "Did you try to move it?"

"What?"

"Did you try to move it? Or did you just look at it and decide you couldn't?" He nodded his head toward the fridge, a mammoth side-by-side for a family that had consisted almost entirely of hungry men. "Give it a shot."

"Is this how you get your jollies? You want to see if I'm stupid enough to try to move something that's ten times heavier than I am? Blondes are dumb, right? This is your test to see if I'm a real blonde. Men always want to know if I'm a real blonde. Well, guess what? I am." She grabbed the handles of the open doors and gave them a dramatic yank, heaving all her weight backward in the effort.

The fridge rolled toward her at least a foot, making her yelp in surprise. The shock on her face was priceless. Travis rubbed his jaw to keep from laughing.

She pressed her lips together and lifted her chin, and Travis had the distinct impression she was trying to keep herself from not going over the edge again.

That sobered him up. He recrossed his arms. "You can't see them, but a fridge this size has to have built-in casters. No one could move it otherwise. Not you. Not me. Not both of us together."

"I didn't know."

"Now you do."

She seemed rooted to her spot, facing the fridge. With her puffy eyes and tear-streaked face, she had definitely had a bad day. Her problems might seem trivial to him—who cared if someone snapped a photo of a famous person?—but they weighed on her.

He shoved himself to his tired feet. "Come on, I'll help you plug it in."

"No, I'll do it." She started tugging, and once she'd pulled the behemoth out another foot, she boosted herself onto the counter, gracefully athletic. Kneeling on Mrs. MacDowell's blue-tiled counter, she bent down to reach behind the fridge and grope for the cord. Travis knew he shouldn't stare, but hell, her head was behind the fridge. The dip of her lower back and the curve of her thigh didn't know they were being fully appreciated.

When she got the fridge plugged in, it obediently and immediately hummed to life. She jumped down from the countertop, landing silently, as sure of her balance as a cat. He caught a flash of her determination along with a flash of her bare skin.

Hunger ate at him, made him impatient. He picked his hat up from its hook by the door. "Good night, then."

"Where are you going?"

"Back to work." He shut the door behind himself. Stomped into the first boot, but his own balance felt off. He had to hop a bit to catch himself. He needed to get some food and some sleep, then he'd be fine.

The door swung open, but he caught it before it knocked him over. "What now?"

"I need groceries."

There was a beat of silence. Did she expect him to magically produce groceries?

"Everything melted." She looked mournfully over her shoulder at the sink, then back at him, and just…waited.

It amazed him how city folk sometimes needed to be told how the world ran. "Guess you'll be headed into town tomorrow, then."

"Me? I can't go to a grocery store."

"You need a truck? The white pickup is for general use. The keys are in the barn, on the hook by the tack room. Help yourself."

"To a truck?" She literally recoiled a half step back into the house.

"I don't know how else you intend to get to the grocery store. Just head toward Austin. Closest store is about twenty miles in, on your right."

"You have to get the groceries for me."

"Nope. It's May." He stuck his hat on, so his hands were free to pick up his second boot and shake the cell phone out of it.

"It's May? What kind of answer is that? Do you fast in May or do a colon cleanse or something?"

He looked up at her joke, but his grin died before it started. Judging by the look on her face, she wasn't joking. "The River Mack rounds up in May."

She looked at him, waiting. He realized a woman from Hollywood probably had no idea what that meant.

"We're busy. We're branding. We have to keep an eye on the late calving, the bulls—"

He stopped himself. He wasn't going to explain the rest. Managing a herd was a constant, complex operation. Bulls had to be separated from cows. The cow-calf pairs had to be moved to the richest pastures so the mamas could keep their weight up while they nursed their calves. Cows who had failed to get pregnant were culled from the herd and replaced with better, more fertile cattle.

Sophia flapped one hand toward the kitchen behind her. "I have nothing to eat. You have to help me."

He stomped into his second boot. "Not unless you're a pregnant cow."

At her gasp, he did chuckle. "Or a horse. Or a dog. You could be a chicken, and I would have to help you. I keep every beast on this ranch fed, but you, ma'am, are not a beast. You're a grown woman who can take care of herself, and you're not my problem."

She looked absolutely stricken. Had he been so harsh?

"Listen, if I'm going toward town, I don't mind picking you up a gallon of milk. That's just common courtesy. I expect you to do the same for me."

"But I can't leave the ranch."

"Neither can I." He touched the brim of his hat in farewell. "Now if you'll excuse me, I've got horses to feed before I can feed myself."

Chapter Four

A pregnant cow.

It was fair to say women pretty much spent their lives trying not to look like pregnant cows. Yet if Sophia Jackson, Golden Globe winner and Academy Award nominee, wanted help on this ranch, she needed to look like that cow she'd hugged in the middle of the road.

She didn't look like that. She looked like a movie star, and that meant she would get no help. No sympathy.

That was nothing new. Movie stars were expected to be rolling in dough and to have an easy life. Everyone assumed movie stars were millionaires, but she was more of a hundred-thousandaire. Certainly comfortable and a far cry from her days pointing at mattresses with a smile, but the money went out at an alarming rate between jobs. Even when she was not being paid, Sophia paid everyone else: publicists, managers, agents, fitness trainers, fashion stylists…and her personal assistant, Grace.

Sophia had to pay them to do their jobs, so that she could land another job and get another burst of money. An actor only felt secure if the next job got lined up before the current job stopped paying. Then, of course, the next job after that needed to be won, a contract signed, and more money dished out.

There would be no new jobs, not for nine months. Sophia slid her palm over her perfectly flat, perfectly toned abs. The whole pregnancy concept didn't seem real. It was a plus sign on a plastic stick and nothing more. She didn't feel different. She didn't look different.

Alex the Stupid Doctor had explained that she was only weeks along, and that for a first-time mother, especially one who stayed in the kind of physical shape the world expected Sophia to be in, the pregnancy might not show until the fourth or fifth month. Maybe longer.

She could have filmed another movie in that time…

But nobody in Hollywood wanted to work with her…

Because she'd fallen for a loser who'd killed her hard-working reputation.

Round and round we go.

Always the same thoughts, always turning in that same vicious cycle.

If only she hadn't met DJ Deezee, that jerk…

She picked up the goose salt shaker and clenched it tightly in her fist. For the next nine months, instead of paying her entourage's salaries, Sophia would be paying rent on this house. The rent was cheaper than the stable of people it took to sustain fame, which was fortunate, because the money coming in was going to slow considerably. Her only income would be residuals from DVD sales of movies that had already sold most of what they would ever sell—and her old manager and her old agent would still take their cut from that, even though they'd abandoned her.

She was going to hide on this ranch and watch her money dwindle as she sank into obscurity. Then she'd have to start over, scrambling for any scrap Hollywood would throw to her, auditioning for any female role. Her life would be an endless circle of checking in with grouchy temps, setting her head shot on their rickety card tables, taking her place in line with the other actors, praying this audition would be the one. She wasn't sure she could withstand years of rejection for a second time.

She shouldn't have to. She'd paid her dues.

The ceramic goose in her hand should have crumbled from the force of her grip, the way it would have if she'd been in a movie. But no—for that to happen, a prop master had to construct the shaker out of glazed sugar, something a real person could actually break. Movies had to be faked.

This was all too real. She couldn't crush porcelain. She could throw it, though. Deezee regularly trashed hotel rooms, and she had to admit that it had felt therapeutic for a moment when he'd dared her to throw a vase in a presidential suite. Afterward, though…the broken shards had stayed stuck in the carpet while management tallied up the bill.

She stared for a moment longer at the goose in her hand, its blank stare unchanging as it awaited its fate. "There's nothing we can do about any of this, is there?"

The kitchen was suddenly too small, too close. Sophia walked quickly into the living room. It was bigger, more modern. Wood floors, nice upholstery, a flat-screen TV. A vase. The ceilings were high, white with dark beams. She felt suddenly small, standing in this great room in a house built to hold a big family. She was one little person dwarfed by thousands of square feet of ranch house.

She heard her sister's voice. Her mother's voice. *You've got nowhere else to go. You cannot live with me.*

She couldn't, could she? Her sister was in love, planning a wedding, giddy about living with her new husband. There was no room for a third wheel that would spin notoriety and paparazzi into their normal lives.

And her mother... Sophia could not move back home to live with her. Never again. Not in this life. Other twenty-nine-year-olds might have their parents as a safety net, but Sophia's safety net had been cut away on a highway ten years ago.

The ceilings were too high. The nausea was rising to fill the empty space, and it had nothing to do with pregnancy, nothing at all. Sophia squeezed her eyes shut and buried her face in her clenched fists. The little beak of the salt shaker goose pressed into her forehead, into her hard skull.

The house was too big. She got out, jerking open the front door and escaping onto the wide front porch. In the daylight, the white columns had framed unending stretch of brown and green earth. At night, the blackness was overwhelming, like being on a spaceship, surrounded by nothing but night sky. There were too many stars. No city lights drowned them out. She was too far from Hollywood, the only place she needed to be. *All alone, all alone...*

This was not what she wanted, not what she'd ever wanted. She'd worked so hard, but it was all coming to nothing. Life as she'd known it would end here, on a porch in the middle of nowhere, a slow, nine-month death. Already, she'd ceased to exist.

She hurled the salt shaker into the night, aiming at the stars, the too-plentiful stars.

The salt shaker disappeared in the dark. Sophia's gesture of defiance had no effect on the world at all.

I do exist. I'm Sophia Jackson, damn it.

If she didn't want to be on this ranch, then she didn't have to be.

You know how to drive, don't you? Turn the car around, then, instead of blowing that damned horn.

There was a truck, the cowboy had said. A white truck. Keys in the barn. She ran down the steps, but they ended on a gravel path, and her feet were bare. She was forced off the path, forced to slow down as she skirted the house, crossing dirt and grass toward the barn.

I don't want to slow down. If I get off the roller coaster of Hollywood, I'll never be able to speed back up again. I refuse to slow down.

She stepped on a rock and hissed at the pain, but she would not be denied. Instead of being more careful, she broke into a sprint—and stepped on an even sharper rock. She gasped, she hopped on one foot, she cursed.

I'm being a drama queen.

She was. Oh, God, she really was a drama queen—and it was going to get her nowhere. The truck would be sitting there whether she got to the barn in five seconds or five minutes. And then what? She'd drive the truck barefoot into Austin and do what, exactly?

I'm so stupid.

No one had witnessed her stupidity, but that hardly eased her sense of embarrassment as she made her way more carefully toward the barn. It was hard to shake that feeling of being watched after years of conditioning. Ten years, to be precise, beginning with her little sister watching her with big eyes once it was only the two of them, alone in their dead parents' house. *But Sophie, do you know how to make Mom's recipe?*

Don't you worry. It will be a piece of cake.

Sophia knew Grace had been counting on her last remaining family member not to crack under the pressure of becoming a single parent to her younger sister. Later, managers and directors had counted on Sophia, too, judging whether or not she would crack before offering her money for her next role. She'd had them all convinced she was a safe bet, but for the past five months, the paparazzi had been watching her with Deezee, counting on her to crack into a million pieces before their cameras, so they could sell the photos.

The paparazzi had guessed right. She'd finally cracked. The photos were all over the internet. Now no one was counting on her. Grace didn't need her anymore. Alex had stuck Sophia in this ranch house, supposedly so she'd have a place where no one would watch her. Out of habit, though, she looked over her shoulder as she reached the barn, keeping her chin up and looking unconcerned in the flattering light of the last rays of sunset. There was no one around, only the white pickup parked to the side. The cowboy must have gone to get his dinner.

Well, that made one of them. Sophia realized the nausea had subsided and hunger pangs had taken its place. Maybe inside the barn there would be some pregnant-cow food she could eat. She slid open the barn door and walked inside.

Not cows. Horses.

Sophia paused at the end of the long center aisle. One by one, horses hung their heads over their stall doors and stared at her.

"You can quit staring at me," she said, but the horses took their time checking her out with their big brown eyes, twitching their ears here and there. The palette of their warm colors as they hung their heads over their iron and wood stalls would have made a lovely setting for a rustic movie.

There were no cameras here, no press, no producers. Sophia stopped holding her breath and let herself sag against the stall to her right. Her shoulders slumped under the full weight of her fatigue.

The horse swung its head a little closer to her, and gave her slumped shoulder a nudge.

"Oh, hello." Sophia had only known one horse in her life, the one that the stunt team had assigned her to sit upon during a few scenes before her pioneer character's dramatic death. She'd liked that horse, though, and had enjoyed its company more than that of the insulting, unstable director.

"Aren't you pretty?" Sophia tentatively ran the backs of her knuckles over the horse's neck, feeling the strength of its awesome muscles under the soft coat. She walked to the next stall, grateful for the cool concrete on the battered soles of her feet.

The next horse didn't back away from her, either. Sophia petted it carefully, then more confidently when the horse didn't seem to mind. She smoothed her hand over the massive cheek. "Yes, you're very pretty. You really are."

She worked her way down the aisle, petting each one, brown and spotted, black and white. They were all so peaceful, interested in her and yet not excited by her. Except, perhaps, the last one with the dark brown face and jet-black mane. That horse was excited to snuffle her soft nose right into Sophia's hair, making Sophia smile at the tickle.

"It's my shampoo. Ridiculously expensive, but Jean Paul gives it to me for free as long as I tell everyone that I use it. So if he asks, do a girl a favor and tell him you heard I use his shampoo."

How was that going to work, now that she was out of the public eye? She rested her forehead against the horse's solid neck. "At least, he used to give it to me for free."

The horse chuffed into her hair.

"I'd share it with you, but I might not get any more, actually. Sorry about that, pretty girl. Before this is all over, I may have to borrow your shampoo. I hear horse shampoo can be great for people's hair. Would you mind?"

"Did you need something else?"

Sophia whirled around. Mr. Don't-or-Else stood there, all denim and boots and loose stance, but his brown eyes were narrowed on her like she was some kind of rattlesnake who'd slithered in to his domain.

"I thought you were gone," she said. She adjusted her posture. She was being watched after all. She should have known better than to drop her guard.

"You are not allowed in the barn without boots on."

The horse snuffled some more of her hair, clearly approving of her even if her owner didn't. "What's this horse's name?"

"No bare feet in the barn." The cowboy indicated the door with a jerk of his strong chin—his very strong chin, which fit his square jaw. A lighting director couldn't ask for better angles to illuminate. The camera would love him.

Travis Chalmers. He'd tipped his hat to her this afternoon as he'd sat on his horse. Her heart had tripped a little then. It tripped a little now.

She'd already brought her ankles together and bent one knee, so very casually, she set one hand on her hip. It made her body look its best. The public always checked out her body, her clothing, her makeup, her hair. God forbid anything failed to meet their movie star expectations. They'd rip her apart on every social media platform.

Travis had already seen her looking her worst, but if he hoped she'd crack into more pieces, he was in for a disappointment.

Sophia shook her hair back, knowing it would shine even in the low light of the barn. "What's the horse's name? She and I have the same taste in shampoo."

"He's a gelding, not a girl. You can't come into the barn without boots or shoes. It's not safe. Is that clear?"

Sophia rolled her eyes in a playful way, as if she were

lighthearted tonight. "If it's a boy horse, then what's *his* name? He likes me."

The cowboy scoffed at that. "You seem to think all of my stock like you."

"They do. All of them except you."

Travis's expression didn't change, not one bit, even though she'd tossed off her line with the perfect combination of sassy confidence and pretty pout. He simply wasn't impressed.

It hurt. He was the only person out here, her only possible defense against being swallowed by the loneliness, and yet he was the one person on earth who didn't seem thrilled to meet a celebrity.

Supposedly. He was still watching her.

The audition wasn't over. She could still win him over.

The anxiety to do so was familiar. Survival in Hollywood depended on winning people over. She'd had to win over every casting director who'd judged her, who'd watched her as impassively as this cowboy did while she tried to be enchanting. Indifference had to be overcome, or she wouldn't get the job and she couldn't pay the bills.

With the anxiety came the adrenaline that had helped her survive. She needed to win over Travis Chalmers, or she'd have no one to talk to at all. Ever.

So she smiled, and she took a step closer.

His eyes narrowed a fraction as his gaze dropped down her bare legs. She felt another little thrill of adrenaline. This would be easy.

"You're bleeding," he said.

"I'm—" She tilted her head but kept her smile in place. "What?"

But he was impatient, walking past her to glare at the floor behind her. "What did you cut yourself on?"

She turned around to see little round, red smears where

she'd stopped to greet each horse. "It must have been a rock outside. I stepped on a couple of rocks pretty hard."

"Good."

"Good?"

He glanced at her and had the grace to look the tiniest bit embarrassed. "Good that it wasn't anything sharp in the barn. If it had been a nail or something that had cut you, then it could cut a horse, too."

"Thanks for your concern." She said it with a smile and a little shake of her chandelier earrings. "Nice to know the horses are more valuable than I am."

"Like I said earlier, it's my job to take care of every beast on this ranch. You're not a beast. You should know to wear shoes."

She wasn't sure how to answer that. She couldn't exactly insist she *was* a valuable beast that needed taken care of, and she certainly wasn't going to admit she'd run outside in a panic. Actors who panicked didn't get hired.

"Come on. I'll get you something for the bleeding."

He walked away. Just turned his back on her and walked away. Again.

After a moment, she followed, but she hadn't taken two steps when he told her to stop. "Don't keep bleeding on the floor."

"What do you want me to do?" She put both hands on her hips and faced him squarely. Who cared if it didn't show off her figure? She'd lost this audition already.

"Can't you hop on one foot?"

This had to be a test, another trick to see if she was a dumb blonde. But Travis turned into a side room that was the size of another stall, one fitted out with a deep utility sink and kitchen-style cabinets.

He wasn't watching her to see what she'd do, so maybe it wasn't a joke. After a moment of indecision, she started hopping on her good foot. The cut one hurt, anyway, and it was only a few hops to reach the sink.

Travis opened one of the cabinets. It looked like a pharmacy inside, stocked with extra-large pill bottles. He got out a box of bandages, the adhesive kind that came in individual paper wrappers. The kind her mother had put on her scrapes and cuts when she was little.

I am not going to cry in front of this man. Not ever again.

He tapped the counter by the sink. "Hop up. Wash your foot off in the sink."

"Why don't you come here and give me a little boost?"

He stilled, with good reason. She'd said it with a purr, an unmistakably sexual invitation for him to put his hands on her.

She hadn't meant to. It had just popped out that way, her way to distance herself from the nostalgia. Maybe a way to gain some control over him. He was giving her commands, but she could get him to obey a sexual command of her own if she really turned on the charm.

Whatever had made her say that, she had to brave it out now. Sultry was better than sad. Anything was better than sad.

She tossed her hair back, her earrings jingling like a belly dancer's costume. She turned so that she was slightly sideways to him, her bustline a curvy contrast to her flat stomach.

"The counter's too high for me. Give me a hand…or two."

Come and touch me. Her invitation sounded welcoming. She realized it was. He was nothing like the sleek actors or the crazy DJs she'd known, but apparently, *rugged outdoorsman* appealed to her in a big way. *You've got a big green light here, Mr. Cowboy.*

"Too high for you," he repeated, without a flicker of sexual awareness in his voice. Instead, he sounded impatient as he cut through her helpless-damsel act. "I already watched you hop up on Mrs. MacDowell's counter tonight."

Of course the counter height had been a flimsy excuse; it had been an invitation. She refused to blush at having it rejected. Instead, she backed up to the counter and braced her hands behind herself, letting her crop top ride high. With the kind of slow control that would have made her personal yoga instructor beam with approval, she used biceps and triceps and abs, and lifted herself slowly onto the counter with a smooth flex of her toned body. People would pay money to see a certain junior officer do that in a faraway galaxy.

Travis Chalmers made a lousy audience. He only turned on the water and handed her a bar of soap.

She worked the bar into a lather as she pouted. Even Deezee wouldn't have passed up the chance to touch her. Actually, that was all Deezee had ever wanted to do: touch her. If it wasn't going to end in sex, he wasn't into it. She'd texted him ten times more often than he'd texted her between dates. His idea of a date had meant they'd go somewhere to party in the public eye or drink among VIPs for a couple of hours before they went to bed together. There'd been no hanging out for the sake of spending time together.

Sophia held her foot still as the water rinsed off the suds. She'd mistaken sex for friendship, hadn't she?

"It's not a deep cut. You should heal pretty quickly." Travis dabbed the sole of her foot dry with a wad of clean paper towels, which he then handed to her. Before she could ask what she was supposed to do with damp paper towels, he'd torn the paper wrapper off a bandage and placed it over the cut. He pressed the adhesive firmly into her skin with his thumb. There was nothing sexual in his touch, but it wasn't unkind. It was almost…paternal.

"Do you have kids?" she asked.

For once, he paused at something she'd said. "No."

You ought to. There was something about his unruffled, unhurried manner…

Dear God, she wasn't going to start missing her father, too. She couldn't think about parents and sister any longer. Not tonight.

She snatched her foot away and jumped lightly off the counter, landing on the foot that hadn't been cut. She held up the wad of damp towels. "Where's the trash?"

"You need those paper towels to wipe up the blood on your way out. I'll get you something to wear on your feet."

On her way out. She was dismissed, and she had to go back to the empty house in the middle of nowhere. She didn't want Travis to fetch her boots; she wanted him to carry her. He was a man who rode horseback all day. A cowboy who stood tall, with broad shoulders and strong hands. He could carry her weight, and God knew Sophia was tired of carrying everything herself.

She wanted his arms around her.

But she'd failed this audition. He wasn't interested in her when she was either bossy or cute. He wasn't fazed by her sultry tone, and he didn't care about her hard-earned, perfect body. He wasn't impressed with her in any way.

She gingerly stepped into the center aisle to see where he'd gone. Across from the medical room was another stall-sized space where it seemed saddles got parked on wooden sawhorses. The next room was enclosed with proper walls and a door, with a big glass window in the wall that looked into the rest of the barn. She could see a desk and bookcase and all the usual stuff for an office inside. She felt so dumb; she hadn't known barns had offices and medical clinics inside.

Travis came in from the door at the far end of the aisle from the door she'd used. He dropped a pair of utilitarian rubber rain boots at her feet. "These will get you back to the house. Return them tomorrow, before sundown."

"So specific. Bossy much?" She could hear the snotty teenager in her voice. Whatever. She hated feeling dumb.

"Whoever brings the horses in tomorrow might want to wear them when they hose down a horse, so have them back by then."

It was a patient explanation, but she hated that he could tell she didn't know squat about how a ranch was run. "Someone else is coming? You're not going to be here tomorrow night?"

"We take turns during roundup. One of the other hands will have a chance to come in and shower and sleep in a bed. Someone's usually here before sundown."

"But I can't let anyone else see me."

He shrugged. "Then don't come into the barn at sundown."

Then turn the car around. Then go to the grocery store. As if life were that simple.

"If you do come into the barn, wear boots. Dish towels are optional. Good night." He walked back into the medical stall, closing cabinet doors and shutting off the light.

Dish towels are optional. The man thought she was a big joke. With as much dignity as she'd once been forced to muster each time a casting director had said *Don't call us, we'll call you*, Sophia stepped into the galoshes and headed for the door, bending over to wipe up little red circles as she went.

Travis returned to the center aisle in time to watch the most beautiful woman in the world stomp out of his barn like a goddess in galoshes. She slid the barn door closed behind herself with what he was certain was a deliberate bang.

Samson, his favorite gelding and apparent lover of women's shampoo, kept his head toward the door, ears pointed toward the spot where the woman had disappeared. Travis realized he and the horse were both motionless for a moment too long.

"You can stop staring at the door. She's not coming back."

The horse shifted, stamping his foot.

"All right, damn it, you're right. Her hair smelled amazing. Don't get used to it. We've got work tomorrow. It'd take more than a pretty woman to change our ways."

Chapter Five

Three days, he stayed away.

The days were easy, filled with dirt and lassos as the animals were rounded up, counted, doctored. Calves bawled for their mamas until the cowboys released them and let them run back to the waiting herd. Travis had to change his mount every few hours to give the horses a rest, so the additional challenge of controlling different mounts with their unique personalities kept his attention focused where it ought to be.

But for three nights…

He'd stretch out on his bedroll and stare at the stars while thinking of one in particular, the star that had fallen onto his ranch. Insomnia wasn't a problem after a day of physical work, but when his tired body forced his mind to shut down, he continued thinking about Sophia Jackson in his sleep. Sophia got flirty, she got angry, she was strong and she was weak, but she was always, always tempting in every dream version of her that his brain could concoct. For three nights, he dreamed of nothing else.

It was damned annoying.

In the afternoon of the fourth day, he rode in with Clay Cooper, the hand who was next up for a night off. As foreman, Travis had to get to his office to keep up with the never-ending paperwork that went with running any business. That was reason enough for him to leave camp for the night. Not one cowboy was surprised when he left with Clay and the string of horses that were due for a day's rest and extra oats in the barn.

But Travis knew the real reason he was going in was to check on the famous Sophia Jackson. He was tired of fighting that nagging feeling that he needed to keep an eye on her, a feeling that hadn't gone away since the moment he'd met her in the road.

The house came into view. Travis's horse perked up. Travis had worked with horses too long for him not to understand what drove their behavior. The horse had perked up with anticipation because the rider had perked up with anticipation.

Travis rolled his shoulders. Took off his hat and smacked the dust off his thigh. Relaxed into the saddle.

There was nothing to anticipate. He was going to see Sophia Jackson soon. No big deal. Sophia was a movie star, but he wasn't starstruck.

The horse walked on while Travis turned that thought over once or twice. It felt true. Sure, he'd seen her in *Space Maze*. It would be hard to find someone who hadn't seen that movie. But from the tantrum she'd thrown about being stared at, and from her sister's fear of the paparazzi, he didn't think the Hollywood lifestyle was very attractive. It would have been better if she hadn't been a movie star.

Better for what?

Just easier all around. He put his hat on his head and turned back to check the string of horses following Clay. All was well.

As the foreman, he was riding in to check on the new person renting the MacDowells' house, same as he'd check on any new cowboy who came to the ranch. Hell, he'd check on any new filly or fence post. Once he was sure the MacDowells' guest had gotten her groceries and her fridge was still running, he'd mentally cross her off his to-do list and move on to the next item: he needed to order more barb wire before they got down to the last spool.

He and Clay rode past the house. Travis had planned to help Clay put up the horses first at the bunkhouse's stable before checking on Sophia, but he noticed that Clay didn't even toss a glance toward the house. It hit Travis that none of the hands who'd come and gone from camp seemed to be aware anyone was living in Mrs. MacDowell's house. Travis would've told them there was a guest staying there. No big deal. But no one had mentioned seeing any signs of life for the past three nights.

There were no signs of life now. No lights on. No curtains open to take in the evening sunset. No rocking chair on the porch out of place. Sophia was keeping herself hidden pretty well, then. Or…

Or Sophia Jackson had left the River Mack ranch.

I don't want to be here, anyway, she'd said, hand poised over the car's steering wheel.

It was the most likely explanation. He'd wanted her to leave when he'd first met her, so he ought to be relieved. Instead, that nagging need to see her intensified. He had to know if she was still on his land or not.

"I'll see you tomorrow," he said to Clay. He let his horse feel his hurry to reach Mrs. MacDowell's kitchen door until he stopped her at the edge of the flagstone patio.

There, stretched out on one of the wooden picnic tables, was Sophia. She was laid out like she was the meal, her clothing white like a tablecloth, her body delectable, but her eyes were closed and her hand was open and relaxed as she slept.

He dismounted and looped the horse's reins loosely around the old hitching post. His horse tossed her head with a jangle of tack and the heels of Travis's boots made a hard noise with each step as he crossed the flagstone, but Sophia remained fast asleep.

He ought to be thinking of Sleeping Beauty, he supposed. Sophia was as beautiful as a princess in her innocent white clothing, if a princess wore shorts and a shirt.

Instead, he couldn't get the idea of a feast out of his head. Here was a woman who'd be a banquet for the senses. Old college memories came back, Humanities 101 and its dry textbook descriptions of Roman emperors who'd held feasts where the sex was part of the meal. The image of a fairy tale princess battled briefly with the Roman feast, but Travis's body clearly clamored for Rome.

He stopped at her side. Looked down at her, but didn't touch. "Sophia."

She didn't stir. He said her name again and waited, wondering how a shirt and shorts could look so sexy. Finally, he shook her arm. "Sophia, wake up. It's Travis."

She jerked awake, then jerked away from him, like an animal instinctively afraid of attack.

Fanciful notions from college studies evaporated in an instant. "Whoa. It's just me."

She rolled off the table, off the far side, so that she stood with the table between them. It was a seriously skittish move.

"What are you doing here?" she asked.

"This is my ranch."

"Ha. You don't spend a lot of time on it." She pushed her hair back with both hands, pausing to squeeze her temples with her palms as she looked around the horizon. "Crap. Is it already sunset?"

"Clay's already taken the horses to the stable."

She looked toward the barn, alarmed. "Did this Clay guy see me?"

Travis didn't envy her Hollywood life at all. She seemed to be on edge all the time.

She wasn't wearing a shirt and shorts, after all. It was all one piece, almost like a child's pajamas. Maybe she was embarrassed to be caught outside in her pajamas. "Don't worry. You're looking at the barn, not what we call the stables around here. The stables are on the far side of the horse pasture. You can't see it from the house."

He paused. He didn't have a reason to tell her more, except that it might buy her some time to ease into being awake. "The stables are close to the bunkhouse. Cowboys living there keep their horses in the stables."

But judging by the way she rubbed the sleep from her eyes, she'd tuned him out after *Clay can't see you*. "I have to go inside. It's sunset."

"No one else is due in tonight." His words fell on deaf ears. Sophia stepped up on the little porch and disappeared into the house.

Travis caught himself staring at the closed door like Samson had the other night. He cursed under his breath and went to untie his horse. He had his answer: Sophia Jackson was still here. She looked fine, better than fine. She looked healthy as all get-out. It was time to move on and order that barb wire.

He led his horse to the barn. Caring for the mare was a familiar routine, one that should have let him unwind, but he had to work to ignore a lingering uneasiness. He unsaddled the mare, stored the tack, then took her outside to rinse the sweat marks from her coat with a garden hose.

The galoshes were sitting neatly by the hose, pushing his thoughts right back to Sophia.

Her presence in the barn that night had been unsettling in general. So had been one of her questions in particular: *Do you have kids?*

For just for a second, he'd thought he'd like to be able to answer *yes*. He was thirty-one and settled. He'd stood there with Sophia Jackson's perfectly arched foot in his hand and pictured himself married with a couple of little ones that he'd have to keep out of trouble. *It would be good to be a dad*, he'd thought for that flash of a second.

In reality, he didn't see himself getting married, and in his world, having children meant being married. He had nothing against the institution; he could understand why men did marry. Many a rancher's wife provided dinner every evening and clothes mended with love. They baked cakes and grew tomatoes in the garden, like Mrs. MacDowell.

Or there were wives who were partners in handling cattle. Travis hired the same husband and wife team every fall when it came time to move the cattle to auction. The two of them seemed happy roping and riding together, and they worked smoothly in sync.

But Travis was fine as a bachelor. He liked his own cooking well enough. Working alone never bothered him. He was where he wanted to be, doing what he wanted to do. In order to even consider upending a perfectly good life, he'd have to meet a woman who was damned near irresistible.

Like Sophia Jackson.

Not anything like her. He'd need to find a woman who

was irresistible but not crazy enough to wear a dish towel on her head and spike-heeled boots on a dirt road.

Unless that's what makes her irresistible.

He turned the hose back on and stuck his head in the stream of water.

Listen to yourself. A rancher's wife and a movie star are two different creatures. Too different.

This woman slept on top of a picnic table in the middle of the day. Crazy. A man did not marry *crazy*. A man didn't want *crazy* to be the mother of his children. Irresistible had nothing to do with it.

He shook the water out of his too-long hair as he unbuttoned his sweat-soaked plaid shirt and peeled it off. He had to lean over pretty far to keep the water off his jeans and boots, but the hose was good for taking off the first layer of trail dirt from his arms and chest.

Feeling a hundred times more clearheaded, he shut off the water and turned the mare loose in the paddock. His office was inside the barn. He kept a stack of clean T-shirts there. While he was at his desk, he'd order a dozen spools of quality barb wire, so he wouldn't have to give it a second thought for the rest of the year. Barb wire would be ordered—check. The MacDowells' houseguest was doing fine—check. He'd move on to the next item on his list.

He shoved the galoshes aside with the edge of his boot and left the darkening sky before the stars could come out and taunt his resolve.

It was useless. As he strode into the barn, he heard a distinctively feminine gasp. In the twilight of the barn's interior, Sophia practically glowed, all silver-blond hair and short, white pajamas. A star, right here in his barn. There was no list; there was nothing else to think about.

She dropped her gaze first.

Slowly.

She took him in deliberately, her gaze roaming over his wet skin, from his left shoulder to his right. To his bare chest. Lower.

I'm not the only one around here who's hungry, then.

The knowledge blinded him for a moment. To hell with the kind of woman he ought to want. Sophia was the woman he *did* want. Full stop. And he wanted her badly.

She came a step closer.

As water drops rolled down his skin, blood pounded through his veins, his desire for her ferocious in a way that was unfamiliar, as if he'd never really wanted a woman before.

She was about to say something, but as her lips parted, her gaze flicked from his chest back up to his eyes. Whatever she saw in his expression made her own eyes open wider. Whatever she'd been about to say turned into a little whoosh of "oh."

He couldn't remember feeling this power before, not for any of the women who'd been so likely to be right for him. After dating for weeks or months or, once, a whole year, none had turned out to be right after all. Yet Sophia had only to exhale an *oh*, and the years of friends and lovers blurred into nothing. This woman was the one he'd been starving for.

Hunger caused problems on a ranch. Stallions kicked out stalls. Bulls destroyed fences.

"Why are you here?" he demanded. *Why you? Why now?*

She took a step closer, and a part of him—too much of him—didn't give a damn about the answers to his own questions. He just wanted her to keep coming.

She hesitated.

Then she took that next step closer, but it was too late. Her split-second pause, the widening of her eyes by a fraction of an inch, had betrayed the tiniest little bit of…fear? Perhaps fear of this power between them. Perhaps fear of him, personally. He was the bigger one, the stronger one, the one with an admittedly fresh surge of testosterone coursing through his body.

But he was no animal, no common beast, just as he'd told her she wasn't. He knew what was in his heart and mind and soul, and she didn't need to fear him.

She couldn't know that yet, not for certain. They barely knew one another. Travis didn't have any kind of minimum time limit in mind for how long he ought to know a woman before taking her to bed, but he did know this: she had to be one-hundred-percent certain of what she wanted. Sophia Jackson did not know what she wanted.

Travis stepped back.

Her frown of confusion was fleeting, replaced by a new look of determination. She sauntered up to him, nice and close. Then she looked down his body again, her feminine eyelashes shading her blue eyes, turning him on as she ran one fingertip over his damp forearm.

"I came out here because it's lonely in that house. Very lonely."

God, that purr of hers…

It was an act. She was a good actress, but he'd seen that moment of fear or uncertainty or whatever it had been. Hunger couldn't be ignored forever, but it wouldn't kill a man to wait. Travis didn't intend to act on it or even talk about it in his barn just because he'd been caught out half-naked by a woman in skimpy pajamas.

He balled up his plaid shirt and used it to wipe the water off one arm, then the other. He pitched it through his open office door to land on his chair. *No feast today, Princess.*

"Did you need something before I go home?" he asked.

Her sexy act flipped to a more authentic anger pretty

quickly. Apparently, she didn't take rejection well. "I don't need anything from you. I didn't even want you to be here. I came to see the horses."

"Is that so? In your pajamas and bare feet?" He turned his back on her and went into his office. He grabbed a T-shirt off the stack he kept on a bookcase. When he turned back, he nearly plowed her over; she'd followed him into his office, all indignation.

"I'm wearing sandals, and these aren't pajamas. You wish you could see me in my pajamas. You wish."

Her attempt at a set down was so childish, it sounded almost cute. Travis had to hide his smile by pulling his T-shirt over his head. No harm in letting her think she'd scored a point against him.

"This is a *romper*," she huffed. "Straight from the runway. By a designer in Milan whom I wouldn't expect you to know. My stylist snatched it right out from under Kim K's nose. She probably died when I wore it first."

He stood with his hands on his hips, looking down at her, wondering what a guy like him was supposed to do with a girl like her. "I don't know Kim, but it looks real nice on you."

"Yeah. Sure." Apparently, she didn't believe his compliment. She turned her back on him and left the office, her designer clothes all in a white flutter.

Travis scrubbed his face with both hands. Then he shut off the lights and left the office, closing the door firmly. The barb wire could wait until tomorrow.

Sophia was nuzzling the spotted nose of a nice Appaloosa Travis had borrowed from the neighboring ranch for roundup. Travis watched her for a minute. The horse was loving the attention. *You're getting more action than I am, buddy.*

Still, Travis had to appreciate a person who had a natural affinity for horses. Her talent had to be natural and not learned, because he didn't think Sophia had ever set foot in a barn in her life before this week. She was wearing flip-flops, for crying out loud.

"Where's my horse?" she asked, keeping her eyes on the Appaloosa.

"Your horse?" He didn't like her wording. She had no idea what it meant to own a horse. To train, to groom, to feed, to care for without fail, to rely on when there was nobody for miles around.

"The boy horse whose name you won't tell me. You left, and you took him with you. You took all of them. I came out here to say hello to the horses, and they were gone. Every single one."

Damn if she didn't sound like she was going to burst into tears.

"They aren't pets. They work."

"I returned the galoshes, just like you wanted, but you took the horses away. Without those horses, I've got no one to talk to. You're not interested in talking to me...or doing anything else with me."

Travis was good at picking up on animal behavior, not a woman's, but he could read her well enough. She felt betrayed. Lonely. Hell, she'd curled up into a ball and cried on a kitchen floor just days ago.

He'd have no peace of mind until he figured her out.

"Okay. You want to talk? Let's talk."

Chapter Six

The cowboy wanted to talk.

Sophia wasn't sure if he was kidding. She combed her fingers through the spotted horse's mane and peeked at big, bad Travis Chalmers. He looked pretty serious. Then again, that was his default expression. He grinned a little now and then, but otherwise, he was a serious guy.

Not a guy. A man.

A serious man who walked around here like he ran the place. Which she supposed he did, but still…

Travis took some kind of rope-and-leather thing that was hanging over an empty stall door and coiled it up. Tied it off. Tossed it into the room where the saddles were. It landed in a crate. It seemed that being in charge meant keeping everything in order.

Deezee would have dumped the crate out, flipped it upside down, and stood on it like it was his stage, whooping and hollering and making sure no one else could talk while he was around.

Travis glanced down the row of stalls to the neat stack of perfectly square hay bales, then leaned back against a support post and gave her his full attention. Apparently nothing else was out of place—except her. "What did you want to talk about?"

She wasn't about to unburden herself to this man. She could pour out her regrets to the horses tomorrow morning. She didn't want Travis to know what an idiot she'd been. What an idiot she'd thrown away her career for.

Yet she'd just complained that she didn't have anyone to talk to, and Travis had called her on it. She had to come up with something to say. "What's this horse's name?"

Travis dipped his chin toward the horse, as matter-of-fact as if her question wasn't childish. "That's Arizona. He was named for the state. Texas isn't really known for Appaloosas. He was bought in Arizona as a wedding gift."

Oh, no. Please don't be married.

Dumb reaction. The man looked hot when he was shirtless. So what? That didn't mean she wanted to have a relationship with him. It didn't matter if he was married or not. Still…

"Not a gift for your wedding?" She tried to sound unconcerned.

"Trey Waterson's wedding. His brother gave him the horse. They own the ranch just west of us."

But Travis had that little bit of a grin about his mouth; he knew exactly why she'd asked. Her acting skills must be getting rusty already. She wished she hadn't run her finger down that muscled forearm, chasing a water droplet. She wished she hadn't made that stupid comment about being lonely.

She wished he hadn't rejected her.

"I'm not married," he said, making things perfectly clear. "Never been."

The horse, Arizona, shook his mane like Sophia wanted to. *That's right, horse. We don't care, do we?*

"So you don't own these horses, then. You're just the babysitter." She sneered the word *babysitter*.

She wished it back as soon as she said it. It was so rude. When had she started responding to everything as if she needed to insult someone before they could insult her?

But the answer was easy: when she'd spent too much time with Deezee and his buddies. Their ribbing and one-upmanship had been constant. At first, it had been a novelty to be treated like one of the guys instead of a flawless movie star, but she'd soon figured out that if she gave them an inch, they took a mile.

So maybe I've thrown up a few walls to protect myself. That's normal.

"Some horses are mine. Some are the ranch's." Travis patted Arizona's spotted neck. "Some I borrow."

His voice was so even. He couldn't care less about her nasty little dig. Did nothing irritate him? Or did he just not show it?

Judging by Travis Chalmers, it seemed the great actors in the movie industry, legends like Clint Eastwood and John Wayne, had acted their cowboy roles with more accuracy than Sophia had realized. They delivered their dialogue in an almost monotone way—never too excited, never shouting. Like Travis. Nothing like Deezee.

It was hard to imagine Travis jumping from a church pew to a communion railing and yelling *Yo, where's the ho?*

Deezee had meant her. Sophia had been standing in the vestibule of the Caribbean chapel, trying not to sweat through her white dress, waiting for the church music to start so she could walk down the center aisle to promise her life to him. He'd meant it as a joke, just another outrageous zinger for his posse's amusement. He hadn't bothered to change into a clean T-shirt. It was just a spontaneous elopement. No need to go to any trouble.

No crying in front of the cowboy.

"What's my horse's name?" she demanded. "And where is he?"

"Samson. He's still at camp. And he's my horse, not yours."

"Why did you ride that other horse today, then, if Samson belongs to you?"

"Because that other horse is mine, too. I own four right now, but you could say I babysit the rest."

Thank goodness the man's only facial expressions were somber and barely-a-grin. She'd insinuated that he owned nothing. If he laughed at her for how far she'd missed the mark, she might go all crazy diva on him. She couldn't stand to be laughed at.

"Four? For one man?" But her sarcasm was stupid, and she knew it.

"You can't ride just one horse all day, every day during roundup. That's why Arizona comes to work with me during roundup, see? So I have more horses to rotate. But Samson, he's a real special cow horse. I save him for when I'm actually cutting cattle out of the herd. It's a waste of talent to use him just to ride in from camp."

"You sound like a coach with a sports team."

"I hadn't thought of it that way. It's like setting up your batting order in baseball, now that you mention it. Samson's my star player. Don't tell Arizona that, though. He's been doing a great job pinch-hitting all week." Travis winked at Sophia, and he smiled. Not a grin, but a real smile that reached all the way to his eyes, a smile like she was in on the joke and part of his team.

Good Lord. The man was beautiful. She'd thought he

looked hot the moment she'd spotted him riding toward her that first day on the road. Kind of stern and remote, but so masculine on horseback that he'd cut through her haze of misery. Today, shirtless and dripping wet, he'd looked like an athlete, a man in his prime, serious and strong. But when he smiled—oh, why would the women of Texas keep a man like this out here in the middle of nowhere?

For once in her life, she was the one doing the staring.

"B-baseball?" she repeated. Then, because she'd stuttered, she sneered a little, just to let him know she didn't care. "What would a cowboy know about baseball? There aren't enough humans around here to get a game going."

She caught the slightest shake of his head as he crossed his arms over his chest—a move that did lovely things to stretch that T-shirt tight around his biceps. His smile lingered. He found her amusing. Damn him.

"True enough. This cowboy played shortstop in college. Was there anything else you wanted to talk about besides horse names and baseball?"

She wondered how much of her thoughts he could guess. Could he see how much she wished she hadn't ruined her chances with a guy like him by making a huge mistake with a guy like Deezee?

You're an actor, Sophia. Don't let him see anything.

It was easier just to alienate people so they'd leave her alone. Her bridges were already burned. To hell with it.

"College? For a cowboy? What do they teach you, not to step in horse manure?"

Finally, *finally*, she'd pricked through his infuriatingly calm exterior. His eyes narrowed as she held his gaze defiantly.

That's right, I am a rattlesnake. You don't want to mess with me. She didn't want any man to mess with her, ever again.

His voice remained even. "My degree is in animal sciences from Texas A&M. They expect students to be smart enough to avoid horse manure before they enroll." He looked at her flip-flops, pointedly, and she fought the urge to curl her toes out of sight. "But I guess some people never do figure out what boots are for."

"Are you going to kick me out of your barn again?"

Please. Put me out of my misery. I'm screwing everything up here. Send me back to that awful, empty house and let me fall apart.

"I'm not your babysitter. You do what you want. If you don't have the common sense to stay out of trouble, well, some folks have to learn the hard way."

"I think I can avoid cow patties, thank you very much. I have eyes."

Travis pushed away from the post. "Then you might want to get going. It's getting dark real quick. It'll be harder to see those cow patties, and critters that like to bite toes will start coming out, too. Those flip-flops aren't going to protect you from a snake or a rat."

A rat. She glanced around the aisle. This place was too neat and organized for rats.

"We keep a barn cat," Travis said, reading the skepticism she hadn't bothered to hide. "She's a good mouser, but she does earn her keep."

He wasn't going to kick her out. She was going to have to force herself back to the lonely house. She acted like it didn't freak her out. "I'm leaving, anyway."

"I'll walk you to the door."

She jerked her arm out of his reach and stepped sideways, the side of her foot hitting a square hay bale. It felt like hitting a porcupine, except for her toes. Her toes made contact with something furry.

"A rat!" She nearly knocked Travis over, jumping away from the hay bale.

He caught her with a hand on her arm, but he was already frowning at the floor, bending down and reaching—

"Don't touch it." She tried to yank him away from the rat. He stood up with something brown in his hand and she let go of his arm. "Ew."

"It's not 'ew.' It's a kitten."

It wasn't moving. For the first time since Travis had woken Sophia from her nap, she felt the nausea rising. "Did I—do you think I… I didn't hurt it, did I?"

She felt him looking at her, but she had eyes only for the kitten, the tiniest one she'd ever seen. Travis pressed its baby paws with his thumb, wiggling each limb as he did. "Nothing seems to be broken or bent. You didn't hurt it."

Thank goodness. She sank weakly onto the hay bale, then leaped up as the hay poked her rear right through her designer romper from Milan.

Travis didn't seem to notice. His attention was on the kitten. He pulled at the collar of his T-shirt and tucked the brown fluff in, keeping it in place with one hand.

"Shouldn't we put it back so the mother cat will be able to find it?"

"He's cold. The mother cat must have abandoned him a while ago. If I can get him warmed up, we might be able to slip him back in with his brothers, but this is the second time the mother has moved him out of her nest."

"Why would she do that?"

Travis shrugged, the kitten completely hidden by his hand. "She might sense that there's something wrong with it."

"But you said it's not hurt."

"As far as I can see. The mother might know something

I don't. Or the mother might have decided two kittens are all she can handle, so the third one gets abandoned."

"She leaves it out to die? That's awful. Can't you do something about that?" Anxiety tinged her voice, but she didn't care. Her anxiety to *not* see a kitten die felt pretty intense.

"I am doing something about that," he said drily. "I've got a kitten stuck down my shirt."

"You're going to keep it?" That sounded good. Really good.

He sat on the hay bale, the heavy denim of his jeans so much more practical than her white silk. "This kitten is really young. His eyes aren't open yet. His best bet for survival is with his mother."

Her anxiety spiked right back up. "But he has a terrible mother. She left him, just left the pitiful thing all alone. He's better off without her."

"No, he isn't." Travis spoke firmly, but he was looking at her with…concern. It took her a moment to recognize concern on a man's face. For the past ten years, the only person who'd ever looked at her with concern had been Grace. Her sister was the only one who'd ever cared.

Nausea tried to get her attention, but Sophia pushed it away. She didn't want to acknowledge it or what it might mean.

"You've never had a cat before, have you?" Travis asked.

"Ages ago, but she was neutered. You should neuter your cats. You have to neuter this one's mother right away. She's a bad mother. She doesn't deserve to have any more babies." Sophia pressed the back of her hand against her mouth abruptly to conquer the nausea.

But it was too late. The thing she didn't want to think about was now at the forefront of her mind: the little plus sign on that stick. Motherhood. Babies.

The word *pregnant* might not seem real to her, but Grace and Alex had been so deadly serious about it. They'd sat her down at Alex's kitchen table to talk through the options.

Sophia had immediately pounced on giving the baby up for adoption. It sounded simple. There'd be this baby that she would never even have to see, really, and the adoption agency would find the perfect couple. The couple would be happy. The baby would be happy. No harm all around.

That pregnancy test had probably been wrong, anyway, but adoption was a simple solution for a simple equation: one unwanted baby plus one couple who wanted a baby equaled success. Sophia would be doing a good deed. End of family meeting.

"Sophia." There was a definite note of concern in Travis's voice now, to match the way he was looking at her. "She might not be a bad mother. Sometimes Mother Nature knows more than we do. But for what it's worth, I agree with you about having cats neutered. This kitten's mother found us a couple of weeks ago. She moved herself in and was already pregnant. Accidents happen."

Oh god, oh god, oh god...

Tonight, faced with a few ounces of fluff she'd almost stepped on, Sophia suddenly realized what she'd left out of the equation: herself. Doing a good deed? She was the failure in the equation, not the hero. She was giving the baby away because she knew, deep down, she would be a terrible mother. She'd tried so hard with Grace, but she'd failed. Grace didn't even want to live with her anymore.

Travis had said the cat might have decided she couldn't handle that baby. Sophia knew she couldn't handle a baby, either. So what did that make Sophia? A terrible, horrible, selfish cat.

Travis tucked his chin into his collar and spread his fingers out, trying to see the kitten. "He's moving around. That's a good sign."

Sophia backed away from him, scared of the little bit of brown fluff and all that it represented.

"I'm going to go now." Her voice sounded thin, too high. "Good luck with the kitten."

She turned tail and ran. And ran. As fast as she could in the stupid flip-flops, she ran so that she was out of breath when she got back to the house.

It helped. It was only a sprint, maybe the length of a football field, nothing like the miles she'd had to put in to prepare for battling monsters in *Space Maze*, but she felt a little more normal. She felt her lungs and ribs expanding, contracting, taking in extra air. Muscles she hadn't used in weeks were suddenly awake, alive. She smoothed her hand over her stomach. The nausea was gone, and she felt hungry.

What she didn't feel was pregnant. Not one bit.

The pregnancy test's instructions had cautioned over and over that the results were not always accurate. Really, all that had happened was that Sophia had skipped a period, which was an easy thing to do. She probably wasn't even pregnant.

She was here to hide from the paparazzi, that was all. Her sister and Alex had both told Travis that. Sophia would lie low here for a few more weeks and let the media turn its attention elsewhere. Once they began a feeding frenzy on some other celebrity couple, Sophia would fly back to LA and start hunting for a new agent.

And you should make an appointment to get your tubes tied, because now you know you wouldn't be happy if you really were pregnant, and you'd be a lousy mother who couldn't take care of a baby, anyway.

She glanced out the kitchen window toward the barn,

where some knocked-up stray cat was apparently her spirit animal. If the kitten-killing cat had been sent to show Sophia how much she was lacking, she'd done her job tonight. It was a good thing Sophia was planning on letting someone adopt the baby, because she wouldn't be a good mother. It was a crushing revelation.

The only light on in the whole house was the little one over the stove. That was plenty. The boxes of nonperishable food were still lined up on the kitchen counter, and Sophia had spent the week working her way through them, left to right. She didn't need a lot of light to pour herself another bowl of organic raisins and bran flakes.

She sat at the table and poked at the dry cereal with her spoon for a while. The organic milk substitute had gotten warm that first day, so she'd dumped it down the drain. Without a housekeeper, a personal shopper, or a sister, it hadn't been replenished yet.

Sophia didn't care. She just wanted to sleep, even after the nap she hadn't meant to take outside today. That had been a stupid slip up. It would have blown her cover if anyone except Travis had come by.

She couldn't get her act together enough to do a simple thing like hide. She'd dared to go outside because the house felt too empty. The sun had felt good on her skin after four days indoors, so she'd stretched out and fallen asleep.

No surprise there. She'd been tired for years. She'd been looking for a break when she'd taken Grace for that vacation in Telluride, but five months of Deezee hadn't been very refreshing. She was more tired than ever now.

Except when she talked to Travis. She'd felt alive and awake when Travis had walked into that barn with no shirt on. Nothing like a half-naked, incredibly buff man to snap a girl out of a fog.

The expression in his eyes had taken her breath away.

Boy meets girl. Boy wants girl. Or rather, man wants woman. Woman had wanted him right back, with an intensity that she couldn't handle.

No surprise there, either. She couldn't handle anything in her life. But she'd felt like she was really alive for the first time in ages, so she'd been determined to see how far he would go.

Not very far. One touch with her finger, and he'd literally stepped back from her and put on a shirt. So much for her bankable box office sex appeal. She'd lost her career, her sister—and her ability to attract a man. She sucked. Her life sucked.

On that note, she left her bowl on the table, stumbled into the living room, and did a face plant on the sofa. She never wanted to wake up again.

Chapter Seven

"Sophia, wake up."

She jerked awake, heart pounding.

"It's just me. Travis. Are you okay?"

She sat up on the couch and dropped her face in her hands, willing her heart to slow down. She hated to be startled awake, because her first instinct was to flail about in case Deezee and his crew were in the middle of pulling some prank, like drawing on her face with a Sharpie just before she was expected to make an appearance. *It's funny, baby, whatchu getting upset for?*

She'd had to cancel that appearance, disappointing fans and angering her manager.

"I'm not okay. You just scared me to death, shaking my arm like that."

"Sorry. Nothing else was waking you up."

She was waking up now, fully aware of where she was and who was standing over her. "What are you doing here?"

"Checking on you."

"What are you doing in my house? Did you just open the door and walk in?"

"Yes."

"What are you, some kind of stalker?"

"No."

His implacable, even tone set her teeth on edge. "But you just walked into someone else's house. You don't see anything wrong with that, do you?"

"I knocked first." His cell phone was in his hand, but he slipped it into his back pocket.

She stood up, furious. "I deserve privacy. I rented this house. I get that you're all Mr. I-Run-This-Place, but the house is mine for the duration. You can't just walk in any time you please. Have you been spying on me while I was sleeping? Standing over my bed without me knowing it every night?"

"Of course not. Quit spooking yourself."

"Spooking myself? What does that mean? That's not even a thing."

"You're letting your imagination run away with you. I walked in just now because we don't tend to stand on ceremony out here in the country. We can't. If someone's in trouble, you have to help. You can call nine-one-one, but it can take a long time for help to arrive. We take care of each other."

The man sounded like he actually believed what he was saying. He was oblivious to the invasion of her privacy. Living in the country couldn't be that different than living in the city.

"You had no reason to think I was in trouble."

"I thought I'd come and tell you some good news, but it looked like nobody was home."

"So?"

"If you hadn't come back to the house, then where were you? You ran out of the barn like a bat out of hell, so I figured you'd made it back to your place in a couple of minutes, but it didn't look like you were here. You'd run somewhere else. It's full dark out there. You aren't wearing much, and a person can start to lose body heat pretty quick once the sun goes down. You only had on flip-flops. If you'd gotten hurt—"

"I was right here on my own couch, minding my own business."

"Good. Now I don't have to saddle up Arizona and go out to look for you."

You would have done that for me? But the calm way he was looking at her, the steadiness of his voice told the truth. Just the fact that it had even occurred to him to go looking for someone who might be missing was…

It made her feel kind of protected. A nice feeling.

Crap. It was hard to stay mad at a man who'd honestly been worried about her. Not just worried, either. He actually would have done something about it.

She crossed her arms over her chest, but she couldn't force any real sting into her voice. "Well, we need to have an understanding that you won't sneak into my house again. Where I'm from, that's called breaking and entering. It creeps me out. Even the paparazzi don't dare to walk in my door. Don't do it, okay?"

He took his time thinking about his answer. "All right."

"I mean it." She didn't need any man mounting horseback search parties for her sake. She didn't.

"This wasn't sneaking in," he said. "You have my word I never will. But if I think you're in trouble, I'm going to do whatever it takes to help you, whether you like it or not."

Sophia blinked. *Why, you bossy son of a—* But then she

realized she was looking at his back because he'd left the living room to go into the kitchen. She hurried after him.

He had already turned on the lights in the kitchen. He picked up her dry bowl of cereal. "Is this all you ate today?"

She stopped cold. There was only one reason a man would ask about that. Only one reason. "The paparazzi got to you already, didn't they?"

His gaze narrowed again.

I'm not the rattlesnake, dude. You are.

"I want to see your cell phone." She was seething. "How long have you been in here, photographing Sophia Jackson's hideout? Documenting Sophia Jackson's Hollywood diet secrets? Did you take pictures of me sleeping? Did you?"

"You're spooking yourself again."

"How much did they pay you? The kid at the deli by my condo got two thousand dollars for writing down my sandwich orders for a week. He took a photo of my sister picking up a bag with subs in it. When I didn't order a sandwich the next day, he lied and took a photo of someone else's sandwich. He got the cash. You know what I got?"

Travis set the bowl down with a soft curse.

He didn't want to hear her story? Too bad. He needed to know exactly what he was doing by giving the paparazzi supposedly harmless details of her life.

"I got reamed by America for setting a bad example for the youth of today. The youth of today! Because one of those youths took a picture of some insanely greasy concoction and claimed it was mine. Then everyone said the only way I could eat like that and keep my figure would be if I abused laxatives or stuck my fingers down my throat after every meal. The fact that they photographed me going in and out of a gym every single frigging day was irrelevant when it came to how I might be keeping my figure, but that's beside the point. I was suddenly personally responsible for every poor teenager with an eating disorder. I know how this game works, Travis. You'll get cash, and I'll get punished."

She nearly choked on his name. Travis—the betrayal shouldn't have hurt this badly. She didn't really know him any better than the deli counter kid.

"I'm not talking to any damned paparazzi. I don't think I've ever said that word out loud in my life. Paparazzi."

"I'm not stupid," she said, feeling very stupid for having let down her guard for an instant. "Since when does a big, tough cowboy suddenly take an interest in what kind of cereal a woman eats?"

"Since the big, tough cowboy got scared. Bad." He started walking toward her, two steps that covered most of the big kitchen. "I didn't just knock. I called the phone, too. You didn't move when I turned on the lights. I had my phone in my hand because I was going to call nine-one-one if I couldn't wake you. My grandpa had diabetes. I've seen what happens when a person's blood sugar gets too low. You scared me. That's all."

He took another step closer. She didn't back up, but she crossed her arms defensively. He was a lot of man, looming over her. A lot of man with a lot of honesty in his voice, and concern in his expression, and really beautiful brown eyes.

He ran his rough-warm palm over her arm, from her shoulder to her elbow, and kept his hand there, firm. "I'm very sorry I scared you in return."

Sophia felt her world turning. Pieces of her mind tumbled and landed in a new order. A better order. If she lived her life a different way…if she didn't always assume the worst…if she could believe someone wanted to help her instead of use her…

She could have a friend.

It was what she'd hoped for with Deezee. Things with him had started out with this kind of instant attraction, this desire to trust a man she barely knew.

Hope hurt.

Sophia took a step back.

Travis bowed his head, a quick nod to himself. When he looked up, he was the remote, stern foreman once more. "Do you always sleep so hard?"

He meant, *Is there something I should know about, because I'm responsible for all the horses and pregnant cows and cats around here?* She could hear it in his voice.

The truth would guarantee that he'd think of her as some kind of crazy diva: *No, I'm just sad. When I'm really sad, I deal with it by checking out of the world and going into hibernation.*

She couldn't tell him that.

"I'm just making up for a lack of sleep. A few years' worth of sleep."

"And do you always eat such a spartan diet? You never went to the grocery store, did you?"

"Don't start with that." This was why she didn't have friends. No one walked a mile in her shoes. No one understood.

She imitated his unruffled, even tone. "'If you need groceries, then go to the grocery store.' Everything is so easy for you, isn't it? You get to come and go as you please on any horse that strikes your fancy. You know what to do if you find a half-dead kitten, so you don't freak out. Of course you can decide whether or not you'll head to the store for more groceries."

She was afraid she might cry, but only because she wanted him to understand.

"Do you know why I have to wait for my sister to bring

me groceries? It's not because I'm a diva. It's because I'll get hurt if I go out by myself. It's happened before." She held out the arm he'd stroked. "See these little half moons? That's how much my fans love me. If I walk down a street, I'll let them take their selfies and then I'll try to say good-bye, and they'll dig their fingernails into me. 'No, wait. You have to wait until my friend shows up.'

"I have to smile. I can't pitch a fit or else I'm a bitch or a diva or a monster. I've been held hostage, forced to wait on a sidewalk for a stranger's friend while people start penning me in from every direction. The police will stop to see what the crowd is about and they'll smile and wave at me. So I just sign autographs until it's the policeman's turn, and then I have to smile while I ask them to keep people from hurting me. 'Gee, Officer, could you possibly escort me back to my hotel?'"

Oh, hell, her eyes were tearing up, but she didn't care. Deezee had gotten off on these stories. He'd wanted them to happen to him. But Travis was frowning, and she didn't know if it was because he believed her or if it was because he thought she was *spooking* herself again.

But she had more proof, a secret that only a few hair-stylists knew about. She turned her back to him and started pawing through her hair, piling her hair up until her fin-gertips found it, that dime-sized bit of her scalp where no hair grew. "This is how much they love me. Right after *Space Maze* came out, I was spotted at a grocery store. Honest to God, I had no idea how much people loved that movie. They pulled the hair out of my head as a souvenir. That's love. Right there."

She jabbed at the spot, such a small scar left after so much blood and pain, but Travis's hand stopped hers. He smoothed his thumb over the scar. She closed her eyes, remembering his thumb on the sole of her foot, smoothing an adhesive bandage into place, making everything better.

"I'm sorry," he said.

She dropped her hands, and her hair fell back into place with a shake of her head, just like Jean Paul had designed it to do. It was such a great perk of fame, those great haircuts and free shampoo. What a lucky girl she was.

"I'm sorry," Travis repeated, gruff words that whispered over her hair.

She felt all the fight go out of her. She couldn't remember what was supposed to take its place. Before Deezee, before the breakthrough roles, before her parents' deaths… what had life been like when she hadn't fought for everything?

She opened the door so Travis could leave, facing him with what she hoped was a neutral expression and not a desolate one. "You don't have to worry if you don't see me around. I think any normal person in my position would stay out of sight. It's just that my future brother-in-law told me that the MacDowells said I could trust the foreman, so I… I showed myself to you. Everyone else will just have to think there's a vampire living in the house or something."

Travis nodded and picked his hat up from the table. He must have tossed it there instead of using the hook by the door. It was the sort of thing someone might do in a rush.

He walked out the door. Sophia realized he already had his boots on. He'd come in without stopping at the boot jack, breaking his own rule about boots in the house. He'd really been worried about her.

A little rush of gratitude filled some of the empty space inside her.

"Travis?"

He turned back to her, his expression serious, illuminated

by the light from the kitchen. Beyond him, the night was black, the night he would have ridden in, looking for her.

"I'm not a crazy recluse. I'm just a recluse, okay?"

"I get it."

She'd been holding her breath. Now she could breathe.

He tapped his hat against his thigh. "I never told you the reason I came looking for you in the first place. That kitten got more lively when he warmed up, so I found the mother cat's new hiding spot. She didn't object when I slipped him in with his brothers."

"Oh." She took a deeper breath. The night air felt fresh. "Oh, that's great news. She's not a terrible mother after all."

"I never said she was. She had her reasons. We just don't know what they were. I put out some extra food, in case she was worried about having enough to eat. The other barn cat will probably get to it first, but it's worth a try. When I left, she was pretty relaxed and letting all three kittens nurse."

Maybe Sophia was crazy after all, because it felt like Travis had just given her the best gift. "Thank you. Thank you so much."

"I wouldn't want you to get too hopeful. That kitten's had a rough time of it so far."

"But now he'll be okay."

"We've given him a chance, at least. I'll see you when I get back in a few days. Good night." He touched the brim of his hat, and walked into the dark.

A few days?

She shut herself in the house.

Chapter Eight

She didn't wake up until noon.

What was the point? Everyone was gone again. Everyone meaning Travis and the horses.

Sophia was willing to bet that Travis had been saddling up those horses before dawn, true to the cowboy stereotype. She looked out the window toward the empty barn and tried not to feel resentful that the horses had been taken away. They had to work.

She wished she had to work. Resentment for her ex bubbled up, a toxic brew that made her stomach turn.

Thanks, Deezee.

Actually, Deezee was probably working, too. The more he partied, the more people wanted to pay him to appear at their parties. The more outrageous he got, the more bookings he got. Busting into that Texas Rescue ball and making a scene had been a smart thing for him to do. During their week in Saint Barth, his cell phone had blown up with offers.

Not hers.

A movie studio didn't make job offers to actors who skipped town without notice. A production couldn't build a PR campaign if their star said outrageous, unpredictable things. What helped Deezee's career killed hers.

Looking back, she doubted Deezee had realized how much he was hurting her. She doubted he would have cared if he had.

But she should have known better. She should have cared.

Deezee had lied to her. He'd cheated on her with other women. But he hadn't forced her to party like a rock star. That was her fault.

Thanks, Sophia.

She couldn't spend all day at the kitchen window, waiting to see which cowboy would come in at sundown. It wouldn't be Travis; that was all that mattered. She couldn't be seen by anyone else. She couldn't make another stupid mistake like she had yesterday, falling asleep on the picnic table. Alex and Grace wouldn't be able to pull another great hiding spot out of thin air. This was it. This was her only place to sleep, eat, hide and sleep some more.

But today, she didn't have the desire to go right back to sleep. She felt at least a little bit rested for a change. She'd slept in a real bed instead of crashing on the couch with the television on.

All week, she'd been avoiding the master bedroom. It was too spacious and too obviously someone else's room, with its family photos of little boys and a handsome father from decades past. She knew Mrs. MacDowell was a widow. She didn't like to look at photos of the dead father. She had her own.

But last night, after Travis had left, she'd wandered into one of the smaller bedrooms, one that looked like it was intended for guests. It had a queen-sized bed instead of a king. It had paintings of Texas bluebonnets on the walls instead of family photos. She'd been able to sleep there.

Great. So now she wasn't sleepy, but she still couldn't leave the house. Her one little foray to the picnic table yesterday had almost resulted in blowing her cover, because she'd lacked enough common sense to come back inside when sitting in the sun made her drowsy. She had no common sense. No self-discipline. She was in a prison of her own making, because she couldn't handle her own life.

Round and round her thoughts started to go. She hated them, because they always led to the same conclusion: she was a failure. She hated herself, and she was stuck.

But a new voice broke through the old soundtrack.

If you want to go outside, then open the door and walk outside.

Travis.

If he saw her standing here, if he could hear what she was saying to herself in her head, he would cut through all the nonsense with one of those infuriatingly simple solutions.

You're a grown woman, he'd say. A grown woman who was standing here, wishing she could go outside for a breath of fresh air but afraid that would be some catastrophic mistake. She'd fall asleep on a picnic table again, and let down Alex and Grace, and be laughed at in the press for being found on a cattle ranch, of all places. If she went outside, it would start a chain of disasters. It made sense to her.

Or it had, before last night. Before she'd spent some time with Travis and realized that all the puzzle pieces didn't have to go together in the complicated order she'd been putting them.

If you don't want to be in here, then open the door and go out there.

She opened the kitchen door, and stepped on a pile of zucchini.

She cursed as the zucchini scattered. She spewed every variation of the F-bomb that Deezee had ever shouted while playing a combat video game. She'd hated the way he'd lost control when he killed animated, imaginary enemies, yet she sounded just like him.

She shut up. It was zucchini, not the end of the world. Heck, her own *Space* character had managed to save an entire civilization without resorting to so much drama.

The zucchini rolled to a stop. A note was wedged into what remained of the pyramid by the door.

Sophia—
    When I got to my house, I saw that Clay had left a bunch of zucchini in my sink. His mother had a bumper crop, and she stopped by the bunkhouse when no one was there and left a ton in their kitchen. I don't think it's breaking and entering if someone's mother does it. The real crime here is that nobody can eat as much zucchini as Clay's mother grew. I'm passing off some of it onto you. It might make a nice change from cereal.
—Travis
P.S. I left you some milk in case you don't actually like your cereal dry. It's in the barn fridge. Please wear boots or shoes. You have enough scars. I don't want you to get any more.

Sophia stared at the letter. The man had been doing just fine, dropping little smart-aleck comments, but then he'd had to finish it up with that line about the scars. She must be crazy after all, because she felt all choked up by a hastily written P.S.

Sophia picked up the zucchini one by one, cradling them in her arm like a bouquet, and carried them into the kitchen. She put the zucchini in the sink. The letter she spread out on the counter. She read it again and smoothed out the crease. Read it again.

Then she went into the master bedroom, where Alex had left her suitcases. She hadn't unpacked them yet. Just reaching in and wearing the first thing she touched had taken all the energy she had, but now she lifted out the neat piles of clothes and carried them down the hall to the bluebonnet bedroom.

Trip after trip, she emptied the suitcases her sister had filled for her. As Sophia's personal assistant, Grace had been packing her bags ever since they'd moved to LA. Maybe Sophia hadn't wanted to unpack these final suitcases. Alex was going to be the person Grace took trips with from now on. These were the last shirts her sister would ever fold for her with care and love.

"This is depressing as hell." Sophia spoke the words loudly, but her voice didn't have to reach lofty rafters in here. The carpet and quilts of the guest bedroom absorbed the sound. The words weren't as scary out loud as they were when they echoed in her head.

Whether or not it was depressing, whether or not it was some kind of symbolic final vestige of her life with her sister, the suitcases had to be unpacked now, because Sophia needed her shoes. The only boots she had were the thigh-highs with the killer heels, but she knew that Grace would have packed workout clothes and a selection of running shoes for Sophia to choose from, depending on her mood and her clothes' color scheme.

She found the sneakers. Sophia left the empty suitcase

on the king-sized master bed. In her bedroom, she changed
into a shirt that had sleeves and a pair of shorts that barely
covered her rear but were made of denim. She laced up her
most sturdy pair of cross-trainers and once more opened
the kitchen door.

She wasn't going to fall asleep or get caught by a
stranger or ruin her career. She was going to get some
milk that Travis had left for her in the barn.

Nothing bad was going to happen.

The fresh air cleared the last bit of fog from Sophia's
head as she walked the hundred yards or so to the barn.

The heat of the day was building. Her yoga instructor
would say every molecule of hot air shimmered with energy that she could welcome into her lungs with intentional
breaths. Sophia could practice here, doing yoga outside on
the flagstone, holding poses that took all her concentra-
tion in the May heat. If she set an alarm clock tomorrow,
she could get up a little earlier and go for a run before it
got too hot.

If she really wanted more work in Hollywood, that
would be the smart thing to do. Having a great body was
an essential part of winning roles. If she let herself go too
long without exercise, she'd pay a price. She really didn't
want to keep paying for stupid decisions. *If you want to
keep your fitness level, then work out.*

She'd have to be careful who saw her. But if only she
and Travis were around, and he should happen to catch
her in the middle of a workout in her painted-on exercise
clothing…her muscles working, her skin glistening…

The possibilities sent a sizzle of sexual energy through
her.

She slid open the barn door, using chest muscles that
still felt strong despite weeks of laziness. Every LA per-

sonal trainer emphasized pectoral tone to keep the breasts high. Having good breasts was part of her job.

She'd only had to reveal them once in her career, during a love scene in a serious crime drama. Her male costar's bare buttocks had been in the frame as well. As makeup artists had dabbed foundation on his butt cheeks and brushed shadow into her cleavage, the two of them had attempted awkward jokes until the director had called for quiet on the set. For hours, her costar kept popping some kind of bubblegum-flavored mints that smelled grossly sweeter with each take. There had been nothing sexy about filming that scene, but the director had known what he was doing, and the final cut had looked scorching hot on the big screen.

The movie had only gotten modest box office distribution, but Travis might have seen it. Had he found it arousing? He must have. One couldn't be human and not find the finished scene arousing.

She shut the door behind herself. The interior of the barn was dim after the blinding sun. She took a moment to let her eyes adjust, leaning against the same post Travis had leaned against last night. He'd given her his time and attention, willing to talk. Only to talk.

Not willing to be seduced. Not even by a movie star.

That sizzle died. When she'd reached out to touch him, he'd pulled on a shirt and left her standing in his office. Unemployed or not, she still looked like a movie star. What had she done that had made it so easy for him to resist her?

She walked slowly down the aisle, evaluating her posture and carriage, working on it as an actor. If she saw herself on film now, what kind of character traits would she be relaying to the audience?

She hadn't been very convincing in the role of seductress last night. She didn't believe she was still a movie star, so she wasn't acting like a movie star. That had to be the problem. Deezee's infidelity had shaken her confidence. The publicity had been humiliating, so now Sophia must be giving off some kind of insecure ex-girlfriend vibe.

Guys hated that. If she could turn back time to the person she'd been before Deezee, she would have Travis eating out of the palm of her hand. He'd be grateful if she chased a water droplet over his skin with the tip of her finger, because the sexy and smart Sophia Jackson would be the one doing the chasing, not the depressed and lonely creature she'd turned into. Travis couldn't resist a movie star.

Could he?

He already had. When they'd met on the road, she'd seen the precise moment on his face when he'd first realized who she was, but he hadn't exactly fallen all over himself to get her autograph. He'd told her to get behind the wheel and drive herself off his ranch, actually.

Don't call us; we'll call you.

She paused at his office window. There was nothing in that functional space that implied he was enchanted by Hollywood or its stars. For the first time in her life, it occurred to her that being a celebrity could be a disadvantage.

She'd just have to make him want her, anyway.

Men had wanted her long before she was famous. Really, that was why she'd become famous. People of both sexes had always noticed her. *Charisma*, Grace called it. An aura. Whatever it was, it was the reason Sophia had been put in films. The public might think movie stars were noticeable because they were already famous, but that wasn't how it worked. The charisma came first. They were noticed first. Stardom came second.

Where did Travis fit in?

The refrigerator was in the medical room. She headed for it while fretting over sex appeal and stardom, wondering if she could stand rejection from a cowboy any better than from a producer, and nearly stepped on the proof that everything she worried about, all of it, was insignificant.

At her feet, curled into a little ball in front of the fridge, was the kitten.

Sophia picked him up gingerly. It was humbling to hold a complete living being in her hand. He was still alive for now, but he couldn't survive on his own. The weight of his impending mortality should have been heavy. It seemed wrong that he was little more than a fluffy feather in her palm.

Travis had said the kitten was weak to start with, and Sophia knew next to nothing about kittens. She was going to lose this battle. It was a pattern she knew too well. Losing her sister, losing her lover, losing her career, failing auditions, failing to keep her scholarship…

Failing. She hated to fail.

She studied the newborn's face. "I'm not a very good mother, either, but I'm going to try, okay?"

Then she slipped the kitten inside her shirt.

Chapter Nine

Travis was not obsessed with Sophia Jackson.

He just couldn't stop thinking about her.

He'd left the milk in the fridge this morning with no intention of returning for the rest of the week, but as the morning had turned into afternoon, he'd already started convincing himself that he should head back to his office this evening. There were too many things on his to-do list that he hadn't touched last night.

He'd touched Sophia's scars instead.

Why had she let him into her personal life like that?

I'm not a crazy recluse.

She wanted to be understood, that much was clear to him. He just didn't know how much to read into the fact that she wanted *him* to understand her.

A pickup truck pulled up to the fencing they'd built for this year's roundup. Travis recognized the pickup as belonging to one of the MacDowell brothers who was coming to work these last few days of branding and doctoring. Travis was grateful for the distraction. He left the calf pen to greet Braden.

Braden MacDowell, like his brothers, was a physician in Austin. He'd taken over the reins at the hospital his father had founded, but he valued his family's ranching legacy as well, so it wasn't unusual to see him here. At least one MacDowell was sure to lend a hand during the busy months, if not all three brothers.

Travis respected the MacDowells. They visited their mama. They knew how to rope and ride. And they'd been wise enough to hire him.

Not to get too full of himself, but it said a lot that they'd asked him to keep the River Mack thriving as a cow-calf operation. They could've just rented the land out to a corporate operation that maintained its headquarters in another state. Travis wouldn't have stayed on the River Mack in that case. He preferred to work with a family that knew how to keep their saddles oiled and their guns greased, as the saying went.

"I just got away from the office," Braden said as Travis walked up to him and shook hands. "I trust there's still plenty of fun to be had?"

"Talk to me tomorrow about how fun it feels. You leave your necktie and briefcase at home?"

The ribbing was good-natured. Braden was in shape, but there was still a big difference between bench-pressing weights in a gym and hauling around a hundred-pound calf who didn't appreciate being picked up.

"I've got aspirin in the glove box." Braden dropped the tailgate and thumped an oversized cooler. "I brought supplies."

Travis helped him carry the cooler full of sports drinks closer to the working crew and then helped himself to one.

He drank while Patch, one of the best cow dogs in Texas, greeted Braden.

They kept sports drinks in the barn fridge, too. When Sophia got the milk, she'd see them. Travis hoped she knew she was welcome to take whatever she needed. He should have told her that in the note, maybe, and damn it all to hell, he was thinking about her again. Would he go five minutes without thinking of her today?

"All right, back to work with you," Braden said to the dog, but to Travis's surprise, Braden didn't head for the work area himself. "How's Sophia Jackson treating my house?"

Travis forced himself to swallow his drink around the surprise of hearing her name spoken. She was a big secret he'd been keeping from everyone, but it made sense that Braden knew. Of course he knew; he must have signed the lease.

"The house looks the same as always. You can't tell there's anyone's living there."

"No sounds of breaking glass coming from inside? She hasn't set the couch on fire or gone rockstar and destroyed it yet?"

Travis frowned at the expectation that she might. The closest thing he'd seen to any wild behavior had been when Sophia had dropped the plastic wedges on the kitchen floor. No harm there. "I'm not one to spy on your houseguests, but there's been nothing like that."

She cries a lot. She sleeps a lot. Those insights were his. He didn't care to share them. It felt like it would be betraying Sophia. She didn't want to be stared at. She didn't want to be talked about. Fair enough.

"She's not my houseguest," Braden said, his tone tight. "She's my tenant."

Travis turned to look over the milling herd and the distant horizon, waiting.

Braden studied the horizon, too. "I was against renting the house to her, but one of the ER docs, Alex Gregory, is engaged to her sister. Alex seems to think she's salvageable. He offered to cosign the lease. If she destroys the place, he's good for it, but if my mother comes back from her year in Africa and finds her grandmother's antiques destroyed, money won't make it right."

Travis kept a sharp eye on the calm herd. There was no reason to believe they would suddenly stampede—but they could. "You got a reason for assuming she'd bust furniture?"

"You don't keep up with celebrity news," Braden said.

"I'm surprised you do." That was putting it mildly.

"Only when it affects me. Twice, Texas Rescue invited her to make an appearance to help raise awareness of their work. Twice, she blew their event. My wife and I were going to one of them. I was expecting this elegant actress. My wife was excited to meet her. Instead, this banshee ruined the ball before it even got started. I should have read the gossip earlier. She'd been trashing hotel rooms and blowing off events for months. Now she's living in my home. I don't like it."

It was incredible that MacDowell thought Sophia would destroy someone's family heirlooms, but Travis had known the MacDowells for the past six years. He'd known Sophia six days.

Travis killed the rest of his bottle in long, slow gulps. It took only twenty ounces for him to decide to trust his gut. Sophia didn't mean anyone any harm. He'd seen the physical evidence of the harm others had done to her, and he'd seen her crying her heart out when she thought she was alone. She was a woman who'd been pushed to the edge, but she wasn't going to destroy someone else's lifetime of memories. She just wouldn't.

"She's serious about hiding," Travis repeated. "She's not going to do anything to attract attention to herself. Your stuff is safe."

Braden was silent for a moment. "She's beautiful, isn't she?"

Travis turned his head slowly, very slowly, and met the man's stare. "We weren't discussing Sophia's looks. If you think my judgment is so easily clouded, we'd best come to an understanding on that."

He and Braden gauged one another for a long moment, until, inexplicably, Braden started to grin. "I trust you on horses and I trust you on cattle. I've known you to have a sixth sense about the weather. Maybe you don't find women any harder to read than that, but as a married man, I'm not going to put any money down on that bet. It puts my mind at ease a bit to hear that you don't think Miss Jackson is going to fly off the handle, but I'm still going to stop by and pick up a few breakables before I go."

Travis saw his opportunity and took it. "She won't answer the door if she doesn't know you. I'll go in with you. I've got work at my desk I can knock out while you're gathering up your breakables. If we take the truck, we can be done and back here inside two hours."

"I'm locked out of my own house, technically." Braden sounded disgusted. "Landlords can't just walk into the property once it's been rented out."

Travis paced away from the kitchen door and Braden's legalities. The zucchini was gone. Sophia had gotten up and gone out, then. He wasn't going to jump to any crazy conclusions. She wasn't dead or dying, languishing somewhere, needing his help.

Where was she?

There were no horses in the barn, or else that would have been the logical place to assume she was.

"Let's hit the barn," Braden suggested. "Maybe she'll show up while you're taking care of your paperwork."

Travis had barely slid open the barn door when he heard Sophia calling out.

"Hello? Is someone there? Can you help me?" The distress in her voice was obvious as she emerged from his office. He'd already started for her before her next words. "Travis! It's you. Thank God, it's you."

She started down the aisle toward him at a half run, clutching her heart with two hands.

They met halfway. He stopped her from crashing into him by catching her shoulders in his hands. At a glance, she didn't seem to be hurt. Her expression was panicked, but her color was normal and she seemed to be moving fine. "What's wrong?"

She peeled her hands away from her chest to show him. "It's the kitten. It's dying."

"It's the—" Her words sank in. Travis let go of her shoulders and turned away for a moment to control his reaction, a harsh mixture of relief and anger. He'd thought she was having a heart attack.

"Do you hear that?" she cried.

He turned to look, and yes, she was really crying. She dashed her cheek on her shoulder.

"His cries are just so pitiful. He's been pleading for help like that for six hours. I can't stand it. He cries until he's exhausted, and then he wakes up and cries again. I don't know what to do for him."

Her distress was real. She was just too softhearted for the hard reality that not every animal could be saved. Travis took off his hat and gestured with it toward the office. "Come on, I'll take a look. Did you say six hours?"

"I came in to get the milk from the fridge, and he was on the floor, just lying out there. I warmed him up like you did, but then I couldn't find the mother cat for the longest time. The kitten started crying while I went over every square inch of this place. It took me an hour to find her, but when I put the baby in with the others, the mother just up and left, like, 'Here, have three babies.'"

Travis pulled out his desk chair. "Have a seat."

"I've been in this chair all day. I couldn't look anything up on the internet about what to feed a kitten, because your computer is password protected."

"That it is."

She sat in the chair he offered, but she glared at him like he'd invented the concept of computer passwords just to annoy her. "You've got all these books on animals in here, but do you know what they contain? Info on how many calories are in a frigging *acre* of alfalfa to calculate how many calves it'll feed. Chart after chart on alfalfa and Bahia grass. What to feed a cow, how much to feed a cow, how much to *grow* to feed a cow. Who needs to know crap like that?"

"That would be me." Travis didn't dare smile when she was working through a mixture of tears and indignation. He let her vent.

"Do you know what those books don't contain? *What to feed a newborn kitten.* Not one word. I couldn't call you for help. You're out on a horse all day."

"I'll give you my cell phone number, but there's no reception out on the range. If you leave a message, it'll ping me if I happen to catch a signal."

Braden strolled into the office with a dish in his hand.

"Looks like you tried to give it a saucer of milk. On my mother's fine china."

Sophia jerked back in the chair, clutching the kitten to her chest.

Travis had seen that skittish reaction too many times. This time, he put his hand on her shoulder, a little weight to keep her from jumping out of her own skin.

"It's okay. This is Braden MacDowell, one of the ranch owners. He already knew you were here. Your name's already on his lease."

She sniffed and looked at Braden resentfully. "I remember you from that stupid ball. You're the CEO of the hospital."

"Guilty."

"You shouldn't sneak up like that. I thought I was alone with Travis. Usually only one person comes in at sundown."

The implication hit Travis squarely. "What if it hadn't been me tonight? You would've blown your cover. I told you it wouldn't be me tonight. You came out of that office without knowing who was here."

"Trust me, I had hours to think about that while this kitten cried his heart out. I knew whoever came in was going to get a big surprise, and then he was going to get rich. I'd have to pay him hush money to keep my secret. It's like being blackmailed, only you go ahead and get it over with and offer to pay them up front." She rested her head back on the chair and sighed. "It's only money. That's the way it goes."

Travis was stunned.

She frowned at him. "What did you expect me to do? I couldn't just let a kitten die because the paparazzi might find me."

"No, of course not." But of course, she could have done

exactly that. She could have left the kitten where a ranch hand might find it and then run away to hide in safety. But she'd stayed to comfort a struggling animal instead of leaving it to cry alone.

"Sorry I startled you," Braden said. "I'm surprised you remember me. We'd barely been introduced at the fund-raiser when you…left."

"I remember everything about that night."

With that cryptic statement, she resumed her tale of frustration, how the kitten hadn't known what to do with the milk, and how she'd tried warming it and holding the kitten's mouth near the surface. Her story was full of mistakes, but it wasn't comical; she'd tried hard to succeed at something foreign to her.

He noticed something else as well. Now that Braden was present, her manner was slightly different. She sat a little straighter and told her story in a more measured way. The contrast was clear to Travis. When she'd thought it was just the two of them, she'd been more emotional. Raw. Real.

Sophia didn't keep her guard up around him. There was a trust between them, an intimacy that she didn't extend to everyone. He wondered if she was aware of it.

"I tried leaving the three kittens together. I snuck away and stayed away for at least half an hour. I wanted to give the mother a chance to come back for them, in case she was just scared of me, you know? But when I came back, they were all crying. All of them. The mother cat didn't come back until I took this kitten away again." Her blue eyes filled with tears, and she quickly turned away from Braden. She spoke softly to Travis. "For a while there, I thought I'd doomed them all."

"You were doing your best. You were being as kind as a person could be." And if he turned his back to Braden to shut him out of their private conversation, well, there was no crime in that.

The kitten began another round of plaintive, hungry mewing.

"The road to hell is paved with good intentions," she murmured. "Listening to this kitten cry has been hell."

"I imagine it has."

She looked up at him, tired and trusting. "I'm so glad you're here."

The words stretched between them, an imaginary line connecting just the two of them for one moment. Then it snapped. Her sleepy-lidded eyes flew open as she realized what she'd said. "To help, I mean. I'm so glad you're here to help."

She was still scared, then. Still unsure of this power between them. It made her nervous enough that she put up her guard, which for a movie star meant shaking back some incredible blond hair and flipping her tired expression to one filled with a devil-may-care bravado. "Besides, you just saved me a fortune in hush money."

Braden chuckled, the expected response, but Travis saw through the act. This wasn't a one-sided attraction on his part, but she wasn't ready to admit it. Now was not the time or place to do anything with the knowledge. He was a patient man. It was enough to know that she wanted to see him as much as he wanted to see her.

She still held the kitten in two hands against her chest, so Travis gave her a boost out of the chair by placing his hand under her elbow. "Come on. Abandoned kittens need a specific kitten milk replacer. Let's see if I have any around here. If I don't, Braden will go to the feed store and get you some."

Chapter Ten

The pickup rocked over the rolling terrain, sending the headlight beams bouncing off fence posts and mesquite trees. Although Braden drove with all the speed one could manage on rough roads, they were getting back to camp far later than Travis had expected. Travis was returning with a hell of a lot more baggage than he'd expected, too, and all of it was in his head.

Maybe in his heart.

Definitely in his body.

Damn it. Every time he thought checking on Sophia would set everything to rest, he got more than he bargained for.

They'd found some powdered milk replacer in the bunkhouse kitchen. There'd been just a few scoops leftover from some other cowboy's past attempt to help out another cat, so they'd taken it back to the barn. While Braden had made the run to the feed store, Travis had taught Sophia how to mix the replacer, how to slip an eyedropper into the kitten's mouth, how to hold the kitten a little counter-intuitively while feeding it.

There'd been physical contact between the two of them, and a lot of it. Shoulders and hips had brushed as they huddled over the kitten. Hands guided hands to find just the right angle or apply just the right amount of pressure. He'd cuffed up his sleeves, and the sensation of Sophia's soft skin on his exposed wrist or forearm ignited aware-ness everywhere. By the time the kitten had been settled into a small box with a bit of an old horse blanket, that in-cidental contact had become so addicting, neither of them had moved away.

Sophia had been nearly as relieved as the kitten when it fell asleep from a full belly instead of from exhaustion. It would have been the most natural move for Travis to drop a kiss on Sophia's lips. Not one of passion, but one of camaraderie, the kind between couples who'd been to-gether through thick and thin.

He'd almost kissed her. *You did well.*

She'd almost kissed him. *Thank you.*

But in the end, Braden had returned with enough milk replacer for ten cats, and Sophia had drifted closer to the light over the barn sink in order to read the instructions on the can. They said a kitten this young was going to wake up and cry for a feeding every two hours.

Travis was used to long nights caring for young or sick animals. Braden was a doctor who thought nothing of over-night shifts, but Sophia...

It turned out that movie production schedules pushed actors to work without sleep as well. Sophia didn't flinch at the schedule.

With his head, his heart, his body, Travis felt himself falling for her too deep, too fast.

Too reckless.

The pickup truck bounced out of the rut in the dirt road, and Travis cracked his head against the side window.

He cursed at an unapologetic Braden. "Your breakables would've been safer in the house. They probably just flew out of the truck bed."

Braden kept his eyes on the road. "I didn't take anything out of the house."

"You're not worried she's going to break everything?" Travis knew the past few hours had shown Braden a different Sophia Jackson than he'd been expecting to see, but Travis wanted to hear him say it. Anyone who maligned Sophia should have to eat his words.

"I've been thinking about that."

Not good enough. Travis managed a noncommittal grunt to keep him talking.

"I did see some pretty incriminating photos, but she was never alone while she was flipping birds and screaming at those photographers."

"Paparazzi," Travis corrected him. But hell, were there photos out there of beautiful Sophia being so ugly?

"That jerk of a boyfriend of hers is behind her in every one, or sometimes in front. Looked like he was shoving her out of his way in one. After seeing the way he crashed that ball, he probably was."

It was the last thing Travis wanted to hear. Not after all that warmth, all that soft skin, all those tears for a kitten. He couldn't let go of that. He couldn't let go of the Sophia he knew. He couldn't accept that she had a boyfriend.

"You got any more details than that?"

"It was a black-tie event. Thousand-dollar donation per ticket. Red carpet to give the guests a thrill for their money. You know how it is."

"Not really." *Get to the boyfriend.*

"Everyone's all pretty and on their best behavior. Every camera in the house is pointed at Sophia. That's what she's there for, to give everyone a little taste of glamor. People pay an outrageous price to eat dinner in the same room as the celebrities."

Had Sophia once enjoyed that?

Don't stare at me. Quit talking about me.

"Next thing I know, some jackass in basketball shoes and a ball cap is jumping on the table. Walking on the silverware, kicking the centerpiece, making a lot of noise. Alex pulled Sophia behind his back. That was the first thing I noticed, Alex keeping Sophia behind himself, so I knew this jerk had come to cause trouble for her."

There was nothing Travis could do about it but listen. His hand was clenched in a fist on his knee.

"My brothers and I were ready to take him out. He was standing on my wife's salad, goddammit, but once every camera in the place was focused on him, he dropped to one knee and started apologizing to Sophia. As apologies went, it was crap. Maybe a sentence. Alex was pissed. Her sister was stunned."

"And Sophia?"

Braden hesitated for only a moment. "She ditched her commitment to Texas Rescue and left with him. She looked pretty happy about it, so no one tried to stop her."

Travis couldn't speak. A knife in the chest would do that to a man. The thought of Sophia choosing to be with an ass who'd destroy the happiness of everyone around him was like a knife in the chest.

"But you see how that turned out. She's here alone. After getting to know her a little bit today, it's obvious the two of them aren't as alike as the photos make it look. My guess is that she's hiding from him as much as the rest of the world."

They hit another pothole, which gave Travis the perfect excuse to curse again. "I should have been told. Alex said she was hiding from cameras."

"If the boyfriend turns up again, things will break. More than my grandma's antiques. That kind of hyped-up guy dances too close to the line."

"Got a name?"

"DJ something. Something inane."

"*Paparazzi* is an inane word, too. I'll let the men know we're keeping everyone off the River Mack ranch whose name we don't already know."

"We would've been here sooner, but the gate at the main road was closed," Grace said.

Sophia nodded at her sister as if that made sense.

"All the gates were closed this time. I had to get out three times to open them. I saw a guy on a horse at the last one, the foreman we met last time. We waved at each other and he rode away."

Grace was talking to her through the open window of Alex's pickup. She'd started talking the moment they'd pulled up, not waiting for Alex to shut off the engine.

"We didn't see any cows, though. Not this time." Grace hopped out of the truck and gave the door a pat after closing it. "But we brought the truck, just in case. We can drive off the road if we have to go around a cow again."

Sophia nodded some more, so full of emotion at seeing her sister that she wasn't really listening to what she was saying. It was just so good to see her face. She'd missed her so much.

Sophia hesitated at the edge of the flagstone. Her sister had been so adamant that Sophia should only call for an emergency, and Grace hadn't called her once, not one single time in the past week to ask how she was doing.

Was this how their relationship was supposed to be now? Polite and friendly visits once a week?

Sophia wanted to run to her sister and give her a bear hug. Instead, she twisted her fingers together as she kept nodding and smiling.

Alex got out of his side of the truck and spoke to Grace. "Sophia looks like she missed you almost as much as you missed her. Is one of you going to hug the other, or what?"

"You missed me?" Sophia asked, but Grace couldn't answer because she'd already run up to the patio and thrown her arms around her.

"I've been so worried about you," Grace said, hugging her hard.

Sophia took a split second to think before blurting out something snarky. *Yeah, I could tell by the way you totally ignored me.*

She pulled back from the hug just far enough to smooth Grace's dark gold hair into place, a gesture that went back to their tween years, when they'd first started playing with curling irons and hair spray. "When you're worried about me, you could give me a call. I'd love to hear from you."

"But—but I have called you. A lot."

"The phone hasn't rung once. I just assumed you were busy with your new job and with…" She gestured toward Alex, who was standing beside the truck. Then Sophia realized she'd made it sound like Grace was busy getting busy with Alex, which wasn't a great thing to think about her sister, even if it was probably true.

Sophia almost blushed. "I mean, with your wedding planning. I thought you were busy planning your wedding." *Without me.*

"I called, but you never picked up, so I figured you didn't want to talk. Or maybe I was calling you too late at night."

"I'm up all night long. I'm taking care of a kitten. It needs fed every two hours. It's pretty exhausting, but I volunteered for it, so…"

"You did?" Grace's amazement was genuine. She wasn't an actor.

Sophia was. She pretended not to be hurt that her sister was amazed she would volunteer to sacrifice her sleep for something besides herself. For years, Sophia had cared for Grace, but the freshest memory was obviously of Sophia blowing off everyone and everything for wild parties.

"It's just for a few days," Sophia said, a brilliant performance of perfect cheerfulness. She didn't sound offended at all, not hurt one bit. "The vet is scheduled to come out then, and Travis is sure he'll know a mother cat somewhere that just had a litter and can take another kitten. This one is so young, its eyes aren't even open yet, so it really needs a cat mother, not me."

"Wow. I'm so impressed. I had no idea you knew so much about cats." Grace gave her arm an extra squeeze. "But I'm not surprised. You've always been able to do anything you set your mind to."

Sophia didn't know what to say to that. It sounded like her sister still admired her. Considering the front-row seat she'd had to Sophia's self-destructing spiral, that was something of a miracle.

Sophia didn't want to start bawling and ruin a perfectly lovely conversation. She blinked away the threatening tears and focused on the barn. "I got a crash course on cats from Travis. The foreman you waved at."

"He promised me he'd check on you. He has, hasn't he?"

Sophia nodded some more and wished he was here to check on her now. It would be nice for him to see that her sister didn't hate her. He'd only seen them together that first day, snapping at each other over a cow on the road.

Well, Sophia had been doing most of the snapping. Travis must think Sophia was the world's worst sister.

Alex was standing back, giving them some personal space. He really was a pretty decent guy. Handsome, too, in a doctor-like, Clark Kent kind of way.

He turned toward the barn. "Speaking of Travis, is he around? Where is everyone?"

"It's May." Sophia said it the way Travis would.

"What does that mean?"

She shrugged. "I have no earthly idea, but it's the answer to everything around here. Apparently, cowboys are scarce on a ranch in May."

"Or else they're out working on the range," Alex said. "I think its calving season. We get a few injuries in the ER every year at this time from roundups."

"I'm dying to see this kitten." Grace sounded as carefree as Sophia could remember her sounding since the day their parents had died. Alex must be more than just a decent guy, because Sophia knew she hadn't taken any burdens from Grace's shoulders, not lately. Alex must have lightened that load.

He picked up some grocery bags from the bed of the pickup. "Let's get these inside and check the ringer on that phone. I don't want you two to miss any more calls."

Sophia reached for one of the bags, but Alex shook his head. "It's okay. I've got it."

"Thank you." She meant for more than the groceries. Could he tell?

He winked at her, his eyes blue like her own. Like a brother might have had, if she'd ever had a brother. "She's happier when you're part of her life. I want Grace to be happy, you know."

"I know."

"Let's go fix that dinosaur of a phone."

Grace opened her cab door and reached for a basket. "I almost forgot. Our neighbor grows vegetables, and you wouldn't believe how much zucchini he had. I brought you some. You don't see this in LA. Isn't it great?"

"Oh, zucchini. Yes. Great."

If she could point at a mattress and smile for fifty bucks, she could certainly beam at a basket of zucchini that her sister thought would make her happy. Apparently, the gift of love in Texas during the month of May was zucchini, whether it was from a mother to a ranch hand, from Travis to her, from Grace to—

From Travis to her?

It would be crazy to think he loved her, just because he'd left her a batch of zucchini.

With a note that said he didn't want her to get any more scars.

As she held the door open for her family with one hand and balanced an overflowing basket of zucchini with the other, she couldn't help but look at the empty barn one more time.

A gift of love? She was being too dramatic again—but something felt different now. The zucchini had marked some kind of turning point. Before, Travis would have expected her to do something simple yet impossible: *if you need milk replacer, go to the feed store.* Instead, he'd sent Braden to get it.

It was almost June. May had been full of loneliness and failure and zucchini. But June might be different. A new month. A new vegetable? A new chance to spend time with Travis.

She could hardly wait for June.

Chapter Eleven

Tomatoes.

June was only half over, but if Sophia saw another to-mato, she might scream. Or barf.

It turned out the potted plants lining one side of the flagstone patio were Mrs. MacDowell's absurdly fertile tomatoes. There were so many, they ripened and fell off the vines, bounced out of their pots and split open on the patio, where they proceeded to cook on the hot stone in the June sun. Every deep yoga breath Sophia took brought in shimmering molecules of hot energy that smelled vaguely like lasagna.

The smell made her stomach turn.

She'd had such high hopes for June. She'd imagined basking in the sun, breathing deeply, feeling the health and strength of every muscle in her body as she went through all the yoga routines she could remember. Travis wouldn't be able to resist spying on her. Drooling over her silver-screen-worthy body, he would spend lots of time with her, and she wouldn't be lonely in the least.

Instead, she was the one who drooled over Travis, spying on him from the kitchen window. June had brought him back from wherever he'd been disappearing to, but although he spent part of every day in the barn, he was never alone. The ranch must be too big for just one person, because there were always other cowboys around. Usually, they left in pairs on horseback, off to do whatever the heck kept ranchers busy in the month of June.

Her eye was always drawn to Travis. She knew the way he sat a horse now, the set of his shoulders, the way a coil of rope always rested on the back of his saddle when he rode away, the way the rope was looped on the saddle horn and resting on top of his right thigh when he returned.

Not today. She heard what sounded like a motorcycle.

She ran to the window in time to catch Travis roaring away on an ATV. He was in jeans and a plaid shirt, as usual, but he wore no hat to keep the wind out of his hair. He drove the four-wheeler the way he galloped a horse, almost standing up, leaning over the handlebars into the wind. He looked so strong and young and free, something in her yearned to be with him.

"Wait for me." But saying the words out loud didn't make them seem any less pitiful than when they echoed in her head.

She put her hand on the glass, well and truly isolated. If only a director would yell *cut*. If only the prop team would help her out of a mock space capsule. If only Grace were waiting to bring her out of her self-induced sorrow, to remind her that it was only a movie, and the real Sophia could have a bowl of ice cream and paint her fingernails and never, ever have to wonder if she'd make it back to Earth.

Normalcy. It had always been such a relief to return to the normal world after experiencing a character's intense emotions. Now her real life was the unrealistic one, and her old, normal life was the fantasy.

As Travis rode away, Sophia kept her greedy eyes on him and indulged her favorite fantasy, the one where she wasn't famous yet and had no reason to hide. If she and Travis had met when she was nineteen instead of twenty-nine, she would have flirted outrageously with him. As a young cowboy, he wouldn't have been able to resist letting her hitch a ride to the barn on the running board of his ATV. She would've been the best part of his day, his pretty blond girlfriend holding on to him so she wouldn't fall off while he drove. He would've saved up his money to take her to the movies.

"Cut," she whispered to herself.

In real life, she was the one in the movies, a Hollywood star who couldn't hide forever. There was no stopping the fame now. She couldn't make people forget her face.

"No, really. Cut, before you drive yourself crazy."

She pushed hard with her hand, forcing herself away from the window. She was dressed for a morning yoga workout, but she hadn't kept track of where the ranch hands were. There were five different guys who showed up at least a few days each week. Who had shown up for work with Travis today? Was anyone still in the barn?

She couldn't go out to the patio if someone else might still be around. A few minutes of inattention while she'd wallowed in self-pity had cost her. Now she was stuck inside for the day. She'd already watched all of Mrs. Mac-Dowell's DVDs and had browsed through some of her bookshelves. There were a lot of Hardy Boy volumes. The cover of a pregnancy handbook was so laughably 80s, Sophia had quickly shoved it back onto the shelf. There were a lot of cookbooks. She could give the air conditioner a workout by heating up the kitchen as she tried every single tomato recipe.

The sound of the ATV's engine surprised her. She glued her nose right back to the window. Travis was driving back at a more sedate pace, hauling a trailer full of square hay bales behind the four-wheeler, but there was nothing sedate about his appearance, nor its effect on her. His shirt was unbuttoned all the way, flaring out behind him like a plaid cape.

Sophia bet it was no big deal for him. The day was hot, the drive was easy, why not unbutton his shirt and let the air cool his chest? But for her, it was a very big deal. The sexual turn-on was instant, a primitive response to the visual stimulation of a man's strong body. Six-pack abs in low-slung jeans were a big *yes* in her mind. Weeks ago, when Travis had come into the barn dripping wet, she'd felt that same instant, heavy wanting.

It was heavier now, because now she knew Travis, the man with the hands that handled kittens and controlled horses. The man with the voice that never tried to shout her down. The man who'd listened when she poured her heart out, then gifted her with those three little words she hadn't known she'd needed to hear: *I get it.*

And yeah, the man with six-pack abs. Hot damn, he looked good. Really good.

He was looking right at her.

She jerked away and dropped the curtain, as if he'd pointed a telephoto zoom lens at her.

That was a mistake. Now he was going to think she was embarrassed, as if he'd caught her spying on him.

He had.

Okay, so she'd been spying on him, but she should have played it cool, like she'd just happened to be looking out the window, checking the weather. It was probably too little, too late, but she did that now, using the back of her hand to lift the curtain oh-so-casually. *Hot and sunny, not a cloud in the sky. Same as always.*

Travis turned the ATV and started driving it straight toward the house.

Ohmigod, ohmigod, ohmigod. He was coming to say hello. She tried to fix her hair with her fingers. She wasn't wearing makeup, which wasn't ideal, but on the plus side, she was in her yoga clothes. He wouldn't look at her face if she exposed enough skin. She started to take off the loose green cover-up she'd thrown on over her black bra top. But wait—he'd already seen her in the window in the green. She couldn't open the door in a black sports bra now. Too obvious.

The engine went silent. Sophia peeked out the window and saw six feet of rugged male beauty striding toward her, buttoning his shirt as he came. He started high on his chest, bringing the shirt together with a single button. Then the next one lower. One button after the other, he narrowed the amount of exposed flesh until only one triangle of tanned skin flashed above his belt buckle, and then that was gone, too.

She steadied herself with a hand on the doorknob. If he took those clothes off with as much swagger as he put them on...

The knock on the door was firm. Suddenly, so was her resolve. She wasn't a giddy nineteen-year-old. She was twenty-nine, and she guessed Travis was around thirty. They were consenting adults, and after the sight she'd just witnessed, she couldn't think of a single reason why she shouldn't smile when she opened the door.

Her isolation had taken a turn for the better.

Travis was here. There was nowhere else she'd rather be.

* * *

"Howdy, stranger. Long time, no see."

Sophia Jackson purred the words as she opened the door.

Travis raised an eyebrow.

She draped herself against the door jamb as if she had all the time in the world. Her thin green top draped itself over her curves. She watched the effect that had on him with a knowing look in her eyes.

Yeah, she knew how good she looked. Travis put his hand on the door jamb above her head. He had no idea why the sex goddess was back, but it sure made ten in the morning on a Tuesday a lot more interesting.

"It's about time you came." She said it so suggestively, Travis knew she was teasing. Her eyes were crinkling in the corners with the smile she was holding back. "You told Grace and Alex you'd check on me. Are you here to hold up your part of the bargain?"

Her gaze roamed over him from head to toe, lingering somewhere around the vicinity of his belt before returning to his face. She'd done so before, after he'd hosed off at the barn. That time, she'd been serious and a little bit scared. This time, she was having fun, evaluating him as nothing more than a hunk of meat. Treating him as nothing more than eye candy.

He liked it.

But he didn't trust it. He waited for that moment of hesitation, her fear of this attraction they shared.

He didn't see it, so he played along, answering her question as seriously as she'd asked it. "A man's got to work sometimes. It's only been forty-eight hours since I talked to you."

She pouted prettily, picture-perfect. "But Grace and Alex were here for their little weekly visit at the same time. It doesn't count as checking on me when they're already checking on me."

"I'll keep that in mind." He shifted so that he leaned his forearm instead of his hand on the frame of the door. It brought him into her personal space. As they talked about nothing, he watched her the same way he'd watch a yearling when he approached her with bridle in hand for the first time.

Sophia didn't flinch from his nearness. "If you didn't come to check me out, then I have to warn you that this house is no longer accepting zucchini donations."

"I'm glad to hear it, because there aren't any left. Someone snuck into the barn and conspired with my horses to dispose of the rest."

She laughed and stood up straight, done with the exaggerated come-hither routine. She was still a sex goddess, whether she tried to be or not.

He stayed lounging against her door frame. "Samson incriminated you. I found zucchini in his stall. I'm surprised he ate any of it. Most horses aren't particularly fond of it, or else people around here would probably grow even more of it than they do now."

"I guess it all depends who's doing the feeding. Maybe some hands have just the right touch."

He didn't know why she was so lighthearted today, but she was irresistible in this mood.

It was a dangerous word, *irresistible*. He could imagine a future with an irresistible woman, but not with a celebrity. Sophia wouldn't be staying in his life, which was one reason he'd been staying away. He needed to enjoy this conversation for what it was and not think about what it might have led to in different circumstances.

"I'll see if Samson likes tomatoes tonight," she said.

"They're going rotten because I can't cook them fast enough."

He got a little serious. "Don't do that. Tomato plants aren't good for horses."

She got a little serious, too. "Okay, I won't. I guess I would've figured it out when they spit them back out at me."

"They might have eaten them. Horses don't always have the sense to stay away from something that might hurt them."

And neither, he realized, did he.

"I didn't know," she said.

"Now you do."

"Déjà vu. Now I know fridges have casters and horses can't eat tomatoes."

He didn't have anything to say to that. If they were a couple, he would've dropped a sweet kiss on her lips and gone back to work. He would've anticipated having her alone tonight, a leisurely feast. Or hard and intense. Or emotional and gentle—any way they wanted it.

She bit the lip he was lusting after, but she looked concerned, not carnal. "So, if you didn't come under orders to check on me, why are you here? I hope the two kittens are okay. I looked when I went to the barn last night, but I couldn't find them at all."

Kittens. Right. He forced his thoughts to change gear.

"The mother moves them every day. She's a skittish one, but the two kittens are doing fine."

Sophia wrinkled her nose, instantly repulsed. "She's a terrible mother. I lost a lot of sleep because of her. I'm glad your vet found a new mother for the one she abandoned."

It was interesting, the way she hadn't forgiven that poor cat for isolating one of her kittens. "In my business, any time offspring are thriving without my help, then the mother's all right. Some cats make one nest and stick to it for a month, some move their kittens around twice a day. The bottom line is that there are two kittens in that barn I don't have to worry about, so she's good enough in my book. Don't be so hard on her."

Sophia put a bright smile on her face, a fake one, putting her guard up. "So, are there any other cheerful topics you'd like to discuss?"

A cat seemed a strange reason to put up walls. Travis stopped lounging against her door. He'd gotten entirely too comfortable when he had work to do. "I wanted to let you know we're burning off some cedar today. If you look off your front porch and see smoke, you don't have to come check it out."

Now she was the one to raise an eyebrow. "You thought I'd come see what's on fire?"

"You should. It's what you do on a ranch. You look out for each other, remember? You go see why someone's laying on their car horn. If something's burning, you'd better know what it is."

"I'm hiding. I couldn't check it out even if I wanted to, *remember*?"

The hiding was of her own choosing, as far as he could tell. She could decide not give a damn about the paparazzi knowing where she was, and she could decide not to care if they did take her picture. Travis had asked Alex and Grace about the ex during their last visit, and they'd assured him that the DJ was too busy partying in LA to give Sophia a second thought.

Yet Travis had seen Sophia's scars, so he didn't feel free to criticize her. Maybe he'd choose to become a hermit, too, if he walked a mile in her shoes.

He simply nodded to let her know he remembered that she had her reasons. "Now you know that if you see smoke today, it's intentional, for what it's worth. I've got to get back to work."

"Hey, Travis?" she called after him. "Are all your cowboys going to be at the fire? If it's safe for me to go outside, I'd like to go see the horses."

"Even if they can't help you get rid of your tomatoes?"

"I need someone to talk to."

He wished it was a joke.

"Yes, you're safe."

Chapter Twelve

The horses were beautiful.

Sophia had only talked to them when they'd been standing patiently in their stalls at the end of the day. Of course, she'd seen them under saddle, working, but she hadn't seen them like this before.

She only came to the barn after sundown. She hadn't realized the horses spent their day in the pasture or the paddock or whatever this huge, fenced-in field was called. It ran from the barn at one end all the way to the stables at the other, a stretch of maybe a quarter mile. The horses were spread out the entire distance, swishing their tails and nibbling at grass. They looked happy and content, so much so that they paid her no attention as she stood on a fence rail in her sneakers and yoga clothes.

That was okay; she had Grace to talk to.

"This is so pretty. I'm glad I came out here on my day off."

Sophia was glad, too. The visit was a total surprise,

which made it all the more special. Alex wasn't here, and Grace wasn't dutifully delivering groceries. This was just about them, two sisters who'd rarely been apart before this year.

Sophia jumped down from the fence and bent to scratch a black and gray dog behind the ears. When roundup had ended and all the horses and cowboys had come in, this dog had come, too, apparently part of the whole gang. Her name was Patch. Travis called her a cow dog, but she seemed keen to be with the horses.

"I brought you some of my neighbor's tomatoes," Grace said. "Don't let me forget to take them out of the trunk before I go. I probably shouldn't have left them in there. The whole car will smell like tomatoes in this heat."

The mere thought of the smell of tomatoes made Sophia want to gag.

Grace seemed extra talkative today, raving about her new job at the hospital where Alex worked. She was writing grant proposals and doing something with research studies, using all the organization skills she'd perfected as a personal assistant to a celebrity.

Sophia smiled and listened, but inside, she was hurting. Grace apparently had forgotten that her old job had been to work for Sophia. When she raved about how cool and great her new boss was, did she not realize that implied her old boss had been not so cool and not so great?

Sophia watched the horses and listened to how much better Grace's life was without her. She'd almost rather talk to the horses. She'd never done them wrong. They didn't care if she was famous or a loser or a famous loser.

"Do you know what I need?" Sophia asked.

Grace went quiet in the middle of her sentence. "What do you mean?"

"I need boots. Western ones, so I can learn how to ride.

Get me four or five pair and bring them out next Sunday. I'll pick one. I need jeans, too. I've got those shredded Miami ones, but I need regular jeans, like Mom used to buy us. Something less than a thousand dollars. I'm not making any money right now."

"Sophie."

That was all Grace had to say. The warning note said the rest.

Sophia shut up, but Grace gave her the lecture, anyway. "I'm your sister, not your personal assistant. I'm not writing this down in a little notebook anymore, so you can stop dictating to me."

Grace seemed to know what kinds of thing sisters should do compared to what kinds of things personal assistants should do. Sophia didn't see this clear-cut distinction. Grace brought her groceries, for example, but when Sophia had handed her a pile of dirty laundry that first week, Grace had grown quite cool and informed Sophia that the house had a washer and dryer.

"I need a personal assistant. You promised to find me a replacement when you left me for Alex." Sophia didn't care that she sounded petulant. Sisters got petulant.

"I didn't leave you for Alex. I fell in love with Alex, and I still love you, too. I always will. Millions of people love their spouses and their siblings, both. I'm one of them."

She sounded so calm, so infuriatingly right. It reminded Sophia of the way Travis had talked to her, until she'd showed him her scars. "How do you suggest I do my own shopping for boots? You know I can't walk into a store. I could shop online, if I had any internet access. You're going to have to get me a laptop or a smartphone. Then I could be independent."

Grace bit her lower lip, a habit that Sophia knew she still did as well. She knew, because cameras caught everything.

"I don't think having internet access would be a good idea," Grace said.

"Why not?"

Grace couldn't quite look her in the eye. "Hackers will use it to find you."

"That's not the whole story, is it? What's on the internet that you don't want me to see?"

"It's just…things haven't really died down the way we'd hoped. Not yet. But they will. Um…when do you want to tell Deezee you're pregnant? Alex and I want to be—"

"I'm not pregnant." There. Those words felt much better out loud than rattling around in her head.

"What?" Grace's arm was suddenly around her shoulder. Her voice was all sympathy, shopping and laundry and every other offense forgotten. "Oh, Sophie. When did you miscarry? Why didn't you tell me?"

"I didn't. I was never pregnant in the first place. The tests can be wrong, you know. It says so in the instructions."

"So you got your period this month?"

That startled Sophia. She hadn't been paying attention, really, but she quickly counted the weeks up in her head. They couldn't be right.

She shrugged. "I don't feel pregnant. Look at me. Does this look like a pregnant woman's body?"

Grace looked at her, but not at her stomach. She smoothed Sophia's hair over her shoulder with an almost painful gentleness. The expression on Grace's face was unbearable. Concern, compassion, pity—just horrible.

Sophia turned back to the pasture and shaded her eyes with her hand. "Where's Samson? Do you see him? He's the big bay with black points." She forced a laugh. "Aren't you impressed with my cowgirl talk? That's just a horsey way to say brown with black trim. Travis left the ATV here. I bet he took Samson out for the day. Anyhow, Samson just loves Jean Paul's shampoo. When I get back to LA, I'm going to ship a gallon of it to the ranch."

"Sophia—"

"Just so he has it to remember me by."

"Sophia, you're pregnant."

She whirled to face her sister. "I am not. I wish I'd never done that test in the first place. It's just making everyone worry over nothing."

"You've missed two periods and had a positive pregnancy test."

Sophia kept her chin high. The fence rail was solid under her hands. She wasn't going to crack. She wasn't going to fall apart.

"I'm not, but it wouldn't matter if I was."

"It matters to me," Grace said.

"I had to get out of the spotlight for a little while, anyway, right? If I am pregnant, which I'm not, then I already told you the plan. I'll just have the baby and give it up for adoption."

"Why would you do that?"

"Why wouldn't I? Some couple is out there just dying to have a baby. I'd be a surrogate mother. That's a really noble thing to do, you know."

"But you're not a surrogate mother. This is actually your baby."

"I don't want to talk about it." She started walking toward the barn, done with the whole conversation, angry at her sister for bringing it up.

Patch stayed with the horses, but Grace dogged her heels. "Well, I do want to talk about it. It's the whole reason I came out here today."

Sophia nearly tripped on those words. She'd been suckered into thinking that Grace had sought her out because she wanted to be her sister and her friend, but it was just a betrayal. She didn't want Sophia's company. It had all been a trap to force Sophia to talk about something she didn't even want to think about.

Sophia broke into a run, sneakers pounding relentlessly into the ground until she reached the barn. Until she reached the office. Until she threw herself into Travis's chair.

"Sophie! Where are you?" Grace stopped in the office doorway, breathless. "Don't do this."

"Do what? Not talk about something I don't want to talk about? If I'm pregnant, it has no bearing on you."

"Yes, it does. I'm trying to plan a wedding. My wedding. And I came here today because I wanted to ask you to be my maid of honor."

Sophia closed her eyes. She'd hated herself plenty of times before, but this one was the worst.

"But we need to talk about your pregnancy." Grace had tears in her voice. "I tried to be flexible. I chose a bunch of different locations, but the soonest I could book any of them was September. You'll be showing in September."

"And you don't want a pregnant cow in your wedding." Sophia murmured the words more to herself than to Grace.

"No. That isn't it at all. If you were keeping your baby, then it wouldn't matter at all that you were showing. You'd have nothing to hide."

Grace took a deep breath, and Sophia knew she was about to hear something she didn't want to hear.

"But if you want to keep everything a secret, then I have to respect that. I tried guesstimating when you were due and how long it would take for your body to recover so that people wouldn't suspect you'd ever had a baby. If you're due in January, I think you probably wouldn't be comfortable trying to pull it off until April, even with the way you work out. I don't want to wait until next April to marry Alex. I want my big sister in my wedding, but it's not just about having a white gown and a party and some photos. It's about actually being married to Alex. I want to make him those promises now. I want to start our lives together now, not next year."

Sophia knew she was supposed to say something, but she had nothing to contribute. Grace had thought everything through while Sophia had refused to think of it at all.

"If you don't want to be seen, I thought about asking someone else to stand up with me. I've made some friends, and…well, I really like Kendry MacDowell. She's married to Alex's department chair, Jamie MacDowell. When Alex was putting out feelers about finding a place off the beaten path, Jamie mentioned his mother's house was vacant, so that's how we found this place for you. His baby picture is on the wall in your house, isn't that funny? Anyway, his wife Kendry is my age, and—"

"I understand." Sophia didn't want to hear it. Neither she nor Grace had been able to make friends outside their two-sister world, not when deli clerks were bribed to expose them. She knew she should be happy for Grace, but she didn't want to hear how Kendry was going to hold Grace's bouquet while Alex put a gold band on Grace's finger and started a new life with her.

Her little Grace had lost the best mother. She'd gotten a skittish big sister as a poor substitute. But Grace wasn't letting anything get in her way now. She was doing so much better out of the nest on her own than she ever had when Sophia had dragged her around the world in pursuit of Hollywood dreams.

"I'm so sorry," Sophia said. She was. About everything.

"Don't be sorry. The wedding will be great. We're thinking about a ceremony earlier in the day. We found the cutest bridesmaid dresses, this lemon yellow that's short and swingy. It would be great for a daytime wedding. Kendry's expecting, too. She's further along than you are, so we were excited to find a dress that will work. Even though it's not a maternity dress, it will look cute on her."

Stop. Please, stop.

Sophia couldn't act her way out of this. *Kendry's expecting*, her sister said, like it was a good thing, something to look forward to. If it turned out that Sophia was really pregnant, there would be no excitement, only plans for damage control.

"It would look really cute on you, too. It's only June. You might change your mind by September. You could be in the wedding, too."

Sophia could only shake her head, a vehement denial, as her tears began falling.

She looked around the office, but there wasn't a tissue box in this male space. She already knew there were textbooks on crops and cows, a computer she couldn't access. There was a baseball on the shelf above the neat stack of T-shirts.

Sophia grabbed Travis's T-shirt and mopped up her face.

"Oh, don't cry, Sophie." Grace's voice was husky with her own tears, a sound Sophia remembered from those awful nights when they'd grieved together. "I just wanted… I wanted to talk to you in person. I've tried to ask you about it before, but you wouldn't…well, at some point, I just had to make the call, so we put the deposit down on this rooftop venue for September."

Sophia stood up, clutching Travis's shirt close in case she couldn't pull off the greatest acting job in her life. "September sounds like a good time of year for something outdoors on a rooftop. It won't be as hot as it is now."

Grace looked so concerned. Sophia was being as unselfish as she could. The least Grace could do was let herself be fooled by the act.

"This is just one day out of our whole lives," Grace said. "It doesn't change anything between us. We're sisters."

"Always." But Sophia felt a little frantic. She wanted to get out of the barn and go somewhere else. Be someone else.

Travis had a digital clock on the wall, the kind that gave barometric pressure and humidity and a lot of other stuff that wouldn't matter to Sophia once she gave up and went back to bed. "Look at the time. I have to go back to the house before anyone comes in from the range. Travis is the only one who knows I'm here. There are other guys working today, and one of them might come in any second."

It was a lie. Travis had told her she'd be safe, but she didn't feel safe. She needed to hide and lick her wounds.

Grace followed her out of the barn. "I've got a little bit of time before I have to go. I'm meeting Kendry at this florist that did her brother-in-law's wedding. Braden's. Do you remember Lana and Braden? They were at your table at the Texas Rescue ball...oh, never mind. Sorry."

"I met them. For about five seconds."

Before Deezee showed up and I made the dumbest decision of my life.

Grace did her best to keep talking as if that hadn't been an awkward reminder of a terrible event.

Sophia let Grace's voice wash over her as they walked side by side in the sunshine. The calm weather made a mockery of Sophia's inner turmoil. If she could just turn back time to the person she'd been before she met Deezee...

She'd thought the same thing after she'd tried to touch Travis's wet body and he'd turned her down cold. She'd been certain the pre-Deezee version of herself would've been more desirable. Yet this morning she'd flirted with Travis, and he'd dropped everything he was doing to stand a little too close to her under that kitchen door awning. He seemed to like the current version after all.

Grace had changed topics from her life to Sophia's. "I don't know how to keep you hidden at ob-gyn appointments, but there are midwives associated with the hospital who make house calls. That might work. They have patient confidentiality rules in place, but I'll look into a more comprehensive confidentiality contract, the kind we had for the housekeepers and staff back in LA."

Before meeting Deezee, Sophia had entrusted her day-to-day routine to her personal assistant, but she'd made all the big decisions herself. She'd set her long-term goals and planned out every strategic move to get there. Her reputation as a smart and savvy actor had been earned. Now, Grace was deciding Sophia's medical care for her.

"I'm worried about the press, though," Grace said. "If they wanted to know what you ate so badly, I can't imagine what lengths they'll go to for baby gossip."

Before Deezee, it had never been her assistant's job to decide what to do next. Sophia had never put that burden on her sister's shoulders.

"Hey, Gracie?"

They stopped by her sister's car.

"You've got enough on your plate without worrying about doctors and confidentiality and all the rest. I'm going to look into it."

"Are you sure? I was going to try making some anonymous calls to a few adoption agencies to see what's involved—"

"Stop, sweetie." Sophia took a deep breath. "You've been an absolute rock for me, but I've got this, okay? I can make the calls, if and when I need to. You, meanwhile, are the bride, and you've got an appointment in town with a florist and some friends. Go."

"Are you sure?"

Sophia nodded. This didn't feel like acting. This felt like being herself. Not her old self, not her new self, just herself.

She used the T-shirt to gesture toward Grace's car as she smiled at her beautiful baby sister. "Go be the bride. Order your flowers. No one will look at them when they can look at a bride like you, but get the prettiest ones you can, anyway."

"Oh, Sophie." But Grace's voice wasn't sad. She was excited. "Thanks for being so understanding. I can't tell you how nervous I was about this. You're the best."

The T-shirt in Sophia's fist couldn't crack. She wouldn't crack, either.

"Oh, I almost forgot." Grace popped her trunk with a press of the button on her key fob. "Look, a whole basket of tomatoes for you."

Chapter Thirteen

We got a visitor.

The text message hit his phone when Travis walked away
from the burning pile of cedar saplings. Cell phones were
unreliable like that out here. One part of an empty field
could get a cell signal and another part couldn't.

The text was from Clay, who was working at the pond
near the edge of the property that bordered the road to
Austin. The time stamp indicated the text was two hours
old, just now reaching his phone.

His cell phone pinged again, receiving another text.

Same car as Sunday.

Grace or Alex had come to see Sophia, then.

Travis put the cell phone back in his pocket. He felt like
more of a forester than a rancher today, since he'd been

swinging an ax instead of throwing a lasso. It had to be done, though. The cedar could destroy a pasture in a matter of years, multiplying and spreading roots that would hog all the water and kill the grass his cattle needed for forage.

Another ping sounded, rapidly followed by more, all the texts that had been lined up, waiting for a satellite to find his phone.

Got another visitor.

The time was ten minutes ago. The text had been sent to all the men working the River Mack today.

Blue 4-door sedan? Anyone know it?

No.

No.

When Travis's voice mail played its alert sound, he was already halfway to the shade tree where he'd left Samson.

He listened to Clay's message as he walked. "We got a visitor, boss. I'm too far away to get a good look, but I don't know the car. It doesn't look like it belongs here. I'm knee-deep at the pond. Might be faster if you could meet 'em at the next gate."

There were three sets of gates on the road that led to the house. The main gate was the one Clay had seen. The second set of gates were about a mile and a half farther into the ranch itself, and the third set of gates were a mile closer to the house from there.

This year's new ranch hand, always called the greenhorn, was standing with a shovel near the fire, his phone in his hand. Clearly, he'd just gotten the texts, too, and was reading.

"You want me to come with you?" he called to Travis, with all the excitement of a first-year cowboy in his voice.

"You can't leave a fire unattended," Travis reminded him as he untied Samson's reins.

"I'm gonna miss all the fun."

"Greenhorns aren't supposed to have fun."

He swung himself into the saddle. His horse's idea of fun was to be given his head so he could run, so Travis pointed Samson toward the ranch road and let him go with a sharply spoken *gid-yap*. They covered the mile or so to the second set of gates in a handful of minutes. The blue car had gone through the gate, but it was still there, waiting for its passenger to close the gate and get back in.

Travis reined in Samson, then walked him to the middle of the road and stopped a little distance away from the car. He didn't recognize it. More than that, he didn't like the look of the man that was closing the gate—or rather, he didn't like the camera that the man held in one hand. It had a two-foot-long lens that looked like it was compensating for some shortcomings in some other department. That, or the man was a professional photographer.

"What's your business here, gentlemen?"

The cameraman looked absolutely dumbfounded to see a cowboy on a horse in the middle of the road. City folk. What did they expect to see on a ranch?

The driver stuck his head out the window. "You're in the way. Move."

Travis didn't bother answering that.

The driver threw up a hand. "What do you want?"

"I just asked you that."

"We're going to see a friend of ours."

That lie didn't really deserve an answer, but Travis supposed he needed to spell things out for them. "You can turn your car around and head back the way you came."

"We're not leaving," the cameraman said. "We're not doing anything wrong."

"That's not for you to decide. You're on private property."

"What's your name?" the cameraman demanded, as if he had the right to know.

That definitely didn't deserve an answer.

The cameraman lifted the huge lens and took a few photos of Travis. "We'll identify you."

It would be humorous if they showed the photos to the local sheriff to file a complaint against him. Travis knew the sheriff and most of the deputies, of course, but it was more than that. This was Texas cattle country. The rules had been in place here for well more than a century. If a cattleman didn't want you on his property, then you got off his property. The sheriff would laugh these men out of his office for complaining about a foreman doing his job.

The driver pulled his head back into his car. Stuck it out the window again. "C'mon, Peter. Get in the car."

Once the cameraman was in, the driver revved the engine. He inched the vehicle forward, then revved the engine some more.

Pushy little bastards.

So these were paparazzi. Had to be. Travis imagined it would be a nuisance to have them following him and taking pictures while he walked down a public street. Coming onto someone else's land and sticking a camera in their face took nuisance to a different level. Trespassing was illegal. Trespassing and then taking photographs took a lot of gall.

Years of this would wear on a person. Travis had a better idea now of just how much it had worn on Sophia.

The car lurched forward a full car length, rushing his horse before slamming on its brakes. Samson threw his head up and gave it the side-eye, but he stayed under control. Travis gave him a solid pat on the neck, turned in his saddle, and pulled his hunting rifle out of its carrying case. He pulled a single bullet out of the cardboard box he kept in his saddlebag.

Carrying a rifle was part of Travis's job. Predators had to be dealt with; they'd found the remains of a calf that had been lost to a predator just yesterday. Travis would never kill a man over photographs, but he'd never let a car kill a horse, either. If he were to fire this weapon, every cowboy in hearing distance would come to check it out. If Travis happened to fire that signal shot in the direction of one of the car's tires, well, things like that happened.

One thing that wasn't going to happen? These men weren't getting any closer to Sophia.

Travis opened the rifle's chamber. Empty, as it should be unless he was about to use it. He slipped the bullet into place and locked the bolt into position. It made a satisfying metallic sound for the benefit of the trespassers. Travis set the rifle across his thighs and waited.

The driver and the cameramen started making incredulous hand gestures. Then the driver laid on the horn, nice and loud. Nice and long.

Travis smiled. Wouldn't be long now.

Clay had already been on his way, so he arrived first. A few minutes later, Buck, a young hand working his second year on the River Mack, rode up. Buck was as good-natured and laid-back as they came, but between the text messages and the car horn, he arrived looking serious. The men stayed on their horses, flanking Travis.

"This road's getting mighty crowded," Travis said.

The driver laid on the horn again, longer and louder.

"Seems rude," Clay said.

"Doesn't he?"

The driver got out of the car. "This is very interesting. What are you guys hiding? Why don't you want us to visit our friend?"

"We may be here awhile," Travis said to his men. "He doesn't understand the concept of private property."

The driver addressed Travis's men, too. "Either of you fellas know Sophia Jackson?"

Well, hell. Now it was like playing poker. Travis had to act like he didn't know the cards he held in his own hand.

"Her sister lives here in Austin. We spotted the sister coming out of a bridal shop, then she drove out here to this ranch." The driver squinted at Clay. "Isn't that interesting?"

"Not particularly."

Travis would have to call Alex this evening and let him know Grace was being followed.

"Rumor has it that Sophia Jackson's sister is planning a wedding on this ranch." He made a show of taking his wallet out of his back pocket. "We're just looking for a little confirmation."

"The movie star?" Buck was genuinely incredulous. "What in the hell is this man talkin' about?"

"I believe he thinks we run a catering service," Travis deadpanned. "You cater any weddings lately?"

Buck laughed, although Travis doubted he'd been that funny. Buck just liked to laugh.

The cameraman gestured to his grandiose lens. "Look, I'm just trying to do my job. To capture all the beauty of a wedding, I need to scope out the venue first. Is there a gazebo? Will there be a reception tent? Is Sophia Jackson going to be the maid of honor?"

Buck leaned around Travis to speak to Clay. "I thought you were digging an irrigation ditch today. Didn't know you built weddin' gazebos for movie stars." He cracked himself up with his own joke.

The driver, however, got impatient or insulted. It didn't matter which. What mattered was that he shoved his wallet back in his pants and got behind the wheel again. With his hand on the horn, he put his car in gear. It rolled toward the horses slowly but relentlessly.

Buck stopped laughing.

"Is he playing chicken with us?" Clay asked no one in particular.

Travis didn't believe in playing chicken. He didn't like trespassers, and he didn't like horses being threatened with a car that could kill them. He picked up the rifle, sighted down the barrel, and fired.

The front left tire deflated instantly.

"Never did like games," Travis said, using thigh and knee to keep Samson calm after the gunfire.

"It's about to get real," Clay murmured.

"Yep."

The driver started shouting, jumping out of his car and waving his arms like a caricature of a New York taxi driver. The cameraman got out and started photographing his flat tire.

"Make sure you get my gate in the background, so you can explain to the sheriff how far onto private property you were when your tire blew up." Travis turned to flip his saddlebag open and get another bullet out of the cardboard box. "I'll say this one more time: turn your car around and get off my ranch."

"But you shot out my tire. You *shot* it." The driver was more incredulous about that than Buck had been about movie stars.

"You got a spare, don't you?" Travis pulled back the bolt

on the rifle and chambered another round. "How many spares you got?"

Clay nodded toward the west. "Company's coming."

Travis glanced at the two riders coming toward them with their horses at an easy trot. "Good. Haven't seen Waterson in a while." He looked back at the driver. "You get to changing that tire. We have some visiting to do."

It took the driver and cameraman longer to figure out how to get their spare out of the trunk and set up the jack than it did for Luke Waterson and one of his hands to reach the road. Luke was one of the owner-operators of the James Hill ranch, which bordered the River Mack.

He rode up to Travis and shook hands. "Happened to be in the neighborhood when I heard someone's car horn get stuck. Then the gunshot made it interesting."

"Nice of you to stop by."

"What do we have here?"

Travis leaned his forearm on the pommel of his saddle, keeping the rifle in his other hand pointed away from men and horses. "I believe this here is what you'd call the paparazzi."

"Paparazzi? Which one of you is famous?"

As the men laughed, Travis spoke under his breath to Luke. "Mrs. MacDowell has a houseguest."

"I see." Luke *tched* to his horse and turned him in a circle, until he stood beside Travis. "Looks like we'll be staying until these paparazzi can get their tire changed and get on their way. How long do you think that'll take?"

"They're a little slow on the uptake," Travis said. "I'm gonna say twenty minutes."

"I'll take fifteen."

Clay was skeptical. "Ten bucks says thirty."

In the end, it took them the full thirty minutes, so Clay collected enough beer money to last him a month. Buck was sent to follow the car out to the county road. Waterson and his man headed back to the James Hill. Clay went back to clearing out pond weeds.

Travis turned his horse toward the house.

He had that impatient feeling again, that need to lay eyes on Sophia. *Need* was perhaps the wrong term. The photographers hadn't made it very far onto the ranch, so there was no need to think she was in any kind of distress. She was probably talking to the horses or taking a nap or even holding those yoga poses that had turned him into a voyeur. Travis *wanted* to see Sophia again.

Want and need were all twisted up inside him when it came to Sophia. If he just checked on her, then he'd be able to put his mind at ease and go back to his routine.

Travis told himself that lie for a mile, until the white pillars of Mrs. MacDowell's front porch came into view, and he saw Sophia standing there, hurling tomatoes at the sky.

Chapter Fourteen

He might as well have been invisible.

He'd turned Samson out to the pasture and put on a fresh shirt. His hair still probably smelled like smoke, but Sophia noticed none of it when Travis walked up the front porch steps and joined her by the white pillars. She didn't acknowledge him at all.

It didn't matter. He leaned against a pillar and felt the tension inside him ease, anyway. She was here. He was here. It felt good.

She continued her little ritual as if she were in the middle of a meditation. She chose a tomato from a basket, examined it carefully, and then threw it with considerable skill.

"Had a bad day?" he asked.

"You could say that."

"I'm about to make it worse."

She paused, tomato cupped in her hand.

"I just met my first paparazzi."

"Oh." Her knuckles turned white on the tomato, but as he watched her, she loosened her grip. "I could crush this, but then I'd have to clean up the stupid mess myself."

"You could throw it."

She did.

"Nice arm," he said.

"My daddy taught me."

Right there, just like that, Travis felt something change. The hard squeeze on his heart was painful.

Standing on the porch less than an arm's length from Sophia, he saw her as a child, one who loved her daddy, a young girl determined to learn how to throw a baseball. She might have had pigtails, or she might have been a tomboy in a ball cap, but she'd been somebody's little girl.

Now she was a too-beautiful woman but a very real person, doing the best she could in the world, same as everyone else. She was mostly kind; she had her flaws.

She was irresistible. And the reason she was irresistible was because he was falling in love with her.

Strangers with cameras came to photograph her because that was a crazy side effect of her job. It had nothing to do with Travis and Sophia, two people standing on a porch, throwing tomatoes.His arm was already warmed up from a day spent chopping trees and handling horses and sighting down a hunting rifle for one easy tire shot. He picked up a tomato and threw it for distance, centerfield to home plate.

"Wow," she said.

"My dad taught me."

"Do you see your dad very often?"

Rather than answer, he picked up another tomato. Although he'd played shortstop, he took his time like a pitcher on the mound. Wound up. Threw.

"Now you're just showing off."

He winked at her, as if he were still a young college jock. "I can throw a baseball farther than a tomato."

She picked up another one. Studied it. Threw.

"Why are you killing tomatoes?" he asked.

"I'm sick of them." Her little hiss of anger ended in an embarrassed duck of her chin. "It's wasteful, though, isn't it? But I'm not a bad person. They were just rotting in place, anyway."

His heart hurt for her again, for the way she didn't want to be thought of as a bad person. The little girl had grown up to be defensive for a reason. She was judged all the time, not just for whom she dated, but for how her face looked, what she wore, what kind of sandwich she ate.

"I'll tell you a rancher's point of view. The tomatoes came from the land, and you're putting them back into the land. That's not wasteful. Birds are going to come out of nowhere tonight and have a feast, and I bet you'll see a few tomato plants popping up here next spring. In the catalog of possible sins a person could commit, I'd say throwing a tomato is pretty damn minor. You're not a bad person."

"I won't be here next spring." She sounded wistful. It was a gentle warning as well, whether for herself or for him, to not get too attached.

"I know." He threw another tomato, a sidearm hard to first base to beat the runner.

"So, do you see your dad or not?" she asked.

"Dad and I are on speaking terms again."

"What happened?"

"He slept with a married woman. It wasn't with my mother."

"I'm so sorry." Her voice, her posture, all of it softened toward him. For him. "That must have been awful."

"Tore up two families with one affair. But it's been fifteen years. We talk. Take in a game together when I'm in Dallas. Do you see your dad?"

"My dad passed away. The same instant as my mom, actually. Car crash."

He couldn't pick up another tomato.

"It's been ten years. I was nineteen. I became Grace's legal guardian. She was all I had left. She *is* all I have left. Now she's getting m-married."

The tiny stutter said it all.

"In September." She took a breath, and a little of the actress appeared. "Grace came out here today to tell me she'd set the date. She's planning everything without my help, since I'm kind of a liability in public, with the mob scenes and stuff. She's running her own life. She doesn't need me anymore, and I'm so proud of her for that. I really am. And she's happy and excited and everything a bride should be, and I'm so happy about that, too."

Travis waited.

Sophia traced the edge of the tomato basket with her fingertip. "But deep down, I wish she still needed me, and that, for certain, makes me a bad person."

"No, it doesn't."

It was shockingly easy to pull her into his arms. It was shockingly perfect, the way she fit against his chest. She burrowed into him, her cheek on his collarbone. She brought her arms around his back, as if they'd always hugged away the hurt like this, as if they'd always fit together.

"Who is watching?" she asked. Not *Is anyone watching?* Just *who*.

"No one. It's only three o'clock. The men are working."

He set his cheek against her hair, the scent of her shampoo less dominant than the smell of sunshine. She'd spent the day outdoors, then, not in the dark and the air conditioning.

He savored the smell of her skin as he held her, but the embrace was not entirely about comfort. Hunger demanded attention. Travis felt her breasts soft against his chest, felt the heat of her palm on his shoulder blade, and told himself it was enough.

"The paparazzi aren't watching?"

"They won't be back unless they can afford a lot of new tires. They got a flat. It will happen again. Every time."

Tension spiked in her every muscle. "But they'll be back. They'll keep coming back."

He hushed her with a *shh* and another, the same way he soothed a filly being approached by a rider for the first time. "They think Grace might be scouting out the ranch as a place to have her wedding. When she gets married somewhere else in September, they'll stop wondering if her famous sister will show up out here."

"Oh. That's possible. You might be right."

"Don't sound so surprised."

She lifted her cheek. "Don't be so nice to me."

"It's very easy to be nice to you."

She set her hand on the side of his face, and he closed his eyes at the sweet shock of a feminine touch.

It had been a while since he'd been touched by a woman, but it was more than that. It mattered that it was Sophia's fingertips that smoothed their way over his cheek, Sophia's palm that cupped his jaw. Sophia, Sophia—he couldn't get her out of his head, not since the moment he'd first laid eyes on her.

When her thumb traced his lower lip, he opened his eyes just to see her again.

She looked sad. "This has no future."

"What doesn't?" He knew, but he wanted all the cards spread on the table.

"This thing between us. It has nowhere to go."

"I know." He bent his head, and he kissed her. Like the hug, it was as natural as if they'd always kissed. Of course he would press his lips to hers. Of course.

"I don't know where I'll be a year from now. I don't know where I'll be a month from now."

"I know where you are this moment." He placed a kiss carefully on her upper lip, to stop the tears that were threatening to start. "We have this moment."

She kissed him. Her mouth was soft but her kiss was strong. No hesitation. When he thought he'd like to taste her, she opened her mouth and tasted him. In contrast to her words of warning, she kissed him without any doubts.

He had no doubts, either. If this kiss on the porch was all they could ever have, he still wanted it. He needed one moment, just one moment, to stop denying this power between them. Want and need were the same thing: he needed to kiss her more than he wanted to breathe. He wanted to kiss her more than he needed to breathe.

The slide of her tongue was firm and perfect. It satisfied him deep inside, a moment of relief because that hunger had been answered. *Ah, finally, a kiss.* But then the hunger demanded more.

He wanted to know the shape of her, so he let his hands slide and explore. Her body was softer than it looked when she saluted the sun in those God-blessed yoga clothes. Her muscles were relaxed, languid. He shifted their embrace from one of comfort to one of desire. Her hips pressed against his hardness, a moment of bliss—but then he needed more.

Her hands tugged his hair harder than he'd expected. It was just what he wanted, just what he needed—for a moment. Then greed built like a fire, consuming them both. She rose up on her toes to get closer to him, so he cupped her backside and held her tightly in place.

Not tightly enough. She could still move, and she did, sliding up another inch along his hard body, straining for more as they stood on the porch, reaching for something clothing made impossible.

"I'm gonna lose my mind if you do that again." He was warning her, or he was begging her.

"I know. I know." Her words were panted out, raw with need, no purr, no seduction, nothing deliberate.

Still a sex goddess. *More* of a sex goddess.

She couldn't go higher on her toes, but she tried, hands in his hair, flexing her arms, seeking him. If they were only horizontal, she could slide up his body, and it would all work perfectly. They'd fit together, they'd find the release that was desperately needed now, right now, if only they were horizontal—

"Please." She panted the word against his mouth, and he knew exactly what the rest of the desperate plea was. *Please fix this. Please finish this. Please give me what I need.*

He kept one hand buried in her hair, cupping the back of her head, and watched her intently as he opened the door, waiting to see if that was what she really wanted.

It was; she told him what he needed to hear. "Yes."

She knew what she wanted, and she took the first step, bringing him with her, like a dancer leading with an arm around his waist. Two steps brought them inside, and he slammed the door.

Clothes were coming off. His hands slid under the loose green top to the black spandex underneath, the kind of sports bra that never came off easily, damn it, until he felt the hooks in back, thank God. She made short work of his

belt with her sure hands while he unfastened her hooks.
Her soft breasts spilled free. He filled his hand with one
breast, a moment entirely of touch because he could not
see her beneath the green top. Not yet.

He kissed her breast through the shirt. In response, she
gasped and her hands on his fly shivered to a stop. She
was his. She was perfect. This was all he wanted. Then
the hunger roared again, and it wasn't enough.

He scooped her top up and over her head. She was so
beautifully cooperative, raising her arms so he could draw
the shirt completely off, shaking her wrist for him when
the bra stuck there.

Together, they tossed away the barriers. She kicked off
her sneakers and went to work on the button of his jeans.
He dragged his shirt over his head while trying not to lose
sight of her bare breasts, as beautiful as the rest of her,
with one tiny, dark freckle on the curve of her left breast,
just off center of her cleavage, a sexy imperfection he
wanted to savor.

She unzipped his fly and slid her hands beneath the
waistband to push his jeans to the floor.

Now she hesitated, but the look on her face was one of
desire, not fear. After a pause to enjoy the anticipation,
she closed the space between them and pressed her nude
body against his.

Yes. Yes and absolutely yes, it felt absolutely right when
she wrapped her arms around his shoulders and wrapped
her legs around his waist. He lifted her higher, holding
her thighs in his hands as she cried an inarticulate sound
that meant *yes*, this was what she'd begged him for. They
needed to get horizontal soon, needed to find a bed or a
couch or hell, the floor would work—

But all Sophia did was take a breath, and it was enough

to align their bodies at just the right angle, with just the right amount of pressure, and he was sheathed inside her.

He rocked backward, leaning against whatever piece of furniture was behind him, completely undone at the sensation. Nothing had ever felt so good, nothing in his life. He couldn't move, couldn't breathe. Sophia was hot and wet and all around him. All his.

Hot and wet, so wet...

He wasn't wearing any protection.

Her breath was in his ear. He rained kisses down her neck. "The pill," he managed to say. "Tell me you're on the pill."

"No. Don't you have a condom?"

He shook his head sharply. It wasn't something a man needed to carry to work on the open range, damn it all to hell.

"Just—wait—don't—" He steeled himself—the coming sensation was going to be climax-worthy, but he couldn't, not without protection—then he cupped her bottom and slid her up and off his body. He was sweating from the effort to keep control, a desperate man. "Do you have a condom? In your suitcase? Anywhere?"

"No. I swore off men. Forever." She unwrapped her legs from his waist but stood on her toes before him, arms still around his neck, their bodies still pressed tightly together. "I didn't know there would be you. I never thought there could be you."

She kissed him again, loving his mouth the way their bodies wanted to be loving. He kissed her the way he couldn't have her, although God knew they were both willing.

Still, knowing she wanted him eased something in his chest, and her skin felt glorious against his skin, so when she ended the kiss, Travis found that he could smile, even tease her. "So when you said this wasn't going any-where…"

She gasped-laughed and smacked his chest, but she was quick with the comeback. "You said we had one moment. It sounded kind of romantic at the time, but…" She made a little *shoo* motion with her hand. "There it was. Hope you enjoyed it."

"Oh, hell no. We're having another moment." There were a hundred ways to please a woman, and he was more than willing to try them all with Sophia.

He pushed her just a foot away, so he could finish step-ping out of boots and jeans. She watched, then she touched, one finger trailing down his arm, then one finger trailing up the hard length of him.

He cursed softly, and she laughed, because she knew exactly what he meant by that curse.

She bit her lower lip. "The MacDowells lived here, right? Three guys. Don't you think they might have left something behind in a nightstand from their college days?"

Travis kicked the jeans out of his way and they held hands, jogging naked together through the house to the bedroom hallway. From one room to the next, he took the nightstand on the left side of each bed, she the right, but their search turned up nothing.

"They would've probably been expired, anyway," she said, hands on her hips, wrinkling her nose in disappoint-ment while she talked to him, as if it were perfectly nat-ural to chat with him in the nude. "Aren't you guys the same age?"

"Give or take a few years. I'm thirty-one, so yeah, we're looking for ten-year-old condoms."

They laughed at themselves, but the sound of an ATV brought them both to the window to steal a peek, side by side.

"The greenhorn's back from the cedar burn."

"Now what?" she asked.

"Now I hope he doesn't notice Samson's out in the paddock, so I won't have to explain where I've been later." Travis ran his hand lightly down her back, marveling again at the dip of her lower back and the curve of her thigh. "Much later, because I'm not leaving now. We've got some creative moments in the immediate future."

She kissed his cheek, such an absurdly innocent move. "You still smell like smoke."

"Had I known the best moment of my life was going to happen today, I would have showered before stopping by to throw tomatoes. And I would have brought a damned condom. Spontaneity isn't my strong suit."

She touched him, fingertips smoothing their way from his smoky hair down his chest. "You could take a shower here, and I could try to figure out just what your strong suit is."

"Is that shower big enough for two?"

"Let's find out."

Shampoo and slippery soap led to more laughter. Hands made discoveries, laughter faded into something more intense. Bodies were finally, shatteringly satisfied. As far as spontaneous moments went, although they'd been caught unprepared for basic necessities, Travis could have no complaints.

When he was dressed once more and walking the familiar path to his house, it wasn't the sex that occupied his thoughts; it was the moment that had come afterward. Under the steady, soothing stream of the shower, he'd cradled her against his body for a long, long time. Neither one of them had wanted to move. The water had run down their skin, and the silence between them had been as powerful as everything that had come before.

He was in love with her.

It could go nowhere. It was a fluke they'd found themselves on the same ranch. She was leaving, had been destined to leave since before she'd arrived.

They'd had their moment.

As he walked into his empty house, he already knew it would never be enough.

Chapter Fifteen

"**I**'m getting married!"

Sophia smiled at her sister's excitement as she pulled groceries out of a brown paper bag. Eggs, flour, real sugar. Sophia had so much time on her hands and such a plethora of Mrs. MacDowell's old cookbooks, she'd decided to try her hand at baking a few things to supplement her frozen dinners. Besides, she could sneak the results of her successful attempts into the barn after dark. Not for the horses, but for Travis, her secret lover for the past two nights.

And tonight. She would definitely find him again tonight after sunset.

With a little thrill inside that she hoped wasn't obvious, she scooped up the five-pound bags of flour and sugar and headed for the pantry, laughing at her excited bride of a sister. "Yes, I know you're getting married. September twenty-fourth. It will be here before you know it."

"No, I'm getting married in five days, and you're going to be my maid of honor."

Sophia stopped in the middle of the kitchen. "What?"

"Somebody had a big party planned at the place we booked for September, and they canceled it. It's Fourth of July weekend, which might not sound so romantic, but I think it will be special. The rooftop patio overlooks Sixth Street. You can see the Capitol all lit up for the night, and the city will have fireworks going off all around us."

"But that's less than a week away. A wedding in a week?" Sophia held the ten pounds of flour and sugar steadily as she stared at Grace. "Is that even possible?"

"The florist said she could do it. The corporation that canceled their party had already booked a bartender and music, so we're just scooping up the people they had reserved. Kendry and Jamie weren't going out of town for the holiday, anyway, so I have my bridesmaid and Alex has his best man. If you're in the wedding, then Alex wants to ask his friend Kent to be a groomsman, so we'll have two girls, two guys. Please say yes. It's perfect."

Alex came in the kitchen door. "I found Travis."

And then Travis was right there, hanging his hat on the hook, and Sophia wasn't sure how to act.

Travis had left her bed at dawn in order to get to the barn before his men, or so he hoped. She wondered if he'd made it there first. If he hadn't, then she wondered how he'd explained arriving from the direction of the MacDowells' house and not from his own. Had anyone arrived early from the bunkhouse?

She couldn't tell from Travis's face whether that had happened or not. He stood near the door with his usual impassive cowboy demeanor, but Sophia knew what he looked like when he laughed. She also knew what he looked like when he was at his most primitive, head thrown back, muscles straining, powerless to stop the climax she'd brought him to.

The flour slipped from her arm. She hitched it back up.

Alex looked like a very pleased Clark Kent. "So Grace told you the big news?"

"Just a second ago. I hardly know what to think."

Alex explained to Travis. "We're getting married this weekend."

"Congratulations." Travis stole a look at Sophia. He knew about September. She'd been throwing tomatoes, wishing her sister needed her in September. She hadn't wanted her sister to need her this badly, though. Not badly enough to ruin her own wedding.

"Are you sure this is what you want?" Sophia asked Grace. "There was nothing wrong with September. I'm afraid you're not going to have the wedding you want if you try to cram this in on short notice. What about your cake? What about your dress?"

"There was something definitely wrong with September. You weren't going to be there. You were so nice about it, but when I drove away, I didn't even make it halfway to Austin before I started crying."

"You seemed so happy when you left."

"Well, a hard conversation was over. You'd been so generous about it all, but I realized that I was settling for something I didn't want. I want you in my wedding. I started feeling kind of sorry for myself, that because of the paparazzi and all the pressure you're always under, I wouldn't get my wedding the way I want it. The bride is supposed to get what she wants, right? Well, this bride wants her sister. I sat down and called all the venues on our list one more time. It was my bridezilla moment."

Sophia couldn't help but laugh at Grace's pride in her supposed diva fit. "That's the sweetest bridezilla moment I've ever heard of."

"Seriously, Sophie, it's going to be one of the biggest

days of my life, and I need you there. I just can't imagine getting married without my sister as my maid of honor."

"Oh, Grace." The tears were instant, blurring her vision. The sugar slipped from her arm, but somehow Travis caught it before it made a spectacular five-pound splatter on the tile. She smiled up at him through her tears. "Thank you."

"You're welcome." He took the flour from her.

Sophia wasn't sure why Alex had invited Travis in for this little family moment, but she was glad he was here. He'd been there for her when she was upset that her sister didn't seem to need her, so it seemed right that he got to share this happy moment, too.

Now that Travis had freed Sophia's arms, she could hug Grace, precious Grace, the sister who still needed her. "I can't believe you're doing all of this just so I can be in your wedding. Thank you." She turned to Alex. "And thank you. You're okay with this?"

The way his expression softened when he looked at her sister made Sophia feel mushy inside.

"I wanted to marry her yesterday," he said. "I wanted to marry her the day before that, and the day before that. I'm very okay with this weekend instead of waiting for September. Very."

Sophia squeezed Grace's hands. "So you're doing this. What can I do? What about your dress? Do you want me to call in some favors? You look so good in Vuitton. I could ask them to overnight me some samples in white. I'll tell them it's for a big event. That's the truth, too. I'm sure we'll be photographed enough to make it worth their while."

Grace squeezed Sophia's hands in return. "I already had Mom's wedding gown taken out of storage and shipped here last month. It just needs cleaned and fluffed. The dress shop is going to detach the old crinoline and I'm going to wear a new one underneath, but they have that kind of thing in stock. It's not a problem at all."

"You're wearing Mom's wedding dress?"

Grace bit her lip. "I should have asked you. The crinoline is a minor alteration, I promise."

"You don't need my permission. I'm not your boss. It's as much your dress as mine."

"Yes, but is it okay with you?"

"You're going to be such a beautiful bride, you're going to make me cry, anyway, but this is really going to be unfair. I'm going to look like a blubbering mess in all your photos."

Because being with her sister felt like her old life, Sophia started brainstorming their usual plans. "We'll have to fly Tameka in to give me bulletproof makeup. If my nose turns red, I'll be in all the gossip rags as a coke addict or something. That's just what we need when I'm trying to let the controversy die down. We can fly in Jolin with Tameka. She does such great hair."

"No." Because this was not their old life, Grace interrupted. "I've already got a hairstylist here. Austin isn't exactly a backwater. My stylist is really good. The only person we're flying in from LA is you."

"Me?"

"It will look that way. We're going to sneak you off this ranch and fly you to the Dallas airport. You'll get a nice first-class seat from Dallas back to Austin. Everyone will text their friends that you're on their plane, and when you land here, the paparazzi will assume you flew in for the wedding. You, me and Kendry are going to set up base in a hotel suite, so that Alex doesn't see us before the big day."

Alex turned to Travis. "Which brings us to why I asked you to stop in. Texas Rescue, completely by coincidence, has decided to conduct a training exercise tomorrow. It involves extracting a practice patient by helicopter and transporting her to the Dallas airport's medevac facilities. We were wondering if we might be able to use this ranch as the starting point. It looks like you've got plenty of room for a helicopter to land around here somewhere."

As Travis and Alex worked out locations and timing for her escape, Sophia stood at the counter with Grace, pretending to be absorbed by their conversation. She really just wanted to look at Travis.

She reached into the brown paper grocery bag, and pulled out a random box. Instant oatmeal. That was fine.

But Travis, ah, Travis, he was more than fine, and he would be hers tonight.

Another box. Toothpaste. Fine.

She would have to make the memories of the coming night last for the next five days, though. The thought of not seeing Travis for nearly a week was hard. She'd just found him. Once she left for Austin—

"Sophia." Grace jerked Sophia out of her fantasy. She was shaking her head *no* as she pushed Sophia's hand back into the grocery bag.

"What is it?" Sophia looked into the bag. In her hand, she held the neat, rectangular box of a pregnancy test. She stared at it in horror; she'd almost taken it right out and set it on the counter.

"Why?" she whispered. "Why would you do this?"

Grace pulled her out of the kitchen with an artificial smile for Alex. "Girl stuff to talk about. Shoes for the dresses. Be back in a second."

Sophia yanked her arm free in the living room, the same room in which she'd stripped Travis just two short days ago, the room in which he'd stripped her. She wanted to stay that way, bared to him, unafraid to be her true self. He'd seen her tears and tantrums, her scars, her fears.

When she'd thought she was being terrible, he'd stood beside her and thrown tomatoes at the world. Dear God, he'd said it was easy to be nice to her. He'd kissed every inch of her body.

Now Grace had brought a pregnancy test into her kitchen.

"Why?" Sophia pleaded.

"You need to know, Sophie. You can't keep telling yourself maybe it was a bad test, maybe you'll get your period. Once you know for certain, you can decide what you want to do."

No! The word was stuck in her head. She didn't dare say it out loud; it would come out as a scream that echoed off the rafters of this great big lonely house.

Grace had it so wrong. Sophia would *not* get to decide what she wanted to do. Once she knew for certain, then she would have no choice but to deal with adoption agencies and obstetricians. She'd have to deal with Deezee in the worst possible way.

What she wanted to do was spend more time with Travis. That would no longer be an option, because what she would have to do was tell him she was pregnant by another man, and her time with him would be over.

She'd always known her time with him would be short. This wasn't her house. This wasn't her career. She could not hide here forever and go broke. But dear God, when she'd stripped herself bare in this room, she'd thought she'd have more than two days. She needed more than two days.

"Sophie?"

"July seventh." The words sounded polite, if stiff. They should have sounded like they'd been ripped from her soul. "I should get my period on the sixth or seventh. If I don't, I'll do the test."

Sophia forced herself to relax her shoulders, and tilt her

head just so, and let the tiniest bit of an encouraging smile reach her eyes. "So in the meantime, let's set that aside and focus on your wedding. I wouldn't want to have to tangle with Bridezilla Gracie. She sounds pretty fearsome."

Judging from the relieved hug Grace gave her, Sophia Jackson had just delivered another Oscar-worthy performance.

Chapter Sixteen

Sunset finally came.

The men left for the day—the young bachelors to crash in the bunkhouse, Clay to his own place off the ranch—and Travis experienced the piercing anticipation of having Sophia all to himself.

At the first sound of the barn door sliding open, he left his office and headed for her, his boots loud on the concrete, and he knew he had the arrogant smile of a man who knew he was minutes away from getting exactly what he wanted with the only woman he wanted it from.

"Sophia."

Her sneakers were silent and so was she, tackling him so that he caught her and they turned 180 degrees, his arms around her body, her hands in his hair, their mouths meeting. It was like this every night now, this first moment of pent-up desire that had to be released in a crashing kiss.

He set her back on her feet, but she began kissing her way from just under his jaw down his neck.

He loved it, but he had to ask. "Are we celebrating a good day or blowing off steam after a frustrating day?"

She shook her hair back. "So many emotions."

"The scene with your sister? That had to be a good emotion." He didn't know why she couldn't have made the wedding in September, but clearly, the coming weekend had worked out for everyone.

Sophia locked her hands together behind his waist, as he did to her. Hips pressed together, focused on one another, they talked among the disinterested horses. Travis enjoyed the prelude; Sophia wasn't the only one who looked forward to having someone to talk to every day.

"I thought my role in Grace's life was kind of over. I can't believe she wants me in her wedding that badly. Just as badly as I wanted to be there."

"I can. If you were my sister, you'd be my hero, too."

"Hero." She wrinkled her nose.

"You stepped in when your parents died. You saved the day when her life could've easily fallen apart. You achieved your own success at the same time, and pretty damned spectacularly. I started downloading the line-up of movies that you star in. I didn't realize there were so many."

"I wouldn't say I starred in them all, if any. Except for *Pioneer Woman*, most were just small parts. Supporting actress or ensemble work, at best."

He gave her a tug, pressing her more tightly against the hardness that was inevitable when she was in his arms. "It's impressive. You're a hero, but I thank the heavens every day that you are not my sister."

She deflected his praise. "I hope I didn't show how surprised I was when Alex came in the kitchen door with you. It was kind of fun to have to pretend we're just neighbors, or whatever we are. You were a very good actor, by the way."

"Poker face. I could hardly look at that blue tile countertop now that I know it is exactly the right height for—"

She stood on her toes and twined one leg around his. "For a midnight snack?"

He dropped that casual kiss on her lips, the one that a man could give a woman when he knew he had time with her. He took her hand to lead her to his office. "We need to talk about who knows you're here, though."

He sat in the desk chair, knowing she'd sit in his lap and drape an arm over his shoulder. She did, but she was frowning. "Who knows I'm here?"

"Just the MacDowells who signed the lease, and Grace and Alex. But someone else who is physically on the property should be aware, for days I'm not here. I want to let… I want…what are you doing?"

"I'm leaving tomorrow for five days. I want to stock up on my moments." She turned to straddle him.

He laughed a little until he realized she was serious. Her hand slipped in his back pocket for the protection he was now never without. She stood to wriggle out of her shorts. When she started to undo his jeans, he didn't object, not in the least, but there was an edginess about her tonight that wasn't familiar.

"There's a perfectly good bed about a hundred yards away from here," he said.

"I want you to think of me while I'm gone. Every time you sit in this chair, I want you to remember a special moment."

That didn't need an answer. It was obvious he'd never look at this chair the same way again. But there was that underlying edginess again, so he answered her anyway. "I'm never going to forget you, Sophia. Not one moment."

She looked at him, blue eyes filled with what he could

only call longing, and he wondered for the millionth time if this thing between them was really destined to end.

She closed her eyes and kissed him as she tore open the foil wrapper. With her hands, she sheathed him. With her body, she sheathed him again, and he was lost to any kind of further analysis except *yes* and *more*.

He unbuttoned her cotton shirt, exposing the inner curves of breasts shaped by pink lace. He kissed the precious freckle first, then tasted as much softness as he could through the lace. She rode him, making him shudder almost immediately with the need to maintain some semblance of control. With his hands, he tilted her hips to make sure she was making the contact she needed for her own satisfaction.

She put two fingertips on his forehead and pushed his head back against the chair, then grabbed his wrist and moved his hand to the arm of the chair. Leaning forward, pink lace so close to his face, she spoke into his ear. "Hey, Travis? Sit back and relax. I've got this."

She did. She definitely did.

He tried to take in the moment, tried to comprehend that this dream was real, so unbelievably, incredibly real. When they reached their completion, Sophia collapsed against him, her head on his shoulder. As her soft breath warmed his neck, he wrapped her tightly in his arms and savored this moment, too.

The tenderness stayed with him, every time. Sophia seemed to want it as much as she needed the physical release. She was a sex goddess who cuddled afterward. He was the man who appreciated just how irresistible that combination was.

It might be impossible to live without it.

She wriggled closer yet, keeping him inside her. His body felt thick and full, but sated—for now. It was clear to him that the hunger for her would never be satisfied for long.

"I can't believe I have to leave you for five days," she said. "I don't want to. Not when we've just discovered each other."

He kissed the top of her head. Twirled a strand of silver and gold around his index finger.

She pouted. "It's kind of like the honeymoon phase, you know? That's a rotten time to be apart. It's not like we're some old married couple and we've been together ten years or whatever. Then five days wouldn't be such a big deal."

Was she trying to convince herself that the power between them was just a novelty, a new toy they'd lose interest in someday? Surely an old boyfriend hadn't lost interest in her and looked for greener pastures somewhere else.

"Sophia Jackson, if you push me into a desk chair and straddle my lap ten years from now, you will get exactly the same response from me. Ten years from now, twenty years from now, I will never have had enough of you."

The moment was suddenly charged with tension instead of tenderness. He'd crossed a line. He'd said something he shouldn't have, not when she'd told him from the first that this thing between them was going nowhere. It certainly wasn't going ten years into the future.

He wouldn't take it back. It was true: he would want her forever. He brushed the lock of her hair across his lips, and let it go.

She picked up her head and sat up a little straighter, then smiled as if she didn't have a care in the world. "I'm looking forward to making more moments. We've got to stock up five days in one night. I hope you ate a big lunch."

It was cute. She was overlooking his serious statement, offering to get them back on track. It was her olive branch.

He accepted it. "We may have to build in a dinner break.

It will be more than five days. I spend a week with my family every Fourth of July."

Abruptly, the conversation was serious again. "You won't be here when I get back from the wedding?"

"Not for the rest of the week."

"No, you can't leave," she pleaded, startling him with her intensity.

He slid his hands up her ribs and gave her a reassuring squeeze. "I can't leave the ranch in May, but I do take time off. July is the slowest month for ranching. The calving's done, the weaning hasn't started. The cattle have plenty of natural grass to graze on. If I'm going to leave, this is the time to do it."

"You won't be here when I get back from the wedding? You'll be gone the rest of the week?"

"Right." He tried to soothe her with a smile. He offered his own olive branch, an easy way to keep things light. "But I'll make it up to you when I get back."

"Can you change your plans?"

The edginess was unmistakable, as if it were critical that he be available this week just so they could sneak into bed together after sunset. As if time were short, and this week in particular was all they had.

Something was so obviously wrong, dangerously wrong.

He held her more tightly. Her ribs expanded with each panicky breath between his palms.

"My family's expecting me. My mom, my grandparents, brothers, sisters. Most of us are in ranching one way or the other, so this is our big holiday get-together. Kind of like Christmas for the Chalmers family."

He shouldn't be able to speak so calmly. How could he explain the mundane routine of his life when the best thing to ever happen to him was literally about to slip from his grasp?

She put her hands on his shoulders, prepared to use him for leverage as she stood, but he stopped her, a reflexive grip to keep her from leaving.

Her fingers dug into his shoulders, as if she didn't want to leave, either. "When will you be back?"

"Sunday." He tried to make it sound as normal as it was.

"What date is that? July tenth? Eleventh? It's past the seventh, for sure."

"Something like that. I'd have to look at a calendar."

She said nothing, but misery was written all over her face.

"For God's sake, Sophia. Be up front with me. Is this your last week in Texas or something?"

"No, it's nothing. I hope. I don't know. I don't know what I'll be dealing with next week. This thing between us…"

She kept stopping, running out of words. He couldn't tell if she was angry or frustrated, nor if it was directed at him or at herself.

"What about this thing between us?"

"I knew it couldn't last long," she said defensively. "I told you there was no future in it."

"This thing." He was disgusted with the term. "You mean this connection. We are connected in every way we can be at this moment. So at this moment, you owe me, Sophia. What are your plans? What's happening after this week? You can't just disappear without a word."

She looked away. "I don't think I will."

"You 'don't think'? What kind of answer is that?"

He deserved more. They deserved more.

"I don't even know how long your lease is for." He was angry that he should have to fight for basic information from her. He released her abruptly, but she clutched him as if he was her lifesaver.

What was going on?

She set her forehead against his, pinning him in place with such an intimate motion. Their noses touched as she whispered. "I have the house until January, the whole time Mrs. MacDowell's on her mission trip."

"But? Talk to me, Sophia."

"I swear I don't know what's next, Travis. The future is really up in the air, but believe me that I'm not ready for this to end. I want to be here when you come back. I do."

He wanted to take all these intense, bewildering emotions and push them into passion, make love to her until they were reduced to what they understood, communication of the most basic needs. His body was growing hard inside her. He couldn't talk like this, and hunger be damned, they needed to talk.

He set her aside, stood and turned his back to her. Got rid of the condom. Tucked his shirt in. Prayed for... God knew what. Just a prayer: *please.*

Please, let me keep her a little longer. She was everything to him.

What was he to her? Someone she might leave, someone she might not?

He turned around. She stood in his ranch office in her sneakers and short-shorts, with her million-dollar hair and lovely features. She didn't look like anything else in his world. She had no connection to his life.

And yet this *thing*, this power, this connection between them existed whether it should or not.

He'd known from the beginning she wasn't going to stay. Knowing it and facilitating a helicopter to take her away were two different things.

He forced himself to ask the question. "Are you going back to LA? Since the wedding forced you out of hiding, are you done here?"

"We'll make it look like I'm flying back to LA, just like we're making it look like I'm living there now. Grace is basically inviting the paparazzi to find her wedding by making sure I'm seen flying in. All I can do in return is try to appease the paparazzi so they don't get too aggressive and ruin her big day. I've got to stop and answer when they shout questions at me, smile while they take photos. They'll tell me to 'look this way' or 'twirl around and show us your outfit,' and I'll have to do it so they'll go away."

She trailed her fingers over the computer keyboard on his desk. "It will help. They love a cooperative star. But it won't be enough to bury all the negative publicity I already generated, so I'll come back here after the wedding. I need to continue staying off their radar."

She flicked a glance his way. He was sure his relief showed. He felt like he could breathe again.

She pushed the space bar on his keyboard, but nothing happened. He'd powered the machine down for the day.

"Have you never typed 'Sophia Jackson' in your search bar, just to see what horrible things I did?"

He shook his head.

"You weren't tempted, even a little bit?"

"Braden told me enough."

"Oh. The ball. I don't think all those Texas Rescue people are going to be too thrilled to see me at the wedding. Alex is one of their doctors, you know. Half of the guest list volunteers for them. Maybe they'll give me a second chance to make a first impression." Her gaze drifted from the keyboard to the floor as she shrugged one shoulder. "Just kidding—I know it doesn't work that way."

Perhaps Sophia had brought it on herself, but Travis feared she was going to be very uncomfortable for her sister's sake. She was going to appease the paparazzi. She was going to spend a night with people who had reason to think badly of her.

There wasn't a thing he could do to erase Sophia's past. Not one thing, but he tried to offer her some encouragement. "Braden had less to say about you than about the guy that jumped on your table."

She looked up quickly at that. "You know about Deezee?"

"Braden said he stepped on his wife's dinner and gave you a crappy apology."

"That's as good a summary as any, I suppose." She gave a halfhearted chuckle.

"Do you think he'll show up again?" Travis had that restless feeling again, that need to keep an eye on her—but Texas was a big state, and he'd be almost three hundred miles away with his family on the wedding day.

"That was all orchestrated by his publicist. Deezee is too lazy to set anything up himself, so I doubt it."

Travis couldn't leave without making sure she had some kind of plan in place. "If he does, don't try to appease him. Don't try to calm him down or take him aside. If he wants attention, you won't be able to save your sister's wedding from his type."

"The only reason he'd be there would be because of me. I think I'd owe it to everyone to try to stop him."

"Let Alex handle it. It's his wedding, not yours. Jamie MacDowell's the best man, right? You're the maid of honor, so you should be near Jamie. And you know Braden."

"He kind of hates me."

"He doesn't. You'll be safe with the MacDowells. Quinn will probably be there, too."

"I take it Quinn is the third one in all the family portraits at the house. I'll only recognize him if he still has braces and a bad middle school haircut."

"I'm serious, Sophia. I don't want you trying to deal with this Deezee jerk."

For once, he wished the paparazzi had been right. He wished Grace had been setting up a wedding tent here on the ranch. He'd be here in September. He'd be here if Sophia got harassed. Hell, she wouldn't get harassed on his ranch in the first place. That was the point of her hiding here.

But now she was going to fly away, without him.

She acted like she didn't care, scoffing like she was some kind of tough street kid. "Deezee's got no game. It would just be a lot of noise. Same old, same old. While you're gone, you can log on to your favorite celebrity site and see if anything exciting happened. If it's really juicy, it might make TV. That would be a fun topic around your family dinner table. 'Look what this crazy chick who's staying on my ranch did.'"

He recognized the voice: she sounded like the woman in the thigh-high black boots, the one who said she didn't care when she cared so desperately. He knew her, and he loved her. It made him sick to think that he might have come home to find her gone to LA forever.

It would happen, sooner or later. In the meantime, he wanted to cherish her while he could, yet they were standing on opposite sides of a desk chair.

"I'm sorry, Sophia."

"For what? I'm the one who hooked up with a loser. But hey, I've helped countless people make a living off entertainment gossip as a result. It's all good."

That scoff. It was such an act. She couldn't hide her pain from him.

He sent the chair rolling and hugged her. She held herself stiffly, as if she didn't need affection. He held her as if they'd just finished another round of amazing sex instead of a round of bad feelings and painful subjects, because she needed to skip right to the tenderness. So did he.

"I'm sorry you can't go anywhere without a camera in your face. I'm sorry you need a place to hide in the first place."

She made a small sound, a yip of pain like a hurt animal, and then she was hugging him back, burrowing into him in that way she had.

He realized she was physically hiding. He wrapped his arms around her more tightly, cupping the back of her head with his hand, letting her hide her face behind his forearm. He was grateful his life's work had given him the muscle she could literally hide behind.

"You've got a safe place here. Go do your wedding and get the paparazzi eating out of your hand. When you're done, come back here, and be safe."

She took a shivery breath. "But you won't be here."

It wasn't just the sex, then. It wasn't even the friendship and the camaraderie. She felt safer around him.

"I'll be back Sunday. Until then, Clay will know you're here. You won't be alone."

She shook her head against the idea. "Don't tell Clay. The more people who know about me, the less safe I am. Grace and I learned that the hard way. It's been just me and Grace for years."

"But now it's you and Grace and Alex and me, and you're still safe. You could depend on Clay, too." He stopped cupping her head and moved to lift her chin instead, wanting her to see that she had options. "You know Jamie and his wife, Kendry. Count on them. Braden MacDowell and his wife. She's a doctor. She knows how to keep someone's confidentiality. Quinn and his wife are trustworthy."

"I've never trusted that many people. Ever."

"But you could. The ranch that owns the Appaloosa is just a few miles away, and the Waterson family is as solid as they come. When the paparazzi came calling, all I had to tell Luke was that the MacDowells had a houseguest, and he was there for me, no questions asked. You don't have to be so very alone, Sophia."

He let go of her chin to caress her face, not surprised his hand wasn't quite steady. He had too much emotion coursing through him. He loved her so damned much, and he wanted to give her this gift. "I'll build you a whole safety net here, baby. You can come here to stay."

She wanted it. He could see it in her expression as clear as day, but she didn't say yes. It hurt her not to say yes, but she didn't say it.

She raised her own unsteady hand to touch his face. "I love... I love that you care."

"I care."

"Did I ever tell you my secret fantasy about you?"

She was done with this moment of tenderness, then. It wasn't enough for Travis, but he was a patient man. He couldn't force Sophia to trust him any more than he could force a horse to trust him. Things took time. Things had to be earned.

For her, he would meet her on her terms. She wanted to talk fantasies.

"Does this fantasy have to do with more office furniture?" he asked.

But her smile was fleeting.

"In my fantasy, you take me on a date. We have a drink together at a place with a nice dance floor, and we talk while we have our first dance. By the second dance, maybe we stop talking, because it's so special to be moving in sync, and thinking this is a person you'd like to know better. You drive me home and say good-night, and you tell me you'd like to see me again. There are no cameras. No one calls me names on social media. No one runs a background check on you. No one cares at all, except the two of us, because we're the ones falling in love."

His heart squeezed so hard, he could only whisper her name.

"But it's a fantasy, you see, because that will never happen. This thing between us, it has no future, no matter how much I wish it did."

They had a future. He just didn't know what it looked like yet. But Sophia was afraid now, skittish and spooked, and he needed to be patient.

"We have this moment," she said.

He tried not to be spooked himself at the way she said the words, as if this could be their last moment.

"How would you like to spend it?" he asked.

"I want to make love to you all night and pretend that I don't have to leave for a wedding tomorrow."

"Then that's what we'll do."

He scooped her up as if she were the bride and carried her out of the barn.

Chapter Seventeen

Sophia was the weird one.

She stuck out like a sore thumb at the reception, and nobody wanted to talk to her. She'd thought she was lonely at the ranch during that first month, but she'd forgotten how lonely she could be when surrounded by people. She just didn't fit in.

It had started at the airport. The flight attendants had been so deferential, but she'd told herself they treated all the first-class passengers that way. Then the passengers had started holding their cell phones at slightly odd angles, and she'd known she was being photographed. *OMG. Look who is on my plane!*

She couldn't even go to the bathroom like a normal person. She had to practically clean the bathroom before she left, careful to make sure she left no drops of liquid soap or a crumpled paper towel that would mark her as a slob. *OMG. Sophia Jackson left the lid down on the toilet. Does that mean she went number two?*

The only time she'd been able to forget she was different than everyone else had been in the hotel, when it had been only her, Grace and Kendry MacDowell. Kendry had overcome that invisible distance between celebrity and fan pretty quickly, and they'd had such fun as co-conspirators, trying to make Grace laugh through her bridal jitters. If only there were more Kendry MacDowells in the world...

I'll build you a whole safety net here, baby.

Travis. That man was something special. That man deserved a good life with a good woman, not with an outcast like her.

OMG. Sophia Jackson is at this wedding reception. She eats only shrimp and strawberries. What a freak.

Sophia stood in no-man's land, somewhere between the bar and the band. It was too embarrassing to sit at the head table, because Grace and Alex were on the dance floor, as were Kendry and Jamie. The other groomsman, Kent, was a bachelor who'd been pulled onto the dance floor by a group of single women who weren't letting him go any time soon. Sophia couldn't sit at the table alone.

OMG. Sophia Jackson is like a total bitch. She won't speak to anyone.

She kept a pleasant, neutral smile on her face and watched her sister glow with happiness.

The wedding ceremony had been gorgeous, a traditional service in a white church. At one point it struck her that Kendry was standing next to her with a tiny life growing in her belly. What if she, Sophia, were doing the same? In the hush of the church, surrounded by flowers and lace, pregnant had seemed like an ultra-feminine, almost divine thing to be. Even if Sophia wasn't going to raise the baby herself, it was a miracle.

Would Travis see it that way?

It wasn't July seventh. She didn't have to worry about that yet. With luck, she'd never have to worry about that.

She glanced at the roof of an adjacent building. She'd been holding still too long. The cameraman had a clear angle to her. She moved to the other side of the bandstand.

"May I have this dance?"

Travis. The man behind her sounded just like Travis, and when she turned around, she saw that the handsome man in the suit and tie was Travis.

"It's you. Oh, it's so good to see you. I'm dying to hug you, but there are at least four telephoto lenses on us right this second from a roof and two balconies."

"I missed you, too. Would you care to dance?"

"That would be lovely, thank you."

The band was playing a slower song, the kind where the man and woman could hold each other in a civilized ballroom pose and sway together, even if it was their first dance. She really almost felt like crying, it was so perfect.

"I didn't know you were here," she said. "I didn't see you at the ceremony."

"I saw you. You looked radiant up there. Whatever you were thinking, it looked good on your face."

This was their first dance, but they weren't strangers. Sophia lowered her voice. "I may have been thinking about you and a certain desk chair?"

"I don't think so."

"You and a kitchen counter?"

"Wrong again."

Oh, this was wonderful, to dance and flirt and feel like she belonged at the party. "How do you know what I was thinking?"

"Because I know the look on your face when you think of countertops and chairs, and that wasn't it. Probably a good thing when you're standing in a church."

It was wonderful to be with Travis, who knew her and didn't ask about filming *Space Maze* or whether she'd done her own stunts in *Pioneer Woman*.

"So what do you think I was thinking?"

"You were probably thinking about the child you helped raise, and how she's turned into a lovely woman. Grace is a beautiful bride. You must be very proud of her. I'm very proud of you."

Sophia felt her happiness dim. She had been thinking about a child, but it was one that, if it existed, would end this fantasy with Travis sooner rather than later.

"Grace was a teenager when I took over, not a child."

"You need to learn how to take a compliment. For example, you look very beautiful all dressed up. I've only ever seen you in yoga clothes and shorts. And one pair of thigh-high black boots. What did you do with those boots, by the way?"

She smiled. "I didn't know you owned a suit. It's kind of surreal to see you away from the ranch."

"Now that is exactly how not to return a compliment. I think you're very intriguing, though. Can I get you a drink?"

That's when it hit her. "Travis Chalmers. You're giving me my fantasy, aren't you?"

But he'd already turned to introduce her to a man he knew. Then a woman. He got the conversation onto a topic that everyone found interesting, and then he melted into the crowd. She hated to see him go, but she knew it would save anyone from guessing they were a couple.

She danced with some of the men she talked to. Then Travis returned for a second dance, as she'd known he would. A drink, two dances, an invitation to go out again: the fantasy she had said would never come true.

They swayed in silence this time, not just because that

had been her fantasy, but because her heart was too full to speak for at least two verses and a chorus.

"This isn't just about my fantasy, is it? You came to make sure that the Texas Rescue people gave me a second chance."

"I think they like you. God knows the men are happy enough to dance with you. They just needed to see me do it first, so they'd know you were a mortal even though you look like a goddess. Beauty can intimidate people."

Tears stung her eyes. That hadn't felt like a compliment as much as a benediction. Travis believed in her. She didn't want to be the weird one, even if it meant she was the beautiful weird one, and he understood that.

"Clay is going to call you to tell you if I make it home safely, isn't he?"

"Yes, he knows you're living in the house now. I told you that I would do anything to help you whether you liked it or not. Telling Clay was one of those things. I couldn't leave you isolated in hiding. Anything could happen, even a house fire, and no one would have known you were there. It wasn't safe. Clay knows, and only Clay knows."

Subdued, humbled, she asked, "Where's Deezee?"

"He's working at a club in Las Vegas tonight. You won't be embarrassed by him, and your sister has already forgotten he exists."

I love you.

She wanted to say it, she was dying to say it, but Deezee did exist, and her sister wouldn't be the only one reminded of it if July seventh turned out the way Sophia feared.

"I'd like to see you again, Sophia. I'll be out of town for the rest of the week, but could I take you to dinner on Sunday? There's a place just outside of Austin that I think you'd enjoy."

She tried to play her role. "Really? Where?"

"My house. Genuine Texas cuisine."

She wrinkled her nose. "Zucchini and tomatoes?"

"Steak and a baked potato. Dress is casual. I'll pick you up at eight."

Her voice was thick with tears as the song and her fantasy ended. "I'll see you on Sunday. Have a nice visit with your family."

By Sunday, she would know one way or the other. Either she'd tell Travis she loved him, or she'd tell him she was pregnant with another man's child.

They had to part without a kiss.

Sophia wondered if she'd ever get a chance to kiss him again.

July sixth came and went without any hoopla. Sophia talked to Clay a bit and to Samson a lot.

The seventh came and went as well. Sophia tried throwing a few tomatoes, but it was too lonely without Travis leaning on a pillar, evaluating her technique. Instead, she breathed in the shimmering hot air as she poked around the front yard until she found the goose salt shaker, dirty but unbroken. She took it into the house and scrubbed it until there was no trace of evidence that Sophia had once pitched it into the night sky.

On the eighth, she had to do the pregnancy test. She'd promised. She intended to, but she felt that need to hibernate. She slept most of the day, and by the time evening fell, she thought it would be best to wait until morning. She'd gone back to Mrs. MacDowell's 1980s pregnancy handbook and flipped through the opening pages gingerly, with one finger. There seemed to be something magical about the first urine of the day. So really, she might as well go to bed and do the test first thing in the morning.

On the morning of the ninth, she took the test. She could no longer fool herself: she was pregnant.

She cried the entire day.

The movies had gotten it all wrong. The end of the world was not an isolated, brown landscape.

Sophia woke to summer sunshine pouring in her bedroom window, mixing with the bluebonnet paintings on the walls. It was beautiful.

But it was Sunday.

Travis was coming back, and at eight in the evening, he'd pick her up to take her back to his house for dinner. There, she was going to tell him that she was pregnant with another man's child, that she'd been pregnant all along but too stubborn and willful to admit it to herself, and because of that, she'd sucked him into a hopeless situation.

It was the end of the world.

Black seemed like the appropriate color. Sophia dressed in black yoga clothes, tied on her sneakers, and went to visit the horses.

As always, Samson liked her best. She leaned on his great, warm neck and wished someone would yell *cut*.

The barn door slid open. After five days back in the public eye in Austin, that old reflex to keep her appearance together had returned. She stood properly, shoulders back and down, ankles together, hand on hip—but with her other hand, she tickled Samson under his chin. She hoped it was only Clay coming back for something he'd forgotten. No matter what Travis said, she didn't want more people knowing she was hiding on the ranch.

"Now, this is a fantasy."

"Travis." She drank in the sight of him as he stood just inside the barn door. He looked so achingly good, as if she hadn't seen him for a year instead of a week. Less than that, since he'd surprised her at her sister's wedding.

"To see a woman as beautiful as you are hanging out in cute shorts, talking to my horses, well, you just know that's some rancher's fantasy. Luckily, I'm a rancher."

She wanted to run and throw herself in his arms the way she always did, spinning him halfway around with the impact.

But she was pregnant. She held still.

Travis had no hesitation. He strode toward her, single-minded, confident. He scooped her up and spun her around, bringing enough momentum for the two of them.

His arms felt so strong. He smelled so good. Somehow, she'd been so focused on how they were going to be apart, it was startling to have him here—and still so happy with her.

Because he didn't know. Not yet.

"I didn't think I'd see you until dinner." How could her voice sound so normal when she was dying inside?

"I missed you," he said.

"I missed you, too." It was true. Surely she was allowed to say that.

He linked his arms around her waist, the way they did when they settled in to catch up on how their days had gone. Had he missed just talking to her? She thought her heart might burst.

"I watched a couple of your movies because I missed you so much."

She was grateful to talk about anything except what she needed to talk about. "Which ones?"

He named the crime drama, the one with the smoking-hot sex scene.

"Oh. That one." She felt her cheeks warm as she looked toward the tack room. She couldn't hold his gaze.

"I want credit for keeping my eyes on yours and not letting them drop lower, but if you don't look at me, how will you know how good I am at pretending I'm not thinking about your body?"

He sounded amused.

She looked at him then. "That scene doesn't bother you? I mean, knowing anyone could watch it?" She knew so many fellow actors whose significant others were bothered greatly by those kinds of scenes, even when carefully arranged bedsheets protected privacy. Her costar's girlfriend had been standing by as they filmed that one, anxious and jealous and making the role ten times harder to play. She'd been far more of a diva than any actress Sophia had worked with.

Travis kept his arms locked around her waist. "I've seen rated R movies my entire adult life without thinking twice about it, but it is strange when you know one of the actors. It took a few scenes for me to adjust to hearing you speak with a Boston accent. If you're worried about the sex scene, don't be. I could tell it wasn't real."

"Oh, it's not. It's really not. There are a dozen people working, and you have to hold yourself in the most unnatural way, and there was this awful bubblegum smell, and I remember being thirsty and worried about how to deliver this line that I didn't think my character would really say, and they put makeup on everything. I mean everything."

"I know."

"You do?"

In the moment of silence that followed, she forgot they had no future. She could only think how lucky she'd be to have such an even-tempered man as her partner in life.

"How?" she asked, holding her breath.

"It didn't look real to me. Not the look on your face,

which was sexy as hell, don't get me wrong, but it wasn't what you really look like with me."

"Oh."

He kissed her lightly. "You look sexier with me."

"Oh."

"I could guess about the makeup because your freckle was missing. The one that's right here." Without taking his eyes from hers, he placed his finger precisely on a spot just above the edge of her bra, on her left breast, exactly where she knew she had a little black dot.

"Oh. They hide that all the time, even if I'm just wearing a low cut gown or a bathing suit."

His grin slowly grew into a smile. "Good. I love it. I'll keep it to myself. The audience doesn't get the same you that I get."

She wanted to smile back, but she was dying inside. *We have no future. We have no future.*

"The movie I'll never watch again was the pioneer one," he said.

"That was my best. Everyone says so." The words came out by rote despite her frantic thoughts.

"You died. I don't ever want to know if that looked realistic. I can't watch that one again."

He kissed her as if he couldn't bear to lose her, and she kissed him back the same way. *No future, no future.*

She would lose him, soon, but she wasn't ready to say the words. She was supposed to have had until eight o'clock to prepare herself to say the words.

"Why are you here? I mean, why did you leave your family so early for me?"

"That was why—for you. I couldn't wait until tonight to see you. I just gave Clay the rest of the day off. I realize your fantasy includes a very traditional dinner that might end in a peck on the cheek, but I was going to try to persuade you to try a different fantasy now."

Her body was her traitor in every way. She knew she couldn't sleep with Travis again, but her body didn't care, pregnant or not. Just being near him was enough to make her come awake and alive once more.

Patch saved the day. With outstanding timing, she ran into the barn to greet Travis as if he'd been gone ten years.

Sophia stepped back to give the dog room. She pretended she didn't see the quizzical look Travis threw her.

"How're you doing, Patch?" He bent down to pet her with both hands. There was something odd about the way he did it, almost like he was checking something, deliberately feeling his way from the dog's shoulders to her tail. "Still feeling good, girl?"

Sophia grasped at the distraction. "Is there something wrong with her?"

Travis stood again. "I wouldn't say it's wrong. She's going to have puppies. Judging from the amount of time she's been spending in Samson's stall, she's planning on having them there. I'll have to move Samson when she gets a little closer. They're best friends, but I wouldn't want him to step on a puppy."

Sophia felt her stomach tying itself into knots. "I can't take another abandoned animal crying from starvation. Is there replacer milk for puppies? Do you have any? We should get some right away. Right away."

She must have overreacted. Travis's quizzical look deepened into concern. "Patch is a good mother. This is her second litter, so I don't anticipate any problems, but sure, we'll keep some replacer milk here. I won't leave you with a starving newborn again, I promise."

He kissed her again, not on the lips, but on the forehead.

She told herself that was for the best. It was already

starting, this transition from lovers to friends that she was going to rely on. She'd had time, too much time, to think about her options, and no matter what Grace had said, there weren't many.

Sophia had nowhere else to hide. She was going to have to stay on this ranch for the duration of her pregnancy, and that meant she was going to see Travis. Staying on good terms with him was essential, because frankly, she was scared to death to be without him.

She had a good speech she needed to be ready to deliver tonight that talked about how they'd be able to coexist quite nicely together despite their history. It left out the part about being scared.

Until tonight's dinner, she needed to not freak out. She smiled brightly at Travis. "First the cat, now the dog. Is everything on this ranch pregnant?"

Travis kept looking at her, but she told herself he was smiling indulgently. "We try to keep it that way."

She tossed her hair, praying for normalcy. "You know that sounds terrible, right?"

"That's the ranching business. We had a ninety-seven-percent pregnancy rate in the cattle last year. That's a very good year. But I don't breed cats. She did that on her own. And I suspect Patch here found herself a boyfriend over at the James Hill."

"If she'd been neutered, then you wouldn't have this problem." She couldn't quite keep her tone light. She'd said the same thing after the cat. She'd thought the same thing about herself.

"I wouldn't say Patch having puppies is a problem. She's the fourth or fifth generation of River Mack cow dogs. She's got real good instincts, passed down through her line. People in these parts are glad to have one of her puppies. This will be her second litter, though, so we'll have her fixed. I don't want her to get worn out. I need her working the herd this fall."

"What happens this fall?"

He was silent for a long time. Then he walked up close to her and, as if she were some kind of precious treasure, held her head gently in his hands and rested his forehead on hers.

"The last time we were together before the wedding we talked just like this. You weren't sure if you'd still be on the ranch this week. You said you'd have a better idea of what the future holds when I came back. I'm back. Do you know? Are you going to be here this fall?"

It was hard, so hard, not to dive into the safety of his arms. He'd hold her close and she'd feel safe and everything would be all right.

Those days were over. Those days never should have been, so she stayed on her own two feet and answered him honestly. "Yes, I'll be here all the way until January."

As close as they were, she could feel the relief pass through his body, but she could see his frown of worry as well. She wasn't a good enough actor to fool him. He knew she was holding something back, but being Travis, he didn't push.

"Well, then," he said. "Would you like to see what the ranch looks like beyond the house and barn? It's a Sunday in July. There won't be a soul for miles around. I'll drive you around and tell you what you can expect from now until Christmas."

And tonight, I'll tell you what to expect.

But she was being offered a reprieve, a stay of execution, and she loved him too much to deny herself his company, just one more time.

Chapter Eighteen

"I didn't realize there were so many flowers."

Sophia looked out the window of the white pickup truck. She was all buckled in, huddled by the door, and sad. The ranch had so much beauty, and she'd missed it all when she'd first arrived.

"What did you think it was if it wasn't flowers?"

"Brown. I just thought I was coming to live in exile on some ugly brown planet. But it's flowers. Yellow, purple and orange." She felt a little defensive. The old Sophia was just so pitiful. "You put those colors together, and you get brown."

"Until you take a closer look. Which you are."

She closed her eyes against his kindness. Of course she was in love with this man. How could she not be in love with this man? And he was going to hate her so very soon.

"Stop being so nice to me."

He drove in silence for another little while. "Why are you finding it so hard to be nice to yourself?"

She didn't answer him. Out the window, there were babies everywhere. Quite literally, every single cow had a calf suckling or sleeping underfoot. She could see the satisfaction and pride in Travis's expression—or she had seen it, before her misery had spilled into the pickup.

Travis slowed down the truck and squinted at a distant tree. "There she is. It's about time."

He parked the truck a little distance from the tree and got out. There was a cow under the tree, sleeping peacefully on her side. "You can come out if you want. Just be quiet about slamming the door."

Travis walked a little closer to the cow, not too close, and then crouched down. He checked his watch. And he waited.

And waited.

The minutes ticked by, until Sophia couldn't stand it anymore. She got out of the truck and practically tiptoed up to Travis before dropping down beside him.

"What's going on?"

"She's the last heifer of the season, and by season, I mean she's so far out of season, she's in a class by herself."

"I don't understand."

Travis checked his watch again as the cow huffed and made a halfhearted attempt to get up. The cow fell still again.

"We have our calving season in April and early May on the River Mack. That's when we want the herd giving birth."

"All at the same time?"

"More or less. You have to ride the herd several times a day, looking for new babies to doctor, making sure the mamas are on their feet and nursing, and sometimes—" he stood up with a sigh "—you have to pull a calf."

He walked back to the truck, dug around the back, and

returned with some blue nylon straps and a pair of long, skinny plastic bags. "This little lady tricked us pretty well. We thought she was pregnant during breeding, but turns out she wasn't. Then a bull jumped a fence, and here she is, totally out of sync with the rest of the herd. Accidents happen, though."

The cow moaned again. Travis shook his head.

"What's wrong?" Sophia stayed crouched on the ground, her fingertips on the grass for balance.

"She's a first-time mother. She isn't doing too well. She must have been at this awhile. See how tired she is?"

And then Travis walked right up to the laboring cow. Sophia stood to see better. There were two front legs poking out of the mother's…body. Legs with hooves and everything. Sophia cringed.

The mother seemed to get agitated as Travis stood there, but then the hooves poked out a little farther and the nose of a cow came out, too. Travis came back and crouched beside Sophia.

Nothing else happened for an eternity. He checked his watch and picked up the blue straps again, but then the cow made a pitiful sound of pain and the whole head of a tiny cow came out with its front legs.

"There you go," Travis said under his breath.

Sophia sat on her butt. "I'm gonna be sick."

He turned his head to look at her. "You've never seen anything being born?"

"No." She couldn't look. "What are the blue straps for?"

He seemed amused, which, given that he was in full cowboy mode, meant one corner of his mouth lifted in barely-a-grin. "You can wrap 'em around the calf's legs and help the mama out. It's called pulling a calf."

"You're kidding me. This is what you do all day? I

thought you rode around on a horse and shot rattlesnakes or something."

He turned back to the laboring cow. "I do that, too. These mamas go to a lot of trouble to have their babies. It's the least I can do to make sure the babies don't get bit by something poisonous."

He would be the best father in the world.

The thought hit her hard, followed equally hard by sorrow at the memory of Deezee. She'd been so unwise, so very unwise.

But then the cow moaned and the entire calf came out in a rush of blood and liquid. It just lay there, covered with gunk, and Sophia's heart started to pound. The world got a little tilted. She grabbed Travis's arm, digging her fingers into his muscle to keep herself vertical.

"Come on, Mama," he said quietly.

The mother wasn't moving. The baby wasn't moving.

Then Travis was moving, on his feet and heading toward them as he pulled the plastic bags over his hands and arms—they were gloves. He grabbed the baby's nose, its lifeless head bobbling as he jerked some kind of membrane from around it. Then he grabbed the hooves in his hands and simply dragged the calf out of the puddle of grossness and across the grass to plop it right in front of the mother's face.

This was birth. This horrible, frightening death and membranes and pain—*oh, my God*. Sophia rolled to her hands and knees and tried desperately not to vomit.

What had she been thinking? That she'd do yoga and eat well and sport a small baby bump? Maybe toward the end, around Christmas, she'd be a little bit roly-poly for a few weeks, but then the baby would be born and go off to some wonderful adoptive family and everything would be clean and neat and tidy. She'd move on with her life.

That wasn't how it was. She had to give birth, she had to *labor*, there was just no way out of it. There would be gushing yuck and pain and exhaustion. And if, at the end of it all, the poor little baby didn't move…

What if the poor little baby didn't move?

She dug her fingers into the dirt and panted.

"Sophia."

She was dimly aware that Travis had come back. She heard him cursing, saw bloody plastic gloves being dumped on the grass. His clean arm was strong around her waist as he picked her up and set her on her feet, but he kept her back to his chest, which was smart because she was about to throw up.

"Baby, it's okay. Look, the mama's taking care of her calf now. She was just too tired to get up and go do it, so I helped her out. It's okay."

"No, it is *not*!" She wrenched free from him and ran a few steps toward the truck, but there was really nowhere to go. "I don't want to do it. I don't want to."

"Do what?"

"You're a man." Her words were getting high-pitched, rushing together. "Would you want to go through that? It's awful. She could've died. That baby could've died. I don't want to do it."

"It's okay. You don't have to do anything." He captured her in his arms again and tried to soothe her, making little shushing noises like she was the baby.

She started to cry. "Yes, I do. I'm the woman."

She could feel him behind her, shaking his head like he was dumbfounded, but how could he be? He was the one who'd just gotten out straps and gloves. "Okay, you're a woman, but you're just spooking yourself. You're not going to give birth anytime soon."

She was crying so hard now, she was doubled over at

the waist. She would have fallen if Travis didn't have his arm around her. "Yes, I am. I have to. I'm pregnant."

Travis was an ass for the next seven weeks.

For the first few minutes, he'd held Sophia as she'd choked and cried, although it was frankly a toss-up which one of them was more staggered.

Pregnant. They'd been careful, except for that very first time. He'd only been inside her for a minute, and he hadn't climaxed—but it was possible. That could be all it took, as they'd been warned in sex ed pamphlets given to them a hundred years ago at school. He'd assumed he was the father.

It would be nice to be able to claim that he'd felt some noble calling or had a divine moment of parenthood fall upon his shoulders at the news that Sophia was pregnant, but in fact he'd been trying to hold a woman who was about to vomit, and he'd been doing math. June plus nine months.

"March?" That had been his first brilliant contribution to her distress.

"January," Sophia had gasped, and his world had gone to hell.

His horse tossed his head. Travis was holding onto the reins too tightly. Again. He tried to relax in the saddle, but it was damned hard when he was getting closer to the house. He hadn't caught a glimpse of Sophia in seven weeks, but that didn't stop him from looking.

The rest of July had been a haze of hurt feelings. One of the reasons she'd come to the ranch in the first place was to hide her pregnancy once she got bigger. *She should have told me. Her sister should have told me. Her brother-in-law should have told me.*

He hadn't questioned that assumption in July, but it was the first week of September now, and he did. Why should they have told him? He was a stranger to them. How did he think that first day should have gone? Grace and Alex, standing by their open car doors, should have said what, exactly? *Are you the foreman? This is our sister, Sophia. She's pregnant.*

August had been hot and slow on the ranch. Travis had only ridden half days as he watched the cow-calf pairs thrive on summer grass. The indignation had changed to something else. *If only she'd told me at the beginning. If only her sister had told me. If only I'd known...*

But it was September now, and he realized he'd never finished the thought.

If only she'd told him at the beginning, *then what?*

DJ Deezee Kalm would still be the father. The week of the wedding, Travis had verified Deezee's schedule to make sure he'd keep away from Sophia and her sister. *If only I'd known...*

He still would have kept Deezee away from Sophia. The man was still a jerk. He'd still made life hard for Sophia in more ways than leaving her pregnant and alone. He'd hurt her career, her income, her self-confidence.

Sophia was planning on giving the baby up for adoption. Travis had been incredulous when she'd told him so on that awful day. His whole life was spent watching mothers rear their young. He couldn't imagine Sophia not wanting to rear hers, but now he wondered what kind of influence Deezee might have been on that decision.

Travis had that impatient feeling again. He needed to lay eyes on Sophia. Seven weeks was far too long.

He let his horse walk faster. The house wasn't far away now. He knew the terrain like the back of his hand. Down this slope, up the next rise, and he'd see the white pillars.

The old lie came to him as easily as it had so many

times before. If he could just check on Sophia, then he'd be able to put his mind at rest and move on.

A gunshot rang out.

In an instant, Travis's thoughts crystallized: the only thing in his world that mattered was Sophia.

She was in danger.

Chapter Nineteen

"Damn, girl. You look like a pregnant cow."

Sophia didn't bother to answer Deezee. She was twenty-one weeks along, halfway through her pregnancy, so of course she had a baby bump. She still wasn't wearing maternity clothes. Her stretchy yoga top covered her fine. Obviously, Deezee had never seen a pregnant cow if he thought she resembled one.

Deezee shut the door to his car, a black luxury sedan. He wasn't driving it, though. That privilege belonged to one of his ever-present buddies. Sophia didn't recognize this particular buddy. The back doors opened and two more men came out.

Afraid to be alone with your own thoughts, Deezee? Still?

But she wouldn't say anything out loud. She'd been expecting her lawyer, the one who was supposed to arrive first with the adoption papers for Deezee to sign with her.

She'd texted Clay that a black sedan would be coming onto the property today, so it had come through all three gates unchallenged, she was sure. She'd never expected Deezee to arrive in such a traditional car.

Her little burner phone could only text and call, but it couldn't do either of those things right now, because it was in the house, and she was on the patio. If she made a run for the door, she had no doubt someone from Deezee's crew would get there before she had the door closed and locked behind herself. She didn't want to be locked in the house with these guys.

None of Travis's men would be coming to check on her. And Travis himself? He wasn't speaking to her. She'd never seen a man as shocked as he'd been when she'd told him the baby wasn't his.

Clay was her only point of contact at the ranch now, and she'd told him she wanted the black sedan to come to the house. Round and round, back to the beginning: Sophia was stuck for the next ninety minutes with Deezee and his posse.

A little shiver of fear went down her back.

"You're early," she said, then immediately wished she hadn't. They were almost three hours early. The lawyer had arranged it so that he'd be here long before they were, and Deezee was never early to anything, until today.

"No prob, girl. Let's check out the new place. What do you have to drink?"

She was an actor. She needed to pull this role off. "I don't have anything you like. I'm pregnant, so…no alcohol." She held up hands and shrugged. "I think if you go back to the main road and head west, the very next road takes you to a local bar. That might be fun. The lawyer won't be here with the paperwork for another hour, anyway. Might as well go do some shots."

One of the backseat buddies liked the idea. *Please, please, please talk your gang into going.* Of course, the next road to the west didn't lead to a bar. It led to the Watersons' ranch, but Deezee would probably drive a good half mile in before he realized it. Maybe the Watersons would detain them.

Travis trusted the Watersons. They would've been part of her safety net, if she'd been smart enough to accept it. She hoped the Watersons would forgive her for sending Deezee onto their property, but if they were friends of Travis, it was her best bet for safety.

"Let's go," the backseat buddy said, enthusiastic to find the bar.

Hope swelled in Sophia's chest.

"Nah-nah-no-no-no." Deezee waved off his buddy with a shake of his blinged-out fingers.

Hope burst like a bubble.

"I gotta check this place out. We are in the *sticks*. Damn, girl, whatchu do out here all alone?"

I cry.

She smiled. "Well, like you said, you've now checked the place out. This is all there is." She snapped her fingers. "You know where there might be some beer? In the bunkhouse. Just go past this barn and follow that fence. You can't miss it."

She knew exactly how the hands who had the day off would react to these four storming into the bunkhouse. *Please, Deezee, go get some beer from the bunkhouse.*

"Why are you so anxious to get rid of me?"

Sophia had not done her best acting. She was nervous. She'd never felt so vulnerable, and Deezee could see it.

"Don't you want to party anymore?" he asked. "Oh, yeah. You got a bun in the oven." He turned to his friends.

"How about that, boys? I'm not shooting blanks. Who knocked up Sophia Jackson? This guy."

The gunshot took her completely by surprise. She jumped a mile. Even Deezee dropped the f-bomb on his friend for the deafening sound.

The man had pulled out a handgun and was aiming it at the barn. "Just testing out the 'you can't hit the broad side of a barn' thing." He fired again. "My father used to say that. I hated my father."

"Stop!" Sophia ran from the patio toward him. "There are horses in there. Dogs. Cats. You'll hurt something."

She grabbed his arm, but he shook her off and fired again.

"Please," she begged. "It's a real barn. You'll kill something."

"Give me that." Deezee held out his hand for the gun. He took more careful aim than his friend. "Calling the shot. Eight ball in the corner pocket."

"*Stop!*" Sophia yelled, lunging for his arm before the sound of pounding horse's hooves could register in her head.

Travis was there, off his horse while it was still galloping. He shoved Deezee's arm down. The gun fired into the dirt, then he twisted it from Deezee's grip. Travis ejected the magazine, cleared the chambered round, and then threw the empty gun as far as an outfielder to first base.

"Sophia, get in the house."

Deezee adopted all the arrogant posture he was capable of, but he backed up a step. "Who do you think you are, ordering my wife around?" He turned to the driver. "Show him the marriage license."

Sophia blinked as Travis decked her alleged husband.

Deezee was out.

"What the eff, man?" the driver said to Travis. "You planning on taking on all three of us now?"

"Yes."

None of the three made a move against him.

"Sophia, get in the house." Travis repeated the order through gritted teeth.

She wanted to stay by Travis's side, but she felt the baby kick. This wasn't just about her safety, so she ran for the kitchen door as more men from the River Mack came thundering up the road.

"I want to go check on the puppies."

"Sophia, please, try to relax. Buck said the animals are all fine. Are you uncomfortable?"

She was lying on the couch with her upper body in Travis's lap and his arm supporting her neck and shoulders. His other hand hadn't stopped smoothing over her hair, her shoulder…her belly. She hadn't been this comfortable since the last time they'd made love.

"I'm fine. How are you? You're the one who had the fistfight."

"You're the one who's pregnant. My God, Sophia…" He cradled her closer for a moment, then put his head back and sighed.

"I'm okay, really." Her heart felt more and more okay each time he did that. "I never threw a punch."

"You didn't have to throw a punch to have all your muscles pumped full of adrenaline. I can feel that my muscles are worn-out from the tension, and yours are way more important than mine right now." His hand smoothed its way over her belly again.

"Thank you."

He was silent.

"Thank you for treating me right, and for coming to my rescue, and for being an all-around decent man."

"I've been an ass. You should be kicking mine instead of apologizing to me. I love you, Sophia. I have from the very first, and I could kick myself for wasting the entire month of August feeling sorry for myself."

"Well, it's kind of a big deal to find out your lover is carrying another man's child. Don't say it isn't."

His hand drifted over her hair again, petting her, soothing her. Loving her. "Okay, let's get this settled. It's a big deal, I agree. But I could have talked to you about it. I could have asked you my questions, instead of asking myself questions over and over that I couldn't possibly know the answer to."

"I know I should—"

"There's more."

He looked so fierce, Sophia's heart tripped a little.

"I apologize for taking so long to realize the obvious. I kept saying to myself, 'if only I'd known,' until I finally realized it wouldn't have mattered. What if I'd known you were pregnant when you first arrived here? I would have found you fascinating, anyway. What if you'd had this cute baby bump when you were throwing those tomatoes? We still would've ripped off our clothes in the living room."

"Travis—"

"What if you'd arrived here with a newborn baby? I still would have fallen in love with you. The key is you, Sophia. I will always love you."

"I'm—I'm—" She gave up and snuggled into his chest, because he was big and strong and she could. "I'm going to live on that forever. That fills my heart up."

He kissed her, which was exactly what she wanted.

"Aren't you angry with me at all?" he whispered over her lips.

"No. I watch you through the window every day. You've looked so grim, and I've known it was because of me. I'm so sorry."

She didn't want him to think the worst of her. "I know this sounds hard to believe, but I really was in denial. I read that the pregnancy test could be false positive, and my brain just seized on that as the right explanation, because it was the only explanation I could handle. My career wouldn't be impacted. I wouldn't be tied to Deezee in any way. You came later, but once I met you, that was all the more reason to just ignore the possibility. I sound like an idiot, don't I?"

"There's nothing about you that sounds like an idiot." He kissed her sweetly, casually, like he had hours to kiss her whenever he pleased. "I'm sleeping here tonight. It's going to be a while before I can let you out of my sight. That's not too rational, either."

"I like that, though. You know you won't be sleeping with a married woman, right? I really want you to know I'm not in denial about that. Deezee is just trying to stir up gossip with that paperwork."

"I know. I'm glad the lawyer is releasing a statement for you."

The lawyer had shown up punctually, only to find himself being asked to clarify all kinds of points of law beyond adoption. A quick internet search had cleared up the alleged St. Barth's marriage certificate. Thirty days' notice was a minimum requirement to marry on that island, and they'd only flown in for the weekend.

More importantly in Sophia's mind, she'd never said *I do*. Deezee's antics at the altar had been her last straw. She'd thrown her bouquet at him when she was only halfway down the aisle, something that had made her look terrible in photos, but it had been her one justifiable tantrum.

She pulled far enough away from Travis to look at him directly. "I'm not married, and I've never been married."

He studied her for a moment. "Are you thinking of my dad?"

"Maybe. Yes. I know you don't admire what he did. I think you would never sleep with a married woman."

He brushed her hair back from her eyes. "If I had to wait for your divorce to be final, I would. After meeting Deezee, there's no way I would want you to stay married to him. Am I grateful that we don't need to wait for a divorce?" He laughed to lighten the moment. "That's like asking me if the sky's blue."

Sophia wished she could smile back. "You must question my judgment for even thinking about marrying him. I do. Grace hated him from the first, but he wasn't always quite so bad. He started using the drugs they sold at his raves. Then he started using even when there wasn't a party on. It got pretty out of control before I left him. It's magnified every flaw a hundred times."

"Sophia?"

"Yes?"

"I don't care about Deezee. You are an amazing woman no matter who you used to date."

Sophia placed her hand on her belly.

She cared. And she was scared.

Chapter Twenty

"I've got an early Christmas gift for you."

"Seriously?" Sophia asked. Travis thought she sounded equal parts excited and skeptical as she dumped the last scoop of oats into the trough in the mare's stall. "Wasn't a house enough?"

She'd fallen in love with the century-old foreman's house. She loved that it had a little parlor and a library and a dining room instead of one expansive space—so Travis had bought it for her. The MacDowells sold it to him along with a dozen acres or so, just enough land to make a nice little residential property along the edge of the River Mack. The renovations, including the baby's room, would be finished by the end of January, when Sophia's lease was up.

Until then, he would continue to live with her in the main house. Never again would he go seven weeks without seeing her. Sophia's next movie would begin shooting in July, and her new manager had added contract riders to keep the future Chalmers family together. Sophia's housing on location would accommodate the baby and a nanny, and Travis would arrive via the studio's private jet midway through the shooting schedule. Private jets and cowboys might seem an odd combination, but Travis figured he could handle the luxury. He'd go through hell to be with Sophia. If he had to adapt to luxury instead, well, there was no law that said life always had to be hard.

He walked up behind Sophia and slipped his arms around her, above her round belly, below her breasts, which had become even more lovely with her pregnancy. "I had a different kind of gift in mind."

"Here in the barn?" she asked, sounding like a sex goddess.

"Like that would be the first time."

Sophia pretended to droop her shoulders in disappointment. "I'm going to have to take a raincheck on that gift. I feel as big as a house this morning."

It was cool in the barn in December, so she wore a fluffy green sweater. Travis noticed that she rubbed her last-trimester belly in a different way today than usual, although the baby wasn't due for three weeks. Maybe the sweater was just extra soft and touchable to her.

Maybe not.

Sophia was adamant that a home birth was the only way to keep her birthing experience private. Her midwife could reach the ranch in a little less than an hour, but Travis didn't find that as comforting as Sophia did. He'd witnessed hundreds of animal births in his life, but Sophia was no animal, and he hoped when the contractions began, she'd change her mind and let him drive her to the hospital. She was no longer placing the baby up for adoption, so secrecy was no longer paramount. Her well-being was.

That was a discussion for next week's appointment with the midwife. Today was Christmas Eve, and he wanted to put a smile on Sophia's beautiful face.

"Close your eyes," he murmured. "Don't move."

He went into Samson's stall and scooped up the black-and-gray puppy he'd hidden there. The pup was four months old and probably fifteen pounds, but it was still a puppy with oversized paws and soft fur.

He placed the soft fur against Sophia's soft sweater. "Happy Christmas Eve."

"Oh! A puppy." Her smile was exactly what he'd hoped for.

For about five seconds.

Then it faded in confusion. "Wait. Is this one of Patch's puppies?"

"Yes. She was returned. I thought you might want to keep her."

"The poor thing. Poor, poor puppy." She buried her face in its fur and burst into tears.

Travis scratched the dog behind the ears. "Baby, the dog is happy. Why aren't you?"

"She was returned because she wasn't good enough, was she?"

"No, Roger just got a job offer in another state, and since he'd only had the pup for a few—"

"You don't have to keep pretending for me." Her tears fell as she kissed the puppy.

Having a fiancée in her final trimester had taught Travis that tears were possible over just about any topic. He wouldn't dismiss every tear as hormones, however, not when he knew the unique challenges Sophia faced.

"Come into the office and sit. You and the puppy." He held the desk chair for Sophia, gave her a tissue from the box he'd learned to keep on his desk now that it wasn't just him in the barn, and then he waited to see if she would tell him what was really bothering her.

She did. "You said that everyone wanted Patch's puppies because she's a great cow dog, but for this litter, the father was a mystery. Now the dogs are being returned. It's the father, isn't it? Even with a great mother like Patch, people assume the puppies just aren't good enough. It's so unfair. The puppies didn't do anything wrong."

He crouched down in front of her. "This is the only puppy that's come back to the ranch, and it's because Roger got a job offer in another state. He'll be in an office building all day. That's it. I wouldn't lie to you, Sophia. That puppy is desirable, I guarantee it, whether we know who the father is or not."

"Maybe I should've stuck with my plan to place the baby up for adoption. No one would have known who the biological parents were. The baby would have started life with a clean slate."

That wasn't coming from as far out of left field as it seemed. "You saw the news today that Deezee was convicted of drug trafficking."

She placed one hand on her belly. "That's this poor baby's father. Everyone knows it. Deezee made sure of that, and now he's a felon. How can I make up for that? I'm not that great when it comes to motherhood material. Here's Patch, this legendary cow dog, and even she can't make up for the father. People think her sweet puppies aren't good enough because the f-father—"

"Sophia, listen to me."

Travis hated the son of a bitch who had just been convicted. He wasn't just a drug dealer who'd come to this ranch waving around a gun that could have injured Sophia, but he was the man who'd messed with Sophia's head, too.

The fact that she'd once considered herself in love with Deezee still undermined her confidence in herself.

"You are going to be a great mother. I know this from the bottom of my soul. The fact that you are worried whether or not you'll be good enough for this baby proves that the baby is getting a mom who cares."

He'd tell her that as many times as it took. Deezee had told her crap for five months. Travis was going to tell her truths for the rest of her life. Travis was going to win.

She let go of the puppy with one hand and placed her palm on her belly in that same low place.

Travis covered her hand with his. "No one is ever going to look at this child and think he or she isn't good enough. Deezee chose to sell drugs for money. That's not DNA. That was a choice. Anyone from any parent could make the same choice, or not. Deezee's not going to be around to teach this baby about bad choices. I'm going to be."

He had to stop and clear his throat. Then he thought better of it. Let Sophia see how much he cared.

He looked up at her, and he knew she saw the unshed tears, because she looked a little bit blurry. "I cannot wait to hold this baby. This is the most exciting thing in my world. I may not have contributed any DNA, but I'm going to be part of this child, too. I'm going to teach 'em when to say 'gid-yap' and 'whoa' and not to let their horse step on their reins and to eat their zucchini and to love their mama. That's you."

Sophia's tears subsided. Her breathing was steady and the puppy in her arm was calm. Travis knew their future was bright. Just when Travis had relaxed, Sophia slayed him. "There are a million reasons I'm going to love this baby, Travis, but here's one of the biggest. If it hadn't been for this baby, I would never have come to your ranch. I would never have met you. For that, I will always owe the baby one."

Travis had to bow his head and clear his throat.

"Me, too, Sophia. Me, too."

Under their hands, he felt her stomach draw tight. She wasn't livestock, not at all, but Travis had felt that same kind of contraction in horses and cows. It could pass and not start again for another three weeks. It could be nothing.

"I don't like the look of the weather out there," he said. "Let's put this puppy back in her hay and head back to the house."

Sophia was suddenly keenly interested in rearranging all the ornaments on the Christmas tree.

Travis ran a ranch. He was a big believer that Mother Nature knew what she was doing, but as far as nesting instincts went, this one wasn't particularly useful.

"I'm gonna call the midwife," he said.

Sophia stopped in the middle of switching the locations of a sequined ball and a glass ball. "Why? I feel fine."

Travis nodded. "That's good, baby. Glad to hear it." He dialed the phone.

Outside, the rain turned to sleet.

The radio announced the highways were closed. Travis imagined that children all around Austin were afraid that Santa wasn't going to be able to get his sled through the bad weather tonight. He was afraid the midwife wouldn't.

He was right, damn it all to hell.

In the end, for all the times he'd insisted to Sophia that she wasn't a beast, he was grateful that there were similarities. It made the whole process a little less bewildering. They'd decided ahead of time which bed to use and had plastic coverings and extra sheets prepared. But as Sophia walked around the house rearranging Christmas decorations, he noticed she kept going into the master bathroom, a room he hadn't seen her use once in the four months since he'd begun living with her. It reminded him of a cow who'd kept returning to stand under a particular tree, or a mother cat who'd decided to leave her nice box for a treacherous rafter at the last minute.

He picked up the supplies the midwife had left last week and carried them into the master bathroom.

"I think I'll take a bath," Sophia said. "Then maybe we can watch a Christmas movie on TV."

She got undressed and sat in the tub, but she never turned the water on. She wasn't having any painful contractions for him to time, and the midwife kept telling him on the phone that a first labor could take twelve hours, easily, if Sophia really was in labor. By then, the roads would surely be open.

So Sophia sat in the dry bathtub and Travis pretended that was normal. Then the first painful contraction hit, and poor Sophia went from nothing to full-out labor in no time.

"I don't think this is right," she said, panting to catch her breath.

"Everything is working just like it should."

The pain was scaring her. "But it doesn't always work out. You lose calves every year. We almost lost that kitten—"

But another contraction hit her before the last one ended, and she started trying to do her *hee hee hee* breaths like the online course had taught them.

Another contraction. God, they were coming hard. Fast. His poor Sophia.

Travis kissed her temple, wet as it was from pain and the effort to handle the pain. He knelt next to the tub and kept his arm around her shoulders. He felt so utterly useless.

The contractions left her limp. He could only support her with his arm.

"That calf," she panted. "Mother Nature would have taken that calf and the mother with it if you hadn't been there to help."

"No, baby. You're remembering that wrong."

"You had those straps."

"I didn't have to use them, remember? I just watched and waited, and that baby was born just fine. Your baby is going to be born just fine. It hurts like hell—" and God, he wished he could do something about that "—but it's going just fine."

The contraction started building again, the pain rolling over her as she gripped his hand and tried to breathe.

"That heifer almost died. She couldn't move. She was so tired." Panic was in her voice. She was losing it, the pain was winning, and Travis thought his own heart was going to break a rib, it was beating so hard. She looked too much like her pioneer movie character, the one that had died onscreen.

Help wasn't coming, not until the sleet stopped. Travis couldn't control the weather. He couldn't control Sophia's labor. This was the most important event of his life, the one thing in his life he absolutely had to get right, and he was powerless.

Sophia lifted her head and started panting. *Hee hee hee.*

God bless her. She was still at it. She didn't have a choice. She couldn't quit.

He couldn't, either.

He shoved the fear and the images from that damned movie out of his head as he shifted his position a bit, leaning over the edge of the tub and adjusting his arm to hold Sophia even closer. Her fingers loosened on his as the wave receded.

She plopped her head back onto his arm. "I can't do it. This can't be Mother Nature."

"Listen to me. You are doing everything right."

But she wasted her precious energy to roll her head on his arm, *no, no, no.* "That calf would have died. You had to drag her over to that heifer."

Travis hadn't realized how heavily that still weighed on Sophia. They'd never talked about it before now. This was a heck of a time to talk about anything, but he didn't want her worrying about what could go wrong.

He kissed her temple again. "Everything is going to be okay. When you saw me drag that newborn calf over to the mama, I was just being helpful. She was tired, so I just brought that baby up close to her so she could take care of it. And you know what? When your little baby is born, if you're too tired to move, that'll be okay, too. I'm gonna scoop up that little baby and hold her right here for you." He brought his other arm across her breasts and completed a circle around her, keeping the woman he loved in his arms. "And it's gonna be you and me and that brand new baby, and the three of us are gonna be just fine."

"I'm sorry. This is…just…" She still looked a little unfocused, but not so panicky.

He could feel her body going under the contraction. "You're doing great."

"…just not how we planned it."

"I wouldn't miss this for the world."

"I love you."

He thought he'd never heard the words uttered in a better way. They pierced his soul. "I love you, too."

She let go of his hand and gripped the edge of the tub. The last of that dazed and confused expression lifted as she frowned fiercely. "I think—I feel like I should push. It hasn't been long enough, has it? What time is it? Ohmigod, I'm not kidding. I need to push. Am I supposed to push?"

Travis nodded. "If you think it's time to push, then you should push. I know you're right."

"Okay. Then I'm going to have a baby now."

He dropped one more kiss on her head. "You do that, Sophia. You do that."

And she did.

In record time, in a bathtub on the River Mack ranch on Christmas Eve, Noelle Jackson Chalmers was born, healthy and loved.

Travis wept. No one had ever been given a better Christmas gift.

* * * * *

*And don't miss the next book in
Caro Carson's* TEXAS RESCUE *series,
coming in June 2017 from
Mills & Boon Cherish.*

MILLS & BOON®

Cherish™

EXPERIENCE THE ULTIMATE RUSH OF FALLING IN LOVE

1216/23

MILLS & BOON®

EXCLUSIVE EXTRACT

When Eloise Miller finds herself thrown into the role of maid of honour at the wedding of the year, her plans to stay away from the gorgeous best man are scuppered!

Read on for a sneak preview of
SLOW DANCE WITH THE BEST MAN
by Sophie Pembroke

Maid of honour for Melissa Sommers. How on earth had this happened? And the worst part was—

'Sounds like we'll be spending even more time together.' Noah's voice was warm, deep and far too close to her ear.

Eloise sighed. That. That was the worst thing. Because the maid of honour was *expected* to pair up with the best man, and that would not make her resolution to stay away from Noah Cross any easier at all.

She turned and found him standing directly behind her, close enough that if she'd stepped back a centimetre or two she'd have been in his arms. Suddenly she was glad he'd alerted her to his presence with his words.

She shifted further away and tried to look like a professional, instead of a teenager with a crush. Looking up at him, she felt the strange heat flush over her skin again at his gorgeousness. Then she focused, and realised he was frowning.

'Apparently so,' she agreed. 'But I'm sure I'll be far too busy with all the wedding arrangements—'

'Oh, I doubt it,' Noah interrupted, but he still didn't sound entirely happy about the idea, which surprised her. Perhaps she'd misread his flirting earlier. Maybe he really was like that with everyone and, now the reality of having to spend time with her had set in, he was less keen on the idea. 'Melissa has quite the packed schedule for the wedding party, you know. She's right—you're going to have to find someone to take over most of your job here.'

Eloise sighed. She *did* know. She'd helped Laurel plan it, after all.

And, now she thought about it, every last bit of the schedule involved the maid of honour and the best man being together.

Noah smiled, a hint of the charm he'd exhibited earlier showing through despite the frown, and Eloise's heart beat twice in one moment as she accepted the inevitable.

She was doomed.

She had the most ridiculous crush on a man who clearly found her a minor inconvenience.

And—even worse—the whole world was going to be watching, laughing at her pretending that she could live in this world of celebrities, mocking her for thinking she could ever be pretty enough, funny enough…just *enough* for Noah Cross.

Don't miss
SLOW DANCE WITH THE BEST MAN
by Sophie Pembroke

Available January 2017
www.millsandboon.co.uk

MILLS & BOON®

Why shop at millsandboon.co.uk?

Each year, thousands of romance readers find their perfect read at millsandboon.co.uk. That's because we're passionate about bringing you the very best romantic fiction. Here are some of the advantages of shopping at www.millsandboon.co.uk:

* **Get new books first**—you'll be able to buy your favourite books one month before they hit the shops

* **Get exclusive discounts**—you'll also be able to buy our specially created monthly collections, with up to 50% off the RRP

* **Find your favourite authors**—latest news, interviews and new releases for all your favourite authors and series on our website, plus ideas for what to try next

* **Join in**—once you've bought your favourite books, don't forget to register with us to rate, review and join in the discussions

Visit **www.millsandboon.co.uk** for all this and more today!